Praise for BECOMING MARIE ANTOINETTE

"Full of sumptuous and well-researched details . . . *Becoming Marie Antoinette* by Juliet Grey, the first novel in a new trilogy, gives readers a more sympathetic look than usual at the ill-fated French queen."

—Examiner.com (five stars)

"In her richly imagined novel, Juliet Grey meticulously re-creates the sumptuous court of France's most tragic queen. Beautifully written, with attention paid to even the smallest detail, *Becoming Marie Antoinette* will leave readers wanting more!"

—Michelle Moran, bestselling author of *Madame Tussaud*

"This is historical fiction at its finest." —A Library of My Own

"Fans of historical fiction will eat this one up. It's engaging, smart, and authentic. Grey has done her homework." —January Magazine

"Grey possesses the rare ability to transform readers to a past only accessible by imagination. *Becoming Marie Antoinette* is sure to appeal to lovers of quality historical fiction." —The Well Read Wife

"[A] lively, well-written promenade through pre-Revolution France . . . It's history with a spoonful of sugar—and that's never a bad thing."

—*The Decatur Daily*

"A thoroughly enjoyable novel, brimming with delightful details. Grey writes eloquently and with charming humor, bringing 'Toinette' vividly to life as she is schooled and groomed—molded, quite literally—for a future as Queen of France, an innocent pawn in a deadly political game."

—Sandra Gulland, bestselling author of *Mistress of the Sun* and the Josephine Bonaparte trilogy

"*C'est magnifique!* A very entertaining read, one that I was hard-pressed to put down . . . [I] am waiting (ever so impatiently) for book two in the trilogy." —Passages to the Past

"Smart, yet extremely engaging . . . *Becoming Marie Antoinette* will please fans of historical fiction." —Confessions of a Book Addict

"A great read that is sure to be requested by lovers of historical fiction, especially those who enjoyed Michelle Moran's *Madame Tussaud* and other novels about the French Revolution." —*Library Journal*

"Everything is so vividly described that you feel as though you are right there experiencing it all. This novel is very well written and it captivates you from the very beginning." —Peeking Between the Pages

"It is a captivating and well-thought-out book, and one that raises this woman of history to the point of a living person, which the reader finds easy to identify with and relate to." —The Book Worm's Library

"Readers will see Marie Antoinette in a whole new light. . . . A sympathetic and engaging read that presents the French queen in a manner seldom found in other novels . . . Anyone interested in French history will savor every page of this novel." —BookLoons

"[A] fine fictional account of this very real, audacious world and the transformation of a naive, unsure girl into a formidable worldly leader! Superbly done!" —Crystal Book Reviews

"A lusciously detailed novel of Marie Antoinette's rise to power and the decadent, extravagant lifestyles of eighteenth-century Versailles." —Shelf Awareness

"Well-researched and lovingly written with sparkling details—this new trilogy is not one to be missed by any lover of historical fiction." —Stiletto Storytime

"Completely enthralling. Although this is written as a work of fiction, every person and event was researched and so the two blend seamlessly." —Ex Libris

"This novel was by far the best I have read that tackles such an interesting and misunderstood queen. Grey weaves fun scandals into the history we all know." —Mostly Books

"A lively and sensitive portrait of a young princess in a hostile court, and one of the most sympathetic portrayals of the doomed queen."

—Lauren Willig, bestselling author of the Pink Carnation series

"Wonderfully delectable and lusciously rich, an elegant novel to truly savor. Juliet Grey's Marie Antoinette is completely absorbing."

—Diane Haeger, author of *The Queen's Rival*

"Maria Antonia, Austrian princess. What an amazing person. I absolutely loved each detail that Grey put into her. I could feel her emotions, and her struggles as she grew from Maria Antonia to Marie Antoinette, Queen of France."

—Reviews by Molly

"A truly engaging novel with fantastic historical details, well-fleshed-out characters, depth and emotion. I can't wait for the second and third books, and even though I know how it will end . . . I keep hoping it won't."

—The Loud Librarian

"Very well written, with fantastic descriptions of life in Vienna and Versailles. Grey has done quite a bit of research, as she explains in her author's note, and almost everything she uses is true to history. She does an excellent job of matching the personalities of Marie Antoinette and Louis XVI."

—Medieval Bookworm

"Meticulously researched, Marie Antoinette comes to life in this first in a trilogy about her life. The reader will never look at the French Revolution in the same way again."

—That's What She Read

"A very entertaining and rich read, filled to the brim with historical detail. Recommended to readers of historical fiction of all stripes."

—Raging Bibliomania

"Grey's novel has a little bit of everything: the glitz and glamour of the French court, young love, and international politics. The most enjoyable aspect of the book is seeing Marie find her own way and becoming her own person."

—Historical Novels Review

ALSO BY JULIET GREY

Becoming Marie Antoinette

DAYS *of* SPLENDOR, DAYS *of* SORROW

DAYS *of* SPLENDOR, DAYS *of* SORROW

A NOVEL OF MARIE ANTOINETTE

JULIET GREY

BALLANTINE BOOKS TRADE PAPERBACKS
NEW YORK

Days of Splendor, Days of Sorrow is a work of historical fiction. Apart from the well-known actual people, events, and locales that figure in the narrative, all names, characters, places, and incidents are the products of the author's imagination or are used fictitiously. Any resemblance to current events or locales, or to living persons, is entirely coincidental.

A Ballantine Books Trade Paperback Original

Published in the United States by Ballantine Books, an imprint of The Random House Publishing Group, a division of Random House, Inc., New York.

ISBN 978-0-345-52388-4
eBook ISBN 978-0-345-52389-1

Printed in the United States of America

www.randomhousereaderscircle.com

2 4 6 8 9 7 5 3 1

Book design by Casey Hampton

For MZR . . .

who made the suggestion that recharted the course of my life.

Merci mille fois.

All Queens should resemble the wives of Louis XIV and Louis XV, who knew no other passions than that of doing good . . . A Queen who is crowned for no other purpose than to amuse herself is a fatal acquisition to a people charged to defray the cost.

—Anonymous enemy of Marie Antoinette, Spring 1774

DAYS *of* SPLENDOR, DAYS *of* SORROW

Prologue

June 21, 1786

On this day the sun casts the longest shadows of the year. But in the cobblestone courtyard of the Palais de Justice, they are made that much deeper by the looming scaffold erected two days earlier—plenty of time to allow a prodigious crowd to assemble, provisioned with thin blankets and enough cheese, bread, and cheap wine to sustain them. Some have come to the Cour de Mai lured by the sounds of the workmen hammering wooden boards into a raised platform that in itself betokens something sensational. There is nothing like a public exhibition to take their minds off an empty pocket. Or an empty belly. It doesn't even matter who will take the stage.

Others know precisely what, and who, they are waiting for, even though officials have refused to announce the date and time of the spectacle in order to discourage the formation of a mob. The justices of the Parlement might have known better, for that's precisely what they've wrought.

Inside her narrow cell within the Conciergerie, the prisoner has lain awake since dawn on the straw pallet that serves as her bed, her stomach thrumming with anticipation, the armpits of her shift moist with sweat. Although she has made friends with her jailers, Madame and Monsieur Hubert, she has deflected their sly inquiries about her husband and her lover. For now, her mind is not on their fates, but on her own. She, too, has heard the hammering, but she hopes it has been in vain, that there will instead be a *lettre de cachet* exiling her to some remote precinct or consigning her to a convent for the rest of her days. Until now she has been certain she could never endure the solitude, the hypocrisy, of an existence amid godly penitents of her own sex, the comforts little better than what she currently enjoys at the hands of the State.

Having lapsed into the twilight between sleep and wake she is rudely startled by the rapping of a truncheon against the wooden shutter covering the small barred window set within the door. The panel affords her a modicum of privacy from the inquisitive eyes of the prison guards. *"Allez-vous,"* a gruff voice commands.

Nothing more? From the tone of those two curt words the woman tries to parse out her destiny. Has she detected a note of cheer? Perhaps the hours ahead will secure her release. Perhaps there will be no convent. Perhaps there will be no punishment at all. The people—the people believed in her innocence. At the trial, she could see it in the spectators' faces; they expected an acquittal instead. Perhaps these past three weeks behind the stone walls of the Conciergerie have been enough to satisfy the authorities.

"Get dressed. And hurry." The guard lingers outside her cell. She patters across the cool earthen floor in her bare feet and reaches onto her tiptoes to slide open the shutter, peering through the bars at the soldier. He grins back through tobacco-stained teeth. *"Bonjour, ma belle."* He flatters her; she knows she is more handsome for her thirty years than pretty.

For modesty's sake she slides the shutter back across the bars, allowing just a sliver of light to illuminate her toilette while she makes her ablutions at the only furnishings in the cell, a small trestle table and a ladder-back chair. She splashes water that has been sitting all night in a porcelain bowl on her face and *poitrine,* under her arms, and between her legs. She removes her nightcap and runs her fingers through her tangle of brown curls. In a moment of vanity, she inserts a gold hoop into each ear, lending her the defiant appearance of a *gitane.* Appraising her image in a shard of mirror, she is pleased. Then she quickly rolls on her hose, securing them with garters of black ribbon, shoves her feet into a pair of worn leather shoes, and slips her stays over her chemise, lacing them tightly in front so that her bosom juts prominently from the contours of the simple morning dress she hastily dons. A wool cape the color of drying blood, trimmed in silver *passementerie,* crowns her slender shoulders. Sliding open the wooden shutter, *"Suis prête,"* she announces. "I'm ready."

The guard, Lieutenant Gabin, ominous enough in his uniform—the deeply hooded blue cape that all but obscures his features—unbolts the iron door and leads the way, down the steeply winding back stairs, the usual path by which the woman descends each morning to take her breakfast—a cup of chocolate and a crust of bread—with the Huberts. He enters a room opposite the jailers' apartment. The woman, close on his heels, follows him, but no sooner does she pass through the open door than she hears it slam shut behind her, and the jagged scrape of an iron bolt imprisons her in the chamber as though she is an animal needing to be caged.

Her heart leaps into her throat as she wheels about to face the sound, only to be brutally spun around again, seized under the armpits by a pair of gendarmes. Her toes scrabble against the stone floor and kick at her captors' shins as she is hauled into the adjacent Hall of Records, where the men bind her hands and arms with cording. But they have not silenced her mouth, and she spews invectives like vomit, calling them curs and sons of whores, insulted when they only chuckle at her distress.

Tossing her head about in search of a champion, her eyes light on the saturnine face and burly figure of Monsieur Breton, the Court Clerk, and suddenly she recalls a conversation with her jailer; Monsieur Hubert had informed her that the secretary would be reading the official pronouncement of her sentence this morning. Surely if there were to be a reprieve she would not have been treated so violently. Aware now of what is to come, her anguished cries echo off the walls and columns of stone.

"*Non, non,* I will not listen to that wicked verdict! I refuse to bend my knee while you read a judgment rendered by a corrupt Parlement bribed by my enemies to rule against me!"

No sooner do these words issue from her lips than her tormentors attempt to force her to her knees. But she is determined to resist them, and is far fiercer than they have anticipated. She fights back with every ounce of strength until she is caught by the elbows and suspended between the guards like an unruly brat while her legs, kicking angrily beneath her skirts, ineffectually pummel the air.

Monsieur Breton's words are never heard, drowned out by the screams of the accused. Her efforts to break free of the gendarmes leave her exhausted, and she is nearly hoarse from shouting when she is dragged out of doors into the bright sunlight of the courtyard. A halter is thrown over her neck and she is tethered inside a cart that draws her to the scaffold like a calf driven to market.

What a rabble has gathered to witness her disgrace! If her hands were free she would lift one to her eyes to shield it from the sun. She would gaze at the rooftops and into the windows of the houses across the *rue* from the Palais de Justice, for at every *fenêtre* people are pressed against the glass, ogling her. It is not merely the canaille, the riffraff of the capital, who have come out to see her shamed, but members of the aristocracy from which she descends, who paid heavily for the privilege. She does not know what a brisk trade there has been selling prime places both in and out of doors from which to witness the execution of her sentence; does not notice a finely dressed gentleman standing behind one of the windows in the company of a particularly attractive young lady. The courtesan's back is pressed firmly against his torso and thighs as one of his hands absentmindedly toys with her breast through her blue silk bodice. In the duc de Crillon's other hand he holds a quizzing glass, usually an accessory for operas and dances, but today it offers a better view of the accused and of her public punishment.

Below the duc, the shadows lengthen as the hour nears noon. The cart draws to a halt near the foot of the scaffold and two gendarmes in their blue coats drag the accused up the wooden staircase to the platform where the *bourreau,* the executioner, awaits. As she fights them every step of the way, they nearly lose their footing, and when they reach the summit she scans the crowd, seeking a friendly face among the thousands of ruddy cheeks and broad grins, among the countless children pressing against the entrance gates and gilt-tipped iron railings that rim the courtyard.

"Save me!" she implores. "Save an innocent woman, a descendant of France's former kings!" Her eyes are wild with panic and she jerks her body to and fro in an effort to break loose from her bonds. Her cries of despair rend the air, but the people—her countrymen and -women who these past few years she has foolishly accounted her friends—have come for a show.

Like a magician revealing an illusion the *bourreau* whisks a black velvet cloth across a table, and at the sight of his instruments of torture, the accused woman unleashes another torrent of abuse against the judges of the Parlement and the Cardinal de Rohan.

But her shouts are drowned out by the din of the crowd as the guards begin to disrobe her. For this they must first cut the cords that bind her arms. The steel blade of a knife flashes, drawn from a gendarme's leather sheath, and in an instant her wrists are free and her nails fly, aiming for the faces of her captors.

"Don't worry, *ma chère,*" the executioner soothes, in a tone one might use to calm an unruly child, but she is sobbing too loudly to hear him. He removes the whip from the table. "It will all be over very soon."

The sight of the lash sends the woman into another agonized frenzy. She recalls the words of her sentence: *Condemned to be flogged and beaten, naked with rods, by the public executioner . . .*

A rough hand grasps the back of her gown, holding it away from her body, and one clean slash of the knife cuts through the layers of silk. But she will not slip her arms from the sleeves, and her flailing fists are too quick for her captors to clasp. The officer warns her, ridiculously, "Stop moving! We do not want to hurt you," but she is like a frightened animal and will not heed.

The sleeves are sliced open, revealing her sweat-stained chemise. The woman tosses her head; errant tendrils fall into her eyes, eyes that are filled with tears of terror and fear. "Snatch me, I beg you, from my executioners!" she cries, reaching toward the onlookers. "It is my own fault that I suffer this ignominy—I had only to speak one name and could have made sure of being hanged instead."

Her back must be exposed in order for the sentence of flogging to be legally fulfilled. With the bravado of a showman at a carnival the lieutenant takes his dagger and splits the laces down the front of her stays. Whistles and catcalls of approval greet his performance. From there it is a simple matter to rend the flimsy batiste of the woman's shift, baring her entire torso and her high breasts.

From his vantage at the window opposite the courtyard the duc de Crillon feels his heartbeat quicken and he pulls the courtesan to him so that her derrière presses against his silken breeches. He had used the privilege of rank to secure this optimal view, having written to the cardinal's attorney, Monsieur Target, *I am consumed with curiosity to see this woman scourged with the rods which you, in a manner of speaking, have prepared for her.* The outer rooms of the lawyer's office, those of the duc de Brissac's *hôtel* next door, and many other edifices with a view of the courtyard, are crowded with men and women of means, nibbling macarons and sipping brandy or champagne as they enjoy the ignominious display.

The accused struggles to cover her nakedness; mothers amid the crowd try to shield the eyes of their children; but the two lieutenants grasp the woman's arms, and by extending them, unwittingly pose her in the tableau of a martyr. Derisive laughter from the rabble degenerates into all manner of blasphemous remarks. "Some Madonna," shouts one man. "*I'd* worship her!" hollers another in reply.

The *bourreau* orders the soldiers to spin the woman around so that the hooting will cease and the crowd may witness her flagellation. His victim's guilt or innocence doesn't keep him awake at night; it is not within his purview. At the first crack of the whip upon her bare back, the woman cries out, "Save me, my friends! It is the blood of the Valois they are desecrating!" The lash falls nineteen times more and with each subsequent stroke, the throng becomes less exhilarated, even bored, daring to surmise that the flogging is being carried out in a most perfunctory way. There is not enough blood. A cabbage head, lobbed from within the crowd, glances off the edge of the scaffold. The catcalls are now aimed at the executioner.

"Rather pro forma, that," remarks a disappointed English journalist, who has traveled across the Channel purely to cover the spectacle for his London broadsheet.

The woman would disagree. She can feel the raw welts rising on her skin with every stinging stroke. At last, the torment is over and she collapses to the floorboards in an incoherent blizzard of curses, cries, and tears. Her hair tumbles down her flayed back in loose ringlets.

But her punishment is only half completed. The clamor of the crowd has drowned out the sizzle of the brazier. The lieutenants hoist the woman to her feet to receive the balance of her public penalty. *To be branded upon both shoulders with a hot iron . . .* The head has already been heating and the executioner raises it aloft so that the crowd can see the shape of the brand: V for *voleuse*—thief. Some cheer; others gasp; still others can be heard weeping.

There is a moment of dreadful, deafening silence as the *bourreau* approaches the woman with the glowing iron. Behind his hood, his small eyes are grim. As he clasps her by the arm the soldier relinquishes his grip, and in that fleeting moment the prisoner slips from their grasp. She bolts across the scaffold and down the wobbly flight of steps as the executioner, branding iron in hand, gives chase. Tripping on the final step the woman falls headlong, scraping her palms, and begins to writhe in agony from the lashing she has only just received. She rolls away from the scaffold, bumping across the uneven cobbles, as if by doing so she could stop the pain, but she only increases her torment. Her mind is a jumble; her only thought, to escape the executioner.

In this she has no prayer. The *bourreau* quickly hauls her to her knees, pressing the brand into the tender flesh of her left shoulder; a pale bluish vapor floats about her mane of curls. The stench causes two onlookers to vomit onto the paving stones. A nearby child hides her face in her hands.

At that moment the woman's body is seized with such a violent convulsion that the executioner is unable to steady the branding iron. The red-hot instrument misses her back entirely. The second V does not land on her right shoulder but upon the delicate flesh of her breast.

She releases a howl that rattles the glass of the windows above the courtyard and sends a shiver coursing through the spine of the duc de Crillon's inamorata. Several women in the crowd are moved to tears, but they are nothing to those that streak the prisoner's face. Her eyes widen and her mouth gapes ghoulishly. After another prolonged spasm, she manages to rise, having harnessed all the fire of the Furies. She places her hands, stippled with blood, on the *bourreau*'s broad shoulders as if to bravely steady herself. And then with a roar she sinks her teeth into his shoulder, biting through his protective leather vest all the way to the skin.

He emits an involuntary cry of shock.

Turning to the mob, the woman shrieks, "It is the queen! It is the queen who should be here in my place! My only crime is that of having served her too well!" Her spittle sprays the crowd and flecks her chin and lips like wet snow. Overcome with pain, she collapses to the ground as the blue sky above her head appears to turn impenetrably black.

How quickly those who had come to enjoy the woman's punishment take up her cry and martyr her instead! The voices of the rabble begin distinctly at first, cursing *l'Autrichienne*—the Austrian bitch. Within moments they have reached a crescendo. "Marie Antoinette is the real *voleuse*! It is the greedy queen who should have suffered this fate! *Monsieur le bourreau,* why did you not brand *her*?"

ONE

Queen of France

⁓ Twelve Years Earlier ⁓

May 8, 1774

TO: COMTE DE MERCY-ARGENTEAU, AMBASSADOR EXTRAORDINARY AND PLENIPOTENTIARY TO THE COURT OF VERSAILLES:

My Dear Mercy,

I understand that the death of my sovereign brother is imminent. The news fills me with both sorrow and trepidation. For as much as I account Antoinette's marriage to the dauphin of France among the triumphs of my reign, I cannot deny a sense of foreboding at my daughter's fate, which cannot fail to be either wholly splendid or extremely unfortunate. There is nothing to calm my apprehensions; she is so young, and has never had any powers of diligence, nor ever will have—unless with great difficulty. I fancy her good days are past.

Maria Theresa

LA MUETTE, MAY 21, 1774

"My condolences on the passing of His Majesty, Your Majesty."

"Your Majesty, my condolences on the death of His Majesty."

"Permit me, *Votre Majesté,* to tender my deepest condolences on the expiration of His Majesty, Louis Quinze."

One by one they filed past, the elderly ladies of the court in their mandated mourning garb, like a murder of broad black crows in panniered gowns, their painted faces greeting each of us in turn—my husband, the new king Louis XVI, and me. We had been the sovereigns of France for two weeks, but under such circumstances elation cannot come without sorrow.

Louis truly grieved for the old king, his late *grand-père.* As for the others, the straitlaced prudes—*collets-montés,* as I dubbed them—who so tediously offered their respects that afternoon in the black-and-white tiled hall at the hunting lodge of La Muette, I found their sympathy—as well as their expressions of felicitations on our accession to the throne—as false as the blush on their cheeks. They had not loved their former sovereign for many decades, if at all. Moreover, they had little confidence in my husband's ability to rule, and even less respect for him.

"Permettez-moi de vous offrir mes condoléances. J'en suis desolée." I giggled behind my fan to my devoted friend and attendant Marie Thérèse Louise de Savoie-Carignan, the princesse de Lamballe, mimicking the warble of the interminable parade of ancient crones—centenarians, I called them. "Honestly, when one has passed thirty, I cannot understand how one dares appear

at court." Being eighteen, that twelve-year difference might as well have been an eternity.

I found these old women ridiculous, but there was another cause for my laughter—one that I lacked the courage to admit to anyone, even to my husband. In sober truth, not until today when we received the customary condolences of the nobility had the reality of Papa Roi's death settled upon my breast. The magnitude of what lay before us, Louis and me, was daunting. I was overcome with nerves, and raillery was my release.

The duchesse d'Archambault approached. Sixty years of rouge had settled into her hollowed cheekbones, and I could not help myself; I bit my lip, but a smile matured into a grin, and before I knew it a chuckle had burbled its way out of my mouth. When she descended into her reverence I was certain I heard her knees creak and felt sure she would not be able to rise without assistance.

"Allow me, Your Majesty, to condole you on the death of the king-that-was." The duchesse lapsed into a reverie. *"Il etait si noble, si gentil . . ."*

"Vous l'avez détesté!" I muttered, then whispered to the princesse de Lamballe, "I know for a fact she despised the king because he refused her idiot son a military promotion." When the duchesse was just out of earshot, I trilled, "So noble, so kind."

"Your Majesty, it does not become you to mock your elders, especially when they are your inferiors."

I did not need to peer over my fan to know the voice: the comtesse de Noailles, my *dame d'honneur,* the superintendent of my household while I was dauphine and my de facto guardian. As the youngest daughter of Empress Maria Theresa of Austria, I had come to Versailles at fourteen to wed the dauphin; and had been not merely educated, but physically transformed in order to merit such an august union. Yet, there had still been much to learn and little time in which to master it. The comtesse had been appointed my mentor, to school me in the rigid rituals of the French court. For this I had immediately nicknamed her Madame Etiquette, and in the past four years not a day had gone by that I had not received from her some rebuke over a transgression of protocol. Just behind my right shoulder the princesse de Lamballe stood amid my other ladies. Our wide skirts discreetly concealed another of my attendants, the marquise de Clermont-Tonnerre, who had sunk to her knees from exhaustion. I heard a giggle. The marquise was known to pull faces from time to time and kept all of us in stitches with her ability to turn her eyelids inside out and then flutter them flirtatiously.

"Who are you hiding?" quizzed Madame de Noailles. My ladies' eyes darted from one to another, none daring to reply.

"La marquise de Clermont-Tonnerre est tellement fatiguée," I replied succinctly.

"That is of no consequence. It is not comme il faut. Everyone must stand during the reception."

I stepped aside. "Madame la marquise, would you kindly rise," I commanded gently. With the aid of a woman at either elbow she stood, and the vast swell of her belly straining against her stays was as evident as the sheen on her brow. "I believe you know the comtesse de Noailles," I said, making certain Madame Etiquette could see that the marquise was *enceinte.* "I am not yet a mother, mesdames, although I pray for that day. I can only hope that when it comes, common sense will take precedence over protocol. And as queen, I will take measures to ensure it." I offered the marquise my lace-edged handkerchief to blot her forehead. "As there is nowhere to sit, you may resume your former position, madame, and my ladies will continue to screen you from disapproving eyes."

I glanced down the hall, noticing the line of courtiers stopped in front of Louis a few feet away. There was much daubing of eyes, yet only his were genuinely moist. Then I returned my attention to the comtesse de Noailles. We were nose to nose now; and I was no longer an unruly child in her custody. One mother who scolded me at the slightest provocation was sufficient; I had no need of a surrogate. "You and your husband have served France long and faithfully," I began coolly, "and you have devoted yourselves tirelessly without respite. The time has come, therefore, for you to take your congé. My husband and I will expect you to pack your things and retire to your estate of Mouchy before the week is out."

Her pinched face turned as pale as a peeled almond. But there was nothing she could say in reply. One did not contradict the will of the Queen of France.

"The princesse de Lamballe will be my new *dame d'honneur,*" I added, noting the expression of surprise in my attendant's eyes and the modest blush that suffused her cheeks. I had caught her completely unawares, but what better time to reward her loyalty?

The comtesse lowered her gaze and dropped into a deep reverence. "It has been an honor to have served Your Majesty." The only fissure in her customary hauteur was betrayed by the tremolo in her voice. For an instant, I regretted my decision. Yet I had long dreamed of this moment. From now on, I would be the one to choose, at least within my own household, what was comme il faut. As the comtesse rose and made her way along the hall to offer her condolences to the king, I felt as though a storm cloud that had followed me about from palace to palace—Versailles, Compiègne, Fontainebleau—had finally lifted, leaving a vibrant blue sky.

At the hour of our ascension to the throne, after the requisite obsequies from the courtiers, we had fled the scene of Louis XV's death nearly as fast as our coach could bear us, spending the first nine days of our reign at the Château de Choisy on the banks of the Seine while the innumerable rooms of Versailles were scrubbed free of contagion. Yet I was bursting to return, to begin making my mark. No one alive could recall when a queen of France had been much more than a dynastic cipher. Maria Theresa of Spain, the infanta who had wed the Sun King, was almost insignificant at court. She spent much of her time closeted in her rooms drinking chocolate and playing cards with her ladies and her dwarves, and had so little rapport with her subjects that when they were starving for bread she suggested that they eat cake instead—this much I had learned from my dear abbé Vermond, who had instructed me in the history of the queens of France when I was preparing to marry the dauphin. The mild-mannered abbé had accompanied me to Versailles as my reader, to offer me spiritual guidance, and he still remained one of my only confidants.

In any case, Maria Theresa of Spain had died nearly a hundred years ago. And her absence from public life had afforded Louis XIV plenty of opportunities to seek companionship in the arms of others. They, not his dull queen, became the arbiters of taste at court.

My immediate predecessor, Marie Leszczyńska, the pious consort of Louis XV who passed away two years before I arrived at Versailles, had been the daughter of a disgraced Polish king, forced to live in exile. She bore Louis many useless daughters, but only one dauphin to inherit the throne—the father of my husband—and he died while his papa still wore the crown. Like the queen before her, she endured a shadowy existence, maintaining her spotless propriety while my husband's *grand-père* flaunted his latest *maîtresse en titre*. No one noticed what she wore or how she dressed her hair. Instead, it was Madame la marquise de Pompadour who had defined the fashion in all things for a generation. And then Madame du Barry, Louis XV's last mistress, set the tone, but there was no queen to rival her—only me. And I had failed miserably, never sure of myself, always endeavoring to find my footing; desperate to fascinate a timid husband who could not bring himself to consummate our marriage. I had wasted precious time by allowing the comtesse du Barry to exert her influence, over the court and over Papa Roi, much to the consternation of my mother.

Yet I was determined to no longer be a disappointment. Not to Maman. Not to France. In the aftermath of Louis XV's demise, the comtesse du Barry was now consigned to a convent. Her faithful followers at court, the "Barryistes," would simply have to accustom themselves to the absence of her bawdy wit and gaudy gowns.

The condolences of the nobility at La Muette marked the end of the period of full mourning. When the last of the ancient courtiers had risen, the king and I made our way outside to the courtyard where the royal coach awaited us. I dared not voice my thoughts to Louis but I felt as though we had spent the past ten days in Purgatory and now, as the gilded carriage clattered over the gravel and out onto the open road toward Versailles where we would formally begin our reign, we were finally on our way to Heaven.

I had first entered the seat of France's court through the back route in every way—as a young bride traveling in a special berline commissioned by Louis XV to transport me from my homeland. How eager he had been to show me Versailles, from the Grand Trianon with its pink marble porticoes, to the pebbled *allées* that led past the canals and around the fountains all the way to the grand staircase and the imposing château that his great-*grand-père* the Sun King had transformed from a modest hunting *boîte* into an edifice that would rival all other palaces in Europe. And oh, how disappointed I had been on that dreary afternoon: The fountains were dry, the canals cluttered with debris, and the hallways and chambers of the fairyland château reeked of stale urine.

How different now the aspect before me as we approached the palace from the front via the Ministers' Courtyard. The imposing gateway designed by Mansart loomed before us, its gilded spikes glinting in the soft afternoon sunlight. I rolled open the window of the carriage and peered out. Then, turning back to my husband, giddy with anticipation I exclaimed, "Tell me the air smells sweeter, *mon cher*!"

"Sweeter than what?" Louis looked as if he had a bellyache, or a stitch in his side from a surfeit of brisk exertion. As neither could have been the case, "What pains you, Sire?" I asked. I rested my gloved hand in his. He made no reply but the pallor on his face was the same greenish hue as I recalled from our wedding day some four years earlier. He was terrified of what awaited him, fearful of the awful responsibility that now rested entirely upon his broad shoulders. And as much as I desired to be a helpmeet in the governance of the realm, I was no more than his consort. Queens of France were made for one thing only. And *that* responsibility, *I* was painfully aware, I had thus far failed to fulfill.

I pressed Louis's hand in a gesture of reassurance. Just at that moment, the doors of the carriage were sprung open and the traveling steps unfolded by a team of efficient footmen. *"Sois courageux,"* I murmured. "And remember—there is no one to scold you anymore. The crown is yours."

The Ministers' Courtyard and the Cour Royale just inside the great gates were once again pulsing with people. The vendors had returned to their customary locations and were already doing a brisk business renting hats and swords to the men who wished to visit Versailles but were unaware of the etiquette required. The various *marchandes* of ribbons and fans and *parfums* had set up their stalls as well. I wondered briefly where they had been during the past two weeks. How had they put bread on their tables while the court was away?

My husband adjusted the glittering Order of the Holy Spirit which he wore pinned to a sash across his chest. But for the enormous diamond star, his attire was so unprepossessing—his black mourning suit of ottoman striped silk was devoid of gilt embroidery, and his silver shoe buckles were unadorned—that he could have easily been mistaken for a wealthy merchant. As we were handed out of the carriage into the bright afternoon, at the sight of my husband a great cheer went up. *"Vive le roi Louis Seize!"* How the French had hated their old king—and how they loved their new sovereign. *Louis le Desiré* they called my husband.

Louis reddened. I would have to remind him that kings did not blush, even if they were only nineteen. "*Et mon peuple*—my good people—*vive la reine Marie Antoinette!*" he exclaimed, leading me forth as if we were stepping onto a parquet dance floor instead of the vast gravel courtyard.

They did not shout quite as loudly for me. I suppose I had expected they would, and managed to mask my disappointment behind a gracious smile. When I departed Vienna in the spring of 1770 my mother had not so much exhorted, but *instructed* me to make the people of France love me. I dared not tell her that they weren't fond of foreigners, and that even at court there were those who employed a spiteful little nickname for me—*l'Autrichienne*—a play on words, crossing my nationality with the word for a female dog. Didn't Maman realize that France had been Austria's enemy for *nine hundred years* before they signed a peace treaty with the Hapsburgs in 1756? Make the French love me? It was my fondest hope, but I had so many centuries of hatred to reverse.

The courtyards teemed with the excitement of a festival day.

Citizens, noisy, curious, and jubilant, swarmed about us as we made our way toward the palace. A flower seller offered me a bouquet of pink roses, but I insisted on choosing only a single perfect stem and paying for it out of my own pocket. Sinking to her knees in gratitude, she told me I was "three times beautiful." I thanked her for the unusual compliment and tried to press on through the crowd. After several minutes of jostling and much waving and smiling and doffing of hats, we finally reached the flat pavement of the Marble Courtyard and the entrance to the State Apartments.

For days I had imagined how it would feel to enter Versailles for the first time as Queen of France. I rushed up the grand marble staircase clutching my inky-hued mourning skirts, anxious to see *my* home, as I now thought of it—*my* palace. Would I view it through new eyes, now that I was no longer someone waiting—now that I had *become*?

Like a caterpillar bursting from its chrysalis, I emerged into the Salon d'Hercule, with its soaring pilasters topped with gilded acanthus leaves, and glided airily through the State Apartments, appraising them with the keen eyes of ownership, noting immediately which wall coverings and upholstery were faded or threadbare—or which simply were not to my taste—and were therefore in need of replacement. I had nearly forgotten how much the chimneys smoked. Something would have to be done about the intolerable soot that coated every surface with a patina of black grime every time a fire was lit.

By now I was trailed by a phalanx of attendants, and suddenly I found myself giving them orders, commanding this *petite armée* to remove this and cover that and "Send for the royal *tapissiers*!" *Everything* would be redecorated, befitting the splendor of the glorious new reign of Louis XVI! My imagination was swirling with color. The Queen's Apartments had not been occupied in six years, and to put it bluntly, Marie Leszczyńska had not been a stylish woman. If I was to give birth to the future king of France in her former bedchamber, much would need to be ameliorated. Hues that were dear to me—cream and gold and pink—and floral motifs, should abound. "Make a note of it!" I instructed the princesse de Lamballe, my pulse racing with anticipation.

That night, long after the tedious ceremonial business of our respective *couchers,* in which we were formally undressed and put to bed in the presence of any number of the highest ranking members of the nobility, Louis visited me in that great bed. I had lain awake so long, I feared he might have fallen asleep or decided not to honor me with his presence. "Where did you come from?" I asked him.

His face, illuminated by the candle glow, looked bemused. "My bed. Where should I have come from?" The corners of his full, soft mouth suddenly turned downward and his expression became crestfallen. "You didn't think I was with anyone else . . . ? Another woman?" He extinguished the candle with a pinch of his fingers and drew the hangings, cocooning us in a waterfall of brocade.

"Mon Dieu, non!" I gasped. The thought had never occurred to me. "I meant the great bed of State where Papa Roi used to hold his *levers* and *couchers,* or the bedchamber in the king's private apartments. The one where he . . ." I didn't finish the sentence, unwilling to contemplate the image of the old king's passion for the vulgar, voluptuous comtesse du Barry.

"Neither feels right to me. Not yet," Louis admitted. His voice was barely above a whisper. "It's almost as though I can feel *Grand-père*'s shadow."

"Then you must take a deep breath and step into the sun," I whispered. "We are the future of France now. It is here." Timidly, I reached for his hand and placed it over my belly, resting his palm on the soft cambric of my nightgown. Our first night in Versailles as the new sovereigns of the realm. Wouldn't this be the perfect time to finally consummate our marriage and start a family to continue the Bourbon line?

But Louis froze. Although he did not snatch away his hand as he had always done when I had tried so valiantly, so patiently, to encourage him in his marital duty, his fingers became like a claw, stiff and unyielding. I agonized over his reluctance to embrace me. Our attempts had been rare, clumsy, furtive, and fruitless. My husband would moan, or even cry out in pain, as if I were doing him some injury, then turn away from me and refuse to discuss the matter. I was left to gaze at the underside of the embroidered silken canopy, stifling my tears, fearful about being sent home to Austria, falsely accused of barrenness.

I tried to hold his hand. "What is the matter, *mon cher*?"

"Rien," he groaned, clutching his arms to his chest. "It's nothing. Let's go to sleep."

I couldn't mask my disappointment. "Will you kiss me good night first?" He obliged by turning toward me and placing his lips on my forehead. Then he rolled away. Side by side, for several minutes we lay completely still in the darkness. Dozens of questions were dancing inside my mind. Finally I summoned the courage to address them—and my reluctant spouse.

"If you did not want to . . . to love me . . . then why did you come to see me tonight?" I could barely squeeze the words past my lips so great was my humiliation, accumulated over four years of celibacy with only the scantest of attempts at intimacy. Maman had counseled me to employ caresses and *cajoleries* but even the gentlest of inducements had been met with rebuffs.

"I do," Louis insisted, after a considerable pause. "And I love you. It's just that . . . I've told you before . . . I can't explain it . . . it hurts."

"But I didn't even touch you," I replied. "Touch you *there,* I mean. I had thought, perhaps. *Hoped.* You know."

"I did, too," he confessed with a ponderous sigh. "Which is why I am here. Do you have any notion how mortifying it is to creep from the King's Bedchamber to the Queen's, tiptoeing past the sentries, knowing how they will snigger?"

When they learn, as the entire palace will, that our sheets remained unsoiled for yet another night. Ever since our nuptials my mother had insisted that it was unnatural for us to have separate quarters, that we should share a connubial bedroom as she had done with Papa for the entirety of their marriage and the birth of their sixteen children. It was the Austrian way. But such informality was not comme il faut at the French court.

"If it hurts, then promise me you will speak to *monsieur le médecin.*" Louis was silent. *"Mon cher?"* It pained me to know he was suffering, but it was not the first time I had encouraged him to seek the advice of his personal physician.

"I promise," Louis grumbled. It was the sound of a man who wished to avoid the whole unpleasant business. I knew then to leave well enough alone. But there was another subject that weighed nearly as heavily upon my chest, and one that was almost as personal, for there was scarcely a single thing we did, from getting dressed in the morning to retiring at night, that was not also a matter of State.

"Louis?" I whispered, staring into the blackness overhead.

"*Oui?* Are you not tired yet?" Spoken like a man prostrate with fatigue.

"*Non*—not just yet. My mind is racing."

"*Eh bien*—catch it, then."

I giggled. "Is that an order, Sire? I am hurt, too," I began, slowly, "but in a different way. I thought this was to be our world now. And, to that end, I have been wondering . . . why . . . after you finally recognized what a detestable man your former tutor the duc de la Vauguyon is . . . why one of the first things you do as king is to name two of his friends as your top ministers." I had hoped that he would recall the duc de Choiseul, who had been an architect of our marriage and a trusted minister of the late king until Madame du Barry forced his removal. This my husband had agreed to, but only in part; Choiseul's involvement in the new government would be nominal at best.

"Toinette, why do you raise this now?" Louis was at this instant completely awake, and his voice had become guarded, despite his use of the same pet name for me that my favorite sister Charlotte had always employed.

"Why *not* discuss it now? When else can I speak to you utterly alone? When there is no one to overhear us? When I feel I have your complete confidence and trust?

"The comte de Vergennes?" I murmured. "How could you select a Foreign Minister who is not a friend of Austria when your wife is a Hapsburg? And I thought you hated the duc d'Aiguillon as much as I did and yet you allowed your aunt Adélaïde to bully you into sending for his *uncle,* the comte de Maurepas. You have chosen for your Chief Minister a man who is old enough to have been the father of Papa Roi!" As a way of asserting his dominion (and, to my mind, further separating me from the seat of power), the elderly minister had immediately taken over the comtesse du Barry's suite of rooms, a hidden warren that lay just behind the King's Apartments. My husband had not uttered a word of remonstrance regarding this act of audacity. "Where is that new beginning we planned? And how can we ever hope to achieve it when you are holding the reins while facing backwards?"

No sooner had these words escaped my lips than I knew I had said far too much. My husband's silence hung in the great bedchamber like a third presence. He sighed heavily and I was punished for my mistake by twin pools of tears that stung my eyes.

Finally, he spoke. "I had not thought to ask you. I am sorry.

In France the queen is not consulted in matters of State." Louis's voice was soft but firm.

I knew this; I had just hoped we would be different. There were so many things I wished to change now that we were king and queen. And wasn't that, in some measure at least, what being the sovereign was all about—the ability to make the rules? Why carry on with the ones you never liked? Nowhere did it say that kings (or queens) had to martyr themselves to etiquette—or law—even at Versailles. In 1771 Louis XV had even exiled the Parlements, France's judicial bodies, for refusing to ratify his edicts; and instead overrode them in a *lit de justice* where he reposed like a Roman Caesar on a bed of cushions. Papa Roi had made a number of enemies with this exercise in autocracy, even among the Princes of the Blood, his own cousins. My husband, unlike his *grand-père* in nearly every way, in one of his first acts as king, recalled the Parlements, believing it was better to rule as a friend of the people, with a firm but just hand. I wondered if he had done the right thing. It seemed as though the king of France could never make everyone happy at once, for whatever decision he made was bound to anger the clergy or the nobility or the trade guilds or the merchants or the farmers or the army; yet even as I saw that Louis was already seeking to improve the lives of our subjects, one faction or another vociferously resisted his new programs and sought to prevent him from achieving them. But why must I be excluded from these plans? At Maman's skirts I had been inculcated with the lesson that it is the Christian duty of a princess, no less a queen, to give charity to those who were born under less fortunate circumstances.

At least my husband had bowed to my wishes and recalled my distant relation, the unctuous prince de Rohan, from his diplomatic post. I had met him only once, when he had greeted me upon my arrival in France, but the single occasion sufficed to make me dislike him. A particular favorite of Madame du Barry (for they shared a louche manner of living), at her instigation Papa Roi had named him his ambassador to Austria. Maman had been appalled by the appointment, for the prince had nothing good to say about the Hapsburgs, and was particularly insulting to her. In a letter to the old king's *maîtresse en titre,* the prince de Rohan dared to repeat a joke that Frederick of Prussia had made at Maman's expense after the partition of Poland was affected. "The Devil," as my mother called Frederick, had jested that in one hand my mother held a handkerchief and wept for the poor innocent Poles, while in her other she wielded a sword against them.

According to Maman, who minced no words on his account, the prince had arrived in Vienna in January 1772, and proceeded to install himself like an Oriental pasha, setting up a private brothel in his residential mansion. Maman, a devout Catholic, remained further offended by the prince's cavalier attitude toward the Church despite his aspirations to a sinecure in it. He rode booted and spurred through religious processions, hunted on Sundays, and harbored an unhealthy fascination for mysticism and the occult. He illicitly funded his extravagant mode of living by smuggling silk and then selling it at a tremendous profit, in violation of religious custom. And still, according to Maman, he had amassed enormous debts although he refused to economize, attended as he was by scarlet-liveried servants whose uniforms were trimmed in gold lace.

It was a small victory, but at least I had been able to do something for Austria. Yet my mother expected much more. As my sister Charlotte had so swiftly managed to achieve once she became Queen of Naples, Maman wanted me to master my husband.

Several minutes of painful silence elapsed. I found myself

counting Louis's ragged wheezing breaths. At length, he reached out and stroked my hand. "I'll make it up to you, Toinette. This I promise."

In the darkness, the grim expression on my lips metamorphosed into a hopeful grin. "Does that mean I get to choose the next minister?"

The enormous bedchamber echoed with my husband's braying laugh, as though I had just told him the silliest joke. "No, of course not—but I assure you, it will be something wonderful. I have just the present in mind; and I do not think you will be disappointed."

I fell asleep anxiously endeavoring to imagine what he had conceived, for I knew what Maman would think of Louis's attempts to mollify me. What could be a satisfying substitute for power?

TWO

Le Grand Mogol et le Petit Trianon

June 14, 1774

My Dear Daughter,

Although you are surely feeling a certain headiness now that you preside over the most illustrious court in Europe, allow me to offer a few words of advice to ease your transition from dauphine to queen. As the reign of Louis XV was a lengthy one, many of the nobles have been accustomed for decades to a certain manner of doing things. For the time being, change nothing. Otherwise, chaos and intrigue will become insurmountable, and you, my dear children, will find yourselves in such a tangle that you will be unable to extricate yourselves.

What I fear most, Antoinette, is that you think of nothing but pleasure. Now more than ever you must learn to interest yourself in serious matters, for this may be most useful if the king should seek your counsel. Be careful to avoid misleading him into any great or unusual expenditure.

Maria Theresa

"Look!" I exclaimed to the duchesse de Chartres, as we strolled by the window of a shop in Paris. "That's the eighth display we've seen this morning!" I could not wait to write to my mother. She would be delighted to hear that portraits of Louis and me were displayed prominently in nearly every merchant's window. The outpouring of love for us in the capital had been so gratifying. At the opera and the theater my appearance was greeted with cheers, as was my husband's, of course, but he did not accompany me often. Try as I might, I still could not disabuse the king of his conviction that the soprano arias resembled the cries of tormented cats.

A gloved footman, as splendidly liveried as any employed by the nobility, reached for the polished brass handle and beckoned the way into the lush salon. Another servant invited us to make ourselves comfortable on a plump divan upholstered in saffron and gold brocade, while a third offered to bring us a pot of coffee. *"C'est divine, n'est-ce pas?"* sighed the duchesse.

"I cannot believe you have kept le Grand Mogol a secret from me, Louise!" Pastoral landscapes and imposing portraits of prominent aristocrats reposing in heavy gilded frames dominated the cherry damask walls while grand beveled mirrors reflected our images and that of Mademoiselle Rose Bertin's myriad fantastical creations, which she had artfully arranged throughout the emporium. *Grandes pandores,* like the dolls that had once modeled my trousseau, displayed the latest fashions in gowns, headdresses, and accessories. Redolent of a pasha's seraglio, the shop was a tasteful mélange of color and texture, demonstrating how the tactile surfaces of silk and velvet, taffeta and batiste that adorned a woman's body could be enhanced with just the right configuration of spangles, feathers, ruching, lace, or gemstones. I recognized a gauzy white gown with a broad pastel-pink sash on one of the *pandores.* The comtesse du Barry used to receive her guests in such a simple style, her full bosom and unbound blond curls spilling over its décolleté. I shuddered at the memory of my rival. Apparently, she, too, had shopped here, as did, *évidemment,* all the women of fashion. The duchesse noticed my frown. *"Elle a partie,"* she said with a dismissive wave. "She is gone. It is you who should set the tone now."

I rose from the sofa and removed a glove. I wanted to touch everything; to own it. It was all so exquisite. I took a turn about the shop, fingering the fabrics, inspecting the lace, examining the gems. And after several moments, I had the distinct sensation that I was being watched. Turning to my companion, I exclaimed, "Good heavens, you don't think they believe that the Queen of France would steal something?"

"Most certainly not. I merely wondered, as would any proprietress worth her salt, what the Queen of France thinks of my merchandise." A large-boned woman, not too many years older than I, rose from a chaise longue that had been placed in the shadows. Her cheeks were quite red, owing to a robust complexion rather than the circles of rouge applied by women of means at their daily toilette.

"I find it breathtaking," I replied. My eyes lingered over the embellishments she had made to a dozen gowns, and as many bonnets and headdresses, capes and capelets—each one adorned uniquely. "*Absolument magnifique.* Not one bead too many or too few. Your sense of proportion . . . your eye . . ." I gazed about the room again. By now a trio of shopgirls had emerged, each wearing one of the original, enviably beautiful, creations. "It is perfection," I breathed.

The duchesse de Chartres stood. "Mademoiselle Rose Bertin, allow me to present you to Her Most Illustrious Majesty, Marie Antoinette."

The *vendeuse* did not curtsy to me, even after she saw the glimmer of shock in my eyes at her transgression of etiquette. Instead, "I agree with you," she said, towering above me. In her two-inch heels she was nearly my husband's height. "It *is* perfection," she echoed proudly. "Which is why I have the most exclusive clientele in France."

"Do you sew everything here in this atelier?" I asked, wondering what lay behind the lush Orientalism of her décor, the opulent palette of jewel tones that soothed the sensibilities of the browser as it undoubtedly blunted the blow to one's purse.

"Regrettably, the garments themselves are not manufactured here," Mademoiselle Bertin explained, adding with a touch of asperity, "The tailors and seamstresses of France hold a monopoly from the Crown on the construction of clothing. And as an unmarried woman I am denied entrée into the guild." Noting my surprise, she added, "Enhancements and adornments are another matter entirely." In this province an unwed woman could make a mark for herself as a *marchande de modes,* or stylist, retailing her good taste in addition to the separate, and quite costly, trimmings and accoutrements she affixed to the garments and accessories, transforming them into unique, and quite spectacular, ensembles. The *marchande* herself was an advertisement for her wares, proving in her gown of cadet-blue moiré, exquisitely embellished with two slimming lines of ruching that ran from the neckline all the way down the front of the robe to the hem, that a woman with a fuller figure need not fear furbelows.

"*Eh bien,* and what do you think of the duchesse's hair?" asked Mademoiselle Bertin slyly. I wondered if she noticed that I had been staring at her—the *marchande,* not the duchesse—for I was trying to equate the young woman's exquisite sense of style with her somewhat coarse appearance, her features far from delicate, her limbs scarcely dainty. I was also struck by her audacity in daring to speak to me as if I were merely anyone, heedless of conventional manners.

I glanced at the duchesse, whose coiffure, towering several inches from her scalp, was a veritable work of art. For several months now, she had favored similar confections, each of which boasted a narrative or commemorative motif. Last October, her elaborately detailed coiffure announced the birth of her first child, a son. At the time, I was delighted, even envious of the duchesse; but my private jealousy was doubly pricked by her husband's gloating and his clear intimations of superiority over the barren Bourbons. On my first night at Versailles as the fourteen-year-old dauphine, a foreigner amid my new husband's extended family of Princes of the Blood, my *dame d'honneur* had warned me about the duc de Chartres and his equally ambitious and powerful father, the duc d'Orléans, explaining that the long-standing rivalry between the two branches of the royal family precluded their socializing, except for the most formal of occasions. Yet the duchesse and I, who knew nothing of our husbands' affairs, enjoyed a perfectly pleasant friendship.

"Mademoiselle Bertin calls them her *'poufs aux sentiments.'*" Louise touched a lavender-gloved hand to her hair, careful to avoid dipping her finger in the pool of water precariously nestled atop; it resembled a miniature summer garden, complete with gateposts, trellises, climbing vines, and a tiny mobcapped figurine dangling a watering can. "*C'est charmant, oui?* I think she should design one for you. You must have her come to Versailles and discuss it."

"Perhaps Mademoiselle should create a pouf to commemorate my husband's inoculation against the smallpox!" I exclaimed gleefully. I spoke half in jest, relieved to have finally convinced Louis to be vaccinated, against the remonstrance of Mesdames his maiden aunts, his sour-faced ministers, and the entire court—how behind the times the Bourbons were, when we Hapsburgs had all been variolated as children! Ah, then, but what a lark it might be. To become a walking gazette with the latest news atop my head!

How people would talk! I imagined meandering through the verdant paths of the Bois de Boulogne with my attendants or enjoying a charming fête champêtre of strawberries and champagne on the grass in full view of my subjects, or promenading amid the shops at the Palais Royal, or attending the Opéra—and every day, my coiffure would tell a new story! "Come to the palace tomorrow morning," I instructed Mademoiselle Bertin. "I will speak with you after my *lever.*"

"*Votre Majesté,* I have a distinguished and demanding clientele," she replied. "I cannot drop everything on a whim and ignore their custom to do a queen's bidding. And *I* am queen of le Grand Mogol," she added, gesturing expansively about her shop. "Moreover, I would lose nearly the entire day in traveling the ten leagues each way to and from Versailles, which means that I will expect to be compensated for a day's worth of business. So, perhaps *you* would prefer to visit *me* tomorrow."

Who did the woman think she was? I glanced at the duchesse de Chartres but she averted her gaze, evincing no desire to become involved in this contest of wills. "I, too, have a full calendar every day," I replied, eager to assert myself with this provincial tradeswoman (for her accent was not that of a Parisian), no matter how stylish her modes or how singular her coiffures. "I rise and choose the four gowns I will wear during the day from the *gazette des atours;* my tub is wheeled in for my bath; I return to my bed to rest until my breakfast of toasted bread and chocolate—or coffee, if I am in the mood—is brought to me; I receive visits from my closest friends, members of the royal family, and the royal physicians, if necessity dictates—those who have the privilege of *petite entrée* for half the morning; and then at noon it is time to attend to my grand toilette and my formal *lever,* at which I entertain the ministers and diplomats, foreign dignitaries and Princes of the Blood—all those who have the right of the *grande entrée.* So you see, my every moment is accounted for. What some deride as frivolity is in fact a most delicate form of diplomacy. And I ride to the capital at my pleasure, mademoiselle, not at the behest of others. I will see you therefore tomorrow morning during my *lever* in the Queen's Apartments at Versailles and we will discuss your compensation then." My pulse was racing. Why did I feel as though I was at the gaming tables?

Finally, Rose Bertin sank into a curtsy. Lowering her head she murmured, "It is a great honor to have had the pleasure to meet you, *Votre Majesté,* and to dream that I might someday account you my grandest client." She lifted her chin and her eyes met mine. They were sparkling with triumph.

"Where have you been?" Louis quizzed, when I returned to the palace that afternoon. "I have been waiting for you."

"Paris," I replied breathlessly. "With the duchesse de Chartres. I am still so excited that I think my heart is tingling. See!" I clasped his hand and brought it toward my breast but he made an odd face and pulled away.

Changing the subject, he said with a shy grin, "Remember the gift I promised you?" I nodded. "May I present it to you now?"

I expected a bracelet, or perhaps a necklace. But when the king produced a length of purple silk from the pocket of his coat and insisted on fastening it about my head as if we were about to commence a game of blindman's buff, I was truly intrigued. He dismissed our attendants and guided me himself, with one arm about my waist, clasping me by the elbow, as we promenaded through the State Apartments. Heaven knows what the myriad courtiers and visitors who thronged these halls thought to see their sovereigns in such an undignified manner. I heard murmurs of curiosity, and more than one dismayed cluck of disapproval. But the stiff-necked centenarians already thought we were children; why shouldn't we humor them?

Louis gingerly guided me down what I supposed was the

grand staircase just outside the Salon d'Hercule, and out of doors into the Marble Courtyard. A gentle breeze riffled through the pale blue plumes in my hair. We walked for several yards, until the paving stones changed to gravel, and I surmised that we'd reached the Cour Royale. My husband instructed me to gather my skirts and I was handed into a carriage; Louis settled his bulk beside me; and with the exception of a good day's hunting, he was giddier than I'd ever seen him. After docilely trotting for some minutes the coachman drew his team to a halt and the door was sprung open. I reached for the knot behind my head, but Louis playfully caught my wrists.

"Ah, non! C'est défendu, ma chère."

"Forbidden? But why?"

"Not just yet." He took my hand and led me across another expanse of gravel. A heavy iron gate swung open as if it had not been employed in quite a while. "You'll have to tell someone to oil the hinges," I said to my husband.

"Not I," he insisted. "I'm afraid you're responsible for the upkeep from now on." He tugged at the silk blindfold and when the knot would not come undone, clumsily wrestled it over my coiffure, fracturing the delicate spine of a feather. Too curious about the surprise to be upset with him for mussing my hair, I adjusted my vision to the sight before me.

"You like flowers. Well, I have a whole bouquet for you," he said, blushing. When I made no reply other than to gape in astonishment at the prospect before me, he added somewhat breathlessly, "What do you say?" He tilted his head and looked down at me like a large hound who hoped desperately to please his master. "It's all yours, Toinette."

I continued to gaze at the little square villa with openmouthed amazement. It was a perfect jewel box. As the gardeners had not tended to the exterior in some weeks, the creeping ivy and wild roses had begun to spread over the high walls flanking the *petit château,* lending it an overgrown, enchanted aspect that reminded me of the cottages in the Vienna Woods. The waning afternoon light stained the honey-hued stones of the façade coral and violet. "You are giving me le Petit Trianon?"

"Because you were so cross with me for appointing Maurepas and Vergennes."

"Cross" was hardly the word I would have chosen. It didn't begin to define my disappointment. And Maman's. As I admired Louis's attempt at amelioration—bequeathing me the villa that Louis XV had constructed for Madame de Pompadour—I wondered whether it was a fair exchange for influence.

The empress of Austria would say *nein*. But, brimming with curiosity, I could not wait to step inside the late king's former pleasure palace. "Is it true that the dining table is on winches so that it can be raised or lowered from the subterranean kitchen?" I had heard the stories of how Papa Roi had enjoyed many a private repast in the company of Madame du Barry without the servants hovering about them. Evidently, the table could arrive in the salon fully laden, including the illuminated candelabras, so that their trysts would not be disturbed by the intrusion of others.

I was intrigued by any invention that might afford me some measure of privacy in a world where nearly every moment of my life was witnessed. Apart from all the courtiers and family members, my own household numbered five hundred retainers and I was followed everywhere by numerous armed guards—a "detachment of warriors," as abbé Vermond called them. But my husband shrugged. He, too, had never crossed the threshold. Architectural gem that it was, the Petit Trianon had, during the previous reign, been a den of immorality and neither of us had been invited to visit, nor (disapproving as we did of the king's liaison with the du Barry) would we have accepted the offer, had one been extended. But now, as Louis and I promenaded up the walkway toward the entrance to the château, I imagined what *I* might make of it—an exclusive retreat from the bustle of the court and the backbiting of its nobles, as well as from the overbearing etiquette that threatened to strangle me. Here, I thought, as we strolled through the small but perfectly proportioned chambers, the rigid propriety of the palace would be relaxed and the necessary servants would be selected by me for their discretion. Sweet simplicity would reign beside charm. Even the décor, as I immediately began to re-envision it, would dispense with the overblown sensibilities of the rococo. The palette should soothe the spirit with shades of dairy cream, celadon, and robin's egg blue. As ideas took shape in my head I began to chatter of such things to Louis, but he interrupted my oratory with an amused wave.

"It's entirely yours to do with as you wish." Considerable renovations would need to be undertaken. I would not entertain upon any upholstered or lacquered surface chosen by the late king's former mistress, nor sleep in a bed where they indulged their passion for each other. And on inspection, the unremarkable grounds and gardens could, with a healthy dose of imagination, be transformed into a charming fairyland reminiscent of my Austrian childhood. I would speak with Louis's cousin, the prince de Condé, who some years earlier had commissioned an adorable rustic village or *hameau* to be built on the grounds of his Château d'Enghien. Rather than the manicured precision that had been de rigueur at Versailles for centuries, my *hameau* would feature all the accoutrements of the English gardens that were currently the rage in France. I would have follies and little waterfalls . . . and, as I lapsed into a reverie, a little Roman temple dedicated to Love. And a summer house open to the elements where I would eat strawberries, sip orangeade, and play cards *en plein air* with only a few chosen companions. There would be no one to complain behind my back that I had robbed them of yet another perquisite.

Once outdoors again, I tilted my face to the warm waning light, as if to thank the Almighty for the gift of such a splendid day. Louis and I were facing the parterre at the rear of the château. Just at the horizon line seemed the ideal place to erect a theater where my little company would amuse ourselves by performing plays that we had attended at the Comédie-Française. My head was spinning with ideas. Surely being Queen of France was the most delightful occupation imaginable—or could be, if one refused to fade into the shadows. Sinking into a curtsy before my husband, I exclaimed, "I am most beholden to you, Sire, for this magnificent honor."

Louis smiled, shyly relieved. In the four years we had been married I had learned to read his looks. He was thankful to have found something that might occupy my time and distract my thoughts from weightier matters. But my mind was not so lightly disposed as he surmised. If only persuading him to converse with the royal physician were as easy as it had been to convince him to eliminate most of the *grands couverts,* so that I rarely had to stomach the horrid ritual of eating in public, I should be merry indeed!

"I am terrified of being bored," I admitted during my *lever* the following day to Papillon de la Ferté. "And so I intend to banish tedium. It is time that France's queen is seen in public and sets the tone. For far too long, this court has been the domain of harlots who have eclipsed the role of the rightful and virtuous consorts. But I mean to show the world that the court of Louis and Marie Antoinette can be just as full of delights, without the taint of scandal or immorality." I applied rouge to my cheeks and lips, a blend created especially for me by the *maître parfumier* Jean-Louis

Fargeon, while a bevy of courtiers hung upon my every word as they sipped coffee and cups of bittersweet chocolate. Papillon, the Steward of Small Pleasures, took notes on a portable writing desk, scratching away furiously with a quill fashioned from a vibrant yellow plume. All of the court festivities and amusements lay within his creative dominion; judging from the furrow in his brow, never had so much been demanded of his delicate nerves.

"I should like to host two suppers a week with the king," I told him. "And in addition, two dances, one of which will be a masquerade. I will set the theme with you in advance and then you will advise the court of it. Monday evenings are perfect for the masked balls because it commences the week with an element of fun. I think it would be delightful to dress from time to time like some of our delegations from foreign lands. They are so marvelously exotic—the Finns, the Tyroleans, the Lapps—"

If there was anyone at Versailles more adventurous and flamboyant than I (and he wore far more rouge), it was the forty-eight-year-old Papillon, but he had a way of becoming unhinged at the slightest provocation. His pen ceased its furtive scratching. "*Pardonnez-moi, Votre Majesté,* but did you say Lapps?" His lips quivered nervously, alternating between a grim line of fear and a petulant moue.

"*Oui,* Lapps. From Lapland. It's very cold there all the time, so they do remarkably clever things with leather and fur." Clapping my hands excitedly, I turned away from my mirror and spun in my chair to face him. The marquise d'Abrantes sprayed my neck and shoulders with *eau de lavande.* "Can you imagine all of us dressed like that?"

From his shocked expression, evidently Papillon could not fathom such a costume, especially when multiplied by the hundreds, for in addition to superintending the décor it was his responsibility to see that all of the invitees to a *bal masqué* were appropriately attired.

I scanned the faces of the courtiers at my *lever*. The younger ones, such as the princesse de Lamballe, the duc de Lauzun, and the comte d'Artois, seemed intrigued by the idea of so many fêtes, but the old guard, those relics who had passed their greener days during the early reign of Louis XV, regarded me as though I had just compelled them to eat a wedge of fresh lemon. The duchesse de Villars, my mistress of the robes, who had performed the same role for Papa Roi's consort, Queen Marie Leszczyńska, appeared particularly put out. I decided then that I would have to find a new *dame d'atours*. I could not countenance such a sour face every day; it made me melancholy.

What a bunch of hens they were! Even the men—with their dreary gossip and their enameled snuffboxes! "They are grumpy because I have replaced their beloved cavagnole with dancing nearly every night," I said to Papillon. It remained a mystery to me why the lottolike game had been so popular at Versailles. Never was there a pastime more tedious. When I was preparing to become dauphine, every evening in Vienna my mother had forced me to play round after round until my eyes were dry with sleeplessness. I was as fond of wagering as anyone, except perhaps for Louis's youngest brother, Artois, who was the most avid gambler I'd ever seen, but there were card games aplenty, such as piquet and écarté, that were considerably more entertaining.

A few days earlier I had confessed to Louis that perhaps nothing had tickled me more about becoming Queen of France than putting an end to the nightly games of cavagnole.

"You have made enemies," the king had cautioned.

"Really? Over such a trifling matter as that?" In the past I'd often overheard the backbiting chatter of the courtiers—issued mostly from the lips of the older ones who disapproved of me because I was foreign, because I was young, because I was pretty—but for some reason the whispers had become fainter of late. Perhaps they did not wish me to know their views so soon into our reign, as it might be expedient to change them.

"Vraiment, ma chère," Louis had assured me. "Really."

I thought about it for a few moments. Did I care about their opinion? I knew that some courtiers at Versailles had always disliked me and an amendment to the evenings' customary diversions was unlikely to alter their view. *"Tant pis,"* said I. "Too bad. It is a stupid, dreary game. We are France, and France is a young person's kingdom. Dancing is much livelier. And they will come around, you will see. Because they will want your favor."

And now, as I admired my reflection in the mirror and caught the anxious glance of the Steward of Small Pleasures, he looked as if he, too, might have been mourning the monotony of interminable rounds of cavagnole. Before he could nervously echo the word "Lapps" again, or wonder what I meant when I suggested that we all don Indian costumes one night (turbans and wide breeches that hugged one's ankles and yards upon yards of brightly colored silks—whatever did he think I intended?), a footman announced the arrival of Mademoiselle Rose Bertin and a small, elegantly attired gentleman wearing a suit of lilac moiré and a pale pink *perruque.* "Monsieur Léonard Hautier, *Votre Majesté.*"

"He does not have an invitation to my salon," said I.

"Monsieur Léonard est avec moi," came the stentorian reply. Tightly laced into a robe of lawn-green silk spangled with paillettes of mother-of-pearl, and balancing an ostentatiously plumed hat on her lightly powdered curls, Mademoiselle Bertin swept into the room as if she owned it, causing a flutter of alarmed murmurs and curious whispers. Several of my ladies recognized her from le Grand Mogol, which only heightened their disdain. Who did this tradeswoman think she was, to speak so brusquely

in the presence of the highest woman in the realm? Moreover, what was she doing at Versailles, and at the queen's *lever,* where one's noble pedigree, and years of service to the Crown won them the privilege of *entrée*? I detected a number of glowering looks. By inviting a *marchande de modes* into their rarefied midst, once again I had robbed them of another perquisite of rank to which they had so long been accustomed.

Mademoiselle Bertin lowered her large frame into the smallest of curtsies, while the slender Léonard made an elaborate bow. "May we sit?" the *marchande* inquired, inciting another flurry of exclamations after I insisted that my visitors be accommodated, for my mother taught me to have respect for everyone, regardless of rank—unless of course, like the comtesse du Barry, their morals were beneath reproach.

"Monsieur Léonard is one of the most talented *artistes* in Paris," Mademoiselle Bertin informed me smoothly.

Although her tone brooked no contradiction, "I am sure he is," I replied, smiling serenely, "but you see, Sieur Larsenneur has been styling my hair since I was a child in Vienna." With a flourish of the wrist I introduced them to my coiffeur, who with an extremely proprietary air began to restyle a perfectly arranged knot of curls.

Léonard pursed his lips and looked as if he detected the aroma of decaying fish. "I am no mere *friseur,*" he said haughtily. "I am a Physiognomist." He glanced expectantly at Rose Bertin.

"Monsieur creates the spectacular heads. While the poufs are the children of my imagination, it is Léonard whose magical fingers bring them to life." She was a temptress, dangling his unique gifts before me like Circe luring Ulysses with her siren song. And I knew that the pedestrian talents of the aging Sieur Larsenneur, to whom I felt a tremendous loyalty, but whose efforts had never pleased me, did not compare.

"The Queen of France must set the tone, not follow it," said Mademoiselle Bertin silkily. "I took the liberty of bringing some sketches that might please Your Majesty," she added, and at my behest, opened a large leather satchel containing mouthwatering renditions of embellished gowns, hats, cloaks, robes, gloves, shoes—entire ensembles, cap-à-pie, illustrated to the minutest detail. Affixed to each sketch were swatches of the silks, satins, velvets, lace, and brocades.

It was difficult to disguise my admiration as I thumbed through the samples. With each extraordinary design I felt my heart quicken; it was the same sensation that coursed through my veins when I placed a prodigious bet at pharaon, or rode at breakneck speed beside the comte d'Artois in his curricle, a two-wheeled lightweight rig that could travel with such velocity that it had been nicknamed *"le diable."* I had nearly overturned us the first time he handed me the reins as we cantered through the Bois de Boulogne; but we were laughing so hard at the time that Charles didn't realize my distress, utterly unaware that I had no control of his bays.

Coloring slightly as I studied the sketches, I confessed to the *marchande,* "I fear I am as the mouse to the eagle, your unsuspecting prey, for there is not a single creation I would not wish to wear. Therefore"—my fingers lingered over a few inches of striped silk the color of a newly hatched robin's egg—"I am offering you an exclusive appointment."

The incessant chirping of the courtiers diminished to a pregnant hush.

Mademoiselle Bertin shook her head.

"*Quoi?* You refuse the Queen of France?" My hand flew to my breast. Rarely had I been so shocked.

With a benign smile and a tilt of her chin, she said, "Were I to accept such a magnanimous offer, *Majesté,* it would stand neither of us in good stead." To my raised eyebrow, she added, "Here, as magnificent as it is, I would be isolated. Only from Paris, where I am exposed daily to the latest modes, and where I would have so many disparate inspirations, can I create unique ensembles that will not mimic the latest fashions; they will spark them—which is, after all, what the queen must do."

I considered her rationale. She was right. "And of course the balance of your clientele will wish to emulate me."

"Which inures to us both, Madame."

But I had conditions, too. And I could not let her see she was winning. "I see the merit in maintaining your shop in the rue Saint-Honoré—on one condition. No one is to own an article similar or identical to the one you create for me until two weeks after I have worn it first."

The *marchande* smiled. "Done."

"However," I added, "you have my permission to model some of your *grandes pandores* as my likeness, to dress them in creations similar to those you have designed for me, and to publish the philosophy of your art in *Le Journal des Dames* so that people may come to understand what sets your practice apart from the mercers, the tailors, and the seamstresses." I began to discern murmurs of disapproval, even from my own entourage.

But their censure only served to augment the *marchande*'s extraordinary sense of privilege. "You do realize, Madame, that I will need time to discuss these vital matters of the royal wardrobe with you. This morning's tête-à-tête is but an amuse-bouche."

Rose Bertin had indeed whetted my appetite. And how she had managed to enter my salon merely for an interview and in a matter of minutes upend my world, so that I heard myself offering her a private audience two mornings a week, was rather stunning. And, oh, the gasps and exclamations *that* elicited from my aristocratic visitors! Mademoiselle Bertin would have to become truly creative, however, for the period of "little mourning" for the former king would not end until November.

I also gave leave to Monsieur Léonard to return.

"A thousand thanks, *Votre Majesté,*" he said, as his hands fluttered about like a pair of songbirds. "But *bien sûr,* you do understand that I have my *own very* busy shop in the capital. I cannot work exclusively on *la tête de la reine,* because, like Mademoiselle Bertin, I cannot afford, as an *artiste,* to lose the custom of my regular clientele. And, *naturellement,* as soon as they see how I have styled Your Majesty's hair, they will want the very same, which means every time we will always be imagining something new!" His eyes were shining with ideas and silver *écus.*

Finally, the *friseur* and the *marchande* were ushered out of the salon, and as the great doors closed behind them, and I was presented with the basin for the formal washing of my hands, I was treated to yet another earful of astounded remarks, uttered by a panoply of aristocrats whose presences had been sullied by the very persons whose skills they relied upon to dress their hair and clothe their bodies so stylishly. But I had little time for their petty griping. My mind was too occupied with the unpleasant prospect of pensioning off dear Sieur Larsenneur. The poor man had stood mutely by while these two forces of nature with their outré creations had swanned into my *lever* and sailed out again with the promise of royal favor. "I am sorry, monsieur," I said softly, taking his hands in mine. But I saw so clearly now that his talents belonged to another place and time. He had served me, and the House of Hapsburg, faithfully. Although I had never been fond of his coiffures, when I was a slip of a girl he had disguised the flaws of my disproportionately high forehead—*trop bombé,* the French called it—to satisfy the Bourbons' notions of beauty. His handiwork was one reason I had become dauphine and why I was queen today. But to open a new door, I would have to close an old one. Sieur Larsenneur would be compensated handsomely. His retirement would be a comfortable one, yet I always felt a sorrowful pang at giving a loyal retainer his congé. Moreover, inasmuch as I kept Maman apprised of events at Versailles, I dreaded the reply from Vienna.

But I was not as immune to the rumblings of disapproval within the court as I had assumed. I knew there were those who resented the curtailing of the *grands couverts* because it robbed them of the ancient perquisite of watching the royal family dine. And those who grumbled most were hardly the ones we invited to the intimate *soupers* that replaced the public meals. The king chose the female guests for these little suppers; I selected the gentlemen. At Louis's behest, among the frequent guests at our table was the comte de Provence—known as Monsieur, now that he was the next oldest brother of the reigning monarch. But try as I might, I could not bring myself to trust him. When I first came to Versailles, I found his quick wit refreshing, especially when I was forever comparing his silver tongue to Louis's leaden one. The former Provence used to pen wicked little verses about the ministers and courtiers we didn't like—particularly the comtesse du Barry.

But Monsieur was a schemer. I had married the better man by far. He, too, had been well mated, with a squat, swarthy Savoyard princess whose looks and temperament were as foul as her hygiene. The pair of them, after disparaging the du Barry as much as I had, had then joined her coterie. Although the comtesse was now in a nunnery, some of the "Barryistes" remained at court, led by the duc de la Vauguyon, the former tutor of my husband and his brothers. A couple of years ago, Louis and I had caught him in the act of spying on us.

One evening during supper, as the serviette was unfolded and placed in my lap, a little scrap of paper fell to the floor. The footman bent to retrieve it and gave it to me. I unfolded the note and read what had been ominously scrawled upon it in a hand I did not recognize.

Little queen of twenty years
You who treat the people so badly
You'll cross the frontier again.

My eye caught Monsieur's as I slipped the paper into a pocket of my gown, and gently pushed my plate away. Although I kept my head held high, I had no stomach for food.

THREE

The Bees Will Buzz

August—the long, lazy days of summer drifted into each other in a languid haze. With a husband who saw his queen's role as marginal, except in the domestic sphere, but with no children as yet to occupy my hours, I made the etiquette that ruled my days more tolerable by forming a vibrant coterie of my own, surrounded at my *lever,* at fêtes champêtres on the manicured lawns, and on the Grand Canal, by a circle of gallant admirers. They made me laugh—and laughter was the best way for me to forget the burdens of celibacy that clouded my brow. In my salons the sun always shone; showers came in the form of compliments. It amused me to watch my adherents vie for my attentions—Count Esterházy, handsome, but with the look of a pugilist about him; the sardonic prince de Ligne, who proclaimed himself "an Austrian in France and a Frenchman in Austria"; the duc de Coigny, a dashing Field Marshal; the honey-tongued but mercurial comte de Vaudreuil; baron de Besenval—my "dear old lion," I called him—stout, over fifty, and always pontificating about some sort of nonsense with a great deal of authority; my brother-in-law, the comte d'Artois, ever on the lookout for a wager; Montfalcon, the comte d'Adhémar, who played duets with me on the harp; and the man who had secretly set my untried heart atremble, the duc de Lauzun.

In the twenty-six-year-old duc, Armand Louis de Gontaut, I saw a man of the world, chivalrous, cultured, charming. He was the nephew of my dear friend, the duc de Choiseul, whose restoration to the government I continued to champion. Mercifully, the darkly handsome Lauzun bore no physical resemblance to his pug-nosed, russet-haired relation; but I had privately asked myself if I had been drawn to the nephew because of my gratitude and esteem for the uncle.

I had taken to inviting the duc de Lauzun to ride with me every day—yet another joy of being the queen. As dauphine I had been scolded for riding astride, and Maman had penned countless letters from Vienna deriding my equestrian activities. Back then, I had ridden in an effort to captivate my husband. If I could make him love me, I reasoned, he might be less afraid to touch me and might finally consummate our marriage. A wife in name but not in deed, I lived in dread of the Bourbons' displeasure and the possibility that they would send me back to Austria for failing to conceive an heir.

Yet the anonymous note I'd received just a few weeks earlier had sent a shiver along my spine, a chilling reminder that even as queen, my position remained precarious, albeit for different reasons, as it was Louis who continued to balk at performing his marital duty.

One sultry afternoon in early summer, very much like many others in recent weeks, at my invitation the duc de Lauzun met me at the royal stables where our mounts awaited. I anticipated these encounters with a thrumming in my chest, and wondered if Armand felt the same way. The duc's manner was so sure, so confident, so unlike my husband's, that I also found myself guiltily imagining what it might be like to be wed to a decisive man.

A gentle breeze riffled the plume in my deep blue tricorn, and I stepped upwind of the unpleasant odor of ordure. I glanced shyly at the duc. As always, I refused the grooms' assistance, permitting Armand to steady the stirrup and help me into the saddle, holding the horse completely still until I secured my leg over the pommel. In his hands I felt safe. Once I was comfortably positioned, the duc gazed at me in his unsettling way, his dark eyes brimming with a look that blended fire and solicitousness. It nearly put me off balance and I reached for the reins to steady myself. He placed the whip in my gloved hand and as he closed my fingers about the leather handle, I found myself hoping they would linger over mine. But the touch passed in an instant, and minutes later we were cantering side by side toward the Bois de Boulogne, as I stole glances at his noble profile and wondered what color his hair was beneath his powdered periwig.

Like the most successful courtiers at Versailles the duc was an accomplished flirt, always ready with an ingratiating compliment and a winning smile. Often during our afternoon rides, we would dismount and enjoy a peaceful stroll through a quiet glade, our sleeves so nearly touching that I could feel the heat from Armand's body filling the narrow gap between us. These afternoon idylls offered me an escape from the perpetual whirl of court life and the constant scrutiny of courtiers and visitors. The duc was as kind to me as the princesse de Lamballe, but with an altogether more cheerful disposition; moreover, I found his words as irresistible as ambrosia, for he seemed attentive to my every mood. Would Louis have noticed, whenever I overheard an unkind slight to my character, that my eyes were rimmed with red? Had I been weeping? the duc would ask solicitously. Was I unhappy? Was there anything he might do to make me smile? "Name it!" he'd exclaim, and that remark alone could tease my lips into a grin and lift my spirits.

"Will you promise me a dance at Monday's masquerade?" I asked him, knowing he could not refuse the Queen of France. "The theme is the Orient and I will be wearing a ruby the size of a pigeon's egg in my hair. My gown will be of gold tissue hand-painted with bamboo ferns—there will be nothing else in the world like it, Mademoiselle Bertin has assured me, and my mask will be encrusted with seed pearls! Just wait until you see it!"

The duc laughed. "*Votre Majesté,* I would recognize you if you were clad as a penitent in sackcloth and sandals."

I giggled. "Oh, tell me it is not because of my chin—everyone mocks it. Maman calls it the 'Hapsburg jaw' and says I should be proud to wear my ancestors' face." I began to natter on nervously, for the duc's proximity, much as I craved it, unnerved me. "My sister Charlotte, the Queen of Naples, has a worse time of it, for her subjects call her *polpett mbocca*—which translates in their local dialect to something like 'turkey mouth.' Can you imagine? How disrespectful!"

A silence descended between us, made all the more awkward by my previous exuberance.

Finally, I slipped my arm through his and took a step forward. "Shall we continue?" The duc hesitated, his body stiffening alongside me. I pretended not to acknowledge it. How could such a man of the world be uncomfortable in my presence? I tilted my head and gazed at him, finding it difficult to tamp down my admiration. I was sure that his profile was perfection; not the sort one finds on coins, but the kind one sees in an artist's atelier.

"I—I am so grateful that you take the time to accompany me so often, monsieur le duc," I added cautiously, scarcely daring to voice my deeper thoughts, to admit what was in my heart. With each passing week, Armand's presence had grown more important to me. I had not realized it until he had been absent from my *lever* one morning and I became so out of sorts for the remainder of the day that the princesse de Lamballe, in her gentle, solicitous manner, inquired if I was unwell. I found myself dressing to please him, eager to hear his opinion of my coiffure or a new gown, for each morning my *dame d'atours* presented me with an enormous portfolio representing the contents of the royal wardrobe and I would make my selection with the prick of a pin. Never had I worn the same ensemble twice.

"A good courtier is always at the service of his queen," the duc replied gallantly. His smile could have melted the snows of the Grossglockner. Unlike many nobles who were merely sycophants and employed flattery as currency, Armand de Gontaut always appeared sincere. I knew, just from the expressions on my attendants' faces, that he caused many a lady to sigh rapturously, sending hearts aflutter, which made his esteem all the dearer to me. I yearned to be more special to him than they were, and not because I was queen. I wanted to earn his affection, just as he had won mine with his attentiveness, his darkly handsome countenance, his graceful figure, his ready wit, and his insouciant charm.

"When I awaken, I find myself counting the moments until I see you," I murmured, fearing to meet his gaze. Instead I followed the progress of a squirrel as he scampered across the forest floor, darting his head anxiously to and fro in search of food.

"Your Majesty is the soul of generosity. I cherish your words and will carry them forever in my heart." I felt my cheeks grow warm. Did he notice me blushing? "And I can say without reservation that it is always the brightest part of my day when I see *you,* Madame, for you illuminate every place you enter—even," he said, gesturing expansively toward the leafy canopy above us, "in a shaded grove. Now, tell me, what did you think of the Marivaux last Tuesday? One of his best comedies to date, *oui*?"

"La! I have never seen you change a subject so swiftly! And with so little wit."

The duc frowned. "You are disappointed."

"I had hoped that you would fill my head with compliments and tell me a million inconsequential things to divert my thoughts from deeper matters." He looked at me as if I had told him a joke. And so I turned my head away and let it pass. Perhaps I had already said too much.

I confided later in the princesse de Lamballe, who could always be counted upon to sit beside me with a fresh handkerchief. Although she was the picture of kindness and her devotion to me was that of a sister, the princesse herself always appeared close to tears. For a sunny soul such as I, it was beginning to weigh heavily upon me to have such a doleful *amie,* for I spent a good deal of time endeavoring to cheer her.

We were alone in my private drawing room, a cozy octagonal chamber that I had nicknamed "la Méridienne," because it was my favorite location for a quiet afternoon nap. It was the first room I had redecorated after Louis's ascension, as I longed for a place to escape the perpetual strain of public life.

"Have you ever been in love?" I asked the princesse. She was seated beside me on the silken daybed nestled into a mirrored alcove of the room. I anxiously twisted my golden wedding band about my finger. Marie Thérèse did not ask me why I posed the question. Instead, her large, sad eyes grew larger and sadder. "With my husband." She nodded. "In the beginning. But then, when I began to learn about all the women . . ." She swallowed hard. "I was very young and very stupid and I thought that because I loved him it meant that he must love me, too. But he never did, of course." I took her hands in mine; with her halo of flaxen tresses and a perpetually sorrowful cast in her eye she looked so seraphic that I could not imagine anyone knowingly causing her pain. "And now he is dead." She sighed. "And I don't expect to ever love again." She placed our clasped hands in her lap. "It is too costly.

"The duc de Lauzun has an eye for the ladies, too," she added cautiously, stroking my hair the way my older sister Charlotte used to do. "He has quite a reputation, you know." She paused, waiting for me to react.

I nodded reluctantly. Tears formed in the corner of my eyes, and I insisted, "He does not look at me or treat me the same way as the women he makes love to. I am different. The time we pass together is out of the ordinary." At least that was what I believed about our chaste canters through the countryside and quiet strolls through sylvan glades.

Marie Thérèse's mouth had not softened into an expression of approval, despite my rapturous defense. "I had hoped you would feel differently about him," I said, much disappointed. "For my sake I wish that you would not judge him, but love him as a brother." Yet I did not understand my feelings for the duc. I secretly desired him in my dreams; but if he were ever to offer himself to me or made any overt declaration, I would have become horrified and found an excuse to flee his presence. I might even dismiss him from court for daring to speak to his queen so rudely. Although adulterous liaisons were practically de rigueur in the French court, I would never commit the sin of violating my marriage vows. Even if I were the sort of woman who did not take the commandments seriously, I was still a virgin, and if I became *enceinte,* the world would know that I did not carry my husband's child. For such an indiscretion a queen could be sent back to her homeland in disgrace or banished to a convent for the remainder of her days.

Yet images of Armand filled my mind; I remembered everything he wore, and how he looked (down to where he placed his *mouches*). And I frequently found myself drifting into reverie in order to relive our conversations, even when I was in the company of my husband, sensations that mortified my still naïve sensibilities.

"What should I do? Should I tell my confessor of my attachment to the duc de Lauzun?"

Marie Thérèse gasped. "*Mon Dieu, non!* There are some things that the Queen of France must keep locked inside her bosom. Can you imagine how dangerous it would be for people to know? What they would say about you?" She gazed at me with a look of alarm. "Speak directly to God if you will, but please promise me that you will not use an intermediary. Gossip is currency at Versailles. Or if you must, then share your secrets with no one but me."

Perhaps it was precisely because the duc had his well-known *affaires de coeur* that I had mistakenly believed that my affinity for him would be taken for nothing greater than a royal mark of favor or distinction. But one dismally gray afternoon I received a visit from the Austrian ambassador to Versailles. Comte de Mercy was a dear old friend, and when I was dauphine he had been one of my only allies at court; but he could be a bit of a scold, and I often wondered whether he conferred with my mother about my activities, for the pair of them had an uncanny way of chastising me for the same transgression within days of each other.

I had been resting in la Méridienne, playing with my pug, Mops, and discussing my latest plans for a masquerade with the sweet-natured comtesse de Mailly, the witty duchesse de Picquigny, and my dear Lamballe, the trio I had retained nearest my hand after dismissing most of my superfluous entourage as spies and gossips. Abbé Vermond was delighted that I had rid myself of those leeches, as well as the armed battalion that had shadowed me since my ascension. I had replaced that bodyguard with a trio of footmen, which engendered a *petit tempête* of sorts. It was considered beneath a queen's dignity to travel anywhere, even room to room, without an army behind her. The greater the entourage, the higher the rank.

A footman scratched at the door with the nail of his little finger, seeking admittance. Behind him stood the comte de Mercy, resplendent in a suit of evergreen-colored ottoman satin, his diamond-encrusted ambassadorial orders on his red sash of office winking in the soft candlelight. One glance and I knew he wished me to dismiss my attendants. With a rustling of taffeta they disappeared through a secret panel in the wall that led to my private bathroom.

The comte inclined his head in a subtle bow, and I beckoned him to a padded armchair upholstered in turquoise silk. "What do you think of the new décor?" I asked cheerfully. "I was inspired by the sea, though I have never seen it. But I thought of Venus at her toilette on her native isle of Cythera. The gilt on the boiseries is meant to represent the shafts of sunlight, and the cream-colored walls are the pristine sands—"

"Your eye is excellent, *Votre Majesté,*" Maman's ambassador replied begrudgingly.

"But you do not come bearing compliments," said I, reading between the lines of his furrowed brow.

"When was the last time the king visited your bedchamber?" Mercy asked me pointedly, settling into the chair. Sometimes I think he looked at me and still saw a child of fourteen, his countrywoman and a foreigner in the Bourbon court, in need of a father figure to maintain discipline.

"Shall I check my journal for you?" I rose from the divan. "It is not in this room." I gestured beyond one of the walls of the octagonal salon. "I keep it locked in the escritoire in my library."

Mercy crossed one leg over the other, making himself comfortable. "If it is necessary to review your journal, Madame, then it must be some time since you and His Majesty have been *intime.*" He cleared his throat. "I understand that you have not encouraged him of late to visit you. I have heard that you have a thousand excuses to keep him from your bed nowadays: that you have the headache; that you are fatigued from dancing; that you overexerted yourself with walking earlier in the day; that you must rise early to meet with Mademoiselle Bertin to discuss some new fashion, or to order another eighteen pairs of scented gloves from Monsieur Fargeon." He leaned toward me and lowered his voice. "May I suggest, *Votre Majesté,* that the truth lies closer to your passion for *riding*?"

Startled, I said, "I don't take your meaning, monsieur le comte."

Mercy smiled. "I think you do."

I glanced at the golden clock on the marble mantel, then at the turquoise silk drapes, then at the black marble figurine on the table across the room, then at my satin slippers, before meeting the ambassador's gaze. "I-I have never even kissed the duc de Lauzun," I confessed. "And he has never so much as touched me, except when we dance. But," I breathed, "he is all I can think about."

The comte chuckled avuncularly. "When you and Louis first were wed you lacked the maturity, physically as well as emotionally, to become parents, even though it was possible for you to bear a child. Your mother and Louis Quinze grew concerned when the union was not immediately consummated, but accepted the delay because you were both so young and inexperienced. However, more than four years have passed and little has changed."

I was certain Mercy knew that when Louis's physician, Monsieur Lassone, examined him in the autumn of 1773, he measured his height and his burgeoning girth and, putting the problem down to an excess of rich foods and exercise, had instructed my husband to curtail his appetites. But that only made him grumpy; and when the pain persisted nonetheless, Louis refused to submit to another examination.

"Need I remind you, Madame, that you must do everything possible to encourage an already reticent husband to come to your bed? The one thing you have managed to do, which I confess has surprised us all, is to form a true friendship with your *mari,* something that is not to be lightly dismissed. However, withholding your body from the king might dull his genuine affection for you and set back the consummation of your marriage even further, something France—and the Hapsburg court—can ill afford."

The ambassador helped himself to a pistachio macaron from a silver tray piled high with confectionery. "Allow me, *Votre Majesté,* to offer a word or two of advice from a man of the world: Entice your husband to resume his conjugal visits as often as possible. And, in the dark, behind your closed eyelids, if you imagine that the face and body beside you belong to someone else, as long as you do not give voice to these fantasies, your secret remains buried in your soul. Not even God will guess it. And perhaps," he added, as a sly smile crept across his narrow lips, "France will thank you for it in nine months' time."

He rose from the chair and made a shallow bow. "I hope I have made my position clear, Madame. And that of Austria." Wordlessly, I watched him depart the Méridienne, then sank back onto the divan.

Austria meant Maman. And everything I was I owed to her. The last thing on earth I wanted was to disappoint her.

Eleven days (I counted, *bien sûr*) passed before the duc de Lauzun appeared again at my *lever.* It was difficult for me to speak to him with any degree of intimacy because my salon was always so crowded and noisy, and it took some persuasion, despite my rank, to convince him to come riding with me the following day. This time, accompanied by the princesse de Lamballe, who made a discreet exit once we reached our destination, we went only as far as le Petit Trianon, for I wished to find a private place to speak with him.

Sunlight filtered into the airy salon that I intended to redecorate and employ as my music room. I stood by the window where I knew that the light would most flatter my complexion.

"Where have you been?" I asked the duc. "I missed you greatly."

He remained on the opposite side of the room. "I had to return to my estate. I don't know if the news has reached your ears, *Votre Majesté,* but the harvest was a bleak one this year and the people are afraid they will starve. Fueled by rumors that they will not have enough flour to make bread, there have been rumblings of discontent."

I hadn't heard. Louis had brushed aside my attempts to glean any knowledge of current affairs. "And is everything settled now?" I asked gaily.

The duc chuckled. "If only things could be resolved as easily as Your Majesty would wish it." He parted the cerise-colored drapes, focusing on something out of doors. "People would sooner believe a silver-tongued rabble-rouser than their own eyes. I fear it will develop into a genuine crisis. I will need to return to my regiment there." He paused for several moments. "It may take a number of months to maintain order and keep the peace. I will not be coming back to court for some time."

I felt my chest tighten. A gasp escaped my lips. "Oh, *non*! Can't someone else"—I began to fight for words—"make the situation better in the countryside?" In three strides I was across the room and had clasped his arms. "Why must it be you?"

The duc gazed deeply into my eyes. "People are talking about us," he said quietly, firmly.

"There is nothing to say," I replied, my voice quavering.

"When has that stopped tongues from speculating? We spend time alone; you have clearly marked me for your favor. And try though you might, you do not conceal your delight when I am in the same room. My amorous reputation is well known. And it will only tarnish your own unblemished one. I cannot let that happen. Especially when it is fully within my power to prevent it."

I threw my arms about Armand's neck and pressed my face to his chest. "Do not abandon me. I beg of you—what will become of me if you abandon me?" If he departed, leaving me nothing to look forward to each day but the temporary thrill of selecting my wardrobe from the *gazette des atours* and the applause that greeted my arrival at the Opéra, I was convinced I would go mad before I turned twenty.

He held me until my sobs subsided. "It must be this way, *Majesté*. In time you will understand why. And I am honored, touched beyond all measure that you hold me in such esteem. Surely," he added with a hint of a chuckle, "I don't merit such regard." When I began to protest, he placed a finger to my lips. His riding glove smelled of almond and clove. "*Shh*. It is all for the best this way. The unrest in the country is much talked about in certain circles and it will come as no surprise that I have had to return to my estate." He pulled away and regarded my tearstained face. "But perhaps you will give me a souvenir to remember you by."

I reluctantly broke our embrace and fetched my riding hat from the little console table. Removing the white heron feather, I playfully stroked his cheek with it. "My panache," I said softly, presenting the plume.

He took my hands in his and pressed his lips to them, not once, but three times. With a tinge of melancholy, he said, "*Merci, Majesté.* I will cherish it forever. And I will cherish, too, our friendship."

He thought it was best if he departed alone, and so I waited while he cloaked himself; then I followed him outside and watched him mount his horse. With a quick kick of his heels and a spray of gravel he spurred his mare toward the Château de Versailles, growing ever smaller, until he was just a tobacco-colored speck on the horizon.

I dried my tears and stood for several minutes in the courtyard of le Petit Trianon. Armand had been right; that I knew. So, too, was the comte de Mercy. And the princesse de Lamballe. I had risked my untested heart on a handsome courtier because I was lonely and eager to be loved. But the passion, or even affection, that I dreamed of would not come from the duc de Lauzun and I could not hazard a scandal. It was a bitter cordial to swallow, but where was it written that this precious and lofty commodity called love was a queen's prerogative? As Mercy had so succinctly reminded me, I had allowed myself to become distracted from my primary obligation. It was time to adjust the compass before my marriage was blown off course completely.

FOUR

The Covenant of Abraham

November 23, 1774

To My Most Esteemed Sovereign King Carlos III of Spain:

It is with the best authority that I tender the following information:

After four and a half years the marriage remains unconsummated. If the queen were to be as fertile as her sister the Queen of Naples (though the latter, being married to your son Ferdinando, has enjoyed the advantages of wedlock to a youth of fire and temperament), she should have sired a trio of *niños* by now.

As matters currently stand here, stains have been observed on the queen's bedsheets, which proves that emissions are taking place outside the proper place.

I shall continue to keep abreast of the situation and inform you accordingly.

Respectfully,

Don Pedro Pablo Abarca de Bolea, 10th Count d'Aranda
Ambassador Extraordinary and
Plenipotentiary to the Court of Versailles

Within the vast hive of Versailles, it was nearly impossible to maintain a secret. As we had done nearly a year earlier, on the first occasion when Louis had been persuaded to be examined by his physician—after considerable haranguing by two sovereigns, his *grand-père,* and my maman—we waited until the small hours of the morning when even the most inveterate of wagerers had laid down their cards and gone to bed. Our night rails masked by heavy cloaks, lanterns in hand we tiptoed up the narrow staircase that led to the King's Apartments, the informal private suite that Louis had redecorated to his own taste. As we climbed the wooden treads our lamps illuminated the walls of the dark stairwell, casting an eerie glow on the unseeing glass eyes of my husband's hunting trophies, the antlered heads of half a dozen majestic stags and a pair of wild boar. Although I had joined the hunt on occasion, I would never get used to it. What must these noble creatures have thought in their final moment when the fatal blow came? To display their heads on the wall, stuffed with sawdust, was an insult to their dignity.

We crept noiselessly across the thick Aubusson that carpeted the floor of Louis's library, a room decorated entirely in pale blue and gold. It was twice the size of the others in the private apartment, for it had to accommodate his eight thousand volumes. Unlike me, my husband was a great reader and possessed not only the classics of antiquity, countless treasures of history and verse that stood like so many Spartan soldiers in serried ranks, spine to spine with his initials embossed in gold, but Dante and Shakespeare and Hume and hundreds of volumes in English—even spicy novels like *Tom Jones,* which Maman would have a conniption if she caught me perusing—and the writings of some of our own philosophers whose views were often anathema to the Crown. I knew my husband had read Diderot, Voltaire, and

Rousseau. I would not have said Louis's mind was quick, but it was curious.

He turned the gilded handle on the library door and led the way into his study. The eyes of the Dutch humanist Erasmus in Holbein's portrait seemed to follow us as we crossed the room, wending our way about the globes and maps and armillaries that so fascinated my husband. Louis's passion for order was evident everywhere: atop the enormous writing desk neat piles of portfolios on one side awaited his perusal; on the other, a stack arranged just as tidily represented those he had already reviewed. There must have been hundreds of documents, and I had never been invited to take so much as a peek at a single one. My role as a mere consort was clear—which made this clandestine appointment all the more vital.

As we approached the king's bedroom, with each step Louis grew more anxious. I slipped my arm through his. *"Sois courageux,"* I whispered. "Be brave. The remedy might be simple."

We entered the chamber and Louis rested his lantern opposite the canopied bed. He began to pace, while I clutched my cloak to my chest and stole a glance through the draperies. The late autumn night was clear; the crescent sliver suspended in the indigo sky reminded me of the hair ornaments that became all the mode after my childhood music master Herr Gluck presented his *Iphigénie* at the Paris Opéra.

Moments later, a discreet scratching at the door announced the arrival of Monsieur Lassone, the king's *premier médecin,* or first physician. Even in the dead of night he was clad from head to toe in his habitual black suit with a pristine white jabot at his throat. Rising from his reverence, the doctor read the expression of terror on the king's face. "Please, sit," he said gently, gesturing to the bed.

Louis hesitated, then perched tentatively on the edge of the embroidered coverlet. I sat beside him and took his hand in mine. Before the *médecin* could ask a question, I volunteered, "Things have been no better. It is not the king's habits of exercise—not his enthusiastic hunting, nor his . . . his gourmandizing, that are the problem. He gave them up when you advised him to do so last year, and our . . . difficulties have remained the same."

The doctor took a step back and regarded the pair of us with paternal concern. "And what difficulties are they—exactly? How then, would you describe their nature?"

I glanced at my husband. "I . . . can't," he whispered.

Monsieur Lassone lowered his chin to his chest and studied the king gravely. "What is it, Sire, that you cannot do? Is it that you do not have the words to explain, or that you are unable to . . ." He hesitated, searching for the best way, even for a man of medicine, to address the sovereign of the realm on the most sensitive, but vital, subject facing the House of Bourbon—the future of the dynasty itself.

Even in the golden lantern light I could see Louis's full cheeks flush a deep shade of carmine. He lowered his gaze. "I love my wife," he began, so softly I could barely hear him. "But every time I try to . . . to do my duty . . . nay, not a duty, for I *wish* to make love to her . . . I find that my . . ." his voice trailed off, and he placed his hand lightly in his lap, as if to protect himself. "It hurts, *monsieur le médecin.* I cannot account for it, for the will is there. It begins with a throbbing, and as my desire increases, the pain becomes so sharp, so intense, that it is impossible to bear and I cannot continue."

For months Louis had been telling me "It hurts," but would say nothing more, refusing to discuss it. I felt relieved that he was finally confiding in Monsieur Lassone. But was there a remedy? My chest felt constricted. I realized I was holding my breath.

Louis turned to face me and took my hands in his. "Do you

remember the day we met, Toinette, that first afternoon in the forest of Compiègne?"

I nodded. How could I have forgotten? He had been dressed like a tradesman in a suit of brown ratteen with an unadorned tricorn. Even his shoe buckles had been of plain silver. He'd hung back by the coach while Papa Roi embraced me like a daughter long lost to him. And all during the ride to the hunting lodge of Compiègne, the dauphin hadn't uttered a word that wasn't prompted by his *grand-père.* I attributed his reticence to shyness; after all, by virtue of my proxy marriage in Vienna a month earlier we were already married, and yet we were complete strangers to each other.

"When I first saw you, I thought you were the most beautiful creature on earth, and I . . . *it* . . ." he emphasized, moving his palm to his *pénis,* "it became the way it does when it . . . when it *grows* . . . when I prepare to make love to you . . . and when . . ." he blushed deeply, "whenever I think about you—or look at you. Which is very often, you will admit. And whenever that happens to me—to *it*—the discomfort and then the pain become so awful that I can no longer bear it." He tugged off his nightcap and placed it protectively in his lap, covering his privates.

A spontaneous cry escaped my lips; I raised my fist to stifle the sound. "And all this time—for more than four years—I thought you found me so repugnant that the very sight of me made you flinch."

Louis looked aghast. "My poor queen. The torment I have put you through. When quite the opposite is the case."

I pressed his hand to my lips and bathed it with my tears, even more ashamed of my girlish *tendre* for the duc de Lauzun. "I understand now," I murmured, weeping. "But don't you see . . . I was so afraid you would send me back to Austria."

A man of science, Monsieur Lassone appeared at a loss in the presence of such sentimental confessions, but by now he clearly comprehended that something quite tangible must be the source of Louis's inordinate physical discomfort. I could see that he dared not tell the king of France that his condition was not normal. At length, after my husband and I had managed to compose ourselves, his doctor asked him to disrobe.

Louis balked, but I insisted. I am not the daughter of the pragmatic empress of Austria for nothing. To afford the men their privacy I took a chair by the window and allowed Monsieur Lassone to reposition a large floral screen about the foot of the bed so that he might examine the king in strictest confidence.

I waited anxiously. From the opposite side of the screen, I could hear Louis petulantly kicking the side of the bed with his large feet, an annoyed boy rather than a head of state, grumbling that Monsieur hadn't managed to get *his* wife with child in three years, despite his boasts of sexual prowess; and yet no one was up in arms about Stanislas Xavier's failures in the boudoir.

"With your permission to reply, *Votre Majesté,* that is because Monsieur is not the king of France," the doctor said calmly.

"But *he* will be the next king of France if *we* don't produce an heir, *mon chou,*" said I.

Louis groaned as Monsieur Lassone touched him, poking and prodding his delicate anatomy. After several more minutes, the *médecin* offered his diagnosis. "Well, I think I have discovered the source of our woes."

I rose from the padded armchair and stepped behind the screen.

"Non!" Louis cried.

"*Shh,* I am your wife," I murmured, taking his hand in mine. "Ailments and illnesses, and even unpleasant news are facts of life. If there are obstacles to be overcome, there is strength in doing so together."

Pulling away, my husband hid his face in his hands, mortified that I should see his naked flesh. Monsieur Lassone placed his fingers beneath the king's penis and gently raised it. As our amorous efforts had always taken place under the sheets and brocade coverlet, and we never would have dared to remove our nightshirts, I had never seen a man's private parts before; it looked like a bone with a funny little nipple at the tip.

"*Vos Majestés,* I regret to inform you that the king is suffering from a condition known as phimosis," Monsieur Lassone began. "As you can see, the prepuce, or foreskin, does not retract from the member. This would render the act of copulation, or even the occasion of an erection, an immensely painful event. Am I correct, Sire?"

Crimson with embarrassment, Louis slowly nodded his head. Louis stared dolefully at his penis as if it were a young child that had disappointed him. He crossed his hands over his lap, unable to withstand further humiliation. *"Ça suffit,"* he said weakly. "Enough. I don't want to hear any more." A large tear trickled down the side of his face, followed by another, and another. I read the thoughts between his falling tears: *Tant pis*—too bad—if it was not considered manly to weep. With such a deformity, he might as well have not been a man at all.

I wondered why this issue had not been diagnosed during Louis's childhood. He had once told me of submitting to the humiliation of having been stripped naked at the age of five and having his limbs examined for their soundness. No mention was made of this phimosis at the time, unless the report had been suppressed. Could it have been because the *pénis* of a boy of five was tiny enough that the doctors didn't take notice of an abnormality, were too busy looking at his arms and legs and spine, or were too embarrassed to poke about the privates of a prince? Or perhaps, as his older brother was then dauphin, the *médecins* didn't concern themselves with what they saw, or wished not to alarm the royal family; and consequently, little thought was given to any future difficulties he might have in the boudoir and how they might impact upon the kingdom? Or, *c'est possible* . . . maybe maybe the physicians believed that his situation might resolve itself as he grew older.

"Is there a remedy?" I inquired softly. "We cannot go on as we are if the pain renders His Majesty incapable of sustaining . . . well, France must have an heir! And I very much want a child." I looked imploringly into the doctor's eyes. "What can be done for the king?"

Monsieur Lassone steepled his fingers and brought them to his lips. He remained lost in thought for a moment or two. "There is only one remedy, Your Majesties, which would entirely alleviate the issue of pain on erection and copulation. And that is circumcision."

Louis's hands closed over his nightcap, his knuckles whitening. "The Covenant of Abraham? Will you turn me Jew?" he exclaimed.

The *médecin* cleared his throat. "Although I can, *ahh,* recommend certain positions that might be more comfortable than the traditional one, without the procedure you are condemned to endure this excruciating pain in what should be, Your Majesty, a highly pleasurable experience. Especially with a beautiful wife. The recuperation period would span less than a month and there would be few sacrifices expected of you. You could not ride or hunt, and as you enjoy both to excess, perhaps the coming winter would be the best time . . ."

The physician's voice became an incoherent drone. Louis's eyes widened; he clutched his penis and cods more tightly, as if to protect them from imminent torture and a procedure that would undoubtedly be bloody, agonizing, and, given his lack of confidence in sterilization procedures and the unhygienic conditions pervasive at Versailles, perhaps even fatal.

My husband and I had grown close enough over the past few years that I could safely hazard a guess as to what he was thinking. *Would they really do this to him?* No doubt he envisioned the cold knife, soaked in vinegar to sanitize it, pressing against his most tender flesh the way he insinuated the blade of his penknife into the rigid carapace of an oyster shell to shuck out the succulent meat, slicing—

"Non!" The king exclaimed.

"Well, it is not a decision to be taken lightly," Monsieur Lassone admitted. "It is not imperative that Your Majesty undergo such an operation, and I must advise you that there are as many risks as there are rewards." As if he anticipated my question, the *médecin* added, "There will be blood. I would be remiss in my duty if I did not tell you that it is quite possible that His Majesty could lose a good deal of it."

Louis blanched and I clutched his hand. The stakes and consequences were higher than any decision we had ever faced. On one hand, my husband would be risking his life; on the other, the future of his dynasty.

"You need not arrive at a determination tonight. It is of course a weighty one, which must be thoroughly discussed between you—"

The king raised his hand to call for silence. "I'll do it," he said quietly.

FIVE

Pastimes and Polignac

According to my husband's ministers, Louis XV had left France's treasury in a woeful state. The expenditures of the royal family, and even those of the thousand courtiers who resided at Versailles, were paltry, they said, when compared to the disbursements necessary to rule the nation, but the deluge must be stanched somewhere. *Mon mari* began his reign as *Louis le Desiré*—the Desired One—a sobriquet his subjects bestowed upon him in the hope that he would restore morality and economic sanity after decades of flagrant excess during his grandfather's reign, and he was anxious to retain their goodwill. But he quickly learned that the business of governance often resulted in disappointing, if not outright angering, a substantial portion of the populace.

Soon after he inherited the throne, Louis confided miserably, "I feel as though I carry the universe on my shoulders. Still, a king must be just and make his people happy." Eager to earn their love, my fastidious husband immediately sought ways to trim the fat, as he put it. He commissioned only six new suits, and those were of such a modest cloth that his courtiers, who continued to live so far beyond their means that their debts encumbered them like iron shackles, blushed to see him.

Other members of the royal family had long been accustomed to having separate establishments; their apartments even had kitchens and larders. When Louis was dauphin, Monsieur and Madame hosted their own lavish suppers, while the comte d'Artois and his wife, who was Madame's younger sister, did the same. Louis's sisters, the princesses Clothilde and Élisabeth, were dependent on him for their well-being, and so they had always dined *en famille* with us or with Papa Roi when he was alive.

But Louis decided that it would set an example to the realm if the Crown were the first to make sacrifices. So he commanded the members of his immediate family to take all of their meals with us henceforth. Food would no longer go to waste and fewer cooks, footmen, and other servants would be required, thus saving the monarchy a fair number of salaries.

But this was not perceived as a pragmatic attempt to economize by my *beaux-frères* and their wives. Louis's brothers, particularly Monsieur, viewed the king's thrift as a punishment and in our presence their displeasure was thinly veiled. Behind our backs Stanislas and Marie Joséphine spread the word that no attendant's job was secure—but how could my husband (who hated to rob someone of his employment) maintain the status quo for the aristocratic residents of Versailles and still satisfy his ministers' urging and his subjects' demands for fiscal restraint? Pleasing everyone at once was an impossibility; but if the king let things continue in the same vein as his grandfather had done, the Finance Minister warned that they would grow even worse, for money did not buy nowadays what it had done in the time of Louis XV.

Monsieur knew this; he was a clever young man. But he

derived enjoyment from seeing his older brother squirm. And where he was arrogant and demanding, Louis was obliging and conciliatory. My husband once told me about the time Stanislas ordered him to fetch something—and as he was about to do so, their tutor reminded the youths which one of them was going to become king one day.

So there we sat, over ortolan stuffed with wild mushrooms and chestnuts, one evening in early December. The king's youngest sister Élisabeth was hanging on his every word as he discussed the latest work of some English philosopher he had read; none of us understood what he was talking about, except perhaps for Monsieur, who claimed to have enjoyed it in the original tongue. Madame was smirking beneath the dark downy hair on her upper lip and rolling her eyes at her sister Marie Thérèse, who was seated across the table. The comtesse d'Artois had been insupportable ever since her delicate condition had been made public and sharing a meal with her was most unpleasant, for she insisted that the aroma of everything, whether sweet or savory, made her want to retch.

Fifteen-year-old princesse Clothilde, who accepted a third helping of the fish course before tucking into the fowl, was discussing her impending nuptials with the heir to the throne of Sardinia, who happened to be the brother of Madame and the comtesse d'Artois. She was to wed on the twenty-seventh of August and would likely never see her family again. Every time I looked at her I was reminded of my own departure from my homeland to wed a foreign prince I had never met and how I anguished over leaving Austria. But Clothilde, whose gustatory passion had earned her the nickname Gros-Madame, one she cheerfully embraced, seemed quite complacent about her forthcoming marriage, chattering away, between mouthfuls, about her trousseau, and whether she, like I, would be able to order a dozen new gala dresses every season.

"I want twelve of everything, just like you have, *Votre Majesté*—formal day gowns, dishabille, ceremonial, and evening, and all of the informal gowns as well. If you never wear the same ensemble twice, why should I?"

With her girth, a trait she shared with two of her brothers as well as an equal number of their maiden aunts, she would keep the mills busy.

The comtesse d'Artois and her husband Charles, who was the handsomest of the three Bourbon brothers—and one of the more scintillating lights of my salons, for we always comprehended one another's jests—were barely disguising their boredom. I knew the comte was keen for the meal to come to an end and for the gaming to begin. He had won and lost more at écarté in the past week than a baker earned in a year, and had come begging at Louis's door to discharge his debts; but my husband, troubled by his brother's losses at a time when he should be thinking about his responsibilities as a father, assured Artois that the strings of the privy purse would remain taut the next time he dared to make such a request.

Stanislas began to push his chair away from the table. The buttons of his embroidered vest were straining to contain his belly. I hadn't realized quite how large Monsieur had grown in the months since Louis's accession. Both he and his wife resembled a pair of Sèvres soup tureens. "*Eh bien, mon frère,* I hear you are going to undergo the knife." Stanislas tilted his head and regarded the king with a grin, illustrating his remark with a crude gesture.

Where had Monsieur received this intelligence? He was the last person at Versailles whom Louis wished to know about his nocturnal consultation with Monsieur Lassone.

"It is the right decision of course, though I think you are very brave," Stanislas continued. "With my horror of blood I should probably turn white and faint at the sight of so much of it. Of course the stakes could not possibly be higher." From the look on Louis's face I could see that his brother's antagonism was proving successful.

At the word "stakes" the comte d'Artois perked up. Pity his interests were so prescribed. But then I was not one to cast stones, and besides he was still only seventeen years old. There was plenty of time for him to mature.

"Do you worry about becoming a widow?" Marie Joséphine asked me solicitously. A ponderous silence descended. Madame might as well have plunged her fruit knife between my ribs. "What happens to dowager queens?" she continued mildly, as if nothing was amiss. "Would you go back to Austria? Or remain here, *une étrangère* in a foreign land once more?"

Louis's cheeks began to twitch in agitation. He rose from his chair, which meant that everyone in the room was compelled to do so as well. Wordlessly he shambled out of the room, his shoulders stooped with defeat, and did not reappear later for cards.

December 17, 1774

My esteemed Maman,

I am sure you will have much to say on this score and so I mean to rebut your arguments before you have the chance to make them. Although the royal physicians were not in agreement (mine did not believe the procedure that we corresponded about was necessary, but it would be helpful, and Louis's *médecin* cautioned that there were as many drawbacks to having it performed as not to do so), the king was prepared to undergo it nonetheless. But when Monsieur Lassone opened his bag and removed his surgical instruments and his bottles of tincture, my husband's resolve was utterly shattered. No amount of persuasion could bring him around.

It is not that he lacks the stomach to withstand the course

of action proposed, although the knife and tourniquet and the bowls of leeches, milk, and salt were not for the faint of heart; but when faced with the prospect of infection, or worse, and with the memory of his *grand-père*'s final illness so fresh, Louis refused to jeopardize the Crown.

Monsieur is clever, but malicious, and Louis fully believes that it will be detrimental for France if he should become king. Though my husband is awkward at expressing his affection for me, he did admit that it would break his heart to know that he would have left me alone and bereft if he did not survive the procedure. And what of the Franco-Austrian alliance guaranteed by our marriage? Would you and Joseph and the comte de Mercy truly expect Louis Stanislas Xavier to uphold it?

And so we are back where we started, even though it means the sacrifice of his own pleasure, for Louis will be compelled to have marital relations with me no matter the pain. If only he drank, for a few brandies might not only dull the discomfort but quicken his blood. *Hélas!* That last was a jest, Maman.

Mercy has proposed the construction of a secret internal passage connecting the King's Bedchamber with my own, which will eliminate the embarrassment he endures every time he visits me, when every guard must know his business. The renovations cannot begin until some time next year, but both the king and I believe that the plan is a sound one.

Your devoted daughter,
Antoinette

• • •

February 17, 1775

My dear daughter,

Imagine my surprise when I unwrapped the miniature you sent me and saw your hair teased eighteen inches off your forehead and topped with a coronet of feathers—were there ten of them? I tried to count. I thought I had been mistakenly sent a portrait of an actress and not the Queen of France. Take care how you present yourself to the public, for people will comment and the results will not always be complimentary. Mercy tells me that Louis's aunts view these outré plumes as "ornaments for horses," and although Mesdames were never in the vanguard of fashion themselves, they do represent the views of those whose opinions it does not become your dignity to mock and whom you can ill afford to alienate.

Mark me, Antoinette, such cavalier behavior will lead to your ruin. I read in newspaper accounts that these coiffures, ornamented with all manner of toys, gimcracks, and gewgaws, such as sailing ships, gardens in bloom, and mechanical figures on springs—some depicting tableaux of adulterous courtships—have reached such towering proportions that you and your fashionable friends cannot even lie down properly, or ride in a carriage without kneeling on its floor. I can only imagine the state of your gowns once you reach your destination. So much beauty and expense worn once, and then fit only for the dustbin.

Rumors of the architectural renovations that are being made to accommodate these foolish "poufs" astonish me. Tell me, is it true that the entrance to the boxes at the Paris opera have been altered to form archways? A young and pretty queen, full of charm, has no need of all this nonsense.

Your doting mother,
Maria Theresa

• • •

February 25, 1775

Ma chère Maman,

Yes, it is true about the opera boxes, and I'll allow that the poufs also make it a challenge to get a good night's sleep; but you are making far too much of things. They are the popular fashion nowadays and how could the Queen of France possibly be expected to eschew them when the most stylish women in the kingdom vie to outdo one another for originality? The creations I wear announce noteworthy events. When I finally persuaded Louis to be vaccinated against the smallpox, the *Pouf de l'Inoculation* that Léonard and Mademoiselle Bertin designed for me became all the rage. Science triumphed over Evil and heralded the age of Reason. You would surely have admired it: Threatened by a blossoming club, a snake coiled itself about a ripe, blooming olive tree, representing the cadeusus of Aesculapius; and above it all shone a rising sun. You must admit it was genius. And you must allow, too, that Versailles is very different from the Hapsburg court. Everything, from the pace to the fashions, has a *tempo con brio* here; the Hofburg is a stately pavane by comparison. How can I make you see it, Maman? I enclose a copy of a poem penned by an anonymous hand that is readily for sale in the shops of Paris praising "the coiffure of our queen" and her "perfect taste."

You taught me well, my dearest mother. And for that I remain as mindful as I am grateful. So you see, it is quite possible to be at the same time fashionable and not neglect one's duty to those less fortunate.

Your devoted Antoinette

April 1775

As the cold earth began to thaw, yielding to the crocuses and yellow buttercups, and the trees became once again stippled with buds, I decided to host a ball in the Hall of Mirrors in honor of Flora, the goddess of spring.

I had obliged Louis's requests for economies by curtailing the number of masquerades; we had them now only twice a month instead of every Monday. For the vernal fête, I instructed Papillon de la Ferté to inform the guests that in the tradition of my Winter Ball where everyone had to dress in white, this time everyone was compelled to wear green. *Tant pis* for my Savoyard sisters-in-law, who, with their sallow complexions looked positively bilious in every version of the hue. This was my gentle revenge against them for daring to complain about dining with us from now on.

Outside, although it was too brisk to stroll along the parterres, the topiaries twinkled with countless fairy lights. To reflect their glow I'd ordered the gravel along the *allées* to be painted gold, and in the distance myriad paper lanterns danced from the boughs.

Beneath the thousand candles that flickered from the Hall of Mirrors' forty-three chandeliers, the bespoke perfumes of hundreds of members of France's aristocracy commingled.

Attired in verdigris satin, my hair adorned with a pouf that featured a naturally blooming garden of miniature tea roses, I found myself admiring the ingenuity of some of the costumes, for although I had not specified masquerade dress, a dozen or so courtiers had elected to pay homage to a salient event in the reign of Louis XV—the Yew Tree Ball. It was one of many dances that honored the nuptials of his only son, my late husband's father, to the Infanta of Spain in 1745.

The ball derived its unusual nickname because Papa Roi and a number of his attendants had arrived identically garbed as topiaries. The king was seen spending the better part of the night flirting through his unwieldy headdress with a married young woman whose acquaintance he had made some time earlier. Soon, as Madame de Pompadour, she would become the most powerful woman in France.

At my Homage to the Rites of Spring I, too, became utterly captivated by a stranger. Even in the crush of people, she stood out, for this striking young woman, with her flushed cheeks and cloud of unpowdered chestnut hair, was dressed from head to toe in a color I would have described as *yellow*.

"That poor woman!" exclaimed the princesse de Lamballe. Her emerald velvet gown embroidered with golden threads set off her pale blond hair to perfection. She clasped me by the elbow and drew me toward the perimeter of the Hall where we might derive a modicum of quiet. "Everyone has been talking about her all evening," the princesse informed me. "Of course, one can never know how much to believe from the gossip one hears in a ballroom; but they say she is the wife of comte Jules de Polignac, an army colonel whose debts are so burdensome that he cannot afford to keep his wife in the latest fashions, and that it is a wonder they dare show their faces at court at all."

The princesse unfolded her fan, peering above the arc to observe the newcomer while discreetly concealing our conversation behind it. "When her wrap falls away from her shoulder, you can see where the taffeta has been patched by an inexperienced tailor." The sensitive Marie Thérèse dabbed at her eye and whispered in my ear, "Surely something can be done for her, *Majesté*. She looks so kindly. See how she blushes for shame from their cruel remarks."

I followed Lamballe's gaze and found myself thunderstruck by the comtesse's fresh, natural beauty, made all the more alluring in a world of such studied artifice.

Had I been a man, I should have called this sudden rush of emotion the *coup de foudre* of falling in love.

Clasping the princesse by the wrist, the pair of us threaded our way through the crowded ballroom, for I had to speak to comtesse Jules. I wished for all to see that Madame de Polignac was welcome at Versailles and so I impetuously threw my arms about her waist and kissed her on both cheeks.

The comtesse reddened deeply and sank into a reverence. "I do not know what I have done to deserve such an honor," she breathed. Her voice was soft and musical.

In an instant her husband, attired in a suit of olive velvet, was at her elbow. After introducing himself with a bow, "Allow me to present my wife, Yolande Martine Gabrielle de Polastron," he said, and urged her forward with a nudge at her slender waist.

"But you must call me Gabrielle," the comtesse insisted. Lowering her eyes modestly, she apologized for her gown. "In the light at home, it looked chartreuse. I don't know what you must think of me, *Votre Majesté*. I know everyone is talking. I am sure they all must believe I intended to attract your notice by deliberately wearing the wrong color."

I searched the depths of her extraordinary violet-blue eyes for a lie—I have no tolerance for dissemblers—but all I could read there was a sweet simplicity and a willingness to please. There was something about Gabrielle I could not quite identify, but I felt as though we were already kindred souls. "*Dîtes-moi,* when is your birthday," I wished to know.

"The eighth of September. I will be twenty-six this year."

The princesse de Lamballe gasped and brought her gloved hand to her breast. "Why, I was born that very day!"

I joined their hands. "Then it is destined: you will be great friends," I said, "not only of mine, but of each other."

SIX

Coronation

During the spring of 1775, unrest over the poor harvest of the previous autumn had spread as far as the capital. Louis's Chief Minister, the comte de Maurepas, attempted to convince the king that under the circumstances, it would be appropriate to be crowned in Paris, which would bolster the mood of the people and bring much needed revenue into the city. But overanxious about the potential for unpleasant or even violent demonstrations or disturbances, Louis insisted that tradition be upheld and the coronation take place at Rheims, where every French monarch had been crowned since the year 1027, and which lay nearly twenty-four leagues from Paris, a few days' journey from the instability.

As Minister of Finance, Anne-Robert Jacques Turgot, the baron de Laune, had also urged fiscal restraint in the coronation expenditures, reminding His Majesty that he would also be expected to host a grand fête in honor of the child of the comte and comtesse d'Artois, who was due to be born in August.

The homely little comtesse's flaunting of her fertility, which I found to be exceptionally distasteful, was the subject of our discourse one afternoon as I strolled with the comtesse de Polignac about the Neptune fountain. Displaying a deep décolletée enhanced by a purple ribbon about her slender neck, Gabrielle wore a new *robe à la française* of the latest hue, a shade of gold with undertones of apricot called *Cheveux de la Reine,* named for the color of my hair. I had purchased it for her, feeling ashamed on her behalf for the shoddy condition of the chartreuse gown she had worn to my ball in honor of the Rites of Spring.

Gabrielle had been so grateful for the gift that she nearly burst into tears. Was it not honor enough that I had found an apartment at Versailles for her family? Never had someone been so kind, so generous, she insisted. But when she made a point of showing me her other gowns, and her linen, I was mortified to hear her confirm the rumor that the comte de Polignac did not give her a proper allowance, compelling her to make do at the most elegant court in the world with petticoats that were worn and frayed, silk stockings that were threadbare at the heels, and dresses with trimmings that were faded and woefully out of date. Gabrielle's children, too—seven-year-old Agläié, who had her mother's beautiful eyes; and her brother Armand, only four, practically resembled ragamuffins I'd seen begging for bread crusts near the Palais Royal. So I commissioned Rose Bertin to create a full wardrobe for my new friend. I also permitted the comtesse to have the first selection of my own discarded gloves and shoes, for it was a perquisite of my attendants to claim them after I had worn the accessories a requisite number of times, either to make use of the accoutrements themselves, or to sell them if they needed the money. The comtesse de Polignac clearly required both. Her son and daughter I would look after as if they were my own. Agläié had just lost her two front teeth; there was nothing I wouldn't have done to see her smile.

A gentle breeze riffled the edges of our parasols and I tilted mine toward the sun to deflect its glancing rays. I slipped my arm through Gabrielle's and gazed toward the honey-colored wing of the château where my in-laws resided. "As the most junior member of the family, Marie Thérèse should be far more deferential to me, and most certainly to the king. Why her newborn should deserve any great honors beyond its baptism is lost on me." A great pageant for Louis's future niece or nephew only served to emphasize my lack of fecundity and his failure in the boudoir.

Before the comtesse de Polignac could offer her reply, we heard a great commotion coming from the direction of the Ministers' Courtyard. A trio of footmen clad in the red and blue Bourbon livery dashed across the wide gravel parterre, descending the broad stone steps two at a time, shouting breathlessly, long before they were able to reach us. "*Votre Majesté,* madame la comtesse, you must come indoors immediately—His Majesty's orders."

Clutching yards of silk, we hitched up our skirts and raced to meet them. The men's faces, though damasked with exertion, were clearly alarmed. "What is going on?" I demanded.

The reply came in a series of halting gasps. "Rioters, Your Majesty. Eight thousand strong. Marching from Saint-Germain. They managed to force the gates and press into the courtyard."

There had been bread riots in the village of Saint-Germain the previous day. Louis had told me about it. But he had also assured me there was no cause for alarm, for the disturbances had been sparked by false rumors of shortages.

Another footman, Denis, took up the story, as the three of them swiftly ushered us toward the palace. "They came here looking for bread, and finding the marketplace of Versailles shut, pillaged it. The stalls, the wagons, the sacks; everything was smashed, slashed, and torn to bits. The merchants will have nothing to return to on the morrow."

"And the king?" I asked anxiously. Eight thousand angry,

hungry souls. Enough to fill the Paris Opéra several times over. Blaming my husband, a twenty-year-old man, for nature's uneven bounty. A sour taste spread from my stomach into the back of my throat and I quickened my step.

"The protesters are demanding that he step onto the balcony and speak to them," said Denis.

Gabrielle clutched my arm as I faltered and stumbled, restoring me to stability. My foot had come out of my shoe and she knelt and slipped it back on for me. "Steady, *ma chère amie,*" she said, rising, "you have the strength to surmount this ordeal." I withdrew a cambric handkerchief from my bodice with my cipher worked in white thread and pressed it to my nostrils, inhaling the calming scent of lavender. "I will stand beside him," I insisted, as we pressed on.

Once inside, the comtesse de Polignac and I found ourselves surrounded by a flurry of frightened attendants, concerned as much for my safety as for their own, and none more so than poor gentle Lamballe. Her countenance was as pale as her hair. "I tremble for you," she murmured, taking my arm.

"I must see the king!" I declared.

"He is in the Salon de Mars, *Majesté,*" replied Lamballe. I glided quickly toward the room where Louis held court; its walls of bloodred damask and dais draped in an ermine mantle embroidered with golden fleurs-de-lis provided a stark contrast to their beleaguered embodiment of authority. The king was slumped on the throne, his elbows resting on his knees, his large head buried in his hands. "I don't know what to do," he muttered.

I knelt beside him and placed my hands in his lap. "Where are Turgot and Maurepas?"

"Gone to Paris. To quell the disturbances there. We are all alone." His watery blue eyes met mine. I had never seen him look so helpless.

I rose to my feet and extended my hand resolutely. "Come,

Sire. You must show them you do not fear them. We will go onto the balcony together. The presence of a woman will soften their hearts and tame their zeal." I feared my words were hardly convincing. I scarce believed them myself.

Louis reluctantly stood. He knew his duty but feared making a misstep; still, in my view, inaction was worse. As I urged haste, we made our way through the enfilade of State Apartments until we reached the leaded glass doors that opened onto the balcony on the south façade. Even from inside the château we could hear the shouts of the multitude, and the efforts of one man to appease them. Louis threw open the doors and the sound multiplied tenfold.

I had never seen a mob before. I had expected fire in their eyes and menace in their looks. I had imagined that they would bear sticks and crude homemade clubs; instead they carried placards denouncing the Bourbons as a degraded and corrupt family. Some of the protesters, farmers I would have guessed from their attire, brandished rakes and pitchforks; but their demeanor was strangely jovial, as if they were at a country fair. Many of them did not wear hats. I was surprised by the number of women in the crowd. On their arms were wicker baskets lined with colorful cloths of toile de Jouy and stuffed with moldy loaves of bread.

Louis stepped forward and held his arm aloft, indicating that he desired to address them, but the jeering persisted. Rioters shook their fists at him and pointed to me as though we were freaks at a traveling circus. I believe they may have been deriding us for the powder that dusted our hair, which they undoubtedly believed was concocted entirely of flour. Finally the king began to speak, raising his voice in an effort to be heard above the din, but to no avail.

A desperate young man in the blue and white uniform of the royal bodyguard stood below us in the courtyard, frantically gesturing to the horde, as a number of his unit unsuccessfully endeavored to dissuade him from his mission. "How much would you like to pay for bread?" he shouted to the crowd.

"Who is that?" I asked my husband.

"Two sous to the pound," came the reply, shouted from the center of the throng. A cheer went up.

Louis raised his hand to shade his eyes. "That is the prince de Poix, a colonel in the royal bodyguard," he replied.

"Is he authorized to make such a negotiation?" But the answer was apparent. The mob began to pelt the young prince with flour. "If they don't have it to bake bread, then why are they wasting it so?" I demanded.

The prince de Poix turned toward us and opened his arms in a gesture of supplication. His face and uniform were so coated with flour that if his life were not in jeopardy the sight would have been comical. Louis nodded gravely and the prince once again faced the rioters. "*Très bien.* Very well. Two sous it is, then. Now disperse at once. Return to your homes in peace." He did not threaten the mob with violence although it seemed like an eternity before they agreed to depart. Louis and I had long since retreated to safety inside the palace.

Yet the incident was far from over. Monsieur Turgot advised Louis to disregard the prince de Poix's proposal, sticking to the figure of three and a half sous for a one-pound loaf. Believing the Crown had betrayed them, there were riots in Paris the following day, despite Turgot's efforts to stave off the violence. A hundred and sixty-two protesters were arrested and Louis summoned Paris's judicial body, the Parlement, to Versailles, to warn them not to interfere in this affair, as he intended to mete out the rioters' punishment himself. But only two men were sentenced to death for pillaging, a gauze maker and a wigmaker; the other troublemakers received far more lenient treatment. By May 9, the price of a loaf had dropped by a sou without being artificially manipulated, and by the sixteenth of the month, the bread riots were over.

Yet there was something that did not quite tally about the whole business. The bakers' shops had been well stocked, even in Paris. The granaries were full and flour had been plentiful. The crowd that marched on Versailles had been exceedingly vocal, but otherwise rather docile, apart from pelting the prince de Poix with flour. But they had not thrown stones—and where had so many likely illiterate people gotten those placards criticizing the king? And then there was the matter of the barley bread the soi-disant rioters had brandished in our faces; it was almost artfully moldy. Louis and his ministers had their suspicions. The king's cousins, known as the Princes of the Blood, had never been supportive either of Louis or of his *grand-père,* Louis XV. It nearly tested my friendship with the duchesse de Chartres, for I knew that wealthy rabble-rousers like her father-in-law, the duc d'Orléans, and the prince de Conti believed that if the power had lain within their hands instead, they would have wielded it with more dexterity. These men had the means to cross hundreds, if not thousands, of palms with silver coins; and even a few sous will buy as much loyalty as bread to a starving man.

Nevertheless both cousins were ostentatiously in attendance at Rheims along with every other member of the royal family, save the *enceinte* comtesse d'Artois, for my husband's coronation on Trinity Sunday, June 11.

We'd set out from Versailles for Louis's hunting lodge at Compiègne on the fifth of June, leading an opulent procession consisting of the entire court. Nobles clad in silks, velvets, and taffeta glittered with a kingdom's worth of precious gems on their wrists, bosoms, and fingers, on their chapeaux, and in their towering coiffures surmounted with foot-long plumes that dipped and fluttered in the gentle spring breeze. They were followed by a parade of clerics in cassocks and soutanes of scarlet and violet. Those who rode were borne in a cavalcade of carriages burnished with ebony and gold drawn by glossy-coated horses, their manes and tails braided and perfumed. For much of our dry and dusty journey the route was lined with people who had clearly never seen such splendor; but my mood rose and fell nearly as often as my breath, for we were not greeted with universal admiration. While some faces, from ruddy to fair, wore proud broad smiles beneath their tricorns or straw chip hats and muslin bonnets, others peered through narrowed eyes, their lips pressed together in grim disapproval, begrudging their monarch the pageantry that had surely been the prerogative of his predecessors. More than once along the roadside—which Turgot grumbled would now have to be repaired twice—laborers knelt in supplication as we passed, outstretching their arms for bread. But at least they did not throw stones, although a few epithets were hurled at us.

"I overheard Monsieur say that Turgot artificially inflated the price of bread and that is why some are starving," I said to Louis. "Tell me, is that true?"

His dark look told me not to stick my nose where it did not belong. "There are reasons for everything that are not always readily apparent, *ma chère,*" my husband answered, somewhat condescendingly. "Sometimes a decision is made that is misunderstood because it does not appear to be in the best interests of the populace, when in fact the opposite is true. You of all people should know better than to credit propaganda."

I should know better than to believe Monsieur. *He* did not have his *brother's* best interests at heart. But I did not trust Turgot. He continued to press for financial reforms that were certainly unpopular among the nobility, and the king could ill afford to lose their support.

The court rested for two days at Compiègne. Louis was visibly anxious, eating even more than usual, while I could barely touch a morsel. As was the custom, we kept separate chambers but he did not visit my bed. I lay awake praying for the health of the kingdom, asking the Almighty to send my husband our subjects' love, for Louis's task was so immense and burdensome that he needed the patience and understanding of his people. If only they comprehended that he cared deeply for their welfare and appreciated how difficult it was to please everyone at once. It was inevitable that someone would end up disgruntled.

In the company of my brothers-in-law and Madame, I departed Compiègne just after sunset on June 8. Aided by the glow of a resplendent moon our procession traveled by torchlight through the falling shadows as the dusky night sky was transformed from lilac to indigo. I wore a gown of palest blue accessorized with a suite of flawless diamonds from the court jewelers Herren Böhmer and Bassenge, while overhead the twinkling constellations illuminated our way northeast toward Rheims.

We arrived before dawn and were shown to charming lodgings in the center of the city. I scarcely had time to sleep before I was expected to greet the local dignitaries and members of the aristocracy, which I had to do on my own, as Louis's entourage had not yet arrived. Maman would have been proud of me that day. I recalled her parting words to me when I left Vienna: *Let the people of France say I have sent them an angel.* And I believe the courtiers of Champagne were not displeased at the reception I accorded them, offering each a unique and personal welcome which truly came from my heart. I was surprised that the women, whom I had expected to be garbed somewhat provincially, were instead dressed in the latest fashion, from their feathered headdresses to the colors of their gowns, the soft shades we now favored at Versailles and Fontainebleau, including dairy cream, pale turquoise, and pea shoot.

Louis did not reach Rheims until one o'clock that afternoon. I waved to him from a balcony as his gilded coach, followed by a dozen beautifully caparisoned outriders, approached at a majestic pace. The glass carriage was pulled by four perfectly matched teams of white horses, their red, white, and blue plumes bobbing gaily in the breeze; and the beasts pranced and snorted almost as if they knew all eyes were upon their magnificent passenger. The citizens of Rheims had planned for the king's arrival in much the same way as the kind people of Strasbourg had greeted me when I first set foot in France as a naïve girl of fourteen. Floral garlands bedecked the facades of the brick and half-timbered shops and residences; allegorical statues graced the square in front of the medieval cathedral; and leafy arches had been constructed bestriding the cobbled *rues* so that Louis's carriage would rumble beneath them like a triumphant Caesar.

The following day we attended Vespers at the cathedral in preparation for the coronation ceremonies the next day. As queen consort I had no ceremonial role, nor would I be crowned. I jested with Louis that I would be known as the First Spectator. I scarcely slept, for the proceedings began at seven A.M.; and Mademoiselle Bertin and Monsieur Léonard, who had traveled with me, at state expense, toiled all through the night to dress my hair in a style that Rose had dubbed the *"Coiffure à la Révolte,"* in honor of recent events—the Flour Wars. The very artificiality of the pouf subtly mocked the false pretenses under which the protests had been staged at our doorstep.

Léonard, his suit of peacock-blue satin protected by a gray cotton smock, availed himself of the lower treads of a wooden stepladder to tease my hair high above the crown of my head, securing a pad of horsehair. This would eventually form the stage for the inventive tableau that would be affixed to it with a number of long metal hairpins. Then he slathered his hands with bergamot-scented pomade and began to work them through the flamelike cone of hair before using a rattail comb to section off strands which he would then frizzle with his hot iron.

Once his task was completed it was Rose's turn to work her magic. She positioned the figures in each tableau: the farmers with their sheaves of wheat; the rioters destroying mills and markets and granaries only to discover that there were stores aplenty after all; and the strangely convivial assembly with their placards and artfully moldy bread who had come to Versailles, ostensibly to demand a lower price per pound. Mademoiselle Bertin's miniatures were tiny feats of engineering, from the gristmill's fully functioning water wheel to the leaded mullions on the doors that opened onto the balcony of the château to the downy mold on the infinitesimal baguettes.

There was tremendous precedent for the robing of the gentlemen at a coronation, but no queen had been present since 1547, because the last several kings had been unmarried when they were crowned. I suppose I could have paid homage to the era of Henri IV with my wardrobe, which was how the men were garbed, Henri being universally regarded as the wisest and most just of all French monarchs. For some reason, the Age of Chivalry held an uncommon allure for the enlightened denizens of the eighteenth century. But I decided to embrace the present and look toward the future, rather than cast a backward glance at the past.

I was gowned in cloth of silver with close-fitting sleeves and an underskirt of white, embroidered with a bejeweled motif of roses and lilies, the symbolic flowers of Austria and France. The *robe à la française,* a special commission from Mademoiselle Bertin, was so heavy that she suggested we transport it to Rheims on a special stretcher, but my *dame d'atours,* the duchesse de Cossé, refused to comply, so great was her disdain for the gendarme's upstart daughter who had dared to insinuate herself with the queen. My nerves grew so frayed from trying to make peace between the *marchande de modes* and the Mistress of the Robes that I ended up traveling with my coronation ensemble in my own trunks to prevent the lofty duchesse from becoming overburdened.

Attached to my shoulders was a twenty-five-foot satin train that weighed nearly as much as I did. At my throat was a necklace of sapphires and diamonds. Owing to the vast height of my coiffure and the width of my gown, my face appeared to be nearly at the midpoint of my body.

It was still dark at five-thirty, when my ladies and I ascended the stairs to the grandstand from which we would witness my husband's coronation. Even at that ungodly hour it was already unnaturally hot for the season, but I was determined not to show my fatigue. Countless delicate linen handkerchiefs were at the ready to blot the slightest glow of moisture from my brow or *poitrine*.

The entire nave of the High Gothic church, with its soaring marble columns and stained-glass windows refracting the light like countless brilliant gemstones, had been transformed into a sort of rococo theater. It seemed as though the aim had been to eliminate the cathedral's medieval heritage, even as the men's ceremonial garments deliberately paid homage to it. Along the aisles, the torchières had been cunningly disguised as angels sculpted in neoclassical robes, while plump cherubs clasped the burners of pungent incense in their chubby fists. The drab walls of gray stone were relieved by buntings of purple and gold satin; untold yards of violet brocade draperies with the fleurs-de-lis of France woven into the cloth and trimmed with fringe of pure gold, cascaded down the columns and puddled to the floor.

Hidden behind a curtain in the gallery, where I was to witness the coronation, was a completely furnished apartment, as comfortably appointed as any to be found at one of our châteaux. Here, the archbishop informed me, was where I might retire with my attendants to seek privacy, even a nap, if I so desired. Papillon de la Ferté, our Steward of *Menu Plaisirs,* assured me that the apartment had been furnished with "English-style facilities," by which he meant a commode. I sighed with relief that I would not be forced to negotiate with a chamber pot in my weighty robes of state.

At precisely seven A.M., the enormous doors of the cathedral were opened. By then the church had filled with spectators and as the pipe organ resonated through the vaulted interior from the altar to the entry, every head turned toward the procession as it approached the nave, led by a delegation of bishops, resplendent in their ceremonial vestments of gold and purple. Then, representing Charlemagne's original peers, came twelve noblemen, including the king's brothers, costumed as they would have been in the time of Henri IV, with long tunics of cloth of gold, and sweeping violet mantles lined in ermine. Even the headgear hearkened back to the days of chivalry, from the burnished coronets that graced the heads of my brothers-in-law to the flat velvet caps with jaunty plumes worn by the Princes of the Blood to the Guard of the Seals' golden toque.

A moment of silence preceded the entrance of the king to allow him to appear silhouetted in the doorway with the morning sunlight falling on his lightly powdered hair. The orchestra joined the organ as a hundred musicians raised their bows and lifted their trumpets and reeds to their lips.

I felt my heart thrumming within my breast, excited, thrilled, and a bit frightened for Louis, knowing how painfully shy he could be, especially amid a sea of strangers. He was never at ease when all eyes were upon him; and, with the possible exception of our wedding ceremony, during which he had sweated profusely and shifted his weight about, looking rather miserable, this was the most significant day of his twenty years.

A pair of bishops flanked him as he walked with great solemnity toward the altar. I stole a secret smile. They would catch him if he went weak at the knees. Considering his everyday preference for the simplest of garments, I wondered what Louis thought about his regal wardrobe—the purple velvet cloak and heavy ermine cape embroidered with gold fleurs-de-lis, the violet boots with red heels in the manner of the Sun King, and his white satin suit shot through with silver threads that shimmered as they caught the light.

As the hour grew later and the morning light streamed into the cathedral, the heat became oppressive. I pitied the seventy-eight-year-old Archbishop of Rheims who performed the ceremony as much as I did Louis in his weighty coronation robes kneeling before the altar on a crimson velvet cushion, rivulets of perspiration snaking from his hairline along the contours of his full cheeks. Visibly embarrassed, he mopped them away.

A lump rose in my throat when the archbishop took the ampule of holy water from the Master of Ceremonies—the same vial that had been used to anoint King Clovis nearly thirteen hundred years earlier—and asked my husband to open his scarlet chemise and bare his breast. How pale his hairless skin looked against the carmine silk. Although the kings of France ruled by divine right, the sight of Louis's white and tender flesh had never made him seem more vulnerable.

In a ritual that was centuries old, he was anointed on his chest, shoulders, and arms and the sign of the cross was made upon his brow. Intoning the words he had committed to memory, Louis pledged, "I solemnly vow, before God and before France, that I will do my utmost to prevent violence and injustice, to exterminate heretics, and to rule my people justly." His high, slightly nasal voice was clear and without any sign of hesitation or nerves. My breast swelled with pride. How I wished that my mother could be standing beside me to witness this moment!

The reedy tenor of the aged archbishop invoked the coronation prayer. "May the king have the strength of a rhinoceros, and may he, like a rushing wind, drive before him the nations of our enemies, even to the extremity of the earth." Lofty poetry, with a touch of the absurd; and yet, swept away by the pageantry of the day, no one seemed to give it a second thought.

Now came the moment of the coronation itself. I realized I was holding my breath. A staff was placed in each of Louis's hands; one, the six-foot golden scepter and the other, a jewel-encrusted rod known as the hand of justice. And then, just before the church bells tolled noon, five hours after the ceremony had begun, the heavy crown first worn by the great Charlemagne, thickly studded with priceless uncut gems, was lowered onto the king's head. Louis grimaced. *Oh non.* Was I the only one in the cathedral who heard him gasp, "The crown is hurting me!" How my heart went out to him, but oh, how I wished in that most glorious, triumphant moment of his young life, he had shown more fortitude.

With the weight of the kingdom so ponderously upon his head Louis was led to the throne. The archbishop bowed in reverence to his sovereign, then rose and turned to the spectators declaring with both solemnity and relief that the lengthy ritual was finally drawing to a close, "*Vivat Rex in aeternum*—May the king live forever!"

At this the music crescendoed and the doors to the cathedral were thrown open, admitting a flurry of doves, released by the royal fowlers. I could no longer contain my emotions. Sobs choked my throat; my cheeks became stained with salty tears, marring my rouge. I rose to my feet and drew my handkerchief from my bosom, not to blot the damage at first, but to salute my husband. He caught my eye and I waved to him with such gusto, my little square of linen might have been a flag of surrender. The crowd cheered for the both of us, but I was too overcome with joy and pride to remain, and retreated behind the curtain to the apartment in order to compose myself. I dried my tears, drank a glass of lemon water, and repaired my maquillage, but it took some minutes before I was able to return to the grandstand, gratified beyond measure by the applause of the throng below. At the thought of my husband's immense dignity and grace throughout the ceremony (apart from the momentary business with the crown), and the delighted reaction of our subjects, my weeping nearly began afresh. I looked down and noticed that other faces were bedewed with tears; one of the visiting dignitaries, the ambassador from Tripoli, was openly sobbing.

Outside, the church bells pealed from every steeple, competing with the artillery fire of the military salutes. Louis was fêted at a dinner hosted by the archbishop, where I was once again only a spectator; but that evening toward dusk, after the king was finally able to doff his formal coronation robes, we promenaded arm in arm through the square in front of the cathedral accepting the hearty congratulations of the citizens. It was a sultry evening, the day's heat still hanging heavily in the air. Men dared to appear without their coats, and some of the noblemen even elected to leave off their dressed and powdered wigs, strolling about with bare heads barbered nearly to a stubble, lending them an unfortunate resemblance to baby porcupines.

We were greeted with broad smiles and deep reverences from members of all strata of society, from merchants with fat purses to mothers with rosy-cheeked children on their hips to goggle-eyed apprentices—a hulking sixteen-year-old youth named Georges Jacques Danton had walked all the way from Troyes just to witness the spectacle—and our hearts were gladdened by such a warm reception; but perhaps somewhere deep within me lay the acknowledgment that the adulation of the people was both fickle and fleeting. I had only to look to the reign of the late Louis XV for that lesson. I had once admired him deeply, arriving at the French court a starry-eyed bride, mesmerized by the power of his magnetic personality. Yet before long, the scales had fallen from my eyes, and I recognized that he was no better than a pleasure-seeking adulterer who had allowed his passion for his mistresses, as well as for sport, and his natural inclination toward indolence to govern his temperament, leaving the greater responsibilities of kingship to his ministers, whose poor advice had led the country into financial ruin.

With regard to the temporary affection of the Rhéimoise or of any of our subjects, I could not share such dark thoughts with Maman for I hated to burden my family with my doubts or sorrows, especially my mother who would undoubtedly return the missive with a flurry of admonishments rather than any expression of sympathy. I would continue in my way, writing to her only of our triumphs in Rheims, of the applause our subjects showered upon us for my display of uncontrollable emotion and Louis's promise to be a fair and wise ruler. My plan proved to be sound, for I also omitted to inform Maman of a conversation I had with the duc de Choiseul.

Like a canny diplomat, I had deliberately chosen my moment, when Louis was basking in the afterglow of the coronation, to request his permission to meet with Choiseul. Relishing my victory, I wrote to a friend, Count Rosenberg, to confide, "You will never guess the skill I used, so as not to appear to be asking for permission. I told the king that I wanted to see Monsieur de Choiseul and that I was only wondering on which day I should do so. I managed it so well that the poor man himself fixed the most convenient hour for me to see the duc. I rather pride myself in thinking I took full advantage of my female prerogatives at that time. My sister Maria Carolina, the Queen of Naples, who long ago mastered the skill of controlling her husband Ferdinand, could have done no more with him, I think, than I contrived to do with clever timing and a few smiles."

I should have known better. Even when I withheld information from my mother she would discover it in time. Count Rosenberg evidently, and none too discreetly, passed along my letter to the empress. Though the fact that I met with Choiseul cheered Maman, I received not one, but two reprimands from Vienna.

From my brother, the Emperor Joseph II, came the letter:

> Madame my dear sister,
>
> Could anything be more unreasonable, more improper than what you wrote to Count Rosenberg? If a letter of this kind were ever to go astray, if you were ever to let such ill-conceived and disrespectful comments slip in the presence of your intimate confidantes, as I am almost certain you do, I can already envision the misfortune it will bring you; and I must admit, being attached to you by blood and by sentiment, I am gravely distressed by it. You must pay more heed to your words, for they have consequences, often unintended, and it is your enemies who hope to profit by them and most desire the destruction of your influence with the king. Rather than indulge in idle gossip, for gossip cannot be anything other than an empty use of your time, *read*. Keep busy by improving your mind in a hundred ways; give yourself talents so that years hence when you must rely upon inner resources, the well will be full.

Not content with a scolding from my older brother, Maman wrote to the comte de Mercy, who was quick to share with me the contents of her diatribe.

> "The poor man"? What frivolity! What is she thinking? Where is the kind and gentle heart of the Archduchess Antonia? This is the sort of low, persecuting spirit I would expect from a Pompadour or a du Barry, utterly unfit for a queen, a great princess of the house of Hapsburg, who I know to be full of kindness and decency.
>
> Where is the respect and gratitude she owes the king for all his kindness? This only confirms my fears that she is headed straight for her ruin.

Although the frequent backbiting of the French courtiers bore a sharp and painful sting, it was often ridiculous enough to ignore. But my family's barbs had truer aim and never failed to wound the most tender parts of my anatomy.

SEVEN

Summer Idylls

The court spent a few weeks at Marly during the summer of 1775, enjoying the comparatively rustic atmosphere. As the *pavillon du Roi* originally constructed by the Sun King was modest in size with only twelve smaller outbuildings designed to house courtiers and servants, the Château de Marly, surrounded by its famed hydraulic waterworks, assumed an air of exclusivity and privacy. Yet even there, where one day I rose early to greet the dawn, inviting a number of my intimate friends—among them the princesse de Lamballe, the comtesse de Polignac, little princesse Élisabeth's *gouvernante* the princesse de Guéméné, the duc de Lauzun, and the comte d'Artois, whose wife was due to give birth any day—our morning constitutional on the misty lawns was transformed by an anonymously printed pamphlet into a bacchanalian orgy. I was ascribed a lecherous hunger for lovers of both sexes, naming nearly every member of my coterie. One would have thought my bedchamber was as crowded as the Oeil de Boeuf, with courtiers pressing for my favors. Even Mademoiselle Bertin was identified as one of my tribades.

Upon our return to Versailles a copy of the disgusting tract, mockingly titled *Le Lever d'Aurore*—a play on words for the sunrise as well as my formal toilette—was left for Louis to discover beside the globe in his study. My mother received a copy in Vienna.

"What sort of ill-humored, malevolent creature would go to the expense of posting it to Austria?" the sympathetic Lamballe wondered aloud.

"Only someone with deep pockets could finance the printing and such vast dissemination of these ugly *libelles,*" I reasoned. There could be any number of suspects. I knew that a large number of older aristocrats, having taken umbrage at being eliminated from my entourage and denied invitations to le Petit Trianon, had chosen to depart Versailles for good, leaving no end of insults in their perfumed wake. And courtiers who had been loyal to my former nemesis Madame du Barry still lingered as well. Perhaps my propensity for mockery as a release from the rigid court etiquette had offended some ancient marquise—one of the crones who forgot to change her rouge in the evenings, playing cards in the same blend that she had worn all day, and I had remarked upon her garish appearance in the amber candlelight.

Louis sought to suppress the pamphlet, although he never discovered the source. Maman was of course appalled. "My poor queen," she commiserated. But I refused to permit the vitriol of a few scandalmongers to dampen my spirits. Had the older courtiers made the effort to befriend me when I first came to Versailles, offering me the respect that was my due as dauphine, despite my tender years, they might have received a warmer embrace once I became their queen. But I could not play the hypocrite. These painted grande dames and chevaliers, with comically placed patches that unsuccessfully disguised their smallpox scars, called my frankness and honesty "Austrian," and considered it an insult.

And when they failed to wound my pride by disparaging my birthright, they took to inventing and disseminating ludicrous tales. One evening when my fiacre broke an axle in the middle of a muddy *rue* in Paris and I feared missing the opening notes of the opera, I insisted on racing down the narrow, foul-smelling lane to the Palais Royal with my cloak billowing about me, clutching a fistful of the voluminous calèche hood to my face to keep myself from retching, so pungent was the odor of the streets. The following day, everyone in Paris believed the preposterous fiction that I had abandoned my party to rush off to a clandestine assignation.

Predictably, the news, even more lavishly embellished, reached Vienna; this time, Maman was unsympathetic. As had become my wont, I had traveled to the capital not with Louis but in the society of my usual circle of friends—how could I admit to the patroness of Herren Mozart and Gluck that one reason for the king's absence was his general dislike for opera? My mother saw only that I was continuing to indulge in an endless round of pleasures outside my husband's company. She recently had an earful about the amount of time I had been spending in the company of the comte d'Artois. Our shared passion for fast-paced indulgences had led to my newest obsession—the sport of kings, as he and his English confederates called it.

Wildly fashionable across the Channel, horse racing combined Artois's favorite passions—speed and wagering—and he was determined to popularize the pastime in France. No less a personage than His Brittanic Majesty's brother the Duke of Cumberland had advised him on the purchase of horseflesh and the proper management of a racing stable. Maman was appalled that not only did I sit in the wooden grandstand among women of questionable repute, but accompanied my brother-in-law onto the turf itself to inspect the horses and mingle with the jockeys, trainers, and touts, as the English called the wagerers, all men of dubious character, in Maman's view.

But little could compete with the thrill of dozens of thundering hooves spraying up the dirt as the challengers flew by, and the excitement of cheering for the mount I had wagered on. *"Allons! Allons!"* I would cry, shouting the name of the horse I had chosen until I lost my voice. I would return to the palace spattered with mud, my gown much darker and my purse, more often than not, much lighter than when the day began.

"The newspapers used to be filled with stories about your kindness and generosity of heart, yet they have suddenly changed their tone," my mother lamented. "I now read of nothing but horseracing, of turning night into day with masquerade balls and gaming parties that last until dawn, so that I can no longer bear to look at them."

The manicured gardens and airy salons of the Petit Trianon had by then become my haven and provided the solitude I sorely craved when the comtesse d'Artois began her confinement, for the anticipation surrounding Marie Thérèse's impending childbirth merely accentuated my own superfluousness.

I was already commissioning improvements to the little château itself, inspired by Louis XV's dining table that could disappear entirely out of sight. Every window would have cleverly constructed mechanical blinds that remained embedded in the sill until it was time to employ them. When I desired privacy the blinds would be unfurled from within their hiding place, revealing a mirrored exterior. Anyone rude enough to come sniffing about my business would be confronted with his own curious, envious reflection.

But when the time came for the comtesse to be delivered of her child, I departed the quiet comforts of le Petit Trianon and my private gardens there, swallowed my humiliation, and according to custom, attended the birth with the other members of the royal family. As it was the first week of August, her bedchamber was already stifling hot. It was made stuffier by the fifty or so noblemen and -women in their silk-satin suits and wide skirts who crowded into the room to formally witness the birth; but the doctors and Monsieur Laportère the *accoucheur* (for the nobility of Versailles considered themselves too grand to use a female midwife to deliver a child) refused to open a window for fear that the slightest breeze might endanger the health of both mother and infant. It was the Bourbon way. Maman, who had given birth sixteen times, and who was a great believer in wide-open windows—the chillier the better—would have scoffed at the antediluvian methods of the French physicians.

In the enormous bed, propped against numerous down-filled bolsters, tiny Marie Thérèse looked like a child swimming in a sea of white linen. She was soaked with perspiration. Her dark hair clung damply to her forehead; sweat beaded upon her upper lip; and her dressing gown was discolored with stains. Although she was nineteen years old, she had such a girlish mind that rather than fear the dangers of childbirth she had only been delighted to hear in her final weeks that she would not be forced to swallow any "black medicine."

"What can I do to help?" I asked the *accoucheur,* willing to cool my *belle-soeur*'s forehead with a damp cloth, fetch her a glass of lemon water, sit at the bedside and hold her hand—whatever would allow me to fix my thoughts on her, rather than on my own conjugal woes. All eyes were upon me as well. I knew they were waiting just as eagerly for me to display some show of weakness. It was written in their expectant glances and narrowed gazes. How would the childless queen react to the birth of an heir not her own? But I knew that as long as I remained occupied I could push these distractions from my mind.

The afternoon dragged on as the sun drenched the parterre in amber light. Outside the windows fat black flies flitted and hummed about the sashes, seeking a point of entry and a respite from the heat. The clock on the mantel chimed three times.

According to the doctors, Marie Thérèse's labor was an easy one; unusual, they said, for a first child, and I hoped that I would one day be as fortunate. She suffered only two or three strong pains toward the end and then scarcely a minute later Monsieur Laportère announced that the baby's head was crowning.

Soon we heard the lusty cries of the newborn. "It's a boy—a healthy boy!" the doctor proclaimed. The cord was cut and tied and the infant, resembling both of his parents with a head of downy dark hair, was held aloft, squinting and kicking blindly, for all of us to see. The comtesse d'Artois dragged her arm across her brow and declared with a profound sigh of relief, "*Mon Dieu, que je suis heureuse!*—how happy I am!" As the first of the Bourbon wives to bear a child—moreover, a son—one who might someday sit upon the throne of France, her eyes shone with triumph, humiliating both me and her older sister with her proud gaze.

I searched the cheering throng of courtiers—how many of them adored the new father, the handsome, carefree comte—for my husband. He was standing beside his brothers, offering Artois a hearty clout on the back. Louis's expression registered nothing but a benign complacency. Did the king not notice the sorrow in my eyes? Or recognize the import of the tiny Bourbon's birth? Already, only minutes in the world, the boy had a title, the duc d'Angoulême.

What would Louis write in his journal for today, August 6, 1775? True, it was primarily a hunting diary that recorded the day's kill. But I recalled at that moment what he had written after our wedding night. *Rien.* Nothing. When nothing indeed had transpired in the marital bed.

Should I simply leave matters to Providence and wait submissively for some happy outcome? How many more nights of nothing would there be? We had been married for more than five years and a third, by now the sovereigns of France for fifteen months, and our nursery was empty while Louis's youngest brother and his wife, still in their teens, welcomed into the world—for now—a future king.

I pressed through the crowd of ogling, chattering, nobles cooing over the infant duc, while the comtesse de Polignac murmured, "Her Majesty is feeling faint, please give her some air," parting the way for me to exit the birthing chamber, followed by the princesses de Guéméné and de Lamballe, their wide taffeta skirts rustling in tandem as we glided through the corridors of the château toward the Queen's Apartments. I blinked back the tears that stung my eyes. The halls remained thronged with visitors who had been waiting for news of the birth since the early hours of the morning. As the word spread that the comtesse d'Artois had borne a healthy son, the celebratory whoops and hollers echoed through the high-ceilinged galleries, ringing in my ears like the din of innumerable church bells.

When I sailed around a corner through the Salon de Guerre into the Galerie des Glaces with my ladies at my heels, the aroma in the room, for everyone wore a tremendous amount of scent, underwent a sudden and startling transformation—from lilac and tuberose to that of mussels and brine.

"And where is *your* son, *Majesté*?" This rude address came from a *poissarde* who had traveled to Versailles with a delegation of fishmongers, still reeking of the marketplace. Her uncombed curls tumbled from a discolored mopcap and her striped apron was spattered with blood. And yet, not much older than I, she was vain enough, or perhaps thought to emulate her betters, by staining her cheeks with large circles of cheap red wine as a substitute for rouge.

"Yes, why, after all this time is there no dauphin?" Brandishing a knife used for filleting the belly of a fish, another *poissarde,* older and stouter, took up the cry. The princesse de Lamballe turned pale and clasped my arm. Beneath my gown my legs were trembling, but I would not let these querulous fishwives see my fear. So *sympathique* were my attendants that we could communicate with the slightest gesture. A nearly imperceptible tilt of my chin commanded them to make haste with all due speed for my apartments and the safety of my inner rooms, which lay behind a secret panel in my bedchamber. But as we glided through the Hall of Mirrors with such velocity that we caught the air beneath our skirts, the *poissardes* gave chase, angry fists raised against me, whistling and hollering insults and obscenities.

"You dance until dawn with men other than the king!"

"You play hand after hand of cards when you should be opening your legs!"

"Who do you frolic in the bushes with at dawn, *Majesté*? And who is in your bush at night?"

"Will the comte d'Artois be the father of your child, too?"

"They say she loves riding in his carriage. No wonder they call it 'the devil,' for he will give his brother horns!" From one mirror to the next the reflections of the fishwives' crude, mocking gestures simulating the act of copulation dogged our quickening pace, as their cries grew bolder and more shrill. My ladies and I had no royal bodyguards to protect us, and the sentries stationed by the doors to the State Rooms stood in useless awe of this antagonistic army. Although I was queen, the manners of the court in many ways remained a mystery to me. I could not put on my own chemise in the morning until it passed through three sets of aristocratic hands, or drop one of Monsieur Fargeon's aromatic pastilles into the bathing tub of my own volition, and yet the palace was open to the public and anyone could observe the daily life of the royal family. It was an ancient prerogative of the fishwives of Paris to gather in the halls of Versailles whenever there was a royal birth. Yet I was appalled to discover that as long as the *poissardes* made no direct move to attack me, the guards permitted them to stampede through the Hall of Mirrors, terrorizing their queen!

"Remember their names," I muttered to Gabrielle de Polignac, indicating the sentries, "for I will speak of them to Louis. Is this how they protect *la reine de France*?"

At last we reached the end of the Galerie des Glaces and sped through the Salon de la Paix, turning in to my pink and gold bedchamber with the *poissardes* hard upon us, the terrifying sound of a hundred wooden *sabots* thundering upon the parquet. Clutching at our trains to tug yard after yard of fabric through the doorway before we were beset upon, for who knows what they might have done had they caught up with us, we four—Lamballe, Guéméné, Polignac, and I, breathless with fear and soaked with perspiration—unlatched the heavy doors and pressed our weight against them, bolting them shut, just as the fishwives reached the threshold. They pounded on the doors, hurling angry slurs and frustrated cries accusing me of entertaining my ladies in my bedchamber with all manner of unnatural acts, until finally we heard the raised voices of the sentries commanding the vicious hags to disperse.

Trembling from my fingertips to my knees, I begged Gabrielle to unlace me so that I could lie down, and when her dexterous fingers had completed their ministrations I prostrated myself across the gold brocaded bedspread and wept loudly and freely, staining the silk with my salty tears.

EIGHT

Whispers and Rumors

NOVEMBER 1775

Thanks to the comte de Mercy's clever interior staircase connecting my bedchamber with the king's private apartments, Louis could arrive at any hour without his movements being known by anyone except Monsieur Cléry, his chief *valet de chambre.* My husband would turn a handle on a panel in the inner stairwell and it would open into my room, and once the little door was closed, it discreetly blended into the gold brocade wall covering. The privacy was a blessing but it did not turn Louis into a confident lover. He tugged the fabric of his nightgown above his midsection and straddled me as if I were a horse. I tried to yank my own nightshirt out from beneath him, while he whispered apologies as if they were endearments, his breath, smelling of clove-scented tooth powder, warm on my chest and face.

Placing his hands beside my shoulders to steady his weight on the feather mattresses, he struggled to insinuate himself between my legs, but after several seconds of frustrated fumbling, he released an uncharacteristic roar.

"Shh!" I was afraid he would frighten the royal bodyguard and they would burst into the room, pikes at the ready.

"I can't do this," he grumbled.

"Yes, you can," I soothed. I reached for him, not knowing myself what to do to prepare him in the right way—I seem to be lacking in nature's gift of fire—but I thought if I were to stroke him gently, perhaps he might become less panicked over the whole business.

"*Non*—don't touch me," Louis protested. "Please."

I propped myself against the silken bolster and buried my face in my hands, squeezing my eyes tightly shut so I could think more clearly. Light danced behind my lids in streaks of pink and yellow. Every dilemma had a resolution. This one came to me in a burst of inspiration, recalling some of the vile caricatures I had seen of myself and the duc de Lauzun or the comte d'Artois. Because of our known fondness for riding, we were depicted in an obscene sexual posture, with the gentlemen mounting me as if I were a mare. Louis's physician Monsieur Lassone had even mentioned that he might be more comfortable in certain positions. . . .

I clenched my fists, imprinting my nails into my palms, ashamed of what I was about to do. Maman would probably scold me for behaving like a harlot; this would hardly have been her interpretation of *cajoleries.* Moreover, would God forgive me for asking my husband to imitate the image on a lewd cartoon, the theme of which was adulterous, if it might lead to the consummation of our marriage? Positioning myself on all fours and raising my night rail to expose the bare cheeks of my derrière, in a strangled whisper I urged Louis, "Come, why not try it behind me then?"

He gasped, clearly appalled. "Like dogs or horses? Toinette, what has come over you?" Stung, even though I had anticipated as much, I hung my head in humiliation, my coiffure weighing me down, then scrambled, mortified, onto my side.

I scrubbed away a tear and took a moment to compose myself. Haranguing him would only make things worse. "Forgive me, *mon cher,* I don't know what else to do. I have been patient. I have been gentle. We could speak to Monsieur Lassone again . . . the circumcision. I would have thought, after the comtesse d'Artois had a son, you might reconsider."

Louis shook his head vehemently. "My concerns remain the same. He may be my brother but where the fate of the kingdom is concerned, Stanislas and his coterie are as vile as any bowl of leeches."

He was right. Not too many months ago, Monsieur had endeavored to ingratiate himself into my circle of intimates, hoping to become as welcome as Artois. But I had allowed myself to be persuaded by the pretense of amity; and while I had gone out of my way to be cordial to Monsieur and Madame, my kindness had been repaid with spite. They had enlarged their own coterie, comprised primarily of former Barryistes, whose chief occupation was to invent and disseminate hurtful propaganda. There was no disguising it anymore: Louis's brother had a weak and dishonorable character.

I sighed heavily, feeling my stomach turn queasy. "Then what is your remedy?" He turned away, shrugging his shoulders. So that was my answer. We would continue as we were, then, trying, failing, drifting apart, rather than solving our dilemma together as we must. I feared that after so many years we had reached the apex of our effort, and like two lines on an artist's canvas we had finally converged at a midpoint, only to split apart, as we headed for the horizon.

JANUARY 1776

One frigid winter afternoon I returned to the palace utterly exhausted, and so chilled that I no longer felt any sensation in my toes, the soles of my white leather boots being too delicate to withstand any time at all upon the icy ground. Abbé Vermond was already waiting for me; I was late for our customary hour together. When I was dauphine he would read to me from a devotional or from the *Lives of the Saints* in order to improve my mind—one day, soon after our arrival at Versailles, I'd become so bored by the rigid court etiquette that I slipped a copy of the lurid novel *La Princesse de Clèves* inside his prayer book just to see him blush when he began to perform his duty.

The music room was as silent as a mausoleum. "Have you been entertaining my ladies?" I inquired gaily, approaching his chair. The past few years had not been kind to the poor cleric; streaks of gray now frosted his curly russet hair, and his shoulders were beginning to sag where his carriage had once been as perfect as a soldier's.

"I brought you a gift from Paris," I whispered in his ear, pressing a bag of sugared almonds into his hands. "I know how much you love them."

His cheeks flushing slightly, Vermond nodded his head in thanks and immediately untied the ribbon. "How are things at the Palais Royal?"

I looked about the salon. In one corner the princesse de Lamballe, settled upon a tabouret with her furbelowed ivory satin skirts billowing about her, was embroidering a section of a fire screen. The comtesse de Polignac was seated as far from her as possible without placing herself anywhere near the abbé. Each of them had a coterie of pastel-clad ladies about them, like the stigma of a blossom surrounded by its petals.

"Yesterday's fire did quite a bit of damage," I told the abbé. "It evidently began where the trials are held, and unfortunately it spread very quickly to the shops because it was too hard to fetch the buckets of water with so much snow on the ground. As soon as I heard the news, I gave two hundred louis for the needy and displaced." I chuckled bitterly. "From the moment of the fire the same people who had been repeating the talk and the songs against me were praising me to the skies." The Parisians who frequented the salons and coffeehouses of the duc d'Orléans derived a sense of pleasure from criticizing me or those I favored; it seemed as much a form of entertainment to them as a novel or a performance at the Opéra. And in many ways they were complicit in their own jest, deriding Monsieur Léonard for driving a six-in-hand from Paris to Versailles every morning to dress my hair, yet demanding that he duplicate his creations on their own aristocratic heads.

As I indicated that I wished to remove my gloves, from either side of the room came Lamballe and Polignac, rising with rustles of satin and taffeta, each discreetly endeavoring to disguise the fact that she was racing to reach me first.

"May I, *Votre Majesté*?" Gabrielle offered sweetly, taking my hand.

Marie Thérèse de Lamballe uttered a faint cry of disapproval. "In the absence of the *dame d'atours* and the First Lady of the Bedchamber, it is my responsibility as Her Majesty's *dame d'honneur* to relieve her of her glove." For the faintest moment, the sweet Lamballe reminded me of my former *dame d'honneur,* the comtesse de Noailles—"Madame Etiquette." Taking my other hand, the princesse gently tugged at each of the fingers of the lemon-yellow glove. In response to Madame de Polignac's glower, she added, "It is not your office, Madame la comtesse. Besides, I know why you wish to help. You have apprehended the gloves the queen has worn every day this week and most of the days last week as well."

I had never heard her speak severely to anyone; her sobriquets at court were "gentle Lamballe" or "tender Lamballe," and yet she was teetering on the edge of accusing Madame de Polignac of misappropriation.

Carefully rolling the glove over my palm, the princesse apologized. "Your Majesty, I would not trouble you with such trifling matters, but I have heard complaints among your other attendants that they have not been able to avail themselves of the right of the queen's gloves, because one lady has been claiming them time after time." She glared at Gabrielle de Polignac. "Unfortunately, it is the same situation with the right to the candles at the end of the evening."

At the close of day, every one of the tapers at Versailles, whether they had been lit or not, were taken by our courtiers and servants from their sconces and candelabra and used by them or sold to line their pockets. I hadn't realized that the comtesse de Polignac was helping herself to more than she should. I knew she saved the lengths of ribbons from my *robe à négligée,* for I retied it with a fresh yard every day after I was bathed and changed out of the wet gown into my chemise, hose, and *négligée*. The ribbons, too, were a perquisite, as were the two yards of green taffeta cut each morning to cover the osier basket containing my scented handkerchiefs and gloves and the *gazette des atours* from which I selected the garments I would wear that day. An additional two yards covered the basket that was used to collect my accessories every evening.

The princesse de Lamballe relieved me of my right glove and I thanked her for her assistance before inviting the comtesse de Polignac to join me at the window where we could speak more privately. Snow blanketed the courtyard below us. It tipped the iron railings and frosted the trees and the parterres beyond, cocooning the vast estate in uncommon silence. Such weather was rare for Paris and its environs. I was reminded of my childhood in Vienna, of our family sleigh rides and the forts I would build with my brothers and sisters. Knowing my fondness for snow, if the winters were too mild in the capital, my papa would command the servants to bring great wagons of it from the nearby mountains so that we would have enough to play in.

I gazed out the mullioned window into the middle distance and tried to imagine us as we were then, my father, portly and pink-cheeked, hoisting me onto his shoulder and tossing me back into an enormous snowdrift of his own manufacture, just so he could hear me laugh. I found myself rationing my memories of Papa because they were so few. He died of an apoplectic fit on the eve of my brother Leopold's wedding in 1765; in my life just nine winters, and three of them I was far too little to recall.

Gabrielle did not impress me as greedy. She must have needed the gloves and candles. But I could not fail to contrast the scene I had just witnessed, which to anyone who did not reside at Versailles would have seemed the height of childishness, to the despair on the faces of those who had lost their livelihoods in the shops at the Palais Royal.

"Your Majesty?"

"Ah, *oui,* Gabrielle." The reverie was broken, evanescing. I glanced over at the princesse de Lamballe who had taken up her needlework in an uncharacteristic sulk. It pained me to see her displeased about something. No matter the circumstances, an aura of *tristesse* swathed Marie Thérèse de Lamballe, but she had a docile and compliant nature and was not the sort to complain or tattle. If the comtesse had hindered her ability to perform her obligations as *dame d'honneur* of my household or had created dissension among my entourage, I would have to step in and make peace. Their rivalry perplexed me, as I was conscious of showing neither of the women any mark of favoritism above the other, for they were the two confidantes I most relied upon. I could not imagine a day without their companionship—the princesse so gentle and amiable, and the comtesse so lively and charming.

I reached out to touch the latter's sleeve affectionately. "Gabrielle, I hope you realize how much I cherish your friendship. Your presence is a breath of sweet, pure air amid the fetid odors of Versailles." At my compliment the comtesse smiled demurely, her teeth perfect and white, as rare, too, as the heavy snowfall. "But it troubles me to discover that there is ill will among any of my ladies. I have broken court etiquette and angered a good number of people by choosing each of you because you please me, because I can trust you, because you are my true friends—in preference to those whose ancient coats of arms have granted them the privilege of attending me at my *lever* or in my bedchamber."

Madame de Polignac's violet eyes dimmed with tears. "Have I then *dis*pleased you, *Majesté*?"

"You must not be seen to appear eager to obtain your perquisites. It is appropriate to share and wait your turn."

"I can explain," she whispered, desperately clasping my hand. "It is not all for me, you see." She tossed a sidelong glance at the abbé Vermond. "I know he thinks I am grasping—*non,* you do not have to deny it—I have overheard him say as much to the comte de Mercy. But they do not understand my situation." She tightened her grip, entwining our fingers. "If it were for myself alone, I would hardly have such need. But you know my husband is deeply in debt, and Armand and Agläié must eat of course, and be clothed according to their station in life or the humiliation would be insufferable."

I secretly envied the comtesse the happiness of having two beautiful, healthy *enfants.* Her greatest gift to me had been to allow me the pleasure of their company whenever I wished. How amused the abbé Vermond was when he found me teaching Armand to read! The good cleric regarded us as if he surely expected the roles to be reversed. Agläié was fascinated by my poufs and always asked to play *friseur* with me. We spent countless hours dressing her chestnut curls into all manner of elaborate styles, limited only by the bounds of her imagination. I would have traded almost anything to be in Gabrielle's shoes—and I would have emptied my purse on the spot if her children required anything, as I had done when I first met the comtesse and her family; but before I could open my mouth, Gabrielle continued, "I have a cousin just outside Versailles, in Marly. And another in Languedoc; she is at the same convent where I was educated after my mother died. And I wish for them to one day be able to make good marriages, but for that one needs money, and so I send them the candles and taffeta and ribbons and gloves, because everyone wants something that was touched or worn by the queen." She anxiously fingered the lilac-colored bow at her breast. "I meant no harm, *Majesté;* I only desired my impoverished *cousines* to have the same advantages as I have had—to be here at court—" She broke off, and turned away, casting her gaze on the floral medallion in the center of the Savonnerie carpet so that I would not see the shame that colored her cheeks.

I slipped my arm about her waist and drew her into a comforting embrace. *"Ma pauvre petite,"* I soothed, though she was taller than I. "Why didn't you just come to me and tell me about your cousins? I will find places for them here at Versailles, and in time, who knows?" I jiggled her about the waist in an effort to make her smile. "They may meet some handsome courtier with a good stable and a fine estate, and soon the abbé Vermond over there, waiting so patiently for me to sit by him and listen to his homily, will be ringing the banns—well, not him of course, the archbishop would do so—but there will be a happy ending; so you see, all you needed to do was speak to me directly, *ma chère,* and I will grant all of your wishes. For what is money, when happiness is at stake?" I clutched Gabrielle's wrist to pull her close again. "But you must not make it difficult for the dear princesse to perform her duties—and you must also assure me that you will be more considerate of the other ladies in the future."

She nodded contritely and sank into a deep reverence, kissing my hands in supplication when I assured her that arrangements would be made to bring her relations to Versailles as soon as it was practical to do so. But now I felt compelled to play the peacemaker with the soulful princesse de Lamballe, bent intently over her embroidery frame, undoubtedly pretending not to eavesdrop.

The fire crackled and blazed in the marble hearth. The room would have been a cozy retreat, had it not been for my closest friends' chilly animosity toward each other. How could two such lovely women, born on the selfsame day, behave like rivals when I loved them in equal measure?

I settled into the fruitwood armchair beside the princesse and spoke to her in a voice so low and gentle that even the amiable abbé could not hear me. "*Ma très chère amie,* when I was a stranger in a strange court, sixteen years old and still a virginal bride after nearly two years, you were the only woman to extend her hand in friendship. And from that moment you have been as close and as dear to me as a sister. If you wish the queen to bend her knee to you, she shall, for I beg of you not to be jealous of others—it does not suit your impeccable dignity."

The princesse smiled wanly, not entirely convinced that I honored her no less than Madame de Polignac. How I envied the comte de Mercy at that moment for his diplomatic talents. Eventually I mollified Madame de Lamballe the way one does a child, with the promise of a sleigh ride at dusk; for at Versailles, a courtier lived for those private moments spent in the presence of the sovereign. However, the internal strife among my entourage still weighed heavily upon me. While there was little amity between the princesse de Lamballe and the comtesse de Polignac, covetous of my close bond with a lowly cleric of no birth, they were united in their lack of respect for the abbé Vermond. Their hauteur troubled me greatly because he remained my only connection to Austria and my girlhood.

Except of course, for the comte de Mercy and Maman.

NINE

Excess Is Never Enough

July 16, 1776

Your Imperial Majesty:

I regret to inform you that the Queen's taste for jewelry is far from sated. Her Majesty has recently purchased diamond bracelets worth nearly 300,000 livres, in exchange for which she gave the court jewelers some stones which they appraised at a very low value, but she was compelled to make a large deposit for the balance. This sum, combined with her old debt of 300,000 livres for a pair of earrings, leaves her with an aggregate of 100,000 livres owing to the jewelers, in consequence of which, she has nothing left in her allowance for current expenses. In addition, she long ago exhausted her annual wardrobe allowance of 150,000 livres; she has become a slave to her *marchande de modes* Mlle. Bertin.

The Queen most reluctantly (and at least shamefacedly) asked the King to give her 2000 louis to settle the debt with

Herren Böhmer and Bassenge. The sovereign greeted her request with his usual kindness and affability, but was overheard murmuring to Her Majesty that he was not at all surprised that she had run out of money, given her fondness for diamonds.

The queen's income has more than doubled, and yet now she has debts. At first the public was pleased that the King had given her le Petit Trianon as a country retreat, but now it is alarmed at the amounts of money being spent there. Antoinette ordered the gardens to be redone in the English manner, which is expected to cost at least 150,000 livres. She also had a theater built at Trianon for her private performances, but thus far she has given only one play there, followed by a supper, and the costs for one evening were considerable. Moreover, the servants at Trianon wear her own livery of red and silver, rather than the Bourbon uniforms, giving rise to further criticisms about the château's exclusivity.

In addition to her acquisition of diamonds, her passion for gambling is an expensive one. She no longer plays ordinary games such as cavagnole where one cannot lose very much. Lansquenet and pharaon are all the rage, and the king has even taken steps to prohibit the latter game, which may have an effect elsewhere but not at court, and certainly not when his wife sits at the baize-covered table. These games are concealed from the king as much as possible, as the high stakes displease His Majesty.

However, the courtiers have grown worried about the astronomical losses they risk if they are invited to sit down to play with the queen, and yet how can they refuse?

The dissension in Her Majesty's entourage has other roots as well. The princesse de Lamballe, by multiplying her claims and defending them arrogantly, creates endless conflicts within the Queen's Household whose ladies are complaining about her despotism, and Antoinette is continually forced to adjudicate. Frustrated with her *dame d'honneur,* for now, anyway, she has returned to her taste for the comtesse de Polignac, in whose coterie intrigues of all sorts are born, and where, regrettably, Her Majesty's frenzied spirit of dissipation is encouraged.

Your Obedient Servant,
Mercy

I felt so useless. I had come to France more than six years earlier to produce children and still had none. That was my role and as it remained unfulfilled, I tried to create a new one. How else might I be of service to my husband, to my friends? Louis and I routinely gave alms; but I yearned for other ways to enrich our subjects.

Maman grew livid when I advanced one of my favorites, our ambassador to England, the comte de Guines, insisting that Louis offer him a dukedom, even as the Contrôleur-Général, Monsieur Turgot, was investigating him for some sort of misconduct. The minister's agenda of financial reforms had displeased me—for I knew it would be highly unpopular with the nobility, and my husband needed as many friends as he could amass in these antagonistic times. It was perceived that I had forced Turgot's resignation—which prompted the inevitable dressing-down from my mother.

July 26, 1776

Madame my dear daughter:

Unlike the Queen of Naples you lack the talent for political intrigue; however, were you to apply yourself to anything substantive you would be your sister's equal and advance our relations with France instead of creating an embarrassment. If you would have looked through the eyes of an administrator and not with those of a spoiled and petulant child who is denied an increase in her allowance, you would have seen that Turgot's plans were in fact the king's best hopes for reining in the morass of France's economy. You have no business interfering in such matters, and it is such naïve meddling that has lost you the support of those upon whom you should most rely. I hear you are taking delight, even credit, for the fact that an excellent and beloved minister has retired rather than accept dismissal, while an unscrupulous *ami* has been made a duc. I can only sigh in amazement and wonder where is the Antonia I sent across the border.

As to your ongoing frivolity, I cannot conceal my fears on this subject. To go into debt over a few trinkets? A queen only degrades herself in adorning her body with all that tinsel, and even more if she spends exorbitant sums of money on it. Everyone knows that the king is very moderate in his expenditures, and therefore the entire blame will be laid at your feet. I hope I shall not live to see the consequences.

Your loving Maman

As wise as Maman was, she refused to comprehend my world. At Versailles, everyone vied to outdo their rivals and wore their family's wealth about their wrists, throats, and fingers, and sewn onto their gowns, coats, cuffs, and bodices. It shouldn't have to be spelled out for her that the queen of France had to sparkle with far greater effulgence than her courtiers. The price of asserting my dominance was certainly worth a few hundred thousand livres. And times were hard, it was true. But in my view this dazzling competition could only benefit the merchants who catered to the nobility. If I set the tone for lavish diamond bracelets, or for anything—then everyone from Paris to Marseille knew that a clamor would ensue to possess whatever was being worn by Her Majesty. And, by increasing the income of these *marchandes* and *vendeuses,* their coffers were enlarged, thereby enriching others, from fellow merchants to farmers to craftsmen. Everyone in France ultimately stood to profit.

The golden cupids on the mantel clock struck the center gong, tolling the hour of ten.

"Heavens, how late it has grown!" the king exclaimed. "I hadn't thought it possible I'd remained in this pleasant company for so long." He stifled a yawn. "But you must excuse me, madame," he said, turning to address me directly, "for it is time for me to go to bed."

"Yet Your Majesty has just arrived," chirped the comtesse de Polignac. "Though you are hardly dressed to join us at the masquerade, unless, saving your honor, you are in disguise as a notary." At le Petit Trianon, she dared to laugh at the king's expense.

Louis managed a chuckle as well. Gesturing about the room full of sartorial popinjays, brightly clad in shades of mustard, peacock, fuchsia, and garnet, he jested wryly, "I know when I am beaten. I would never, madame la comtesse, endeavor to compete with such splendor." Appraising her pouf with a narrowed gaze, he remarked, "What will you do if your headdress hatches while you are in the carriage bound for Paris tonight?"

High atop Gabrielle's brow perched an actual bird's nest in which a trio of eggs, covered in glittering diamond pavé, were guarded by a gold filigree songbird. If the comtesse were to touch a spring hidden in her hair, the bird would appear to fly above her coiffure and sing a charming air composed by my childhood friend Herr Mozart. The mechanism was the clever invention of Sieur Beaulard, one of Léonard's rivals. Beaulard had made a name for himself among the fashionable women of Paris with his whimsically named *coiffure à la grand-mère,* because a lady could lower his stratospheric creations by as much as two feet by pressing upon the hidden spring, thereby appeasing even the most disapproving grandmother. I had worn a few of Sieur Beaulard's mechanical coiffures myself. But not tonight. I would have to kneel on the floor of my carriage in a most undignified manner if I expected my puce-colored ostrich plumes to survive the journey intact.

"Must you depart so soon?" I said, lightly touching my husband's arm. It was all for show, a pantomime we had played for the benefit of our courtiers countless times over the past two years. My husband would arrive at le Petit Trianon toward the end of the gaming, and when the clock struck ten he would apologize for retiring so early while I would make a great display of regretting that he would miss the rest of the night's adventures. But my friends knew something about these nightly charades at the Petit Trianon that Louis did not; it was not ten P.M. at all. It was only nine. I deliberately set the clocks ahead an hour so that he would plod back to the palace thinking it was his bedtime, and we could continue our fun. *Le pauvre homme* never noticed and never suspected a thing. In our artificial sphere, lies lay cocooned inside of lies, and it was the most natural thing in the world to maintain them.

Drawing my husband toward me, I murmured in his ear, "I will return late. You needn't visit me tonight." I winced at his expression of palpable relief and suddenly began to feel less guilty about resetting my clocks. He wished me *bon soir* and turned to leave, shambling away. I watched his retreating form, grown even stouter of late from his diet of charlotte russe and meringues, and surreptitiously brushed away a falling tear. Then, addressing my devotees, I clapped my hands and announced gaily, "Who will come with me to the masquerade? My *carosse de gala* will hold eight!"

The comte d'Artois rose immediately, as did the duc de Guines, and an old friend lately returned to court, the duc de Lauzun. The comtesse de Polignac and the princesses de Lamballe and de Guéméné folded their hands of cards and collected what winnings they had amassed. "Well, then, I suppose the pair of you will have to draw your swords for the last place in my carriage," I jested, glancing at the dear old baron de Besenval and the duc de Coigny.

"I believe that age should have the prior claim," said the Field Marshal gallantly, "and so I will defer to the baron."

"Try not to look so disappointed, sister," Artois whispered to me.

I playfully rapped him on the knuckles with my fan. "Mustn't start rumors! But everyone must have dominoes!" At the opposite end of the room a panel cleverly concealed a cabinet. Inside it hung an array of splendid cloaks and masks, from pure black silk to silver tissue. "Help yourselves!" I declared. "And make haste, or we will be late."

I called for my coach and the eight of us piled inside the gilded conveyance. Giggling, glittering, and spangled, dripping with feathers and jewels, we resembled an opulent gypsy band.

"You must open the windows so we ladies can stick our heads outside," insisted Gabrielle de Polignac.

Lamballe frowned prettily. "But the horses mustn't go too quickly or our poufs will be destroyed by the breeze." Atop her head was a spring garden of fresh vegetables to match her gown of lawn-green faille.

"If they don't, Marie Thérèse, we shall never get to Paris. The three of you must do as I do—come!" I crouched on the carriage floor, and still, my coronet of feathers brushed the velvet underside of the roof. "The ladies must arrange themselves first, and then the gentlemen must make do around us." And oh, what a jumble of limbs we made, as elbows brushed thighs and knees found breasts, and tight sleeves and corseted torsos made it all the more difficult to extricate ourselves. I think we laughed for leagues as the heavily sprung *carosse* jounced along the road. Artois entertained us with a string of bawdy jokes as the comtesse, the pair of princesses, and I bounced about, our derrières rising from the floor every time the wheels hit a rut. "My eggs!" cried Gabrielle, as she reached up to steady the bird's nest.

"Oh, yes, by all means, the fertile bird must protect her brood," jested my brother-in-law. His own fertile bird was whiling away the evening hours with her sister and the vile coterie of former Barryistes, who now made Monsieur and Madame the center of their social circle. I knew that Stanislas, for all his wit, was not to be trusted when he'd one day compared my own bold fashions to those of a royal mistress rather than those of a queen. It had not been a compliment, accusing me—by dressing with regal splendor—of emulating the ostentatious du Barry when everyone knew I thought her nothing but a gaudy harlot. And then upon reflection, I realized—this was Monsieur's intended insult!

But I knew it was a lie. I was as chaste as the day I was born and as true to my husband as Penelope to Ulysses despite being surrounded daily by a circle of ardent admirers. During every unoccupied minute my thoughts were overtaken by the *rien* in my bedchamber, the courtiers' mockery, and my mother's entreaties to manage *mon mari.* Yet, to stave off even a moment's ennui I had become determined to dance nearly every night in the guise of a stranger until the soles of my slippers were nearly transparent, and to hazard the contents of my purse, or the jewels at my throat, if it would bring me a momentary thrill.

It was raining in Paris. My ladies squealed at the gentlemen to close the windows of the carriage because their silken cloaks were becoming splashed and their elaborate poufs were in danger of ruin. The unpaved *rues* had turned to mud striated with veinlike rivulets released into the streets from dozens of drainpipes.

The duc de Lauzun poked his head out of one of the windows. "It looks like we're stuck; we may have to walk."

He was met with a chorus of objections. "Not in these shoes!" Gabrielle exclaimed.

"How far are we from the Palais Royal?" I asked.

"A quarter of a mile or so, I should think," Lauzun replied.

"Each of us can carry a lady on his back!" Artois proposed.

"Perhaps you young bucks can perform such feats, but I am an old stag," the baron de Besenval chuckled.

"Then you will have to bear the lightest one!" concluded the duc de Guines.

And so we arrived at the Opéra ball that night, bedashed with rain and spattered with mud, my attendants and I each a jockey on her mount: I on Artois, as it did not seem seemly—*un*seemly as the whole notion was to begin with—for the queen to straddle a man who was not at the very least a relation; Gabrielle on Lauzun; Guéméné on the duc de Guines; and Lamballe, being most petite, struggling to stay on the broad, if somewhat stooped back of the complaining baron.

Oh, how we laughed! Our domino cloaks were drenched, but our dancing slippers were dry and that was all that mattered as we minced and twirled anonymously through minuets and gavottes and polonaises. I spied Dugazon, the popular actor, and saw through his disguise immediately, because he affected it so often. Yet it made me shudder, for he was garbed *en travestie* as a *poissarde*.

I had been dancing for upwards of an hour, and soaked with

perspiration, had found a place behind a pillar to discreetly daub a bit of orange blossom scent on my wrists, inside my elbows, behind my ears, and in the crevasse of my cleavage. All about me assignations were being arranged in hushed whispers; papers pressed into palms disappeared discreetly into pockets. *Bals masqués* were delicious occasions for such diversions because the parties traveled incognito. And yet, a fine lady might be identified from her expensive pouf, even as she trysted with a gentleman of a lower social order.

Having refreshed myself, I whirled about the marble column and made for the dance floor, my voluminous black hood and mask in place, when I came face-to-face with a trio of women. All were bejeweled and expensively gowned, but dresses could be rented and in the soft candlelight what passed for fine gems could have been merely glass. "If it isn't the queen of France herself!" exclaimed one of the trinity, peering at me through her sequined mask.

"You have failed your duty as a good wife and are a disgrace to the kingdom," spat one of her confederates, snapping open her ivory-handled fan. "Disporting yourself at masquerades till all hours with the king's brother, while the king himself no doubt lies abed alone at Versailles." She pressed a paper into my hand. I refused to accord her the satisfaction of glancing at it and shoved it into the pocket of my gown.

"I have seen common harlots behave with more dignity!" agreed the third woman. She was wearing a pouf embellished with countless blue butterflies, quite similar to one I had worn just two weeks earlier. Her voice sounded familiar, yet I could not place it. I could have heard it anywhere—in the halls of Versailles or in the shops of the Palais Royal. But it had a sinister edge to it that sent a shiver running along the length of my spine.

I could not wait to leave. But I would do so with my chin held high. These harpies would not witness my discomfort.

I called for my carriage, then threaded my way through the throng, grateful for a breath of cool night air. In the flicker of the link boys' torches I read the pamphlet that had been so rudely thrust upon me. It was the most recent issue of the *Gazette de Paris* and although the watermark was unfamiliar, it would not have surprised me to learn that it had been printed within steps of where I stood, somewhere within the bowels of the duc d'Orléans's Palais Royal. Louis's cousin detested him, and his favorite way to undermine the sovereign was to malign his wife.

I read the paragraph that had been circled with a heavy hand.

> The Queen, although unwittingly, has done irreparable injury to the nation. In the passionate desire to copy her example, women's dress has become so enormously expensive that husbands generally are unable to pay for what is required, so lovers have become the fashion. As a consequence, Her Majesty is dangerous to the morals of her people.

The paper felt like it was burning my fingers. I blinked back tears, anxious to hide them from my companions. My hasty departure had already disappointed some of the party, particularly Artois, who had not wished to quit the ballroom so soon. It was barely one A.M.; the night was still in its infancy. That word . . . that thought . . . perhaps it was time for another discussion with Louis and Monsieur Lassone.

Safely back home, in my empty bed with its golden canopy I wept for the children I should have been kissing *bonne nuit.*

TEN

Indulgence

~ October 30, 1776 ~

My, but we all looked so beautiful bathed in candlelight; the cerise-hued drapery of the Trianon's card room made every punter appear more youthful. Even the craggy-faced baron de Besenval looked quite majestic as he surveyed his hand of cards, flexing his fingers so that his ruby signet ring would catch a shaft of light and blink at his partner, Gabrielle de Polignac. I was certain it was a signal and they were conspiring to cheat, for she was never terribly lucky at the gaming tables. How many times since the summer had I paid her debts for her? But wouldn't any friend do as much for another if they could? At her elbow sat the table's dealer, the comte de Vaudreuil, her adversary for the night, but only at lansquenet. I had not been alone in noticing the furtive glances, the subtle gestures, the barely suppressed sighs that passed between them. I was scarcely surprised to see that she had slid her foot out of her pink brocade slipper and was subtly exploring the comte's well muscled calf with her stockinged toe. Everyone at court was talking of their affair, and frankly, the gossip offered a welcome respite from the ridiculous lampoons that depicted *me,* ruffled silken petticoats raised to our derrières, as her Sapphic paramour.

The comte de Vaudreuil removed the ivory toothpick from his mouth, tugged at the spill of lace peeking out from the right cuff of his coat, then touched the large diamond pinning his frothy jabot in place before leaning carelessly over the table. I was certain at that moment he had deftly palmed the *portées*—a winning hand of cards he had already prepared by surreptitiously removing them from the deck as he dealt. He must have placed them in his sleeve. They were *all* cheating.

The air was heady with the scent of tuberose from the aromatic pastilles burning in a perforated cachepot to mask the pungent odors of perspiration. Chinese vases filled with lush arrangements of hothouse blooms—peonies, irises, and roses—were placed throughout the room. Rather than take a seat, as their hostess I continued to thread my way between the baize-covered tables, studying the painted faces of my intimates as they scrutinized their hands, feigning more, or less, than they held, their rouged mouths, shaped like cupid's bows, made more prominently carmine in the golden light. With their coiffures elaborately powdered, and suited and gowned in fabrics that shimmered and clung like a second skin, they resembled exotic beasts of prey, their maws bloody from a fresh kill.

Silent though it was, as cards were dealt, drawn, and discarded, the room was alive with a language all its own—not merely the prearranged signs between partners, but a player's "tells," those tics that indicated he was bluffing. Opened or shut, ladies' fans were drawn across the owners' fingers or lips, or along her cheek, below her eyes, perhaps even in the cleft of her bosom, every gesture a sentence pregnant with intent. *Not tonight; I have another engagement. Meet me later. Are you available? I must, regrettably, decline.*

Across the Petit Trianon's card room, the princesse de Lamballe sat amid her own coterie. To my sorrow, her rivalry with the comtesse de Polignac had only increased with time, gaining momentum as each of them won adherents. The two factions displeased me; I was ignorant of neither their existence nor their combined efforts to influence me. With a crow of triumph the comte d'Artois, seated by her elbow, startled everyone in the room. All heads swiveled to regard him as, grinning at the dejected princesse de Guéméné, he swept up a pile of louis from the center of the table.

At another table, the talk had turned to serious matters. The duc de Guines was still lamenting his removal as ambassador to the court of St. James, for during the summer England's American colonists had declared war on their fatherland in protest of King George's high taxes.

"Perhaps it is because you would not be so welcome anymore at Whitehall," opined his partner, the duc de Coigny. In the candlelight his eyes were as green as a cat's. "I understand the revolutionaries have appealed to His Majesty for aid against the British." He drew on his clay pipe, emitting a spiral of purple smoke into the thickly perfumed air.

I whirled on my heels, unwilling to believe what I'd heard. My cheeks grew warm and my breath quickened. Louder than I had intended, I demanded, "Do you mean, *messieurs,* that the king of France is entertaining the prospect of providing military aid to a discontented rabble that has overthrown their sovereign?"

The duc de Lauzun nodded. "Although it sounds like madness, there be method in't," he said, sounding as though he was quoting someone else.

"Madness indeed," I agreed. "But I see no method. His Majesty and I do not condone such a revolution, of course, and if we are seen to fund it—?"

The duc de Coigny exhaled another plume of smoke and cocked his head to regard me. "'The enemy of my enemy is my friend,' *bien sûr.*" He palmed de Guines's discarded eight of hearts from the baize and slipped it into in his hand, fanning it out for a better view of his cards. "France has much to gain if her age-old adversary is forced to spend a fortune fighting a foreign war."

"Well spoken, *mon ami*!" The murmur of voices gossiping and placing bids suddenly halted. With a scuffle of court heels, the gamesters pushed themselves back from the tables so they could rise to greet the king. He was dressed in one of his brown ratteen suits, barren of all adornment. Even his shoe buckles lacked diamanté embellishments. Monsieur Léonard, my physiognomist, looked far more glamorous when he came every morning to dress my hair, but then again, Léonard purchased the most dandified courtiers' castoffs.

"There is no need to stand on my account. *S'il vous plaît, recommencez,* my friends," Louis said jovially, although the corners of his mouth turned down when he noticed the amounts of money tossed into the centers of the gaming tables, and the perspiration on the handsome brow of his brother Artois. All of the winnings the comte had amassed that evening had been re-staked. Louis meandered between the tables and came over to kiss my hand. "At le Petit Trianon, the queen makes the rules. We are all of us here, myself included, by Her Majesty's invitation, and because she insists that her guests continue to go about their business when she enters a room, I do not expect you to stand on ceremony when I do."

My husband turned to regard me more closely. "You are looking quite charming this evening, *ma chère.* Pray, what does Mademoiselle Bertin call that ensemble?"

I giggled at the compliment. "'Indiscreet Pleasures.' And yesterday's gown—the one with the fawn-colored stripes that you said reminded you of the chase, was called 'Masked Desire.'"

Louis glanced at the dashing gentlemen seated at the table beside me—Lauzun and Coigny. "An apt description, if one were to credit the pamphlets making the rounds of all the salons in Paris."

"The pamphlets you are endeavoring to suppress and destroy," I amended lightly. "But I think 'Indiscreet Pleasures' might best suit the gaming, in my case. The hue is all your own, you know. It was you who said one day that my gown was the color of a flea—who would think of such a thing except a man who spends his days staring into microscopes?—and so we called the color 'puce.' Now puce is all the rage."

I slipped my arm through his. "But on to the affairs of men," I said gaily. "What is this I hear about your aiding the American revolutionaries?"

The ducs de Guines, de Lauzun, and de Coigny laid down their hands of cards and regarded the monarch expectantly.

"As a student of the English Civil War and its unfortunate result for the Stuarts, I am well aware of what can happen when a king's subjects become discontented." Louis took my hands in his. "I hope, *ma chère,* that you do not imagine that I, for one moment, countenance revolution, or worse, the overthrow of one's sovereign, but our friend Coigny the Field Marshal speaks astutely. It would suit France well to see the English overreach themselves militarily. They have the most superior navy in Europe; their army, too, is nearly unparalleled, and is surely better trained and equipped than a few thousand rebels, even if they know their own terrain. However, if the revolutionaries were to receive a bit of aid from those who stand to profit from King George's downfall, then France might become the greatest European power."

And perhaps the French would look upon Austria more favorably instead. Yet I still could not support the reasons for the revolt in the first place. I glumly refilled the men's brandy glasses.

The duc de Lauzun raised his goblet in a toast. "And if France becomes involved in the conflict, men like us"—he glanced at Coigny beside him—"will have the opportunity to cover ourselves in glory."

I couldn't imagine anything gloomier—for me—than my beloved coterie donning four-cornered hats and tight blue coats trimmed with silver buttons, with sabers at their hips—riding off to war with mad dreams of returning a hero. But I knew they would go if the chance arose. The life of a courtier—day after day of angling for preferment and sycophantic posing, whiling away the hours in the feminine pursuits of gossip, music, cards, and dancing, swanning about the royal châteaux in their finest garments and incurring endless debts—was not a fulfilling existence for men such as Lauzun or Coigny. The excitement they craved came at the head of a regiment amid smoke and gunpowder, not lazing in a gondola on our Grand Canal or flirting amid the candlelit, perfumed headiness of a masquerade ball. Yet while there were *bals masqués* still to be enjoyed, we would attend them!

Not tonight, however. "Have you come to join us for my birthday game, *mon cher*?" I asked my husband gaily.

He regarded me quizzically. "Are you not playing already?" he inquired.

"*Oh, non,* Louis, this is a *different* game! We have not yet started the other." I glanced at the clock. "The first bets will be placed at seven." I took his hand in mine and turned to address my guests. "*Mes amis,* I am certain you will all agree that I have the kindest, and most generous, husband in the kingdom." The king blushed. Murmurs of assent greeted the tinkle of crystal brandy snifters meeting in a toast. "And when he asked what I desired for my twenty-first birthday, 'just a game of pharaon,' I replied."

Gabrielle de Polignac gasped. Louis's antipathy for high-stakes wagering was well known. He enjoyed a good game of cards as much as the next man, but had a horror of high play, having once hazarded everything he had on a single hand, only to lose it all.

"Will you send me a message when you have finished?" Louis asked.

Ah. "Gladly; but I would retire at the usual hour, if I were you, Sire. Don't wait for me," I added, with a whisper in his ear. I grabbed the red velvet purse with my cipher worked in silver bullion from my place at the gaming table. It was empty. With a wink, I showed it to my husband, asking sweetly, "Will you stake me then, as part of my gift? I think 15,000 livres should be sufficient."

He paled momentarily, then reached into his pocket for his own purse. It was heavy with coins. He placed it in my hands. "There are thirty thousand in here. I counted them this morning. I would appreciate it if you would endeavor to do me the honor of returning as many of them as possible." He lowered his head to kiss my brow.

I dropped into a curtsy. "And I shall endeavor to do my best! Are you absolutely certain that you don't wish to remain?"

Louis chuckled, then shook his head. "Absolutely. *Mais, bon anniversaire, ma belle femme—et bonne chance!*"

He turned on his heels just as the clock struck the seventh hour. The tables were moved to form one oblong, and the players took their places as the suit of spades was laid out for pharaon. Louis had prohibited the courtiers of Versailles to act as the banker, for that player invariably came away vastly enriched at the expense of the others at the table. I rang the silver bell on the table beside me and one of my red-and-silver-liveried servants entered the room. A word in his ear and he returned a few moments later with Monsieur de Chalabre, a Parisian well known at the tables in the Marais. Our banker was introduced, the punters purchased their checks, and the first round of cards was dealt.

By midnight I had lost every sou from Louis's purse.

By noon the following day, I had hazarded the diamonds about my neck. At five in the evening, the dear baron de Besenval loaned me ten thousand louis. An hour later I was wearing my diamonds again and I had been able to repay him a quarter of what I had borrowed.

All Hallows' Eve at the stroke of nine. We had been playing for twenty-six hours. I rang for more coffee, lemonade, brandy, and Ville d'Avray water. The table was littered with checks as bets could be placed directly on a single card, on multiple cards, on the high-card bar at the top of the layout, or hedged—on the edges of cards or between more than one of them. The baron de Besenval's own snoring had awakened him, much to the mirth of the rest of the table. The servants brought another tray of cold meats, bread, and cheese.

My purse was empty again. "What will you wager, *Majesté*?" asked the princesse de Lamballe. "Does this mean the game is over?"

"Absolutely not!" My hands flew to my ears. I paused. All eyes were on me. The emeralds had been a gift from Louis. But I could win them back; I was certain of it. I removed the ear bobs, letting their weight rest in my palms. "These cost the king fifty thousand livres," I told the banker, reluctantly forfeiting my jewels in exchange for the commensurate amount of checks.

"And I think I shall cash in some of my winnings. Perhaps . . . fifty thousand," the comte d'Artois drawled lazily. He counted the coins and handed them to Monsieur de Chalabre. "Enough to purchase a pair of emeralds—which would adorn the charming ears of the comtesse d'Artois."

I felt my blood rise and glowered at my brother-in-law. I

had always accounted him a friend. "You daren't!" I cried. More likely he would give them to his mistress! Caught up in the uncontrollable fervor that took possession of his spirit whenever he was winning, Artois laughed uproariously at my distress, which infuriated me all the more. No matter how long it took, I would regain my jewels. "*Ma chère* Marie Thérèse, how much money have you?" I asked the princesse de Lamballe.

All Saint's Day. Two P.M. A single emerald adorned my ear. "Do you have fifteen thousand livres I can borrow, Your Majesty?" The comtesse de Polignac glanced up at me, as she rested her head on the shoulder of her lover, the comte de Vaudreuil. I counted out the checks and slid them across the table to her. The duc de Guines had gone to sleep beneath it. We decided that as long as half the number of punters at the table remained awake, the game was officially still in play; however, no one was permitted to doze for longer than two hours at a time. I drained the last of my coffee and rang for more.

All Souls Day. One A.M. "*Majesté,* perhaps we should end the game soon. It has been three nights. Everyone will want to rest and they will require time to make their toilettes before Mass." Dear Lamballe was always so concerned. But I had not yet won back my other ear bob. And the morning of my twenty-first birthday was dawning. My eyelids were heavy with sleep and my body limp with fatigue, but all the chocolate and coffee I had imbibed kept my heart awake and aflutter. I staked everything I had on my card over the banker's—and won! "Aha! *Un parolet-double!*" I cried, folding back one edge of my card. The thrill of winning a trick after such a dry spell had awakened me like a dousing of icy water. I restaked the lot, hoping to win sevenfold. *"Sept et le va!"*

Monsieur de Chalabre turned a card. "Her Majesty wins again."

I clapped my hands gleefully. The insipid little comtesse

d'Artois would never wear my emeralds! I bent back another corner of my card and bet the entirety of my winnings for a third time. *"Quinze et le va!"* I shouted. This time if I beat the banker I would win fifteen times the amount of my *couche.* My blood was pulsing. My heart thundered.

"It is indeed Her Majesty's lucky day," said the banker, as he turned the next card.

I left the checks where they lay and rose from my chair, too excited to remain seated. *"Trente et le va!"* I cried, vibrating with excitement over the possibility of winning thirty times my stake. My breath was ragged; I clasped the back of the chair for support.

"Her Majesty wins," said Monsieur de Chalabre. I was shaking, near to delirium. I now had 75,000 livres to buy back my other ear bob, and more besides. I triumphantly cashed in the requisite checks and relieved my *beau-frère* of my emerald.

"It was good sport, wasn't it?" Artois said, without a hint of malice.

"Who would you really have given them to?" I challenged.

"Ah—you would have had to wait and see. And so would Louis."

The game continued for two more hours. I did not see the king until we met in the Galerie des Glaces later that morning on the way to Mass. He noticed with a frown my efforts to disguise the ravages wrought by three sleepless nights with the artful application of cosmetics. However, little could be done to mask the violet demilunes of shadow beneath my eyes and the swollen, red-rimmed lids. My hair, too, had not been dressed with its customary creativity and precision. Léonard had scolded me, for he'd not the time to complete my coiffure to our exacting standards. As I fell into step with my husband, I unfurled the tines of my silk fan, stifling a yawn behind them.

"And how did you spend the last two days?" I inquired politely.

"The usual," Louis murmured. "Gamain is teaching me how to construct a lock that cannot be picked. I drew up the plans for a mechanical table I think you might appreciate—it doubles as a work box for your sewing and a breakfast table—and I hunted every day. It was all most enjoyable. You missed an excellent *coquilles à la vielle Russie* last evening at supper. And a very good capon with a *sauce marron.* Did you eat well?"

"I'm rarely hungry when I play pharaon. It's too exciting to think about food. This is yours, I believe," I said, handing Louis his empty purse. "I'm so sorry." He shook his head in disbelief. But I gave myself a secret smile as I touched a gloved hand to my ear. My other secret was that I sent the fifty thousand livres that remained after I bought back my emerald ear bob to the Hôtel-Dieu as an anonymous bequest for the care of the hospital's impoverished patients.

"Pray, what time did the game cease?" he inquired, as our shoulders brushed.

We were walking briskly toward the chapel, nodding to the men and women thronging the halls on either side of us as we conversed. "The punters placed their final *couches* at three this morning." I lowered my fan and winked at him. "You said we could play one game, Sire," I added merrily, "but you never specified for how long!"

I could see that he wished to summon his anger, but all that bubbled up was fond amusement. Louis clasped my hand and briefly brought it to his lips as we made our way along the Hall of Mirrors. Regarding me indulgently, he muttered, "You're all worthless, the lot of you."

January 17, 1777

Your Imperial Highness:

I found the queen worried and embarrassed by the state of her debts, the total amount of which she does not even know. She thrust the sheaf of notes into my hand and I added them up; the total came to 487,272 livres—more than two years' income. Her Majesty, who was somewhat surprised to see her finances in such a woeful state, with great reluctance decided to approach the king to ask him whether he might assume some of her encumbrances. The moment the queen broached the subject, without hesitation His Majesty agreed to pay the full amount. All he asked was a few months' grace, as he wished to pay the sum from his privy purse rather than go through his ministers. He fully comprehends the detrimental effect on the queen as well as the Crown, but he seems powerless to curb her passions.

Nonetheless, despite the rumors that have reached you from Saxony and Poland, Antoinette indeed looks forward to the Emperor's visit to France this spring; naturally she will set aside her usual round of amusements to entertain her brother. She has even indicated that she would prefer to lodge him at the palace so they can spend more time together.

Your humble servant,

Mercy

• • •

February 3, 1777

Madame, my dear daughter:

It delights me that you await your brother's arrival with such anticipation. He and the king are both young and I believe they will have much in common when they meet. A good deal should be discussed; to wit: You will speak to Joseph about your marriage with complete sincerity. We now come to other matters wherein mutual trust is equally essential. I have ordered Mercy to inform you of our Austrian foreign policies and decide with you how your ministers should be handled. There are dissensions between the Turks and Russians and between Spain and Portugal, as well as the war in America, and I fear that Austria may be dragged into one or more of these conflicts in spite of my better judgment.

• • •

February 17, 1777

Madame my esteemed mother:

Although I have little experience of politics, I understand that it would indeed be terrible if the Turks and the Russians went back to war. The French point of view, I believe, is that they want to keep the peace. As for the Americans, in December, they sent over one of their ambassadors, Monsieur Franklin, an odd gentleman who wore no wig, but left his balding pate and shaggy gray hair as nature intended. Nor (as I heard from the fashionable Parisiennes who entertained him in their salons) did he make any effort to improve his tailoring for the French taste, eschewing satins and brocades for simple American garments in somber shades—how close to the king's ratteen suits I imagined they must have been!

But I digress. I have interesting news for you, as they say. The Grand Almoner, Cardinal de la Roche Aymon, is now at death's door. He is to be replaced by Prince Louis de Rohan. I well remember your disgust with him when he was ambassador to Austria, and it pleased me greatly to insist that my husband recall him upon his accession. Yet Louis XV had evidently made some vague promise to Madame de Marsan, the prince's cousin and former governess to the princesses Clothilde and Élisabeth, assuring her that if the post of Grand Almoner should ever become vacant, he would fill it with the prince de Rohan. This, Maman, is the highest ecclesiastical office in France, disburser of the king's alms, making whoever holds it exceedingly powerful, as the Grand Almoner also functions independently of the cabinet ministers. He is also charged with celebrating Mass in the royal chapels on all holy days.

Louis offered to make him a cardinal instead, but this was unacceptable to his illustrious family. "It is the only reward I will ask or accept in return for the services and care I lavished upon you and your siblings when you were children," insisted the comtesse de Marsan.

"But I have given my word to the queen that the prince de Rohan shall not be advanced at court," said *mon mari.*

"*Votre Majesté* cannot have two words of honor," retorted Madame de Marsan. "If the word of a gentleman is sacred, then what is the word of a *king*? Should you fail to honor the pledge of your grandfather, I will of necessity make public the fact that the king has failed in his word of honor—merely to please the queen."

You must know, Maman, that even after the conniving Madame de Marsan threatened him, Louis continued to uphold our wishes. But then his former *gouvernante* made him a promise, on behalf of all the Rohans, "that if in two years my cousin has not had the good fortune to redeem himself in your eyes and restore himself in your favor, he will resign the post of Grand Almoner." My husband took her at her word and capitulated. I suppose Louis was hoping to appease a prominent former Barryiste at a time when it would do well to subdue the voices of my detractors. Now, the king deserves their thanks. But he does not have mine.

My opinion of Prince Louis coincides with that of my

dear mother. I consider him not only an unprincipled man, but a dangerous one, with his grand ambitions and his *petits scandales.* Had the decision been left to me, he would never have had a place at court. Fortunately, as Grand Almoner he will have no contact with me; and he will see the king only rarely, at His Majesty's *levers* and at Mass.

If the prince behaves as he always did, we will have many intrigues. I can only hope he does not drag the king into the mire with him.

ELEVEN

A Visit from Abroad

APRIL 1777

It was really too chilly for a light repast in the Belvedère, but the sunny neoclassical pavilion on the grounds behind le Petit Trianon had just been completed and I was anxious to enjoy both the solitude and the vistas. Each of the eight tall windows looked out onto a slightly different view. The swans glided in the pond below us and the trees were still straining to bud. Beyond, depending on the vantage, lay a grove of trees, rolling meadows, and a charming outcropping. I had asked for my harp to be brought to me so that I might practice my music while the comtesse de Polignac and the princesse de Lamballe joined me for orangeade, strawberries, and confections. At our feet, Jacques and Julie, whom I had met two months earlier during a sleigh ride in the Bois de Boulogne, played with a wooden cup and ball on a string,

"Look!" Gabrielle exclaimed, swiveling in her chair with a rustle of lilac taffeta. "We have a visitor!"

A solitary man, tall, wearing a gray felt tricorn that shaded his brow and a simple, tobacco-colored cloak, trudged up the rocky path with the aid of a gilt-topped ebony walking stick. My liveried footman went out to meet him. The men exchanged a few words. My footman looked sour and shook his head. The stranger became insistent and grew impatient. Moments later, my footman approached. "A Count Falkenstein insists upon having a word with you, *Votre Majesté*. He says you have been expecting him."

I rose and walked to the glass doors, opening them myself. My heart began to tremble, for despite the warning signs posted on the grounds, anyone might talk his way into the presence of the sovereign and I had not been terribly popular of late. Perhaps this stranger meant me some harm. "Count Falkenstein?" I echoed doubtfully.

The gentleman stepped forward and doffed his hat, revealing a head of thinning blond hair, unpowdered, a pale face with light blue eyes, and a jovial smile with a fine set of teeth.

"Joseph!" I flung my arms about his neck and kissed him on both cheeks. When he drew away, he touched himself where I kissed him, and worried with an amused chuckle that he was now splotched with rouge. "What is this 'Count Falkenstein' business? I nearly had you removed from the property as a trespasser!"

"Have you already forgotten that I prefer to travel incognito? As soon as people know they are speaking to the Holy Roman Emperor I am given quite a different welcome and then I have an altogether distorted experience. No, I wish to see the world as any other man of good stature would, and so I kept my *nom de voyage* a secret even from my favorite sister."

I stepped back to regard him more fully. "*Mon Dieu!* Look at you, *mon frère*! So—so—" I had not seen him since I was fourteen years old, on the day I left my homeland for France. In truth Joseph seemed a bit aged for his thirty-six years; perhaps because he was losing his hair and had not the vanity to wear a wig, at least in his disguise. "Come, you must meet my two dearest friends!" I clasped his hand and, suddenly a little girl again with her beloved oldest brother, tugged him up the three stone steps into the intimate Belvedère. On this afternoon in early spring, it was the loveliest spot in France, with its cream-colored walls frescoed with floral motifs in shades of gray and gold. I slipped my arm through Joseph's.

He paused when he saw the two children playing on the floor, surrounded by a half-dozen toys and dolls. "Obviously not yours."

"*Hélas, non,* but loveable all the same." I knelt beside Julie and stroked her dark curls. "They belong to a miller and his wife. The roof of their cottage was in dreadful need of repair—and I offered to ameliorate their lot by adopting Jacques and Julie while the work was being done. Now that the spring has come and the roof has been rebuilt, I must regrettably return them to their parents soon." I cast a mournful glance at the six-year-old boy and his sister. "But I hate to part with them."

"Is Her Majesty kind to you?" my brother asked Jacques.

"Tell *Count Falkenstein* the truth, *mon petit.*"

"Oh, yes. But she doesn't let us eat too many sweets," the boy replied.

"She gave us two pairs of new shoes," eight-year-old Julie volunteered, displaying her ankles. "With diamond buckles."

"Do they play in the palace?" Joseph inquired, uttering the words between his teeth.

"Of course they do; they live there!" He blanched, clearly imagining the pair of them rolling hoops through the Galerie des Glaces. "Where else should they play? In my rooms there are dogs aplenty for them to romp with, and I have seen to it that they shall have no end of other amusements. I wish I could keep them forever." I sighed. "There are so many advantages I could bestow that their parents could not." I drew the children into my arms. "They could neither read nor write when I met them, and already they are becoming proficient." The rush of crimson to my cheeks informed Joseph that Julie and Jacques were not the first children I had adopted and would doubtless not be the last.

"You do have to bring them home soon," Joseph murmured. "Your duty is to bear children, not to borrow them."

I kissed their sweet brows and rose to my feet. Best to change the subject. "Allow me to introduce you, brother, to my two dearest friends. The beautiful lady in lilac with the cloud of dark hair and the indigo eyes is the comtesse de Polignac. Her family is terribly poor," I whispered. "Desperate straits, all of them, so I have found places for several of her relations at court. I have helped those who remain in the countryside with gifts of food and contributions from my privy purse. It's the least I can do to help a friend. Louis, too, has been quite magnanimous, for he sees how greatly Gabrielle's companionship pleases me."

"Ah" was all Joseph said. "And the blond woman in the striped blue dress with the sad eyes. Does she never smile?"

"Rarely," I replied. "Yet that does not mean she is always unhappy. What a tease you are. Such a big brother to say cruel things about *mes jolies amies*—and I have not even introduced them to you! But aren't they the most beautiful creatures in the world?"

Joseph released a little sniff. I'd almost forgotten his annoying way of laughing through his nose. "I couldn't tell," he said wryly. "The three of you look like a trio of painted dolls."

"Now I think you have only come to France to vex me! I know we didn't wear cheek and lip rouge in Austria, but here it is a mark of distinction, rank, and wealth. As silly as they look to you, these big red circles are emblematic of our stature at court and our ability to afford the most costly cosmetic in the kingdom. Now, before you insult me any further, where have you taken lodgings and will you not change your mind and allow me to furnish a grand suite for you at the château?"

When I discovered he had rented a modest hotel room near the Palais Royal for the next two months I warned him not to grow too close to the duc d'Orléans. "For he is ambitious and wishes he were king instead. I am certain he is behind the printing of some of the dreadful pamphlets about me, though we cannot prove it. I suspect that Monsieur has a hand in the *libelles* as well. He is just as cunning and conniving as Orléans." I frowned and turned my attention to the swans, so perfectly paired, as they glided on the pond. Someone once told me they mate for life and are never unfaithful. How unlike the courtiers of Versailles! "To think that my brother-in-law once maintained the pretense of being our friend."

Joseph chucked me on the chin. "I thank you for your counsel, little queen, but I hope you can trust me to form my own judgments."

In his guise as Count Falkenstein Joseph was determined to play the vulgar German in the presence of the French aristocracy, perversely encouraging their negative impressions of our countrymen. At his first royal dinner, having insisted that he not be treated with the deference due to his rank and title, Joseph dined with Louis and me in my bedchamber, the lavishly laid table shoved up against the bed while the three of us perched upon identical folding stools. My husband was indifferent as always when he had food in front of him, and Joseph was amused by the entire charade. I could not stomach any more than a serving of chicken breast, mortified at such a humble reception when my brother was the first emperor to visit a French king in his own palace in nine hundred years. I departed anxiously after the meal to have my hair dressed for the evening, dreading the thought of leaving my brother and husband alone together.

Joseph attended my *lever* the following morning, quipping like a court jester at every turn. I found myself biting my lip at our secret, for no one was the wiser that my uncouth guest with his unpowdered hair and simple shoe buckles was none other than the Holy Roman Emperor. On the subject of the court-mandated rouge, he was relentless. As I carefully applied the two-inch-wide circles with my boar-bristle brush, my brother shocked the distinguished assemblage by declaring, "Lay it on, ma'am. Are you certain your rouge pot contains enough pigment? Perhaps a trowel might be a more useful implement than a brush. Surely the court stonemasons have one they can lend you. Slap some more of your cochineal under the eyes like that woman over there." He rudely pointed to the marquise de Lorillard, legendary at court for the artificial appearance of her visage.

And he took an immediate dislike to Monsieur Léonard, who dressed my hair that morning with a quintet of lemon-yellow ostrich plumes and a topaz and sapphire aigrette. Expecting a compliment when I asked the soi-disant Count Falkenstein what he thought of my feathers, he quipped insultingly, "Too light to support a crown."

But once the sycophants had departed, we slipped through the secret door that led to my private apartments, and there, in the solitude of la Méridienne, we could finally converse as beloved siblings, without pretense, our public masks removed. "Would you like some refreshment?" I began. "Apart from chocolate and coffee, I drink mostly orange water and lemonade. The water from Versailles gives me indigestion, so I import bottles from Ville d'Avray; but I can ring for something stronger if you prefer. *Eau de vie,* perhaps?" I paced excitedly and was about to perch on the edge of my daybed when Joseph spoke.

"Don't sit yet. Let me truly look at you. The Emperor of Austria wishes to admire the Queen of France."

"So *that's* it," I teased, playfully striking a pose at the center of the octagonal salon. "People think my life is effortless because everything is done for me—but they are wrong. Playing the queen takes a good deal of exertion. The constraints are endless; it seems that to be natural is a crime. Now, if I believed that my favorite *brother* wished to appraise *his youngest sister's* appearance after seven springs, an eternity since he last saw her as an awkward, coltish girl, then I might deliver an inventory of her improvements. To begin, you might remind Maman that the bosom which was the subject of so much international agonizing all those years ago, finally developed, arriving without fanfare in 1773."

The passages inside my nose began to sting, a harbinger of tears. I squeezed my eyes shut in an effort to stave them off. "Yet what a cruel joke that was. The Savoyard sisters who married Louis's brothers are dark, squat, hairy little gnomes, but they were wed all the same. It mattered to Papa Roi whether I 'had good breasts.' But Louis is not like other men. He couldn't even glance at me then without wincing. And even after I discovered the reason, it didn't matter, for nothing changed between us, despite his avowals of esteem and affection." My chest rose and fell as I wept, releasing the tears that had been corked up for so long. "Try as we both have, we are ill suited. My tastes do not accord with the king's. He is only interested in hunting and mechanical work." My words came in wet gulps as I sought to explain my marriage to Joseph, for I knew he had heard much, but most of it was fanciful, or at the very least, exaggeration, designed to discredit me. "I know you will agree that I should not look particularly well standing beside a forge, that the part of Vulcan would not suit me; and I fancy the role of Venus would be more uncongenial to *him* than my tastes." I told my brother that earlier in the year, despite his plans to economize, Louis had doubled the number of spectacles at court. Placing my hands over my flat belly, I said, "He feels he must indulge me in other ways, you see."

Joseph remained silent, his arms resting on the padded chair, his light eyes full of concern. He seemed to be studying me as if I were some exotic specimen. "It has not always been easy to be me," I said, with a note of self-mocking.

Reaching into my pocket for a ring of skeleton keys, I unlocked a cabinet inlaid with mother-of-pearl. I withdrew a red leather box containing a sheaf of pamphlets and a number of loose sheets of paper. Some were clearly published professionally; others bore the hallmarks of an amateur press. "Did you know there were printing presses right here at Versailles?" I said rhetorically. "Oh yes, they belong to some of the noblemen who reside here. Louis and I house them, feed them, grant them perquisites, honors, and largesse, and they repay us by printing screeds such as these." I thrust the papers into his hands. "Most of the others are made on foreign presses—in England and Holland primarily. But they are secretly financed by powerful men right here in France." I chuckled bitterly. "Well, I suppose it is only half a secret, for we know about the printings. We just don't know the identities of the instigators."

Joseph was leafing through the pamphlets. "Go ahead; read them," I urged him. "Read them aloud so you can taste the words in your mouth. For only then will you know what it feels like to be on the receiving end of such filth."

"'It is not there that the trouble lies/Says the Royal Clitoris/ But nothing comes out but Water,'" Joseph read, his voice devoid of expression. He thumbed through the loose pages and found another diatribe. "'One says he can't get it up, Another—he can't get it in.'" Muttering with disgust, he picked one of the bound pamphlets at random and read, "'Everyone asks in a whisper/ The King—can he or can't he?/The sad queen is in despair.'"

"She is indeed." I sighed heavily. "One might almost think that last one was published by someone who was *sympathique*—at least to me." I felt the tears well up again. Perhaps it was the comfort of a family member and the privacy of our reunion that gave me the freedom to cry, for I had not wept so copiously in recent memory. "I hope you plan to stay in France at least past the sixteenth of May, for it would be a great honor to her king and queen to join these virgin monarchs for the celebration of their seventh wedding anniversary!" I blotted my tears with a lace-edged handkerchief whiteworked with my cipher.

My brother continued to study me. At length, stating the obvious, he reminded me, "The Austrian alliance depends upon your bearing a son. Tell me," he said, his manner almost clinical, "do you ever make any efforts to seduce your husband?"

Beneath my circles of rouge, I blushed profusely. "For my perceived excesses and an influence upon the king that I do not in truth possess, I have been compared to Pompadour and du Barry by many people—but to have my own brother suggest that I behave like a concubine, I—I am at a loss for words!" I recalled the humiliation I'd felt after suggesting to Louis that we make love *à levrette*. Never again could I abase myself in such a manner or risk another embarrassing rejection of my efforts to excite my husband.

"*Listen* before you dismiss it out of hand," he scolded. "I merely propose that you entice the king to your bed in the afternoon when he still has energy from the hunt or his smithing. After a day of strenuous exercise, how can he be expected to rouse himself in the middle of the night, when you have finally exhausted your round of amusements? And he will be equally useless in the bedchamber right after a large meal, if yesterday was an indication of his daily consumption."

Joseph did not mince words, nor did he spare my feelings. I

nodded obediently. "You have become a beautiful and desirable woman," he added, "with a charm and vivacity that are undeniable. Were you not my sister, and were I considering exchanging my widowed state, I would be delighted to find a bride such as you." He studied me with a long, appraising look. I felt uncomfortable being so scrutinized and glanced away. "You are coloring all the way to your hairline," he observed. "Mercy reports that you have been experiencing sudden attacks of *affectations nerveuses,* and it would appear to me as though you might be about to have one now. He believes that compliments on your beauty from virile gentlemen are the cause. And you have quite a number of handsome admirers."

My breath was catching in my throat. Joseph was right. Feeling light-headed, I sank onto my daybed; la Méridienne became a blur of aqua, celadon, cream, and gold. "What are you saying?"

The emperor was about to rise from his chair, when a familiar face appeared from behind a table and began to nuzzle his leg. "*Mein Gott,* is this Mops?" I nodded and he lifted my pug into the air and gave him a cuddle. After so many years the dog must have remembered my brother's scent, for he eagerly licked his hands and face. "Maman is right," Joseph laughed. "You are unparalleled at deflecting someone's attention from anything you find unpleasant." He allowed Mops to slip from his arms and took a stroll about the room to stretch his legs.

"My point, dear sister, is that you are surrounded by temptation. I expect that you comprehend the dangers of giving yourself to a lover before you have given France a lawful heir. You could be sent back to Vienna, Toinette."

I lowered my head and shut my eyes tightly. "You need not fear my sense of duty. And my faith is just as strong." I sat up straighter. "I am Maman's daughter, not Papa's." Reaching for Mops, I stroked his thick, tawny coat. He was an old boy, now.

Would he live long enough to play with my children? "Besides, there is no one at court who sets my heart aflutter; my *friseur* has more substance. And I do think about how Louis would feel."

Joseph produced a snuffbox from the pocket of his puce-colored coat. The ladies of Paris found him so amusing for he thought he sported the height of fashion, but "flea's thigh," "young flea," and "flea's belly" were hues that were already seasons out of date. Now, "dandies' guts" and *"boue de Paris"*—Paris mud—were all the rage. "In that case, do you ever suppress any of your own wishes for the king's sake? Do you occupy yourself with matters which he has neglected, in order to assist when he has stumbled? Do you ever sacrifice yourself to him in any way, or are all your concerns for yourself? Do you silence those who dare to allude to his errors or infirmities, or do *you* mock them as well?"

His sudden barrage of questions stunned me. "For this is what a good wife does, Toinette. Listen to a brother who loves you, a twice-widowed man of the world who was fortunate enough to once know love. But love is not the principal ingredient of a marriage. Esteem and obligation, as well as trust, are essential."

I wished to remind Joseph that he'd had so little esteem for his second wife, Maria Josepha of Bavaria, that he had a wall constructed on their balcony so that he would not even have to look at her, but he was so intent on reprimanding me that I could not insert a word edgewise.

"Have you ever taken the trouble to consider the effect that your friendships and intimacies may have upon the public when you fail—as you do—to give your high regard to your husband and instead squander your good opinion upon those who are untrustworthy and who encourage you in acts of vice rather than those of virtue? When was the last time you visited a convent as you used to do with Maman? Do you ever reflect upon the disastrous consequences of playing hazard and pharaon, on the bad company that assembles on these occasions, and then bear in mind that the king never plays games of chance?"

Sick of being scolded like a child, I rose from the daybed and began to rearrange the flowers in my vases, glumly plucking the brownish blooms with dolefully drooping heads. "What an old hen you are! You sound like Maman! Do you never dance? Do you never gamble? Or have you forgotten what it is like to be twenty-one years old?"

"It is different for women," Joseph insisted calmly. "You are too old for such unseemly escapades. Why must you feel the need to rub shoulders with a crowd of libertines and loose women when you know it is irreparably harming your reputation, and, by extension, the king's?"

I raised my hand to make him stop, but my brother, still deprived by Maman of the ability to rule the Austrian empire, sought at the very least to govern me. "None of this behavior becomes you. It is the chief cause of offense to those who are sincerely attached to you and whose thoughts run in respectable channels."

I snapped the head off a peach-hued rose and inserted the short stem in my bosom, admiring the way the blossom complemented the cream and salmon satin bodice. "And who might you mean by that? You? Maman? Mercy?"

My brother nodded. "And someone who dares not challenge you because of his own shortcomings." Tossing me a glance, he added, "Look at you, adorning yourself like a cocotte. Have you heard a word I've said? The *king* is left alone all night at Versailles while you defile yourself by mixing with the canaille of Paris!"

He made a shallow bow. "And now, madame, with your kind permission, I will withdraw. I find myself exhausted from my efforts to usher you from darkness to light." He drew a deep breath. "The air in here is stifling; don't you ever feel suffocated?"

I laughed. "You are too used to Maman and her open windows, even in the dead of winter. But if I didn't burn perfumed pastilles and fill my rooms with flowers you would truly find yourself gagging, for Versailles must be the most odiferous place on God's earth." Joseph donned his gray tricorn. "Where are you off to, then, in your quest for fresh air? I can show you the improvements I am making to the grounds of le Petit Trianon. We can have another picnic!"

My brother shook his head. "*Merci, ma soeur.* But I have more mundane pursuits in mind: the waterworks at Marly. Perhaps I can glean something from your civil engineering that I can take home to our backwater empire," he added wryly. "You are welcome to accompany me."

I wrinkled my nose. "Weirs and dams and reservoirs and such? *Pas pour moi.* I'll take strawberries and champagne instead by the Belvedère or beneath the trees in the Bois de Boulogne."

Joseph shrugged. "*Tant pis.* Perhaps, then, I should invite your husband."

Stung, I replied, "Not if you expect clever conversation, for if you find mine frivolous, I can assure you, his is mostly nonexistent. If you wish to enjoy Marly in solitude, by all means, ask the king to join you."

Having reached the door Joseph stopped and turned. "Why did I waste my breath this morning? Your ears are fully open to the barbs of those who wish you ill, but your mind is utterly closed to one who has nothing but your welfare at heart." With an audible click of the latch, he was gone.

TWELVE

Beauty Is Always Queen

The Emperor of Austria stood on a hilltop above the banks of the Seine watching the fourteen whirring paddle wheels of la Machine de Marly and wishing he'd thought to bring some cotton swabbing to stuff inside his ears. A foreman whose accent was so thick the emperor could scarcely understand him had provided him with a comprehensive tour of the complex, explaining that it could add over a million gallons a day to the reservoirs when it was pumping at full capacity, supplying the water not only to Marly, but to the châteaux and grounds of Versailles. *Could Austria do as well?* Joseph wondered. After all, la Machine de Marly was the invention of the Sun King's engineers nearly a century ago. He doffed his hat to blot the perspiration from his forehead, daubing away the sheen with a monogrammed square of Belgian linen—once known as the Spanish Netherlands, those low countries were now Hapsburg territories as well—and cupped his hand to shade his brow. He imagined a painter setting up his easel here; what light he would have, and what a prospect, gazing down over the waterworks and that gleaming white villa that resembled a large mausoleum, so incongruously close to the machinery. How did its residents sleep at night with the perpetual din? On second thought, with the little château looking as it did, perhaps they were dead, consigned to perpetual sleep.

Joseph's painterly eye strayed to an interruption on the horizon; another incongruity. Two figures: a woman, on the tall side, in a billowing white gown with a corona of lemon-blond curls that cascaded nearly to her waist, shadowed by a turbaned youth dressed in the Oriental style with a pair of blousy white pantaloons and a pink vest. Mincing a step behind his mistress, he wielded a parasol to shield her delicate skin. The emperor, an adventurous man who would never tell his little sister that one of the reasons he had selected an unprepossessing hotel and traveled incognito was because he had heard much about the celebrated brothels of Paris, stepped onto the winding path that led down the hill toward the grounds of the "mausoleum." This duo was too intriguing for him to ignore.

Minutes later, he was bowing to the strangers. "If a foreign visitor might introduce himself, Count Falkenstein at your service, madame," he said, removing his hat.

The woman turned her large blue eyes on him. "Your accent is Austrian," she remarked. "I have heard its like before." There was an effortless charm about her, a ripeness, a worldliness, and although she looked as though she might be only a few years his junior, she bore all the hallmarks of having once been an exceptional beauty. Joseph found himself instantly mesmerized. "It has grown warm early today," she remarked. "I am sure you must be thirsty. May I offer you some refreshment?" Her voice was sweet and musical with a hint of a lisp. Gesturing to the neoclassical villa, she added, with a dazzling smile that must have brought countless men to their knees, "My home, Louveciennes, is close at hand, so don't bother to make small talk and protest that it will be too much trouble."

She began to lead the way along the path, but stopped after a few steps. "If I may confess something to a complete stranger, monsieur le comte, the cobbler made these new shoes a bit too large and I am afraid I will slip out of them. Would you mind if I took your arm so that I do not take a tumble down the hill?"

The emperor recognized flirtation when he saw it, not merely in the woman's shining cobalt eyes, but in her faintly suggestive language—"take a tumble"?—yet he would play the gallant for her. "I should be loath to see you thus compromised, madame," he said, as he offered her the crook of his elbow.

Upon entering the little château, he immediately noticed that it was no mere country villa, but a palace in miniature, teeming with servants wearing liveries of crimson and pale yellow. A nude statue of Diana presided over the entrance hall. The boiseries accenting the walls were gilded with pure gold leaf. Enormous crystal chandeliers illuminated every room.

"Zamor, will you order some lemonade for our guest?" said the woman to her nut-brown page. The turbaned stripling bowed and disappeared, his footsteps noiseless on the thick carpets.

Motioning for her visitor to seat himself on a carved divan upholstered in turquoise striped satin, the châtelaine sank luxuriantly onto a low stool beside him, affording Joseph as fine a view of her décolleté as of her opulent collection of bronzes and porcelain objéts d'art. "It's all very beautiful, *n'est-ce pas*?" she said. Her extravagant gesture encompassed the surrounding wealth. "Everything you see here I owe to the generosity and benevolence of the late king, Louis Quinze—to *me* he was *truly 'le Bien-Aimé.'*" When Joseph arched a quizzical eyebrow, the hostess smiled warmly, slyly murmuring, "*Pardon, monsieur;* I thought you recognized me. I should not have been so bold to imagine that my fame had reached the lesser nobility of Austria. *In*famy, some would say, depending on whom you asked. I am Jeanne du Barry."

Joseph was sure his eyes reflected a half-dozen consecutive thoughts, but he merely said, "Then I imagine you are no great friend of the current king and queen."

The comtesse's melodic voice was bitter at first, becoming melancholy as her narrative continued.

"When *le Bien-Aimé* realized he was dying and knew that his soul must be shriven, he could not make his final confession until he banished me from court for the harlot I was. He had raised me to the nobility; made me a comtesse, invented a coat of arms for me—even changed the date of my birth so that everyone believed I was a few years younger. But *au fond,* I was no better than Jeanne Bécu of the rue de la Jussienne, natural daughter of a provincial friar and a seamstress. I had known many men before *Son Majesté,* yet he was always gracious enough never to mention my past—although Mesdames, his daughters, and la dauphine, Antoinette, made sure that no one forgot it."

Joseph eyed the comtesse sympathetically. "Then do I take it that you and the dauphine never—"

"I wished to become her friend," his hostess said tersely. "At least in the beginning; when she first came to Versailles, and knew no one. I would have been glad to take her under my wing. But, *hélas,* she turned out to be a condescending little prig, with her haughty German morals—no doubt learned at her mother's inky skirts—and refused to have anything to do with me after my initial overture of amity."

Joseph chuckled at her rather accurate reference, both to his little sister and to the empress. "We have a word for that back home—*hochnäsig*. It means 'high nosed.'"

"Whatever you call it, *I* suffered grievously, I assure you."

Madame du Barry pursed her full, sensuous lips into a petulant, rather kissable, moue. Joseph felt his thigh begin to twitch. "When the time came for me to leave court forever, I learned that the carriage was not to transport me here to Louveciennes but to a convent. I was certain that it was the new queen who forced her husband into signing the *lettre de cachet* consigning me to that bleak fate." The comtesse's eyes grew moist. "Because I had been privy to state secrets, I was dispatched to a place where I could not make trouble for the Crown."

Madame du Barry gazed down at her white skirts, smoothing her palms along the fabric. "I remained in the convent at Pont-aux-Dames for an entire year," she said, her tone embittered once again. "But even after my release I was ordered to keep at least ten leagues' distance not only from Paris, but from Versailles; as Louveciennes is clearly within the environs of the palace, I was unable to return to my beloved villa until last October." She forced a laugh. "Quite a lot of dust had settled in the chandeliers."

Joseph continued to regard the former favorite, wondering if she had always been so unguarded, especially at the vipers' nest of Versailles. The woman who sat beside him clearly retained a good deal of anger toward the royal family; but she hardly seemed the manipulative Jezebel of his sister's correspondence. Now, at any rate, she was a creature who dwelled in the past, surrounded by relics of her former triumphs. His first impression of Louveciennes had been correct after all: it *was* a mausoleum. Parched from having spent the better part of the afternoon strolling about Marly, he downed his entire goblet of lemonade in a single gulp, but his hostess saw that his glass was refilled immediately.

"A few weeks ago I received a visitor," the comtesse continued, her voice strained and tense. "An old friend—the duc d'Aiguillon, who still owes me much for his appointment as Louis Quinze's Chief Minister."

Changing the subject for a moment, she gestured to a three-tiered stand of gold-rimmed Sèvres plates laden with delicate, multicolored macarons. Joseph tentatively helped himself to a crunchy pillow of pink meringue and almond flour, filled with violet-flavored cream.

Tinged as it was with sadness and regret, the du Barry's voice was also spiked with a distinctly acidic note. "After all this time, the duc finally gained the nerve to tell me what no one else ever had."

Joseph noticed her increased agitation; as she spoke, she twisted a sapphire set in vermeil about her finger. What purpose could the comtesse have in sharing such a discommoding encounter with him? "When the old king was dying, the Grand Almoner of France, Cardinal de la Roche-Aymon, refused to grant him absolution or to perform the last rites unless *le Bien-Aimé* punished his paramour, by turning a prostitute into a penitent." The comtesse blinked back tears. "Madame la dauphine, or the queen, I should say, knew nothing about it, as it turned out, although she delighted in my disgrace. To this day I am certain she believes her husband was responsible . . . when all the while it was my own beloved—Louis Quinze himself—who, as the moment of judgment neared, feared that his soul would never fly to heaven if he did not consign his *maîtresse en titre*'s body to a convent. And so, monsieur le comte, for years I have borne this misplaced animosity toward your countrywoman. I have so recently been disabused of my thoughts that, although Her Majesty can never hear the words from my lips, as I cannot return to court, at least I may apologize to a fellow Austrian for my hasty judgment."

Joseph swallowed hard, debating whether it would be kinder or crueler to continue to dissemble in the face of Madame du Barry's intriguing confession. He rose and paced about her sun-drenched salon for several moments, pausing to gaze out the tall mullioned windows toward the waterworks in the distance.

He realized, then, that he heard nothing of la Machine from inside the château. At length, he spoke. "Forgive me, madame la comtesse; you have been so candid with me this afternoon, baring your soul and sharing your most intimate recollections of your years at court, particularly as you have confided the nature of your difficult relationship with the Queen of France, under the assumption that you were addressing an unknown foreign visitor." The du Barry artfully posed by the room's majestic hearth, draping her arms across the marble mantelpiece, as if to martyr herself to the verbal assault she undoubtedly anticipated.

"Comtesse, I am not Count Falkenstein. The Queen of France is my youngest sister. Allow me to properly introduce myself." He bowed deeply to his hostess. "I am Franz Joseph, Emperor of Austria."

Madame du Barry released a little gasp as the color rose to her cheeks. Not only was she surprised by her visitor's identity—but that he should pay her such homage when he need not have so much as inclined his head to her. "I am the one who must beg *your* forgiveness, Sire. I have been so indiscreet." Her eyes darted about the room, surveying her treasures, as if she expected to be relieved of them at any moment. She sank into a deep reverence. "I ask your prudence, Your Excellency," she added anxiously. "I beg you not to convey my remarks and opinions of the queen to Her Majesty. I enjoy my life here and do not wish to poke the hornet's nest." Her fair skin remained a charming shade of rose; perspiration beaded on her brow and settled upon her ample *poitrine*.

"My fan," she breathed, and hunted for the delicate lace-edged accessory. After finally locating it, her high color diminished with her mortification, and she expressed a desire to return to the open air.

"I should be very grateful if you would show me your gardens," Joseph said. They stepped into the golden light of the late afternoon and the emperor offered his arm to the former royal favorite, a woman whose abundant attractions were still in evidence even at the age of thirty-three.

Now that she knew who he was, her coyness of an hour or so earlier evanesced, replaced by awe, out of practice from mingling with monarchs, and genuinely touched that such a great man had spent so much time in her presence and treated her with such kindness. How unlike his sister was this Hapsburg! "Oh, no, Sire! I am not worthy of such an honor," the du Barry exclaimed, glancing at his upturned palm. She murmured that she was content merely to be the aging châtelaine of Louveciennes, dispensing baskets to the village poor.

But the emperor gallantly took her arm and slipped it beneath his. "Please—please," he insisted. "Beauty is always queen."

"How could you visit that creature?" I gasped, shocked that my brother had spent the afternoon in the company of my former rival. "Maman will be appalled when she hears of it. If you wished to have paid a call on anyone in the country it should have been the dear old duc de Choiseul, rather than the woman who orchestrated his downfall." Joseph assured me that he had encountered the comtesse du Barry quite by chance, yet I could not help but be envious that he had whiled away precious hours in her presence, time I wished he had spent in my own company. "I suppose that, like countless courtiers, as well as Papa Roi of course, you succumbed to her allure," I sighed. "Grown men seem to become hopeless under her spell."

My husband, whom I had invited to join us for a stroll and a picnic of strawberries at le Petit Trianon, shook his head like a wet dog. "I never saw it, I assure you," he insisted.

"You wouldn't," the emperor replied. "You two are a pair of children, and wouldn't have understood the ripe appeal of a true woman in all her feminine glory if she fell into your laps. You were blinded, *ma petite soeur,* by your jealousy and self-interest, and you, *mon ami*—well, *you* are just blind to the charms of women in general!"

"I am not!" Louis protested somewhat petulantly.

"Before I utter another word about your marital state—as you are too curious to know my opinion of your notorious du Barry to listen to anything else—frankly I found her rather plain. Toinette, you have far more pleasing features, an equally charming figure, and infinitely more grace." I turned as red as a berry. "Which is why I cannot fathom your childless state." Joseph turned to address the king. "I have spoken of the situation quite candidly with my sister, but I should like to spend some time alone with you, Sire, observing *every* discretion, I assure you, and forgetting for those hours that we are sovereign brothers. Consider instead our ties of blood and my experience of women."

At this suggestion Louis's complexion turned somewhat chartreuse, but I encouraged him to take advantage of Joseph's worldliness. Perhaps he had some sound advice, I reasoned. After all these years of *rien,* things couldn't become any worse.

• • •

TO: THE GRAND DUKE OF TUSCANY FROM JOSEPH II,
HOLY ROMAN EMPEROR: CONFIDENTIAL

Paris, May 2, 1777

My Dear Leopold:

I have now had the opportunity to spend a good deal of time with our sister and the King of France. He is honest and not devoid of knowledge, but he is badly educated, as well as incurious, and the ministers are the masters, making it all the more necessary for the queen to come into her own, and quickly, for Louis is a man too easily led by the nose.

Yet the only place he cannot be led, it seems, is the bedchamber. Physically, he is a strong man, sturdily built, and he looks perfectly capable of fathering a child. Yet he barely seems to know how to go about it! I spoke with him privately and entirely candidly, and he confided that he has very firm erections, but then after he introduces the member he stays there without moving for perhaps two full minutes and withdraws without having ejaculated, although he is still erect. Then he kisses the queen good night.

I find the entire business incomprehensible. He says he sometimes has nightly emissions, but never during the act itself; and he says quite plainly that he does it purely from a sense of duty—that he derives no pleasure whatever from it. To think that there has been no Bourbon heir due to such laziness and apathy. Oh—if only once I could have been there! I would have whipped him until he grew so enraged that he spent like a donkey! Our sister has little temperament; if she were by nature a romantic or a sensualist she might make his task easier, but together they are two complete blunderers.

Their situation is very odd. The king is at present only two-thirds of a husband. He loves our sister, I can see it. Yet he fears her more. She has the kind of power one expects from a *maîtresse en titre,* not a wife, as she compels him to do things he doesn't want to do. Her virtue remains strictly intact; however, she acts as if she gives no thought to next week, let alone the future.

Joseph's departure from France at the end of the first week in June left an aching void that I could not seem to fill, the seven weeks he'd spent with us gone so quickly that it seemed little more than a gauzy dream. My usual round of amusements no longer brought me delight. True, he had employed a good number of our hours together lecturing me on how to be a more amiable wife and a more respected queen, and I was hardly nostalgic for these scoldings.

"What can you be thinking of, to interfere in public affairs, to dismiss ministers and appoint others in their place?" my brother had demanded to know. "Or to create new and costly posts at court when the king is endeavoring to economize?" The comtesse de Polignac had made recommendations (naturally the persons in question were her friends or relations) and I had forwarded them, thinking they were sound. Yet Louis had not questioned them at the time; indeed, he had always encouraged my friendship with Madame de Polignac.

"Have you ever troubled to ask yourself what right you have to intervene in the business of the French monarchy?" Joseph said. His words made me shiver. "Small wonder, then, that the king is afraid of you. And that the caricaturists cannot fill their nibs with ink fast enough."

I briefly lowered my gaze. My cheeks burned. My brother was right, of course. I hadn't at all considered the possibility that my husband had acquiesced to the Polignac promotions out of fear, for I certainly did not see myself as formidable or threatening in any way. Whatever was there about me that Louis could be frightened of? I only wished to help my friends. If someone was not qualified, surely the king would have told me so.

But I could not admit to my brother what I had surmised for the past two years at least—that Louis had altered his original policy against my "intervening," as Joseph put it, gratifying my wish to feel useful, as our childless state left me on the periphery as his consort. My husband understood that I would not seek an active role in the affairs of state if my hours were occupied with the joys of motherhood; and so I believe he became determined to indulge me in other ways.

Resentful at Joseph's presumption, despite my affection for him, and perhaps because his words had hit the mark too well, "I do not wish to appear managed," I said smoothly, promising at the same time to reform my behavior after his departure.

He was not convinced. Seated beside me in the solitude of le Petit Trianon, on a couch upholstered in pale green silk, he took my hands in his and looked deeply into my eyes. "My dear, sweet, charming sister, *reflect* before you act, for every little thing has consequences." He brought my fingers to his lips. "Listen to a brother who loves you and who has only your welfare at heart." His voice was quiet, but firm. "All your beauty and charm is worth nothing if you continue to dance toward an abyss, spurred on by the gossip and backbiting of those you choose to account your companions. In truth, *ma petite soeur,* I tremble for your happiness, seeing that in the long run things cannot go on as they are." He sounded almost regretful. "The revolution will be a cruel one, and perhaps of your own making."

THIRTEEN

A True Wife at Last

Joseph had been customarily blunt to Louis as well, but his words had their desired effect. A few weeks after my brother's departure, when we entertained the king's maiden aunts, Mesdames Adélaïde, Victoire, and Sophie, bitter crows who had retired from court to the Château de Bellevue on our ascension, my husband made sure to demonstrate to them that he was hardly indifferent toward his queen.

Feasting on strawberries and cream in the Bois de Boulogne that afternoon, Mesdames and I were surprised to see the king canter over, dressed for the hunt, with a half-dozen outriders trailing behind. He pulled up his horse and dismounted, handing the reins to a groom. Removing his hat and blotting the perspiration from his brow, he surveyed the four of us in our candy-colored gowns with their furbelowed skirts and ruched bodices, our pale décolletée protected by matching silk parasols.

"How splendid you look!" he exclaimed. "Monsieur Fragonard should paint you just as you are." He took my hands and swung me to my feet as if I weighed nothing, then clasped me about the waist and drew me to him, kissing me fully on the mouth. His lips were soft and tasted slightly of salt from his equestrian exertions. Later in the day, and for hours afterwards, I rustled through my memories: Had he ever before kissed me like that? It was surely not for show because I was in the presence of Mesdames—who, I had learned long after the fact, mistrusted the Austrians, like so many of the French nobility, and had been against our marriage from the beginning. Louis's embrace was born out of pure spontaneity. This rare gesture at Versailles, this tender expression of affection among the sovereigns, won an unexpected reaction, for Mesdames, our footmen, and his grooms and outriders all applauded us!

Joseph had chided me for not showing affection toward my husband, and I had tried to become more aware of demonstrating my esteem for him, not only in public, but in the bedchamber, although I don't believe my brother comprehended how agonizing even the gentlest expressions of tenderness could be. Had Louis confided the specifics of his medical condition, according to the diagnosis of Monsieur Lassone?

Once again I raised the prospect of circumcision. I was reliably informed by those with a good deal of experience that the procedure would make the business of lovemaking more enjoyable for my husband. And in Louis's case, his phimosis was not correcting itself over time, with repeated attempts, however painful, at intercourse, as one of the court physicians had advised. So finally, although he remained loath to consider the possibility of infection, or worse, and the unthinkable likelihood of leaving me a widow and France at the mercy of his brother, Louis capitulated.

Yet the operation was to be performed entirely in secret. Monsieur's coterie of schemers could not be permitted the opportunity to stir the pot of dissension and plot against the king, netting allies like flypaper, should he perish from the procedure.

The procedure was effected in the dead of night in my

small single bed at le Petit Trianon, amid a soothing palette of robin's-egg blue, rose, celadon, and ivory. Nowhere else at Versailles could such privacy be obtained. Rules governing entry were posted at various points about the acreage: THE QUEEN FORBIDS THAT HER GARDEN BE DEEMED A PUBLIC PLACE, ALLOWS ENTRANCE ONLY BY THE GATE AND UNDER THE ESCORT OF A SWISS GUARD; SHE FORBIDS PERSONS ATTACHED TO THE SERVICE OF TRIANON TO BRING THEIR FAMILIES OR FRIENDS ONTO THE GROUNDS ON THE DAYS WHEN SHE DINES THERE ALONE OR WITH THE ROYAL FAMILY; EVEN IN HER ABSENCE SUCH PERSONS MUST BE ACCOMPANIED.

The most illustrious trespasser thus far had been the Grand Almoner. On the night we fêted Grand Duke Paul of Russia, His Arrogance, prince de Rohan, had connived his way into the gardens, which had been illuminated with lanterns cleverly concealed within flowerpots. He had lied to my gatekeeper, and the hapless concierge had admitted him to the grounds; the princesse de Lamballe alerted me to the cardinal-prince's presence when she glimpsed the hem of his red moiré soutane peeking out from beneath his voluminous black domino cloak. I was livid, for the cardinal was the last person I would have wished to entertain. Not only had he not been invited to the Grand Duke's soirée, but the prince de Rohan never had been, and never would be, my guest at le Petit Trianon, or anywhere else where it lay within my power to exclude him. I debated whether to permit the cardinal to remain; but countenancing any breach of the rules of Trianon, and of my privacy and security, would set a dangerous precedent, so I had my Swiss Guards discreetly escort him from the gardens.

Ordinarily quite abstemious, Louis consumed a fair amount of brandy to calm his nerves and blunt the inevitable pain of the surgical procedure. Yet when he undressed and Monsieur Lassone examined him for the final time, to our immense relief the physician found that nothing quite so radical as a complete circumcision would be necessary after all.

Having first made sure that both the lancet and the *médecin*'s hands were scrubbed with hot water and strong Castille soap, I held the candle as he made a few small traverse incisions, in order to loosen the fibers of the prepuce of Louis's *pénis.* I peered over Monsieur Lassone's shoulder, careful not to obscure the light as he explained how the deformity manifested itself. Maman, I thought, would have been proud of me, for I never so much as flinched. "You see, *Votre Majesté,* how the prepuce was forming a corona about the head of the king's member, essentially strangling it. This abnormal, tight skin was preventing His Majesty from obtaining an erection without enduring extreme discomfort." In no time at all, the doctor had pronounced the loosening accomplished, and he began to apply an ointment concocted of wine and olive oil between Louis's glans and prepuce. "Is that all?" my husband remarked, shocked at how quickly, and with such minimal fuss, the greatest burden of his life had been dispensed with. Even the pain, he admitted, though he had been gnawing on the heel of a stale crust of bread, was not as fearsome as he had imagined it would be.

Monsieur Lassone drew my attention to the ointment. "In a few days' time, if you continue to apply this *baume samaritain* as I am doing, you will see that the scabs will heal rather swiftly and you and the king may resume all of your normal activities."

The royal physician was as good as his word. And on August 22, 1777, nearly seven and a quarter years from the day we knelt at the altar together in the chapel at Versailles, the King of France—*finalement*—made me his true wife.

Although our initial efforts as he filled me completely—to the hilt of his sword, he proudly proclaimed—were quite painful for both of us, I gasped in surprise at how elastic *mon vagin* became as we persevered. I wished to show Louis I loved him, so to feel closer, I wrapped my legs around his bottom, only to discover that the position rendered our exertions considerably more comfortable. This enabled me to relax and when I felt more at ease, the king grew more confident and thus we could finally perform our marital duty.

I can only describe it as unqualified ebullience when at long last Louis and I relieved ourselves of the burden of celibacy. The joy and elation of consummation at long last triumphed, trumping every other sentiment and sensation. Louis was so thrilled, relief etched so visibly in his full cheeks and light eyes that he was eager to repeat the deed for several days running, and even gushed with delight to Mesdames, themselves uninitiated in the great mystery, exclaiming that he could curse himself for having denied his body such transcendent enjoyment for so long.

The court was abuzz with excitement, and when many of the courtiers felt robbed of one of their favorite topics of gossip and derision, I became doubly delighted. Monsieur and Madame sourly congratulated us. I was almost positive that they still had never consummated their nuptials, despite Monsieur's frequent boasts of prowess; certainly they had nothing to show for it. "You are catching up, perhaps," simpered the comtesse d'Artois, already twice a mother, and with her belly swelling again. I knew Joseph had written home to Vienna that he found her useless for anything except making babies. But even my prolifically fecund *belle-soeur* could not dampen my euphoria. On August 30, I wrote to Maman with the good news:

> I am in the most essential happiness of my entire life. It is more than eight days now since my marriage was thoroughly consummated, and the proof has been repeated daily. At first I thought of sending my dear maman a courier, but I feared

that it would be such an event that it would cause talk. As it is, nothing remains a secret here for long. I will also admit that I wanted to be quite sure. I do not think I am pregnant yet, but at least I now have that possibility from one moment to the next. How happy my dear maman will be now. May I kiss her with all my heart?

But, *hélas,* not ten days after I had become "fully a woman," as my sister Charlotte would have said, my husband's passion for our newfound marital intimacy waned almost entirely, the way a young child loses interest in a once-favorite toy. I was crushed and when I sorrowfully confronted Louis to ask what had happened to cause so great a change, he could only blush and shrug. He returned to his old ways—long days at the hunt or the forge, conferring with his ministers without including me, and overindulging at meals, surfeiting himself on sweets and sauces.

So I quickly resumed my former routine as well, dancing and gaming until the wee hours, almost afraid to retire for the night, my great bed of state the scene of so much distress that I avoided it for as many hours as possible.

On September 10, I wrote to my mother again, shading the truth about the king's nocturnal visits because I did not want her to know that by the time I finally turned in, he had been aslumber in his own suite for hours. At one point I believed our humiliation to be at an end, and the need for his company obviated, referring to my monthly courses with the sobriquet we Hapsburg women had employed during my childhood. I was unfortunately disappointed—not by my husband, but by my own body:

The birth of a son to the Queen of Naples has pleased me more than I can say. Is it true that Charlotte will have a seat on the Council of State now that she has borne an heir? I love my sister with all my heart but I confess that I rejoice all the more about her newborn baby because I hope soon to have the same happiness myself. I had a moment in which I hoped I was pregnant but Générale Krottendorf has never visited me with any regularity.

Although the king occasionally spends the night with me, he does not like to sleep in my bed. I have encouraged him not to proceed to a complete separation, especially as we have finally done what we must, yet I do not feel it would be proper to insist that he visit me more often, as he does come to see me every morning in my private study. His friendship and his love grow every day.

I send you many kisses.

Your devoted Antoinette

• • •

October 17, 1777

Your Imperial Majesty:

It pains me to relay the unsettling news that the comtesse de Polignac and another of Antoinette's Trianon *cercle,* the duc de Coigny, are becoming more favored than ever, with the most deplorable results. The pair of them perpetually wrench favors from the generous queen, giving rise to numerous, and vociferous, complaints from the public. The protégés of the duc are awarded all the financial offices and the comtesse's creatures are given monetary gifts, sums taken from those who have a right to expect it. It is almost unexampled that in so short a time the royal favor should have brought such overwhelming advantages to a single family; I speak of course of the Polignacs. The queen uses no judgment in these matters and no minister dares resist her desires. As the king cannot make her happy where it signifies most, to the detriment of the nation he feels he cannot deny her.

Your humble servant,
Mercy

• • •

My dear Mercy:

As long as she is pressing her advantage with the king and yielding results—whatever the reason for her success—she should be employing this influence to further the interests of her homeland. We will have to be content with what can be obtained by remonstrating with her.

Maria Theresa

Nothing could have upset me more greatly during the ensuing months than the pressure from my mother to convince Louis and his ministers to support Joseph's unethical seizure of Bavaria. The German duchy's old Elector died at the end of December 1777; rather than support the installation of his heir as the new Elector Palatine in return for a third of the Bavarian territory, my brother Joseph behaved as heinously as Frederick of Prussia had done many years earlier when he took Silesia from Austria. He simply marched his troops into Bavaria and seized the entire duchy.

During those crucial weeks when I should have been capitalizing, as Maman might have put it, on our genuine intimacy in the bedchamber, wooing my husband with patience and caresses, I was being thoroughly schooled by the comte de Mercy in the political ramifications of Joseph's actions so that I could assert Austria's position whenever Louis and I were able to steal a few private moments. It was no secret that Joseph's goals were to expand and strengthen the empire. Mercy believed that my brother's intentions vis-à-vis the centrally located Bavaria were to use it as a bargaining chip, if necessary, with Frederick of Prussia, offering "the Devil" the Austrian Netherlands in exchange.

Unfortunately, things steamed to a head, and my husband and I engaged in a rather heated discussion over the crisis in my study one morning in mid February. I had dismissed my attendants so that we could converse in complete seclusion. Surrounded in this feminine sphere by vases of hothouse blooms in every shade of pink and the repeating pattern of hand-painted floral images on my wallpaper, as we partook of coffee and sweet rolls and I tempted him with sugared almonds, I reminded Louis most pointedly of the importance of the Franco-Austrian alliance. Proud now of my knowledge of our shared history, I called to his attention the Treaty of 1756 which laid the foundation for our eventual union. "France and Austria promised to aid one another in a time of conflict, a day that may well dawn before very long. Have you ever tried a spoonful of *Schlag*—whipped cream—in your coffee? Once you have done so you will never wish to drink it any other way. And instead you are committing—squandering, even—your military might and resources to aid some rabble across the Atlantic Sea who are intent on overthrowing their sovereign king!"

Just days earlier, on February 6, 1778, France had formally recognized the United States of America, the entity formed by the rebellious British colonists against overwhelming odds, and concluded a military alliance with them. A passionate, but untrained, army of farmers, lawyers, laborers, tradesmen, and apprentices could never have managed as well against the red-coated soldiers of England's George III without France's help.

"Squandering? Is that how you see it?" Louis demanded.

"Well—*oui,*" I admitted hotly. "Do you think those savages halfway across the world will ever offer to aid you in return, should the time come? You have seen how much they respect a king! Meanwhile, you turn a blind eye to a neighbor at your border—to your family. If the bellicose Frederick marches into Austria tomorrow and carves off a slice of Hapsburg terrain in retaliation for my brother's incursion, who is to say that he will not desire a taste of France the following week?"

The volatile King of Prussia had reacted swiftly to Joseph's invasion of Bavaria; and Maman, who had not encouraged my brother's gambit, now found herself frantically needing to defend it, not only morally, but perhaps literally as well.

"This could lead to war with Prussia," I said despairingly. I offered the king a croissant, making sure he could detect the delicate fragrance I wore on my wrist: Fargeon's orange flower water, an especial favorite of his. "Frederick is already amassing an army at our—I mean the Hapsburg—borders. France *must* send soldiers to stand with Austria." How could Louis remain cold to my entreaties?

He had blinked, however, at my slip of the tongue, wounded by the uncomfortable realization that there was some truth to my detractors' vociferous claims that the Queen of France was an agent of Austria. Although I had forsworn my native country and my birthright upon leaving Vienna, what else had my marriage been for, except to solidify the amity between our kingdoms? Still, after all I had done ever since to prove that I was thoroughly French, it would never be enough for those who despised me now and had always done so.

"England is an age-old enemy. To aid *their* enemy is to further weaken them, and it is far more likely that France would suffer an invasion from Great Britain than it would from Frederick of Prussia. On the other hand, as far as it concerns Bavaria, it is your family's ambition that is causing all the trouble," Louis replied, his voice as frosty as I had ever heard it, his posture rigid and formal, as though he were armoring himself against me. His gaze never wavered, nor did his tone falter, as it so often did when he was confronting his ministers or speaking to his troops. If only he could be so regal, so confident, in their presence. "They started with Poland back in 1771 when they forced France to support the partitioning of the commonwealth so that Austria would end up with some territory out of the bargain. Now they are doing it again with Bavaria. Austria's immoral expansion is nothing more than a policy of armed robbery." He searched for a handkerchief in a hidden pocket of his amber-colored waistcoat and blew his nose loudly. "I am very sorry for you."

His words stung. I had pushed him away when I most needed to draw him to me. All the perfume and almonds in the world had availed nothing. Nearly eight years had passed since our wedding—which in sober truth was an international treaty signed in the sight of God—and finally, the Franco-Austrian alliance had been consummated, quite literally, in my bedchamber. Yet now my husband sought to turn his back, as he had on me for so many nights, on the other raison d'être for our union.

FOURTEEN

Wherein I Am the Consummate Hostess

At length, mindful of his duty to his country, Louis resumed his conjugal visits and we made love on each occasion. Yet I could not savor the experience when my thoughts were preoccupied with stratagems for securing his promise to aid Austria over the Bavarian crisis.

And still he persisted in entertaining the Americans—in every way. On March 20, the gold-tipped iron gates of Versailles were thrown open in welcome to the diplomatic envoys from the new republic: Silas Deane, the son of a blacksmith; and the elderly, avuncular, and exceedingly flirtatious inventor Benjamin Franklin (who, I would hazard, was the first man without sword or wig to enter Versailles). From these unlikely origins the patriots had risen to the role of statesmen, an utter impossibility here in France, which made the men all the more of a curiosity to the aristocrats who evidently could not get enough of the odd Mr. Franklin. In their honor, we hosted an extravagant supper. Our guests looked quite incongruous seated amid the most glamorous members of France's nobility at a long table in the Hall of Mirrors laden with crystal, Sèvres, and silver. The men, including Louis's cousins the ducs de Chartres and Orléans, and the other Princes of the Blood, were dressed in suits of satin and velvet: snug breeches and long, tight-fitting coats heavily embroidered with gold and silver threads. My husband had deputized me to convince the comte d'Artois and his racy coterie to forgo their current fashion for the evening. The youngbloods of France had adopted an English manner of dress that owed its origins to the racetrack: open jackets with a split seam along the back called frock coats, or *"le frac."* Louis and the older and more conservative minds at court found them indecent; they exposed too much of the chest and torso because they required shorter vests to be worn with them, and they also left the upper portion of the breeches visible. Secretly, I encouraged my brother-in-law to sport the new modes at le Petit Trianon, but tonight, our aim was to be as French as possible. Louis insisted that aping the British fashions, which had become all the rage in Paris, would have been spectacularly rude to our distinguished guests; the blood of these patriots, as they called themselves, was still being shed as their War of Independence from England's sovereignty raged on, with no end in sight. Some of the same French gallants who favored British tailoring—the duc de Lauzun, for example—were champing like racehorses, hoping for a commission to head a mercenary regiment, or at least to serve in an American one, eager to return home spangled with glory. The notion still rankled that my delightful *cercle* of gentlemen might desert me for a cause that sounded utterly antithetical to France's belief in the divine right of kings.

When the elderly American envoy was presented to me at the top of the evening, he had made a sweeping bow and kissed my hand, raising his eyes to mine with an insouciant smile. There was something in Mr. Franklin's manner that put me in mind of the descriptions I had heard of that charming reprobate, Monsieur Voltaire, who was still languishing in his self-imposed exile in Switzerland rather than bend his knee, and his philosophies, to life under a Bourbon regime. I had the sensation that some of this American's eccentricities were merely for effect, calculated to amuse an audience that prided itself on its sophistication and elegance. His true mission in France was to convince Louis and his ministers to give him as much assistance as possible—not only monetarily, but militarily—supplying men and munitions both at sea and on the field of battle, from Canada to the Carolinas. Perhaps his plan was to convince us that the more we gave, the more "French" his countrymen would become, thanks to our largesse.

Multifaceted crystal goblets tinkled as our guests toasted the success thus far of the War of Independence. I shuddered and glanced down the length of the table at the celebrants, barely recognizing some of the women, for they looked as though they were attired for a masquerade ball rather than a state dinner at the palace. When it came to women's fashion I had set the mode for years; yet since his arrival in Paris two years earlier, this eccentric "Monsieur Frankleen," with his shaggy gray hair and twinkling eyes, had so captivated the hostesses of the capital that in due time they had endeavored to emulate his appearance. I found myself trying not to stare at an unseemly number of unpowdered heads, some of which were crowned with only slightly more elegant versions of the diplomat's ridiculous beaver hat. Germaine Necker, the outspoken young daughter of our Finance Minister, looked particularly absurd. Not only was a fur chapeau plunged down over her rather masculine-looking head, but her gown had been constructed to resemble the infant republic's flag, a riot of red and white horizontal stripes set off at her breast by a blue field that was dominated by a circle of stars, representing each of the new states in the American union.

Now I watched this—this septuagenarian satyr ogling the ample décolleté of the maréchale de Millepied, a woman easily one fourth his age, and yet the maréchale, fully aware she was being admired, simpered and giggled, and adjusted her position to afford the envoy a better view as everyone seated within earshot peppered the American diplomat with questions about his savage land across the sea.

"Not nearly as *'sauvage'* as you French imagine it," Mr. Franklin chuckled. "We rarely cover ourselves in animal skins," he said, mischievously tapping his unusual chapeau, "and I have seen more feather headdresses at this table than in an entire lifetime in America." He conceded that the women of Baltimore and Boston, Philadelphia and New York, did not dress quite so extravagantly as the Parisians, practicality being more prized in a lady's character than frivolity. Evidently they were more religious as well.

To the silly comtesse d'Artois, he replied, "Yes, Madame, we have Catholics in America, although I myself belong to the Society of Friends, a peace-loving Quaker." He was then challenged to reconcile his nonviolent beliefs to his advocacy of revolution, before surprising the gathering by informing us that it was the intention of the American founding fathers, as he called them, for their newborn United States to champion freedom of religion: to wit, a man's beliefs would not restrict his access to universities or employment. "It is also our goal for every property-holding man, no matter how much land he owns and no matter the circumstances of his birth, to have a vote in who will represent him in all the governing bodies that affect his life, from alderman to the Continental Congress."

The duc d'Orléans and his son, the duc de Chartres, leaned forward to listen more intently. I found the entire discussion shocking. The Orléans *famille* were troublemakers with broad popularity in the capital and equally deep coffers. I looked down the table, trying to catch Louis's eye, but he was deep in conversation with Mr. Deane. I wondered what the king made of all of this talk of revolution and rebellion. And what of Louis's slippery cousins? When the American envoy enumerated the glorious political reforms that his new United States would embrace, I despaired of the dangerous notions they inspired in Chartres and Orléans.

I could not understand my countrymen and -women's enthusiasm for Mr. Franklin's new nation, nor comprehend the anti-royalist sentiment—nay, zeal—that his revolution inspired in even the most aristocratic of bosoms, particularly while my family in Austria still despaired of our aid, even as the King of Prussia threatened to invade their borders in retaliation for Joseph's incursion into Bavaria. Nor could I imagine decking myself out like Mademoiselle Necker in *la mode Américaine*. But before the week was over, I summoned Rose Bertin to Versailles to design a few poufs commemorating our new alliance and, in my sole concession to the cult of "*le très sage* Sieur Frankleen," I chose to cease powdering my hair. Monsieur Léonard was aghast at my *petite révolte*.

On April 19, as I was composing a letter to Maman, I became overwhelmed by a sickly stench in my study. I glanced about, surveying the lush arrangements of lilies, roses, irises, and tuberoses that filled the room. The last, a flower with an exceptionally heady aroma, had the tendency to turn as it began to die. But the long-stemmed bloom looked as fresh as ever. I lowered my nose to the little vase of violets and lilies of the valley, nature's most delicately scented blossoms, and drew away, nearly wretching with nausea.

On the morning of May 5, my *dame d'atours* arrived with the gazette containing the inventory of my wardrobe and handed me the pin with which I marked my selections for the day. I made my choices and my accessories were delivered to me as usual in an osier basket covered with a fresh length of scented green baize. But the pale blue satin slippers pinched my toes. The measurements had always been infallible. I questioned my *dame d'atours:* Had a new cobbler been employed? She shook her head.

"These shoes were made only weeks ago, *Votre Majesté.*"

I wore a new pair nearly every day. Never before had they been too snug. I ordered another pair to be brought to me, but those were too tight as well. So I asked my *dame d'atours* to bring back the gazette and I would select a different ensemble entirely. Perhaps there was something wrong with the blue satin. I decided to wear buttercup yellow instead; then rose, then olive, and I soon found myself surrounded by a haphazard heap of shoes fashioned of silk, brocade, and satin, elaborately embellished, or barely unadorned—and yet every one of them was ever so slightly too small, just enough to be horridly uncomfortable if I wore them for more than a few moments at a time.

My attendants had been exchanging glances all morning. Finally, dear Gabrielle, the comtesse de Polignac—and shame on the comte de Mercy for trying to turn me against her, as I found her no more grasping than any other courtier at Versailles—inquired sweetly whether I had noticed any other changes in my body.

Générale Krottendorf had arrived earlier than usual on March 3, but she had not revisited me since. Tears sprang to my eyes. My heart's pace quickened. Was it possible? Still, I had been fooled before. My courses had never been reliable. Not only that, my belly would become dreadfully upset whenever I grew anxious about something, and Maman's perpetual haranguing over the situation in Bavaria was a source of undue consternation. If I was experiencing yet another false alarm, it would be better to remain silent. Best not to risk rumors.

By the thirty-first of July, not only had the Générale continued to remain elusive, but there were other signs that confirmed my certainty. I vomited most mornings, no matter how little I ate. Even my usual *petits déjeuners* of dry toast made me queasy. Every odor and aroma seemed ten times more pungent. I ceased wearing some of my *eaux perçantes* because the fragrances were too powerful for me to bear. As dauphine I had disdained the use of stays, although the grandeur of my wardrobe as queen all but mandated them, and I had been compelled to succumb to their torments. Yet now I found my corsets more detestable than ever for it was clear, at least to me, from studying myself every day in a tall glass, that at long last there was something more considerable to constrict. Louis never dared to explore my body whenever we performed our marital duty, but had he ever thought to touch my breasts, I would have complained that they were now tender and sensitive.

But most obvious of all, it had come—"the quickening," as the duchesse de Chartres and the comtesse de Polignac (my pair of trusted mamans) called it: that inexpressible, indefinable moment of joy when an expectant mother first feels the stirrings of life inside her belly.

In those early weeks it had been nearly impossible to maintain my secret, but I had so dreaded a miscarriage I had not even told my mother the news. Not before I announced it to the one person who had most to gain. Tipsy with excitement as I glided through the corridors, I could scarcely tamp down my enthusiasm, but I nearly had to hold my breath; catching the attention of the usual throng gathered in the halls and State Rooms might begin a roundelay of murmurs and whispers, and I wished to conceal the sense that something extraordinary was about to take place.

At the door to the king's private apartments, I requested my attendants to quit me, and they receded, retreating in opulent, beribboned bubbles of cerise, aqua, and apple-green taffeta, satin, and moiré.

I found Louis in his library, alone, squinting over a sheaf of documents. An atlas lay on the desk beside him, its red Morocco binding open to a map of North America. As he looked up, startled by the intrusion, I feigned a terribly incommoded expression and, striking an attitude, declared petulantly, "I have come, Sire, to complain about one of your subjects, who has had the audacity to kick me in the belly."

It took him a moment or two to realize what I had said. And then, as the expression in his eyes transformed itself from annoyance to discovery to unabashed elation, and his small full lips broadened into a toothy smile, followed by an exuberant yelp, I broke my pose and began to laugh and cry at the same time. He came around from behind the desk to sweep me into his arms, but then began to draw back, fearful I would crack, like a Meissenware shepherdess, if he handled me too boldly. "*Ma chère Toinette! Est-ce tellement vrai?* After we have waited so long? Can it really be true?" Tears coursed down his broad cheeks. He clasped my hands in his and brought them to his moist lips, smothering them with *petits bisous.* After so many years as man and wife I still marveled at how tiny my hands looked inside of his, as he caressed the insides of my wrists with his thumbs.

I slipped my arms about his prodigious waist and pressed my head to his chest, staining his yellow brocaded waistcoat with my tears of exultation and relief. As my husband held me in his embrace I could feel his emotion in the rise and fall of his chest against my bosom. "So, you are to be a papa!" I exclaimed, when we finally released our arms. "How does it feel?"

He puffed out his already ample chest, preening like a peacock. "This is the happiest day of my life," he assured me. "More so than the day we wed, for I did not know you then." He grabbed me and kissed me full on the mouth, taking my breath away.

"Louis, I give you my solemn pledge," I whispered, as our lips parted, "and I will say the same to Monsieur Lassone and to Maman, that as it appears God has finally granted me the grace I have so long desired, I will henceforth live otherwise than I have done till now. I will live as a mother. To nourish our son and give time to his education will be my chief pleasures from now on."

I am not sure he took me at my word, for I had not been terribly adept at maintaining my previous promises to curtail my gaming and monitor the expenses of my wardrobe more closely. But how could I, when Mademoiselle Bertin never itemized her invoices? And the previous year, the comte d'Artois had all but goaded me into wagering against his contention that he could build a château in three months' time on the property he had purchased from the prince de Chimay in the Bois de Boulogne. He had built Bagatelle in only sixty-three days and I had lost a fortune. But everything would be different from now on. With the stirring of life within me, I looked forward to a new leaf.

Louis took me by the hand and led me toward the paneled door. "We must announce the news to the court!"

"No," I said, pulling him up short, and placing my finger on his lips. "Let us wait a few days; it will give us the upper hand and allow us the time to plan the appropriate pageantry." We were still hand in hand when we exited the king's private apartments, unsurprised to find a crowd gathered outside the doors, although they jumped back like fleas, embarrassed to have been caught eavesdropping. How we frustrated the gossips by supplying only a pair of enigmatic expressions!

That Sunday a Te Deum was sung at Mass, not only in the chapel at Versailles but at all the churches in the capital. The reason became apparent on the following day, August 4, when Louis and I announced to the court that the queen was with child.

Elation and jubilation spread from the corridors of Versailles across France—to Bretagne and Bordeaux, to Tours and Toulouse, Champagne and Strasbourg and across the border over the Hapsburg territories of Belgium and the disputed Bavaria, across the German duchies; and, thanks to my effulgent letter to Maman, onto her escritoire at Schönbrunn.

I am already beginning to put on weight visibly, especially about the hips. For so long I lived without the hope of being so happy as to bear a child that I feel it all the more strongly now.

I forgot to tell my dear maman that back when I missed my courses for the second month I asked the king for 500 louis, which makes 12,000 francs, to send to the indigents of Paris who languish in debtors' prisons solely because of the money they owe to wet nurses; I also sent 4,000 francs to the poor of Versailles. In that way I was not only charitable, but notified the public of my condition.

As for the situation in Bavaria, I cannot go directly to the ministers to make them understand that what was said and done in Vienna was fair and reasonable, for none are more deaf than those who choose not to hear. I mean to speak to them in the presence of the king to be certain that they will use the right tone before the King of Prussia, and in truth it is for Louis's glory that I want it. It can only enhance his esteem by supporting allies who should be dear to him in every way, and what could be dearer than ties of family, especially now? Besides, he is behaving most perfectly to me these days, and is so attentive and kind.

I kiss you lovingly,
Marie Antoinette

In a gesture intended to honor his family for the abbé Vermond's years of service to me, we selected his brother to be my *accoucheur*.

Amid my old retainer's other duties, the humble and appreciative cleric, ever a comforting presence amid an ocean of doubters and detractors, would often deliver my correspondence when he came to read to me. But that day, when I untied the green ribbon that bound the notes and letters, a scrap of paper floated to the floor. He stooped to retrieve it, gave a cursory glance, and, glowering, shoved it into a deep pocket of his black soutane.

"What was that?" I asked, my interest piqued.

"It was . . . not for you, *Majesté,*" he replied evasively.

I did not believe the look in his light eyes, which would not meet my gaze, nor the angry color that had suddenly suffused his cheeks. "I may not know for certain that you are lying to me, but God will; what is His punishment for a cleric? It must be twice that of an ordinary mortal," I scolded, only half in jest. "Come, now, I am sure the paper was intended for my eyes. Please show it to me."

"I dare not, madame," Vermond replied forlornly.

"Then I will have to command you to hand it over!" I insisted with forced gaiety. I extended my palm and the good abbé had no choice but to relinquish the document. It was a cruel caricature, and there was no mistaking the dramatis personae: the overtly *enceinte* woman dripping in diamonds, her hair coiffed in an outlandish pouf; the stout, myopic young man wearing a sash with the Order of Saint-Louis and a *cornue,* or pair of cuckold's horns; and the slender handsome youth with unpowdered hair, wearing an English frock coat and carrying a riding crop and a betting sheet. In case one might confuse him for one of his *confrères,* in his tricorn he wore a feather that spelled out, in spidery letters, *Artois.*

My heart began to pound with a ferocity I had never before known. I was hardly as companionable with my *beau-frère* as I had been in the past, and had rarely seen him since the announcement of my pregnancy, except at my *levers* and at evening card parties.

But someone clearly wished to revive an ugly rumor, deliberately connecting it to the paternity of the babe in my belly. I rose from my chair and walked to the fire with great dignity, then ripped the heinous drawing into shreds and watched as they floated into the yellow flames. "Do not speak of this to the king," I said. "He has enough to contend with. He will only come to blows with his brother over it, and the comtesse will throw a priceless vase at her hapless husband's head, when in truth the comte d'Artois is as blameless as Louis or I." I had a notion who was behind the caricature. I would observe Monsieur the next time we met to see if he was watching me for a reaction. How like a clever middle brother, seeking to drive a larger wedge between his two siblings, in order to emerge the most popular!

"I am in no mood to be read to today. Forgive me," I told Vermond, preferring instead to return to my correspondence. To my mother's latest missive I made no reply with reference to the Bavarian crisis, but, having digested the philosophy of Rousseau, who disdained the older generations' passion for artifice and advocated instead a return to Nature's bucolic ways, I responded:

> *Ma chère* maman is very kind to worry about my darling future child. I can assure her I will take great care of it. But the way they are brought up now they are less hampered than we were when I was little. They are not swaddled; rather, they are always in a crib or held in the nurse's arms, and as soon as they are old enough to tolerate the open air, they are introduced to it little by little until they become fully accustomed to the outdoors, and after that, they are always outside in the sunshine. I think this is the best way to raise them. Mine will be downstairs with a small grille to separate him from the terrace (so that he cannot get out on his own and do himself some injury); thus he may learn to walk faster than he would on a polished parquet floor.

The king promised Monsieur Vermond a pension of forty thousand livres if he delivered me of a dauphin and heir, and the man was wide-eyed with delight until Louis informed him that he would merit only a modest ten thousand should I bear a daughter of France.

"But Sire," he said soberly, through clenched teeth, "only the Almighty can make such a determination. Would Your Majesty not reconsider rewarding the birth of a healthy child all the same?" Despite his connection to my family, the greedy man was nearly dismissed and another sought in his stead.

Tears sprang readily to my eyes during those months while my body was changing; the slightest thing managed to affect me deeply. Almost afraid to read the worst, I nonetheless pored over the gazettes for news of my Trianon coterie who had left our shores to fight against the English on behalf of the American colonists.

When our frigate *La Belle Poule* defeated the British warship *Arethusa* off the coast of Brest that June, marking the first naval combat between the French and British in the American War of Independence, I celebrated the victory by commissioning a pouf from Léonard and Rose Bertin. Atop a three-foot crest of hair sat a majestic replica of the French vessel under full sail. As I had once been very much against aiding the Americans in any way, I thought Louis and his ministers would be pleased by my obvious show of patriotism. Yet I overheard Madame, who never missed an opportunity to flaunt her intellect, sneering that the pouf was in poor taste because *La Belle Poule* suffered casualties to nearly half her 230-man crew, and was herself nearly destroyed during the heavy firefight.

Not because I wished to silence my detractors but because I was growing heavy and wished to lighten my burdens, soon after this incident I began to forgo my poufs in favor of large caps of fine white muslin or linen. At Maman's insistence I had forsworn long, jouncing carriage rides, which curtailed my excursions to Paris, and thus my visits to the Opéra balls and masquerades. Dancing fatigued me more easily now, and I began to content myself with needlework, setting my ladies to embroidering pieces for my infant's layette. Most evenings we could be found seated about the worktable, needles in hand, rather than before the green baize, holding cards and markers. I was determined to bear a healthy heir for France.

FIFTEEN

An Acquaintance Returns

AUGUST 1778

Versailles played host to an endless stream of visitors. On a given day, all manner of humanity could be found crowding the halls and corridors of the State Rooms—mingling with any number of the thousand members of the nobility who resided at the palace—from petitioners seeking the ear of the king to tradespersons hawking their wares to foreign dignitaries and their delegations to representatives from the clergy to curious travelers, eager to see where the French monarch made his home and how he lived.

Seated upon his raised throne in the Mars Salon, with its red silk damasked walls, Louis would hold his formal audiences, and it was there, on one sultry afternoon near the end of August, that an old acquaintance reentered my life. Having become bored with my usual routine, and in an ill humor from the heat, I chose to observe the proceedings from an armchair beside the dais. Yet even there I could not escape Maman, for a portrait of the empress hung prominently on the wall over my left shoulder. Opposite her, Louis XV, immortalized in oils, and in his prime, surveyed the room as if he harbored a secret about everyone in it that could never be prized from his painted lips.

But my daydreams were interrupted by the formal announcement of Count Axel von Fersen. I had last seen him at one of my *cercles* shortly after our ascension. We had only spoken briefly then, when he told me he was returning to his homeland.

"*Le bel* Axel," as I had secretly nicknamed him when we'd first met four years earlier, was even more handsome than when I had last regarded him. In truth, he took my breath away. I suppose he had entered a regiment, for he stood before us, resplendent in his Swedish cavalry officer's uniform of tight white chamois breeches, blue doublet, and white tunic. Under one arm he carried a dashing black shako trimmed with blue and yellow plumes. His blue cloak, jauntily worn across one shoulder, made his eyes, which I once thought were an indeterminate shade of brownish-green, appear to be the color of delphiniums. When he clicked his heels together in a military bow, his black boots were so shiny that I could almost see my reflection.

"Yes, of course I recall you, Count von Fersen," Louis said. "And I understand you have become quite indispensable to your sovereign."

I had not heard as much. Had Fersen been corresponding with my husband or were these merely diplomatic pleasantries?

The Swede chuckled. "On the stage of his private theater, but not, alas on the field of battle. His Majesty Gustavus the Third, like the Queen of France," he added, with a dazzling smile in my direction, "is quite partial to his amateur theatricals."

I clapped my hands together in amazement. "I hadn't known!" I exclaimed. "Now I want to hear all about it."

Louis cupped his hand to beckon me and I leaned toward him, resting my arm on the throne. He gently placed his palm on my hand and whispered, "I have a few more hours of this tedium. If you wish to entertain our old friend, you have my leave to quit the salon and find a quiet place to converse."

I discreetly nodded my thanks and rose from the chair. At the sight of my body, the count's eyes registered a fleeting expression of surprise, which was quickly replaced with an enigmatic look I remembered well, a gaze that undoubtedly masked a wellspring of emotions. "You have never seen le Petit Trianon, monsieur le comte. I hope you will do me the honor of allowing me to give you a tour of my little idyll."

Count von Fersen clicked the heels of his boots, this time with an insouciant flourish. "Your servant until death, *Majesté.*"

His eyes did not jest, however. And I believed him with every fiber of my soul.

Only Lamballe and Polignac were to accompany us, which was now de rigueur for my little excursions on the mile-long carriage ride from the Château of Versailles to my "little Schönbrunn." After I began to increase I had even less tolerance for a crush of people around me; their suffocating presence made me irritable.

The blazing sun bleached the pebbles of the Cour Royale. Count von Fersen waited to hand me into the coach and for the first time since our reunion, he took the chance to fully appraise me. "You are with child," he murmured politely.

"God be thanked." I nodded. "*Finalement.* The doctors say our little dauphin will be born in December. I can't help measuring myself all the time to see how big I am becoming."

He raised my hand and gingerly helped me onto the coach's traveling steps. "I am very happy for you."

We rode in silence to le Petit Trianon, where Axel observed

with amusement the signs posted upon the iron gates forbidding any trespassers or intruders. “I am gawked at all day like the baby rhinoceros in my late father’s zoo,” I told him. “And yet the same people who criticize me for craving a moment’s solitude, clamor for an invitation to the one place where I have ensured that I will have it. This *petit château,* these gardens, the little country village that Monsieur Mique is designing for me, where twelve impoverished peasant families will finally have a home and a working farm with a dairy—this is my fairyland. It reminds me of my birthplace and my happiest, most carefree days when my sisters and I were young and untrammeled. I am myself here,” I said as we entered the black-and-white-tiled entrance hall.

I asked one of my footmen to bring a tray of refreshments to the music room. The comtesse de Polignac and the princesse de Lamballe retired to a corner of the salon, no doubt to gossip over the handsome visitor, so I asked the princesse to entertain us on the harp, and suggested that perhaps she might require Gabrielle to turn the pages of her music, smiling to myself that it would keep my two *chères amies* better occupied.

At length the refreshments arrived and I sipped my Ville d’Avray water, observing to the count how remarkable it was that all the fatigue I had felt at the palace and the oppressiveness of the heat had completely melted away now that I was at Trianon. “It must be the company,” I said gaily, “for here, I never have to put on a performance. Unless of course I desire to do so. I must show you the little theater I had built on the grounds. Had I known you had turned actor I would have ordered your return and insisted that you play all the leading parts, for I am sure you would be far better at them than either of the king’s brothers. And much more pleasing company.”

Fersen’s cheeks colored slightly. “I am no courtier, *Votre Majesté;* I am a soldier. I would follow in my father’s footsteps, if

I were fortunate enough to advance that far. He was a great Field Marshal in the Swedish army and now he is a statesman, a senator in our Riksdag. But," the count sighed, as he gazed about the room—taking in the cherry silk draperies and white boiserie—so clearly a woman's sphere, "fortunately for the populace, but not for a warrior, there is not much for a Swedish soldier to do."

"So why did you return?"

"Ah, that!" Axel slapped his knees with mock theatricality. "We never got the chance to speak much during your *cercles*—"

"There were always so many people I had to greet; I am so sorry. You are one of the people I have always regretted not getting to know better. And then you returned to your homeland around the same time I became queen. But we can remedy all that, beginning this afternoon. Tell me the story now." I lifted my legs onto the divan and settled into a reclining position. "I want to hear everything," I murmured, closing my eyes.

"*Mon Dieu,* that's quite a lot," Fersen chuckled. "Where to begin?" I found his accent musical and charming; it almost didn't matter to me what he said. And I liked the sound of his voice; so different from Louis's high nasal timbre. "By the time I met you at the Opéra ball that Saturday night in January, 1774—it was the thirtieth, and I will remember it for all my days, for how can an impressionable young man forget the night he meets, and almost dances with, the enchanting dauphine of France?"

I opened my eyes and peeked at him. He was blushing, and surely, I thought, so was I, for the room had somehow grown warmer.

"Shall I continue, *Majesté*?" he asked, catching me watching him.

"*Oui, s'il vous plaît.* It soothes me," I said, leaning back against the trio of blue satin cushions.

"Well, then, by the time we met, I had drunk my fill of the

usual education prescribed for a young man of the Enlightenment: a visit to Florence, Rome, and Pompeii and then on to Greece, observing in person all the great classical art and antiquities; an introduction to the heads of state of every minor duchy along the way; the obligatory call on Monsieur Voltaire in Switzerland—the poor old sage must be sick to death of young pups from every nationality popping in to venerate him as though he is Michelangelo's Moses; and of course a tour of Paris, ending with an introduction, through the envoy to the King of Sweden, to the glittering court of Versailles."

The count's wry humor amused me. It was not so much what he said, but the manner in which he said it: as if, perfectly aware that he was rather a serious type of man, he could gently mock that in himself. "And then, my father wrote to tell me, 'Come home, young man, and find a wife.'"

My eyes flew open and I sat up as casually as I could manage. "And did you?" The room suddenly became silent, the princesse having reached the end of her sonata. "That was a lovely composition, Marie Thérèse. Let's have another—but something more lively this time; the other was putting me to sleep. And *molto fortissismo.*" Outstretching my arm toward our guest, I said languidly, "Come take the chair beside me, Count von Fersen. That way we will not have to shout across the room above the music."

Butterflies danced in my chest as he seated himself and I waited for his reply. "Not for want of trying," I heard him say. He gazed down at his primly clasped hands. "After a few years of numerous fits and starts in Sweden, I met an heiress whose family had made their fortune in England . . . a Mademoiselle Leyell. Despite the fact that her origins were in the so-called merchant class, her father being a director of the Compagnie des Indes, *my* father was willing to overlook her inferior social standing because of her wealth. In April I sailed to London and began to court her in earnest."

I swallowed hard. "And . . . should I tender you my felicitations, monsieur le comte?" I breathed.

Axel glanced away, not daring to meet my inquisitive gaze. "She wouldn't have me. I did everything in my power to please my father and win the girl's consent, but she told me she did not wish to leave her parents." He sighed like a defeated man. "I suppose that a life of parties and balls in the vibrant city of London and all the pin money one could desire was preferable to innumerable Swedish winters with a husband of limited means.

"And so, although I admit that I was brokenhearted, I became determined to follow my initial aim: that of becoming a soldier. But since Sweden is not at war with anyone at the moment, I had to become a mercenary. Here, I had three choices: the American War of Independence continues to rage on; within the past few weeks war has broken out between France and England over France's alliance with the United States; and Austria and Prussia are in conflict over Bavaria. And because I wish to make a career for myself, and because Frederick of Prussia's armies are the best trained in Europe, I am on my way to offer him my services. It was a simple enough matter to secure an introduction, as his sister is the Queen of Sweden, and the king thinks highly of me." He patted the breast of his snugly fitting tunic, where the letter of recommendation lay.

"Oh, *non*!" I gasped, reaching to clasp his hand. "You mustn't! You cannot!" Suddenly I needed air. I rose unsteadily to my feet, my head swimming with images of this man I knew so little yet admired so much, galloping at full tilt on a coal-black steed toward Schönbrunn, bearing down on my beloved family with his cavalry saber held aloft. *"Excusez-moi!"*

I exited the music room with a rustle of taffeta and made for the entrance to the villa, in need of a gulp of fresh air. The count was not three paces behind me, following me into the sunlight.

"I apologize for my rudeness, monsieur le comte," I said breathlessly, "but I—"

"You need not enlighten me as to your distress, *Majesté,*" he replied kindly. He offered his arm, and we began to stroll along the winding lanes. A light breeze riffled the furbelows in my skirts and the ruffle of my linen cap. "No sooner had I spoken the words than I saw the anguish written upon your face. How uncivil, how callous of me to have so enthusiastically mentioned the Hapsburgs' greatest enemy, to tell *you,* of all people in the world, of my intention to fight for him against your mother and brother!" He clapped his forehead with the palm of his hand. "I am an utter fool, Your Majesty. If you chose to dismiss me from your sight at this very moment and never spoke to me again, I should fully comprehend the reason."

I placed my gloved hand on his arm and we halted our progress. Behind us, Gabrielle and Marie Thérèse, having followed us outdoors, stopped as well, several paces behind us. "As I have already expressed the regret that I did not come to know you better when I was dauphine, I should be disconsolate to lose you again so soon after your return," I murmured. A plan began to formulate in my mind. "What if I helped to secure you a posting with a French regiment instead? I hear there are a number of opportunities for a man to distinguish himself." In truth I had not, but I was certain they existed. Otherwise, why would such a large number of French noblemen have taken commissions and sailed for North America? "But for the time being, you would still be able to come to court often and attend my balls and *levers* and I will assure you of an open invitation to le Petit Trianon."

We had arrived at the colonnaded Temple of Love. Sinking onto one of the curved marble benches, I admitted, "I am a bit fatigued from all this walking."

"Can I send your attendants for some water?" he asked solicitously.

"They should be carrying some Ville d'Avray and a couple of goblets in a basket," I replied. "Nowadays whenever I go out for any length of time, someone must always follow me with plenty of water."

We gazed for several moments at the countryside. The gentle breeze weaving in and out of the columns felt pleasant on my warm, flushed cheeks. "What else can I say to induce you to stay in France?" I asked softly. The count's profile, silhouetted as it was, looked so fine and noble and he had such perfect carriage. If this had been the man I met in the forest of Compiègne on the fourteenth of May in 1770 and someone had introduced him as the dauphin of France I would have easily believed him a prince.

"What if I promised to dance with you at my balls, although I do very little of it these days? I tire too easily, yet I do not forget that as dauphine I disappointed you. But I was frightened then," I admitted.

Axel turned to look at me. "Of what?" he asked quietly.

"Many things. But of myself mostly. And of you, too, *peut-être*."

"And you are not afraid now to dance with me?"

"No," I lied. My ancient *tendre* for the duc de Lauzun seemed a child's game to this; yet this was nothing, not even a flirtation. A simple conversation with the Swedish count had put me out of sorts. Or perhaps it was the ease with which we seemed able to confide in each other that stirred something in me, a body already so sensitive to the slightest emotion, so susceptible that laughter and tears might come one after the other in rapid succession, or at the same time in a flurry of mirthful hysteria. Finally I gathered the courage to say the words I had longed to voice for the past hour. "Did you love Mademoiselle Leyell?"

The count gazed into the middle distance where a flock of wild geese had just landed on the grass. "It would have been a good match," he replied. "She had a lively temperament that suited me well. Soft, fair hair. Large blue eyes. And I had been persuaded that she was not indifferent to me." He sighed heavily and raked a hand through his lightly powdered umber hued hair. "I think perhaps she reminded me of someone I'd once met. And so I believed I was in love with her. A young man's heart, even that of a sober Swede, is often given to flights of fancy. And the memory plays tricks on him. A chance encounter late one evening in a crowded, overheated ballroom, the scent of her perfume that lingers long after she has gone. The melody of her voice that never leaves your ears. The cadence of her walk. The tilt of her head. The changeability of her smile. And perhaps when my father saw her bankbook, I thought I saw all those qualities in Mademoiselle Leyell. Clearly, however, the young lady found me lacking."

My ladies must have decided that I had spent enough time alone with the count, for they began to approach the temple with the wicker basket.

Yet Axel had more to say to me. "Nevertheless, however brief an initial encounter may be, I do believe in the *coup de foudre* as the French say, in that 'thunderclap' of becoming love-struck right then and there. I wonder," he added, turning slowly to face me, "whether it is possible for one to ever forget one's first love. That is, if one is wise enough—or fool enough—to recognize that one has indeed fallen in love."

Ever so gently he reached out with his gloved hand and blotted a falling tear that had mutinously escaped my eyes, bringing his finger to his lips. "My secret," he whispered. And turning to face my attendants, he said, "*Ah, bon, Majesté!* Your water has arrived."

SIXTEEN

Motherhood

DECEMBER 1778

Early in the evening on the eighteenth of December I awoke from a nap thinking I had been dreaming of swimming in a lake with my sister Charlotte. My nightgown was soaked through and my thighs were covered in fluid. I shouted for help, thinking something was terribly wrong, afraid I was losing my baby.

The maid who slept in a cot near the foot of my bed rang for the doctors and Monsieur Vermond. Poor thing, she was barely older than a child herself and didn't know what to do either, terrified of touching me, or any of the linens, and making a mortal error.

Several minutes later, the bespectacled *accoucheur* arrived with his box of instruments, his supper interrupted. After briefly examining me by placing his cold fingers on my thighs and blotting the liquid away with a clean, moist cloth, he informed me that it was perfectly normal for my bag of waters to break shortly before the pains of labor commenced.

A few days earlier, *estafettes,* mounted couriers, had been dispatched to the Parisian town homes and country estates of any nobles who were not currently residing at Versailles to inform them of the impending arrival of a child of France, for more than a century of court etiquette granted the highest-ranking members of the aristocracy the right to be present in the queen's bedchamber during the birth.

As an army of maids and footmen bustled about, arranging the rose and cream upholstered tabourets for the duchesses in front of the gilded railing about my bed and setting up rows of chairs for the other nobles as though a play was about to begin, the physician took my pulse and felt my brow to ascertain whether I had a fever. Monsieur Vermond requested me to mind the golden clock on the mantel and mark the amount of time elapsing between the contractions.

This was a simple enough request to comply with, and soon the pains began, mild seizures at first, perhaps a half hour or so apart. But the contractions continued throughout the night as they came closer and closer together and the chamber grew more crowded. There they were—Mesdames Adélaïde, Victoire, and Sophie, Louis's maiden aunts; Monsieur and Madame, and the comte and comtesse d'Artois; the duc and duchesse de Chartres and the duc d'Orléans; the other Princes of the Blood, Louis XV's cousins the prince de Condé and the prince de Conti; Marie Thérèse de Lamballe (one of the only faces I would have desired to see) along with Gabrielle de Polignac. The highest nobles made themselves comfortable on armchairs close to my bed. But where was Louis? My bed curtains remained parted, so they could see me, rivulets of perspiration and tears coursing down my face, as I stifled every urge to cry out, despite the terrifying, and sometimes horrifically intense, waves of pain. I could just imagine the admonishment I might have received from my former *dame d'honneur,* the comtesse de Noailles: "It is not comme il faut for the queen to scream like an animal during childbirth."

My hands and feet felt cold, and yet the room was suffocatingly hot from the crush of witnesses. "*S'il vous plaît, ouvrez les fenêtres*—please, someone open the windows," I begged.

"*Je regrette,* but that is impossible, *Majesté.* The wintry night air could bring on a chill and we cannot put your health and that of the *enfant* at risk."

The windows remained closed. And the pains of labor continued through the night. Dawn broke across the frosty parterres. My stomach lurched from the commingled aromas of fifty unique blends of perfume. My head ached from their myriad conversations; I overheard complaints that I was taking too long to deliver my child. The clock chimed the hour of nine. And then the contractions began to grow further apart. The room grew briefly silent as the *accoucheur* examined me, my modesty shielded only by a tented sheet, and told me that the second stage of my labor had come to an end. Soon the contractions should resume and it would be time to push the infant into the world.

By the time the clock struck ten, I felt the baby's head moving inside me. Monsieur Vermond urged me to begin to push. Those who had been compelled to stand at the back of the room for want of chairs, pressed forward. Some of the assembly climbed atop the seats of their chairs and clambered onto the furniture, hoping for a better view. But by then my body was spent; after so many hours enduring the pains of labor with not so much as a sound, I felt as though I could not continue.

I sat against the bolsters with my knees raised. Push, the *accoucheur* urged me. Suddenly, I broke wind, mortified to have done such an undignified thing in the presence of France's highest nobility. Push! I tried with all my might. He gave me lemon water to sip, and applied cool compresses to my brow, but the bedchamber only grew warmer and more stifling. The clock chimed eleven and a few minutes later Monsieur Vermond announced to the notable assembly that the baby's head was crowning. The crowd moved closer, pressing against the railings around the bed. The *accoucheur* directed me to push harder than ever, but the embroidered roses on the bed hangings began to blur and the crystal chandelier above my head seemed to be falling on me. There were too many people. I wanted to make them all go away. I became nauseous and wished to vomit.

But I had been sent to the Bourbon court at the age of fourteen with the single goal of producing an heir. Finally, at the age of twenty-three, it was happening. Pushing with my last bit of strength as the infant emerged I saw the king's face, his pale eyes wide with concern, his hand clutching a handkerchief to his mouth. The room was so oppressive and the noisy, excited crush of people so close that I couldn't breathe. I heard someone gasp, then a cry went up from the crowd, followed by the unmistakable mewl of an infant. I extended my arm toward Louis, but I never reached him. Instead, I seemed to be receding as everything went dark.

"Air, warm water!" cried Monsieur Vermond. "The blood is going to the queen's head. She must be bled immediately." Several women began to weep.

Louis pressed through the crowd of witnesses. By God, nothing was going to happen to Antoinette. She would not, could not die. Finally, after briskly elbowing Monsieur in the ribs, he reached one of the tall windows of the bedchamber. It had been sealed from top to sash with lengths of gummed paper to prevent the cool air from seeping into the room. Breathlessly, he began to tear at the paper; but finding that he was unable to reach the top of the window, he unseated the duchesse de Chartres, the most obliging of her ilk, from her tabouret, and climbed upon the stool, hoping against hope that it would support his considerable weight. Having stripped off all the paper, he stepped down from the tabouret and with all his might threw open the window, then repeated his efforts with the remaining casements in the room while the nobles looked on amazed and somewhat shocked at the quick thinking, not to mention the strength, of the sovereign they had considered so lethargic.

Louis read the look in their eyes. They hadn't believed in him. Had they not seen him with the masons carting paving stones about the grounds of the château? In any case, what man wouldn't tear the world apart to keep his wife alive?

And his child? What of his child? Daughter—or dauphin? No one had mentioned a word in the flurry to save the queen. The *premier chirugien* was making incisions in the soles of her feet, bleeding her into a white porcelain basin. Louis watched the surgeon at work; briefly glancing at the ceiling, he mumbled a barely coherent orison, praying that the man's hands were clean.

Finally, after what seemed like an agonizing amount of time, Antoinette opened her eyes. The king emitted a hoarse cry of relief and started to go to her, but the *accoucheur* prevented him from approaching the bed.

"She needs air, Sire," he said insistently. "Or she might have a relapse." Did Monsieur Vermond, sweating with palpable relief, not realize that she never would have awakened, had not the king of France himself opened the windows? Antoinette's eyes had closed again. Her face drained of color but for the palest spots of natural pink upon her cheeks, she had drifted into an exhausted slumber.

"My . . . son?" he inquired, then, looking at the infant already gently wrapped within the wet nurse's sturdy arms, for he knew the queen would not tolerate any swaddling.

Monsieur Vermond turned to face the chattering press of aristocrats. He waved his arms and called for silence and they realized the moment had come. Had the queen of France given the Bourbons an heir?

"*Mesdames et messieurs, silence, je vous prie.* Her Majesty, Marie Antoinette has borne a daughter of France."

The bedchamber grew still. And then, the nobles' universal dissatisfaction manifested itself in a collective groan. Awakened by the sound, the queen opened her eyes to the sight of their displeasure.

The *accoucheur* was swiftly at her bedside, taking the newborn from the wet nurse to show to her mother. "It is a girl, *Majesté,*" he said soberly, unable to conceal his own disappointment now that he would receive only ten thousand livres for his services. The queen gasped. No one quite knew how to interpret the sound.

"We must name her," I heard Louis say to me. My ears filled with noise. And disillusioned murmurs. Tart comments from the nobility, even in the presence of my childbed. "Marie Thérèse Charlotte," I murmured without a moment's hesitation. After Maman and my beloved favorite sister. Surely the king would not challenge the selection, for I had not borne a dauphin; only a daughter. Useless to the Bourbons. So what would it matter that she was given my family names? She would be formally styled as Madame Royale, regardless. But even as I honored my mother by bestowing her name upon my long-awaited firstborn child, I knew in my heart that the intended compliment would nonetheless be received in Vienna as a disappointment. The Franco-Austrian alliance would not be permanently strengthened by a child named after the Hapsburg empress. Better I had borne a boy. All the churchbells and cannons and celebratory bonfires could not change that.

"You were not wanted, but you will be none the less dear to me," I cooed to my infant daughter, once I was able to cradle her in my arms. "You will belong solely to me and you will always be under my care to share in my joys and lighten my sorrows."

Relieved that I had survived the ordeal after losing consciousness for three-quarters of an hour, Louis was much more philosophical. He had bet me that our firstborn would be a son and managed to mask his disappointment in losing the wager with a loving and romantic compliment. Taking my hand in his and quoting Metastasio, his favorite poet, he assured me, "I have lost. My august daughter/Condemns me to pay. But should she vastly resemble you,/The whole world has won." I kissed his knuckles, bathing them with my tears.

As I was still recovering from the difficult childbirth I was unable to attend my daughter's immediate baptism. But I heard what took place, an insult that was deeply, and publicly, wounding to both Louis and me. Although Monsieur, as our daughter's godfather, was the host, he nonetheless protested that the "name and quality" of the infant's parents had not been formally given; then feigned innocence at the courtiers' shocked looks, insisting that he was only observing the correct protocol for establishing the princesse's lineage.

Seven weeks later, when I journeyed beyond the confines of my apartments for the first time, traveling to the cathedral of Notre-Dame de Paris to be churched, and receiving the customary blessing of thanksgiving for having survived the ordeal of childbirth, I was dismayed by the frosty welcome from all but the one hundred couples whose weddings, new raiment, and dowries the king and I chose to endow as part of our thanksgiving.

My subjects' cheers were faint and halfhearted. Had they already forgotten the free bread and sausages we had distributed among the populace after our daughter's birth? The wine that flowed from the public drinking fountains as copiously as water?

The free entry into the Comédie-Française, where the king's box was reserved for coachmen and mine for the *poissardes*?

Yet I would not let the worshippers see my tears and held my head proudly—disdainfully, my detractors might have said, mocking my naturally protruding lower lip. "What have I done to these good people?" I later inquired of the comte de Mercy, when we were sitting together in one of my private salons. "And Madame Royale, what has *she* done to deserve their harsh looks, and their disapproval? She is an innocent."

The Austrian ambassador looked as though he were debating with himself whether to be diplomatic or to take advantage of our long-standing acquaintance to be as direct as Maman would have been.

"Look about you," he began. "At this salon. When you became queen you were unhappy with the décor, and so you went to great expense to have the walls covered in blue and white Lyon silk in a design of your own devising."

"Butterflies and flowers," I murmured, nodding in agreement, recalling an incident from my childhood. It had occurred on the very day I learned I was to wed Louis.

"But what happened?" Mercy inquired, knowing the answer full well.

"After a few months' time I grew displeased with the renovation," I admitted, a bit shamefaced. "The color did not look as I had expected it would in candlelight."

"And what did you do?"

I hated it when Mercy and the abbé Vermond would catechize me. They were so fond of this method, of drawing me out and leading me to provide the answers myself. At the age of twenty-three I would have thought this nonsense was over. But I humored the old fox all the same. "I had the blue silk ripped off the walls and replaced with the white *gros de Tours*." I gestured toward the brocaded wall covering embroidered with floral bouquets, ribbons, and peacock feathers.

Mercy sighed. "That is an example of the extravagant expense, the wastefulness that your subjects ascribe to your behavior. They see you as a heedless spendthrift during a time of economic woe for most of the kingdom."

"But that's not true," I insisted. "The blue silk now hangs on the walls at Fontainebleau!"

Mercy perched forward, resting his elbows on his knees. "How much have you spent on your wardrobe?"

"But the queen must set the tone," I argued. It was as true at my ascension as it remained now.

"That may be, and I do not disagree, but it is also roundly perceived that Mademoiselle Bertin, your 'Minister of Petticoats,' as they call her, is your confederate in this profligacy and that you are behaving like a *maîtresse en titre* and not like a queen, concerned more for your own personal beauty than for the welfare of your people. For if the latter were true, you would not be well into debt for purchases of clothing and jewels and fripperies, having to go to the king for additional funds, when your subjects have more need of it than you do."

Nothing could have been more hurtful than comparing me to a du Barry or a Pompadour. I blinked back tears.

Mercy looked grim, but unapologetic. "You wanted to know why the Parisians did not cheer for you as they did five years ago when you were dauphine and had your first taste of the capital." He rose to his feet. "You have much else to occupy you now," he said, referring to the cradle on the floor. It was true; my chief delight lay in visits from my tiny daughter and her nurse. "As do they. The people hear that the treasury is empty; they are angry that the king is fighting foreign wars on two fronts to advance the cause of liberty for men and women an ocean away, while they go hungry and and enjoy no such freedoms of their own. The world has changed since 1773, *Majesté.* A new day is dawning—one in which your 'butterflies and flowers' may not live through the night." He made a shallow bow and quit the room.

SEVENTEEN

Sick and Sick at Heart

Early Winter 1779

I took the comte de Mercy's remarks to heart and resolved to devote myself to motherhood from now on. But I saw little of Madame Royale, as she remained in the care of her wet nurse. After waiting for her for so many years and carrying her within me for nine months, I felt strangely bereft without her. Although they did not entirely assuage the unusual loneliness of being separated from my daughter for most of the day, I found solace in the companionship of my Trianon coterie.

Count von Fersen quickly became a treasured member of my intimate circle, and although he was often among the favored guests at le Petit Trianon, there he managed to recede into the draperies and boiseries, his melancholic Nordic temperament, as he freely admitted, not easily conducive to the sort of giddy romps we enjoyed. But I discovered very soon that, like many men of our day, a sentimental heart pulsed beneath the count's blue cavalry officer's tunic.

One evening, I sat down at my spinet and performed one of Dido's arias from Piccini's *Didon,* where she sings to Aeneas, "*Ah, que je fus bien inspirée quand je vous reçus dans ma cour*—Ah, I was greatly inspired when I received you at my court." My eyes met Axel's and we both knew I was singing only to him. Neither of us could ever hear *Didon* again without remembering that moment.

In my box at the Paris Opéra house adjacent to the Palais Royal, Axel would sit beside me, deepening his appreciation for the music that stirred me so. And in the tragic heroes and heroines of the Opéra, and in the star-crossed lovers of the charming pastoral comedies I so adored and often re-created in my theater at Trianon with my own little troupe of aristocratic actors, I saw my love blossoming for the Swedish count. From their chairs behind us, the ladies who usually accompanied me, Lamballe, Polignac, and Guéméné, could not observe the glances that passed between the count and me, the desire in our eyes no longer concealed, and the sorrow that our secret *tendre* could never be publicly declared. After the performances Count von Fersen and I would often attend the Saturday night balls and masquerades, revisiting the scene of our first encounter. We danced, we gazed, we sighed, but to kiss would have transgressed everything I held holy, a step closer to violating my marriage vows, despite my growing passion for him. We never even touched—beyond the acceptable boundaries of polite society: Axel handing me into my *carosse de gala,* or taking my hand for a minuet. But palm to palm, despite our gloves, the kidskin that covered my flesh offered no protection from the frisson of what the American diplomatic envoy Mr. Franklin had described as an electric current, a palpable, tangible sensation as sudden and shocking as summer lightning.

Spring 1779

The spots began on my *poitrine* and soon spread down my arms and up my neck, spattering my face. I knew it could not be smallpox because I had been inoculated against it after suffering a mild form of the disease as a little girl. When my doctor diagnosed a case of measles, I decided to remove myself to le Petit Trianon for the entire course of my recovery. I had never before spent the night in my modest bedchamber there, no matter how late I stayed. But I thought it was best to absent myself from the court, and especially from the king, for Louis had never had the measles and I dared not risk his health.

I wrote to Maman of my decision, but there was more I left unsaid. Although I informed her of my plan to protect my husband from contagion, I deliberately omitted to mention that we had not been intimate since before the birth of Madame Royale. I had nearly expired in my bed of state pushing tiny Marie Thérèse de France into the world and although I owed it to the alliance to bear a dauphin, I could not bear the thought of becoming *enceinte* again and once more enduring the frightening ordeal of childbirth. Louis had been amenable to visiting my bed, but I had found a hundred reasons to discourage him.

I also neglected to tell my mother that in order to keep my spirits up during my convalescence, in addition to the princesse de Lamballe, the princesse de Guéméné, and the comtesse de Polignac, I had invited a quartet of my most amusing confidants, the corpulent duc de Guines, the silvery baron de Besenval, the ebullient young Count Esterházy, and the square-jawed duc de Coigny to be my companions at Trianon. The gentlemen arrived at seven in the morning and departed as late as possible, while my ladies remained with me through the night, to see to my needs.

On the twelfth day of my self-imposed confinement at le Petit Trianon, I received a message from one of my footmen while I was practicing the clavichord. "The king is outside the gates, *Majesté,* and would like to speak with you."

A fond smile escaped my lips. "Ask him to step into the courtyard. I will speak to him from an upstairs window."

Alone, I climbed the staircase and opened the casement, wondering what Louis would think when he saw me with my hair loose and unpowdered, hanging down about my shoulders, dressed *en négligée* in a loose gauzy gown with a peach satin ribbon tied beneath my breasts. They had grown fuller when I became pregnant and had not lost their ripeness. My face was barren of all cosmetics. Monsieur Lassone had forbidden them until every last sign of the measles had healed.

Louis stood below on the gravel in a suit of olive ratteen. With one hand he shielded his eyes from the sun; the other was behind his back. "I brought you something," he said sheepishly, and revealed the bouquet of pink roses he had been concealing. "I thought they would cheer you, but I don't know how to get them to you." He glanced about. "I suppose I could give them to one of your liveries."

"Too boring!" I exclaimed. "Here—toss them to me!" I leaned forward and reached my arms out the window.

"You are mad—you'll fall out!" Louis cried.

"It's not terribly far," I teased. But when I saw him blanch I added, "Don't be silly, if I can't catch them, the worst that could happen is that they will fall back to the ground." Of course, then I would have felt miserable for damaging the lovely blooms he had made the effort to gather.

It took three tries, which made their arrival in my hands all the sweeter.

"I've missed you," Louis said simply. "You are good company. And the only one at court I can truly trust."

I could not clearly see his face from where I stood at the window, but I think his eyes were moist. "I've missed you as well," I admitted. "I hope you have not been jealous. The men I asked to entertain me here; they are like the court jesters of old. Ask Artois; he has come down here, too. You know he cannot keep away when he hears there is a party. Nevertheless, it's not what I've heard people are saying. Lovers? Orgies? I would hope you know your Toinette better than that," I assured Louis as gently as possible, given the distance from my window to the courtyard.

The king stepped closer. *"Attends!"* he said, holding up his hand. "I almost forgot." I followed his rolling gait as he ambled back to his carriage as briskly as his size would allow, returning with a wicker basket. "You left your *parfums* from Fargeon—the scents he created to help you sleep when you were *enceinte.* Tell me which ones you would like." He opened the basket and held the bottles aloft, squinting as he read the labels to me. "*Eau de la Reine de Hongrie, eau de Melisse*—oh, this one has lemon, cinnamon, cloves, and angelica—*eau d'ange,* and the *eau fraîcheur* and *eau rafraîchissante* for your skin."

I was completely charmed by Louis's earnestness and his desire to please me. He stood in the sun for fully forty-five minutes conversing with me while I leaned out the window. Yes, I had missed him greatly while I was ill; he was the companion of my life whom God, Maman, and Louis XV had given me, and in the manner of two people who are mated by circumstance and must swim together amid a sea of troubles, I loved him—which only made me feel all the more guilty, desperately so, that I did not *desire* him.

"Tell me, why do you never play blindman's buff with the rest of us?" I asked Count von Fersen petulantly. "You remain so aloof from all our games, I worry that you are not enjoying yourself. *Dîtes-moi,* do you regret that you remained in France after all? Because I am not a bit sorry I dissuaded you from offering your talents to Frederick of Prussia, regardless of his relation to your queen."

We were seated on the grass at Trianon, overlooking one of the romantic grottoes. I slid my feet out of my court heels and wiggled my pink-stockinged feet in the cool damp carpet of green.

Axel hugged his knees to his chest. "I am protecting you, *Votre Majesté.* And the king. Louis is a good man, and too much maligned by his own courtiers. I am not even *un Français* and for the sake of his honor I am insulted by some of the things I hear."

I rested my hand lightly on his sleeve and just as quickly withdrew it, ashamed of my own behavior. " *'Votre Majesté'* is too formal. And your generous words about my husband were, I believe, spoken from your heart and not calculated to please me. Will you call me Toinette from now on?" The count gave me a faint smile, accompanied by a little exhalation from his nose—a close-mouthed chuckle. "I was protecting you, too," I murmured, "by not inviting you to nurse me when I had the measles. Not because I didn't wish you to catch it, which of course is true, but because I didn't want people to talk about *you.*" I wanted to rest my head against Axel's shoulder, yet dared not. Despite the idle rumors, the games I played at Trianon were giddy children's romps of the sort I had enjoyed in Vienna, not the variety that courtiers at the palace routinely indulged in—amorous dalliances with other people's spouses and lovers. I was not made for such sport. In the sight of God I had taken vows that I most fervently believed in.

A skylark winged overhead, silhouetted against a soft white

cloud. And in that moment, on the most perfect spring day in memory, I finally understood what Maman had tried to instill in me all those years ago when she prepared me to become a bride, extracting my promise to maintain my good German morals and avoid the enticing vices of the French court.

And yet I loved the way Count von Fersen's skin smelled of Castille soap and the scent of pomade he used to powder his hair. I couldn't seem to drink my fill of the angles of his jaw, the planes of his cheeks, the way his eyes never seemed to be quite the same color. And I could not look at him without feeling tormented by the fact that we could never be together, even in the manner of other aristocratic couples in France who made their tacit arrangements with their respective spouses; and by the knowledge that were we to dispense with caution I would not only be insulting God and be no better than the du Barrys of the world, the women I held in such contempt, I would also be deeply wounding a man who had been nothing but generous to me during our marriage, even if the union had not been of our making. Nonetheless, I would willingly do or give whatever it took to make Count von Fersen happy, except the one thing that we both knew would spell our ruin.

EIGHTEEN

Good-byes

1780

January 1, 1780

Madame my dear daughter,

I cannot begin the year better than to send you my loving compliments and wishes—first for a dauphin, and within the year! Générale Krottendorf has just died; I hope "she" soon will stop visiting you.

But you mustn't indulge in any more journeys in an unheated carriage. No wonder you caught a cold. Could you not have skipped one Opéra ball for the sake of your health? Lassone was right to give you iron; it did wonders for your sister Charlotte, and being bled cannot hurt either. I could always count on becoming pregnant when I had myself bled.

You made no reply when I told you that the papers reported the king intends to give your comtesse de Polignac 800,000 livres for her twelve-year-old daughter as a dowry, in addition to a two-million-livre estate and the promise to discharge the comtesse's debts. I must warn you of the sensation this is causing among the public, especially when the court's expenses are being drastically (and so necessarily) reduced.

I cannot remain silent when I hear such rumors. If I do not warn you about this damage to your character, who else would dare to do so?

As to your current war with Britain, regretfully for France, the Austrian public, as well as our nobility, are very much in favor of the English; that is as much of an old prejudice as being anti-Austrian is for the French. I can at least assure you that my ministers and I do not share the anglophilia and wholeheartedly support you, but I cannot answer for your brother. However, as long as the behavior of your ministers does not always run contrary to Joseph's interests, I will endeavor to guarantee at least his neutrality on the matter. I am not at all pleased with what I have read about the current situation in America, or that of the French fleet; the English fanaticism is tremendous and their resources equally immense. As a partisan of France and mother of her dear queen, I only wish for peace. At least the Treaty of Teschen put that messy Bavarian business behind us.

Your maman kisses you lovingly,
my more than dear daughter,
Maria Theresa

March

"Madame Royale is quite tall for a two-year-old, is she not?" I inquired of the princesse de Guéméné, now governess of my little daughter of France. "In that I think she favors her father."

"I think, *peut-être,* it is because she has never had even a moment's fever," the princesse remarked. "Imagine," she sighed, "soon she will be weaned. Where has the time gone?"

It always filled my spirit to visit my daughter's nursery, such a charming little chamber, its paneled walls embellished with baskets of pink roses that I had painted myself. Of course Marie Thérèse could walk already, although she did not speak much. She had taken to hiding behind the princesse's skirts and peeking her head out like a turtle daring to explore the world outside her shell. I did not see her as frequently as I would have liked, and I feared she was becoming too shy, fretting that if she were kept from me for too long, she might fail to remember who I was.

"I think she knows," said the princesse. She requested one of my attendants to speak to the tot. "Ask her to go to her mother."

I longed to get down on my knees and open my arms to her, but of course that would have constituted a rather large hint and would have made fruitless the entire point of the challenge.

Madame Royale quickly scanned the room, her avid gaze taking in the cluster of ladies in pastel gowns, like a tray of giant macarons. Then, launching herself forward on her sturdy little legs she toddled over to me, gaining momentum with every step, and threw her arms about my knee. I sank down and scooped her into my arms, smothering her with kisses.

"My sweet little Mousseline," I cooed into her fragrant curls. "One day, soon I hope, I will give you a little brother to play with."

She frowned at me. "Am I not enough, Maman?"

I held her even tighter, resting my cheek against the peach-soft skin of her brow because I could not look her in the eye. "*Oh, ma petite,* I wish it were so."

MAY

Some weeks earlier, the comte de Mercy and my dear abbé Vermond had finally persuaded me to resume marital relations with the king, not only for the good of our union but for that of the realm. Not many people apart from Louis knew my secret, but I could not conceal my joy from Count von Fersen. He had guessed it anyway, sensible to the slightest shifts in my mood. Not even Gabrielle de Polignac or the Lamballe was as *sympathique.* And neither of them had shadowed us on what would be our final afternoon together for many months.

"You are even more beautiful when you are increasing," Axel remarked, as we enjoyed our last stroll amid the gardens of le Petit Trianon before he prepared to sail for North America as a colonel in the Royal Deux-Ponts regiment. Eager to keep him in France, I had secured the brevet for him last year, although many Frenchmen were jealous of being commanded by a Swedish mercenary. The count's greatest dream was fulfilled when the Deux-Ponts received their orders to depart for the British colonies; and it would be dishonest to say that I was not secretly delighted by whatever had transpired during the interim to delay their departure until now. The additional months of his companionship had been a beautiful gift, but could never lessen the pain of parting. This afternoon I had resolved to show him only smiles, though I doubted I could keep my pledge.

Axel plucked a peony from a nearby bush. "This is what you look like: full and pink."

I laughed and placed my hands over the wide blue sash just above my belly. "Not full yet, I hope. Monsieur Lassone only just confirmed it."

"But you already look like a milkmaid," he teased, caressing my cheek with the subtly fragrant blossom as we made our way toward the Temple of Love.

I ostentatiously adjusted the puffs of my gauzy white sleeves. "You do not like my *gaulle*?" Before he could offer his reaction to my white muslin, for the comparatively unconstructed gown had raised numerous eyebrows and engendered a considerable amount of *médisance* from those who thought I had forgotten to get dressed and was disporting myself about Versailles in my chemise, I pressed on. "*Tant pis* if you do not, for I intend to wear them all the time from now on. I grew too hot during the summer months when I was *enceinte* with Mousseline."

Axel smiled, amused at my nickname for Madame Royale. "Muslin," he said, "like your new favorite fabric. Does His Majesty object?"

I smiled. "To the pet name or the dresses? In sober truth he has said not a word about either." Although now that we were discussing my husband, Louis had recently made an odd remark to me about Axel's imminent embarkation for North America—something akin to the count's wisdom in pulling his toast out of the fire before the flames could singe his hands. Clutching a folded sheet of paper, his expression most distracted, the king seemed to be searching my face for something; not finding it, he said nothing more about the matter.

I returned to the subject of my wardrobe. "I have never worn anything so comfortable, so light. I think a hundred simple frocks like this would weigh as much as a single *robe de cour*. Mademoiselle Bertin designed these *gaulles* after the gowns the Creole women wear in the Indies. I have always detested wearing stays and in this new fashion the underpinnings are far less confining; and perhaps even better for him," I said, gazing lovingly at my stomach, "when I *truly* begin to grow 'full and pink.'"

"I will miss seeing it," Axel said wistfully.

I brushed away a tear. "And I will miss you missing it," I replied, unable to conceal the catch in my throat.

He stopped and took my hands in his. "But you know it is for the best, Toinette. And I must make something of myself in the world. I am not without my own dreams and ambitions."

I nodded. Wishing he would kiss me, and in the same moment feeling miserably guilty for having such a thought, when I carried the king's child inside me. And yet who knew when Axel and I would see one another again. And what precisely did it mean to be a colonel? Would he remain inside a tent, warm and dry and safe, far from the carnage of battle, or—the alternative was too grim to contemplate, the denouement too horrifying to imagine. Even the journey across the Atlantic had its perils, not least of which were British men-o'-war, their cannon trained on any ship sailing under the flag of France.

I began to weep. "Will you promise to write to me?"

"Of course." Axel threaded the stem of the peony into a buttonhole of his tunic, and flicked away a bee hovering about my cap and the ruffles defining my neckline.

"Every day," I whispered.

He chuckled. "I am not certain I can promise you that."

I looked into his eyes expectantly. "But you will try." I could see my reflection in his pupils. Today his irises were teal blue.

He raised my hands and brushed his lips against them. "That is an order, *Majesté,* which I will be honored to execute."

"More," I murmured.

He drew me toward him and kissed me on the brow. His lips were soft and warm and I closed my eyes and inhaled all the scents that were Axel, desiring to imprint them upon my memory along with the recollection of how he looked at this moment, his brown hair tousled and unpowdered, the planes of his cheeks slightly burnished by the sun. "For now," he said, his voice low.

"And, may God have mercy on my soul, but imagining the first taste of your lips will be my lodestar through all the days of my absence. The prospect of returning to such a reward is enough to keep this man alive through every pitch and roll of a frigate, and every encounter with the enemies of France."

"Pretty words," I mumbled, my face wet with tears. "I don't believe I'll sleep through the night until I see you in these gardens again. Come back to me, Axel. Promise me you will come back, just as you are now."

A few days later he sailed for America. Neither of us could have imagined then how long he would be away.

SEPTEMBER

Preceded by a flourish of trumpets, on September 19, a shiny black coach emblazoned with strange cabalistic marks and Masonic insignias entered the gates of Strasbourg. Inside rode the dusky-hued, mysterious Count Cagliostro and his wife Serafina, a flaxen-blond sylph said to be a Roman noblewoman. Thus far, their tour of Western Europe had been a great success, with aristocratic ladies clamoring to invite the mystic to their salons. Not to be outdone, the prince de Rohan prepared to entertain the couple with unprecedented extravagance. The cardinal had become so infatuated with Count Cagliostro's reputation as both a Mesmeric healer and an extraordinary alchemist that he believed such a man could provide him with all he desired. He was deaf to the rumors that Cagliostro, who traveled in a blue fox greatcoat amid swirls of Oriental incense, and conducted séances swathed in a robe embroidered with ancient runes and symbols, was no more than a mountebank—hardly the self-proclaimed Egyptian who had lived for thousands of years and once mingled with the pharaohs, but a swarthy Italian named Balsamo, and his stunning wife no noblewoman at all, but the illiterate daughter of a blacksmith.

Although he was the highest cleric in France, the prince was fascinated by the mystical alternatives to Christianity that had captured the imaginations of the intelligentsia. Reports of Count Cagliostro's successes in healing the afflicted and his refusal to accept money from his patrons (which inclined them all the more to shower him with gifts and financial largesse) had rendered this magician of sorts that much more attractive in the cardinal's eyes. When he learned that the miracle worker had descended upon Strasbourg, the lure proved irresistible and he insisted that the count and countess become his personal guests—for as long as they desired—their every whim made manifest by the ambitious prince of the Church.

And so Cagliostro's japanned coach with its satin-lined interior clattered up to the Hôtel de Rohan in Saverne, where the count and countess were installed in a luxurious suite of rooms, and provided with a chamber under the eaves in which the exotic healer could practice his feats of alchemy. The cardinal-prince's affiliation with the celebrated Cagliostro increased his cachet among the nobility; several prominent members of the aristocracy, having heard that the mystic had journeyed to Strasbourg, came to the Hôtel de Rohan to be cured. Unfortunately, the prince's illustrious affiliation with the man of the moment failed to ignite the curiosity of the one person in France whom he desperately wished would take notice of him: the ultimate patroness—Her Majesty the Queen.

November

Ever since Monsieur Lassone had confirmed my deepest hopes I had taken Maman's advice to avoid carriage rides, excursions on horseback, and any other strenuous activities. But I could hardly deny myself a visit to the capital in celebration of my twenty-fifth birthday on November 2.

That night the Paris Opéra was presenting Monsieur Grétry's *Andromaque,* and any story set during a time of war held particular significance for me. Count von Fersen's safety was never far from my thoughts. He had written to assure me he was hale, and eating as well as could be expected. I took comfort in the knowledge that instead of living among the common infantrymen, he had become the aide-de-camp to the comte de Rochambeau. As his second, Axel usually dined with the general, who was not one to stint on his gustatory habits.

The night had been mild, the air brisk and bracing, but we were overtaken by a sudden storm on our return journey. The temperature of the air dropped precipitously, and the skies opened, releasing a torrent of rain that landed on my gala coach in giant spatters and splashed our gowns through the open windows.

"*Mon Dieu,* the velvet will be utterly ruined!" I exclaimed, reaching for the window latch. Just then the wheels hit a rut and I bounced back against the seat.

"Allow me, *Majesté,*" offered the princesse de Lamballe, who was seated on the opposite banquette. She began to lean toward the window as I reminded her that I was scarcely an invalid and there was no more Madame Etiquette to reprimand me for doing something myself. As the carriage bounced along and we grew wetter and wetter, I made a second attempt to close the window, only to discover that it seemed to be stuck open.

"This will not do," I insisted, fumbling with the latch, then grasping the pane of glass with my gloved hand to try to release it. "At this rate we shall arrive at the château soaked to the skin, our coiffures long past repair, and have nasty colds to boot." Having decided that the consequences were intolerable, I wrenched the window toward me, tugging it with all my might, but I lost my grip on the wet pane of glass and slid partway across the seat.

"They say the third time is the charm," encouraged the duchesse de Polignac, shrinking away from the open window. Louis had recently elevated her husband to the rank of duc. Having immediately commissioned a new wardrobe, she was wearing one of the confections, a plum-colored moiré *robe à l'anglaise* with an embroidered floral underskirt, which set off her eyes beautifully; as the gown had cost her a small fortune, she was disinclined to come to my aid.

Bowing to her superstitious nature, and determined not to travel the remaining leagues to Versailles getting pelted by freezing rain, I made another effort to close the window. After all, as it was my *carosse de gala,* who would understand better than I how the mechanisms operated? But the window was well and truly stuck. Finally I threw my back into the effort and gave a mighty heave.

"Ach! Gott im Himmel!" I cried, doubling over. The windowpane snapped free and swung toward the interior of the coach.

"What is the matter?" inquired the Lamballe solicitously. "Did you hurt your hands? Come, let me see." She reached across the carriage and clasped my wrists.

I shook my head vehemently. The cramping in my belly had been immediate, sharp, and intense, like the most unpleasant visit from Générale Krottendorf I had ever experienced. By the time we arrived at Versailles a few hours later, the spasms had not abated, and I was desperate to avail myself of a commode.

When I hiked up my skirts and petticoats, I noticed a brownish discharge running down my legs and my thighs were streaked with blood. There were dark stains on the lower half of my chemise as well. I screamed for help and the princesse de Lamballe and my Mistress of the Robes came running. They helped me to my bedchamber and shut the doors against intruders, undressing me with great haste and a frightened expression in their eyes. By then the crimson stain on my petticoat had spread.

"Fetch Monsieur Lassone and the king," Marie Thérèse ordered the Mistress of the Robes, "but take care that you do not seem to alarm them, for Her Majesty will suffer all the more if her condition becomes the subject of idle speculation."

I was trying not to weep, but I knew that something was terribly amiss. Slipping through the door cleverly concealed in the paneling I tiptoed back to the commode, shoving my knuckles into my mouth to bite back the sharp onslaughts of pain.

Only when I stood again did I notice the clots of blood in the basin. Merciful God, this could not be happening to me! How many times had Maman warned me about the dangers of a miscarriage from overexerting myself?

Arriving first, Monsieur Lassone examined me, then inspected my ruined garments and the contents of the basin. To my deepest sorrow, the *premier médecin* confirmed my most harrowing fear. He prescribed at least two weeks of bedrest, although I could not even imagine facing the world again by then.

Difficult to rouse once he was already aslumber, Louis finally entered my bedchamber through the secret door shortly after the hour had struck half midnight. Monsieur Lassone shook his head gravely and showed him the contents of the bowl. *"C'est finis,"* he said sadly. "It's over."

The king sat beside me on the bed, taking my hands in his and pressing them to his cheek. I tilted my head and rested it on his shoulder and he shifted his position to enfold me in his arms.

"I am so sorry, Toinette," he murmured into my hair.

"*Moi, aussi. Je suis tellement désolée.* Louis, I am so sorry." I moaned. "I feel so empty inside." I pressed my hands against his chest and looked into hs eyes, watching the silent tears meander down his face. "What if it had been a dauphin?" As I rested in his arms my thoughts were pulled in a thousand directions. "What if God is punishing us?" I said in a small voice.

"For what?" Louis asked, dismissing the notion with his inflection. "Have you something to be so ashamed of that He would take our child?"

I met his gaze. "Yes," I whispered, momentarily thinking of Axel. Yet my secret passion for him had not been consummated; our lips had never even touched. Our mutual desire had been a pleasant dream and my thoughts of him now revolved around his safety. I had certainly cared as much about the infant I carried inside me, the son I'd hoped to bear for France, Louis's long-desired heir. "Perhaps He was cross with me for denying you my bed for so long after Marie Thérèse was born. And He did this to teach me a lesson."

"Why would He take the life of an innocent?"

"He does so all the time." I wound my arms around Louis's neck and pressed my lips to his cheek. "I have learned the lesson nonetheless," I added tearfully. "And I pledge to you with my entire heart that we will try again, as soon as we can, as soon as Monsieur Lassone tells us it is safe." I felt like a drowning woman, flailing for a passing shard of wood.

Twenty-five years from the day my mother had brought me into the world, I had lost a child of my own, perhaps through my own selfishness in insisting upon celebrating my natal day in Paris. In a few weeks we would resume relations, asking God's forgiveness and praying for His munificence: to let me conceive quickly and bring a heathy babe to term. But this night would remain forever imprinted on my memory and I would never cease to mourn my loss.

Yet before the month was over there would be more to grieve.

DECEMBER

Louis found me in my music room practicing the harp. From the moment he entered the salon I sensed something was terribly wrong. Rarely had I seen his expression so sorrowful. And he had never before interrupted my afternoon lesson. As he crossed the threshold my servants and attendants made their reverences and he dismissed them with a terse "Leave us, *s'il vous plaît.*"

Once the room was empty he walked over to me and proffered his hand, raising me to my feet. The knots inside my belly grew tighter with every step we took toward the sofa. The king seated me as gently as if he were nestling an egg into a bed of straw, and sat beside me, still holding my hands. "I know I have not always been kind when it comes to my opinions of the Empress of Austria," he began. "And I-I," he stammered, searching for words, meeting my questioning gaze. He shook his head dolefully. "I am not terribly good at this . . . and there is no worse role than the bearer of bad news, but it has just reached us from Vienna. The empress"—he broke off, realizing how ridiculously formal he was sounding at such a time.

"I am so sorry to tell you this, *ma chère,* but I thought I should be the one to break the news to you. Maria Theresa has . . ." and then with quiet simplicity he said the words that cracked my heart. "Your mother has died, Toinette."

At that moment, my world ceased to spin. I shivered, releasing a soul-shattering wail. My tears flowed copiously and my breath exploded in ragged gasps.

I knew Maman had felt ill for the past few weeks. I was aware, too, that she always worked herself to the point of exhaustion. But I had always thought her invincible, surviving smallpox and the births of sixteen children as she balanced the extraordinary pressures of governing a vast empire, fending off foreign enemies, and often crossing swords with my brother Joseph. She had never made my life easy, but she made it what it became. I was queen of the most glamorous and sophisticated court in Europe because of her indefatigable efforts to solidify an alliance with the French.

Louis reached over and stroked my hair, endeavoring to soothe me as he spoke. "The note we received from the emperor stated that she had caught a chill on the twenty-fourth of last month. She took to her bed with an inflammation of the lungs, but her physician Herr Stork feared that this time she would not be able to conquer the illness. Forty-eight hours before the end she gave her blessing to her absent children, reciting them by name in the order of their birth. Herr Stork writes that Her Imperial Majesty paused just before your name, and after a moment's silence, shouted with all her breath, 'Marie Antoinette, Queen of France!'"

A cry escaped my throat. My hand flew to my mouth.

Louis softly continued. "She requested that last rites be performed on November twenty-eighth and departed this world for a better one on the following evening at nine o'clock. Your brother was at her bedside; she expired in his arms."

Today was the sixth of December; it had taken fully a week for Joseph's letter to reach us. I clenched my fists and shut my eyes. Although she had often visited Papa's tomb in the Kaisergruft and looked forward to the day when they would be reunited, I did not wish to picture Maman cold and stiff and still. Instead, I searched my memory for reminiscences of our happiest times: the arrival of Louis XV's formal offer of his grandson's hand in marriage; the first visit of Générale Krottendorf after so long a wait. Maman's letters from Vienna had angered me as often as they delighted me, for so many of them bore endless scoldings and warnings; but the realization that she would never pen another, and that she had left me adrift amid a sea of enemies without further benefit of her guidance, wisdom, and experience, was too much to bear.

I didn't think I was capable of rising from the sofa; wracked with convulsions, I had lost the will to go on. How could I face the frivolous courtiers of Versailles the following morning as if I had not received such a blow? The thought of masquerades and games of blindman's buff seemed absurd. Although I was as near to collapse as I had ever been, Louis managed to convey me to my bedchamber, where I hurled myself upon the mattress and buried my face in the silk coverlet, staining it with weeping as I sobbed myself to sleep.

In the middle of the night, troubled by my thoughts, I left my bed and lit a candle, placing it on a table near my bedside. Opening a portable writing desk, I sharpened a quill and uncapped the ink, penning a note to Joseph on the stationery embossed with my cipher.

> Utterly crushed by the most dreadful misfortune, I cannot stop crying as I write this. Oh, my brother—my friend! You are all that is left to me in a country that is, that always will be, dear to me! I beg you to please take care of yourself, watch over yourself: you owe it to all your subjects; to me. *Adieu, mon très cher frère.* I have stained the page with so many tears that I can no longer read what I write. I kiss you. Remember, we are your friends, your allies. Love me.

NINETEEN

My Greatest Dream Fulfilled

1781

In the wake of Maman's death I departed for le Petit Trianon, seeking solace and privacy. And as the months progressed I absented myself with greater frequency from the superficial, if glittering, world of the court. The delights of gossip and fripperies had lost their luster and now seemed a discordant frivolity, an insult to my grief.

Our prayers had been answered as well, and both the king and I admitted our surprise at my ability to conceive within a few months of my miscarriage. Although perhaps it was purely my perception, I seemed to be increasing at a more rapid rate than I had previously done. Rose Bertin's lightweight muslin *gaulles,* with their puffed sleeves and ruffled décolletés, suited both my condition and my moods, for only the pastoral atmosphere of Trianon, which I was continually improving in an effort to recapture the essence of my Viennese summers, could soothe me.

One crisp April afternoon, I summoned Jean-Louis Fargeon to Trianon to create a fragrance for me that would distill the spirit of my beloved little idyll. The trees and shrubs were coming into bloom. "Having experienced, of late, so much loss, the reassurance that the world will become green again after so many bleak days is a comfort to me," I confessed, as we wandered through the gardens. "Smell that," I said, inhaling deeply. "It's so clean and pure." Glancing below the wide pink sash wound about my midsection I sighed. "Another new beginning."

Fargeon, a dapper little man seven years my elder, nodded deferentially. "And may I convey my felicitations and wishes for your continued good health, *Majesté.*"

"*This* is the scent I would like you to create for me with your perfect nose," I said, spreading my arms as if to embrace my entire estate within them. "Top notes from the lawns and gardens, middle notes from the bosky woods and grottoes, and the scents of the interior of the *petit château* at the bottom."

I showed him my *rose-modèles,* where all my favorite varieties grew along white trellises, nine feet long. Then we strolled over to a moss-covered bench facing the Belvedère, my bright and airy little pavilion, and I invited Monsieur Fargeon to sit beside me and soak in the view. He took a small leather-bound book and a stub of pencil from his pocket and began to scribble a few lines. The pale yellow jonquils were already in bloom, and the bearded irises would come in soon enough. Lilac bushes, roses, and myrtle abounded. At night, the sultry fragrance of jasmine wafted through the trees, and with the warmer weather approaching I would be taking moonlit walks again, serenaded by nightingales. Even when I strolled alone, meaning that I was discreetly shadowed by a pair of footmen, I found release there. "And this, all of this, is what I wish you to capture and bottle for me so that wherever I may be, when I wear it, I am at le Petit Trianon."

I was almost loath to return indoors, for the day was such a glorious one, but I noticed the perfumer taking note of the various aromas within the rooms—polished wood, citrus, and beeswax. Meeting another client, the princesse de Guéméné, who had introduced me to his products, Monsieur Fargeon bowed in greeting and said hello to her little charge, *ma petite "Mousseline la Sérieuse,"* who was studiously learning her alphabet.

I stopped to listen for a few moments, partially hidden by a screen so that I would not interrupt the lesson. After she had recited her *A* to *Zed* without a single error I revealed myself and gaily applauded her. "*Très bien,* Marie Thérèse! You are coming along much more quickly than your maman ever did!"

I could tell that Monsieur Fargeon was amused by the sartorial resemblance of mother, child, and *gouvernante,* in our filmy white *gaulles* and pastel-colored sashes. In fact there was no way to distinguish attendant from monarch, for not only were our frocks unadorned with furbelows, but it was not the fashion to accessorize them with a multitude of jewelry. About my neck, instead of diamonds, pearls, or a riot of precious gems, was a pink velvet ribbon with a cameo in the center, depicting me holding an infant.

"Every woman in Paris is wearing gowns like this," the perfumer remarked. "They are calling them *'chemises à la Reine.'* My wife already owns one and she has asked me for the money to buy two more, for the muslin is so delicate that it cannot withstand too many wearings. But she, too, is with child, and is certain the dresses will be more comfortable than a rigidly boned bodice. As for me"—he chuckled and shook his head—"forgive my bluntness, *Majesté,* but I see many women in my shop, from princesses to demimondaines, and I do not understand why great ladies who can afford the finest fabrics would choose to look like peasants. Or exactly like one another, for that matter," he added. Aristocrats had long complained that courtesans frequented the same milliners, seamstresses, and modistes, but at least with an inexhaustible supply of textiles and furbelows in every color under the sun, a woman could display her personal taste. The new fashion for these flimsy white dresses confused him. It would be as if all the women in France wore the exact same scent.

After I had finished conducting Monsieur Fargeon through the château we returned to the Belvedère, not only because I had forgotten to speak with him about its interior décor, which I wished to devote entirely to flowers and fragrances, but because I wished for privacy, as I had an additional commission to give him. "I would like you to create a unique toilet water for a gentleman," I told Fargeon.

He scratched his powdered head. "I could devise any number of blends from hundreds of ingredients, but I would know better where to begin if you were to tell me something about his personality."

I paused for a few moments, not because I did not have a ready reply, but because I feared saying too much. "The recipient is very elegant," I said simply. "But with nothing of the dandy about him. He is virile, as virile as one can possibly be."

And always in my thoughts and nightly prayers, forever in my heart.

Along the banks of the Seine at the Château de Bellevue where Mesdames *tantes,* the king's maiden aunts, had retired after the death of their father Louis XV, the trio, removed from the hubbub and glitter of Versailles, held their own far more informal court. At first their visitors were from the old guard, their *intimes* in the days of the late king; but as the mocking young queen had alienated many courtiers from the most ancient families of France by ostracizing them from her own intimate circle, Mesdames eventually amassed a devoted coterie, all of whom shared a single-minded hatred of *l'Autrichienne,* as Madame Adélaïde herself had secretly dubbed Marie Antoinette after pretending to take the innocent dauphine under her protective wing. Presided over by the three embittered princesses, Bellevue had become a satellite court where *médisance* was always on the menu and the chief subject of most of the backbiting and rumormongering was the queen.

So when a delegation of silk merchants from Lyon sought protectors, and petitioned Mesdames for an audience, they were welcomed with smiles and fine wines. Six men from the biggest factories in the city arrived wearing the fruits of their labors on their backs, richly embroidered suits sewn from mouthwatering textiles of all textures—satiny and slubbed, matte and moiré, damask and brocade.

"In a sentence, madame la princesse, we have come to ask you to speak to the king on our behalf," declared their spokesman, Monsieur Bouleau, to Madame Adélaïde. "This new fashion of Her Majesty's to attire herself like a dairymaid is threatening our livelihood. No one is buying silks anymore because they all wish to adopt the queen's new mode of simplicity."

"Orders are down considerably," interjected one of his confederates, sucking on his teeth. "The *tailleurs* and seamstresses only want muslin now."

"And we cannot sustain ourselves merely on the yardage used to make sashes."

"Of course you will continue to have *our* patronage." The corpulent Madame Victoire, swathed, furbelowed, ruched, and beribboned in a considerable amount of satin, offered the men some cold roast meats. She arched an eybrow. "Is it true what I have read: that women are taking lovers to pay for their dresses because they have already bankrupted their husbands in order to imitate the queen?"

"In that case she is corrupting the morals of France," Madame Sophie interjected tartly.

"*Pardon,* messieurs, but I cannot help but be amused, for that's what everyone said when she was spending so extravagantly on silken confections," Madame Adélaïde snickered. Not bothering to conceal her sarcasm, she added, "Poor lady; condemned for dressing opulently, and damned now for looking like she has forgotten to dress at all."

"You should ask where the muslin comes from," Madame Sophie whispered into her older sister's ear. She darted a wary gaze from one merchant to the other, looking as though she feared one of them might lunge forward and touch her.

The question was put to the delegation. "The muslin mills are in Flanders—the Austrian Netherlands," said Monsieur Bouleau.

Madame Adélaïde considered his reply. "Then perhaps Her Majesty is not as stupid as I believed, for every *chemise à la Reine* that is produced enriches the coffers of her brother, the Holy Roman Emperor. What conclusions might one draw from a Queen of France who pretends to have forgotten her mother tongue and yet chiefly concerns herself with the interests of Austria? I am sure people might be curious to know the origin of these charming muslin gowns that the queen has ensured are all the mode." The princesse extended her hand, sheathed in a scented glove, to the silk merchant. "And, as the daughter of a king, I give you my pledge, monsieur, that they will." She smiled serenely. One word to the duc d'Orléans and his son and it was as good as done.

October 22, 1781

My labor pains commenced on the morning of October 22; but this time, although etiquette demanded that the birth be properly witnessed, I refused to have a noisome throng crowding about me. Courtiers and other curious souls had begun to crowd the

State Rooms and galleries of Versailles that morning, but my bedchamber door was locked, shut to all but an exclusive few; and this time the windows were open. Mesdames *tantes* were in attendance, of course, as were my primary ladies in waiting: Lamballe, Guéméné, the princesse de Chimay, and a trio of comtesses—d'Ossun, de Tavannes, and de Mailly. The comte d'Artois was there as well, and although it was de rigueur for him to attend, given his rank, his presence would unfortunately fan the flames of the gossipmongers, who required little tinder as it was. If they cared about whose bed the comte was really warming in his hours of leisure, they might look no further than the boudoir of Gabrielle de Polignac's sister-in-law Diane.

Unlike the ordeal surrounding the birth of my daughter, the atmosphere in the room was more like that of a party than a circus. A little white delivery bed, surmounted by a coroneted canopy whose bed hangings had been tied into swags so that the witnesses' view would not be obscured, was set up within my bedchamber. It was cozier than the vast bed of state; and in it I felt more like any other mother and less like a national symbol.

The torment of giving birth was not nearly as arduous as it had been the first time, but as I had nearly expired after pushing Madame Royale into the world, they did not tell me right away whether I had given birth to a boy or a girl for fear that I would make myself sick with weeping. The baby was cleaned and loosely wrapped in a soft blanket before I could discern anything; I tried to read my ladies' faces. I did recall that the comtesse de Mailly rushed out of the room, somewhat disheveled and excited, for Louis had not been there at the moment when our second child was born at 1:15 that afternoon.

I sank back against the pillows; Monsieur Vermond, the *accoucheur,* felt my pulse. I was relieved that this time the surgeon's services had not been necessary, and allowed myself a little smile of triumph, as my preferences for a quieter, cooler room had yielded healthier results than the French court's age-old etiquette had done during my first delivery. But still, I was longing to know about my child. "You see how reasonable I am," I assured the medical men. "Monsieur Vermond himself can attest that I am quite calm."

Finally, the door to the Queen's Bedchamber opened and Louis stood on the threshold with our newborn in his arms. His face betrayed no emotion; I feared I had given France another daughter.

And then, just as his eyes began to smile, he announced, "Madame, you have fulfilled my wishes and those of France. Monsieur le dauphin begs leave to enter."

I gasped and my hand flew to my chest. My eyes flooded with tears. "A son!" After nearly eleven and a half years of marriage. If only Maman had been alive to hear the news, to celebrate the happiest, and most important, event of my life. I was allowed but a few moments to hold him before our precious prize was handed to the royal governess, the princesse de Guéméné. "Take him back, for he belongs not to me but to France," I declared, adding with a fond smile, "My daughter, however, is my own."

The tiny dauphin then passed into the hands of the wet nurse, a country woman we had nicknamed "Madame Poitrine," who swore like a sailor, but was the most robust and wholesome woman we could find.

The gilded doors of the bedchamber were opened to the blare of trumpets, announcing the birth of a dauphin. The palace cannon fired a 101-gun salute, the announcement to all within earshot that the queen had borne a son. Versailles was in a gala mood. Men and women laughed and wept, and even the courtiers who so often disparaged me came to offer their felicitations. As the princesse de Guéméné, borne aloft in an armchair, paraded our son through the gilded halls, everyone wanted to touch him, or at least the princesse, or even the chair, as though it might bring them luck.

At the christening that afternoon the dauphin was baptized Louis Joseph Xavier François, but the event was marred by the presence of the two most detestable men at Versailles: Monsieur, who stood as proxy for the infant's godfather, Emperor Joseph II of Austria; and the unctuous prince de Rohan, the Cardinal and Royal Almoner, who had the honor of officiating. I said not a single word to him, glaring at his moonfaced countenance across the baptismal font. Everything about him made my skin pebble with disgust, from the ostentatious lace cuffs beneath his red moiré cassock to the expensive perfume that hovered about him like an aromatic cloud, which always reminded me of the stories about his concubines and his illicit trade in ladies' stockings during his tenure as France's ambassador to Austria. Now that Maman was gone forever his disrespect for her rankled all the more. I did not have much traffic with the cardinal-prince; nonetheless, I had pointedly refused to address him or even so much as favor him with a civil look since his arrival at Versailles.

The following day, a parade of representatives from each of the trade guilds paid us an official visit, bearing a gift from their respective crafts, as if our newbon son was the savior of France. The butchers delivered an enormous ox; the pastry makers, a tremendous meringue; the locksmiths, a cunning lock that displayed an image of a dauphin once it was opened; even the grave diggers came to pay homage, with the present of a coffin—a gift I found particularly macabre, though no one else so much as flinched. And fifty market women from Les Halles, dressed in black and dripping with diamonds, were presented to me.

As soon as I could, I sent the news to Joseph; the forty-year-old emperor was reduced to tears of joy, replying, "My heart is bursting with happiness for my sister, who is the woman I love best in the world."

But perhaps everyone at Versailles was not quite as elated. A satire titled *Les Amours de Charlot et Antoinette* that was making the rounds through the backstairs found its way onto Louis's desk. The plot revolved around the efforts of Antoinette and Charlot (a thinly veiled caricature of Artois) to reach orgasm as they consummated their passion, owing to the continued interruption of a page boy, summoned each time "Antoinette" pressed the bell beside her as she thrashed about in ecstasy. And a scurrilous pamphlet depicting Louis crowned with the horns of a cuckold announced "The queen has finally given birth to a son—but who the devil produced him?" There wasn't a scintilla of truth, of course, to any of it; and my *beau-frère* was hardly my closest confidant, nor had he been one of my favorite companions for years. But I believed that the true intent of the *libelles* was not merely to cast aspersions on my marital fidelity and the paternity of my children, but to injure the king as well, by choosing the one man whose betrayal would wound him the most—his charming and handsome brother.

Louis shared my anguish and tried to comfort me, apologizing for being thus far unable to destroy the poisonous plants at their roots. "I can impound the presses that print the slanderous rumors, confiscate the pamphlets, and burn the caricatures, but cannot seem to stem the tide of pestilential *libelles,*" he lamented.

Confined until I was churched, I had much time to ruminate upon the past several years. Although I had never committed any sins against the courtiers of Versailles or the people of France, my character had for years been painted in an unflattering light and with the birth of the dauphin I was moved to recast it. My elaborate poufs would become a thing of the past—although there was another, more pragmatic, reason for this as well.

"Your hair is so thin and fine now, it is coming out in my hand." During this last pregnancy Monsieur Léonard began complaining that he was having difficulty styling my tresses because they had become so badly damaged. Years of frizzling and teasing had taken their toll and the coiffeur determined that masking the problem with false hair and wigs was no longer the best remedy. "Would Your Majesty permit me to cut it short?"

I had not considered such a drastic solution, but Léonard convinced me. "And if I know you, *Majesté,* you will look upon the new style not as a mark of shame, but as a fashionable new beginning to celebrate the birth of a son of France."

And he was right: *"Coiffure à l'enfant,"* as we dubbed it, along with a spate of fashionable new textile colors (such as the ochre-brown "caca Dauphin"), soon became the rage, with the most elegant women in Paris having their long locks cropped into the short, feathery style.

This new mode was not, however, the way our court painter, Madame Élisabeth Vigée-Lebrun, was determined to immortalize me with her brushes and oils. In 1782 she decided to depict me in one of my white muslin *chemises à la Reine.*

The portraitist scheduled several appointments, and finally dared to admit (for she was anything but modest about her talents) that I was the most difficult person she had ever endeavored to limn. "Your complexion is entirely without shadows; it has a delicateness and translucence that defies interpretation with an artist's meager tools. I apply paint to canvas and believe I have captured it, only to discover that I have still missed something. Not only that, Your Majesty's countenance can shift in an instant. When you see your children, your face is lit from within and one can see the playful girl inside you. And in the next moment, when a minister or dignitary wishes to speak with you, you assume the most striking dignity and poise I have ever seen."

"But if I were not the queen they would say I looked insolent, *non*?" I half jested. I remembered that some of the servants at the Hofburg had whispered as much about me when I was a girl, owing to the shape of my protruding lower lip. If only *that* had changed with childbirth, I mused, instead of my body. My shape had thickened after bearing two children and by now the size of my bosom, which I once feared would never grow, was considerable. In the span of a few of years I had watched myself transform from sylph to matron.

One morning as I made my toilette during my *lever,* I found myself startled by the reflection in my mirror. Although Maman had been gone for nearly two years, it was her face that gazed back at me.

TWENTY

May God Forgive Me

1783

It had cost France some 772 million livres to aid the American revolutionaries and help the fledging nation become and remain independent, an unfathomable amount—far greater than anything we had spent on a foreign conflict, including the Seven Years' War, which had effectively bankrupted the treasury of my husband's predecessor, Louis XV. But now our mercenaries were coming home and there was one face and figure I looked forward to greeting more than any other.

Much had happened even in the past year. After the prince de Guéméné was compelled to declare bankruptcy owing to a financial scandal, the princesse resigned her position as governess to the children of France. The prince retired to his estate in Navarre, while his wife decamped to Brittany, surrounded by her two dozen lapdogs. It was frightfully embarrassing for all of us, for the nobility, as well as the monarchy, lived almost entirely on credit. The comte d'Artois was indebted for twenty-one million francs, and yet he continued to buy horses and carriages and clothes (and to support at least one *maîtresse,* Diane de Polignac).

I replaced the princesse with my beloved *amie* Gabrielle, the duchesse de Polignac—tearfully convincing the king on bended knee not to name his conniving maiden aunt Adélaïde instead—but the appointment of the duchesse created a scandal of its own. Gabrielle and I had enjoyed a brief falling-out—her avarice, not merely for herself, but for her friends and relations, had touched a nerve; moreover, I distrusted her lover, the comte de Vaudreuil. But a few months' absence began to heal my wounded sensibilities and I realized that I greatly missed her sweet melodic voice, and her vivacious presence in my rooms. And so I invited her to return to court. But her plum assignment as royal governess and the attendant perquisite of a capacious thirteen-room suite at Versailles engendered a spate of malicious gossip.

However, there was no one more deserving of the position, for the duchesse had been one of my dearest companions for years, had witnessed the births of the royal infants, had watched them grow, and loved them with all her heart.

I found myself at the center of another maelstrom as well. In May, after being accepted to the prestigious Academie Royale de Peinture et de Sculpture, Madame Vigée-Lebrun had placed on display her portrait of me *en gaulle,* wearing a broad-brimmed straw hat trimmed with a blue ribbon and a pair of fluffy egret plumes. But neither of us could ever have imagined the outcry it generated; men and women from every stratum of society criticized the canvas—not for the artist's talents, but for the mode in which I was depicted. To all the world it appeared as though the queen of France had demolished the dignity of her rank by appearing publicly in her chemise. Kinder critics thought I was dressed like a child, for the lightweight frocks were a customary fashion for little girls. And there was a universal hue and cry over the pink rose I held in my hands as roses were symbolic of Hapsburg Austria, although it had been a hallmark of portraiture for centuries to portray the subject with a prop that signified their origin or profession. To the French, however, the rose was not an allusion to my family and place of birth, but a sinister coded image, conveying my ongoing allegiance to my homeland over that of my adopted France—for if this was not the case, why did I not hold a lily?

It was Trianon where I found myself more and more, devoting my time to my children and my music, escaping the poisonous air of the palace, both literally and figuratively. The dauphin was, alas, a sickly little tot, smaller than many children of his age, and his lungs were not developing properly. Fetid gossip aside, the air at Versailles was unhealthful for his delicate condition and I would soon have to find a more salubrious location where he might grow stronger and thrive.

Motherhood suited me as I had always known that it would. And I had finally given France her heir. In that respect I had much to be content about. And when I heard the news in June that Axel von Fersen's regiment had landed safely in Brest, the American War of Independence finally at an end, my heart soared with delight and anticipation. I began to count the days until his arrival at Versailles, paying especial attention to my daily toilette, and choosing my wardrobe with particular care, never sure when he might return to court.

One day in early July, he found me in the orangerie at le Petit Trianon. I was picking fruit for a summer punch, when I heard a warm baritone voice declare, "I am sorry to have kept you waiting, *Majesté.*"

I spun around, nearly dropping the osier basket. Our eyes met for the first time in three and a half years. He saw a young matron in a beribboned straw bonnet and yards of featherlight muslin. I saw . . . a much changed man; a bit older of course, and a bit thinner, perhaps from want of good food; but much of the youthful vitality had waned from his eyes, replaced with the world-weary expression of one who has suffered and seen much. The hollows of his cheeks had become more pronounced; his color, once high, had grown somewhat sallow. And yet, his face and figure could still bestir my heart as no one else's ever had.

Appraising each other's appearance, we drank in the sight for several moments. His blue coat was nearly the same azure as the sky, the froth of lace at his throat as full, yet insubstantial, as a cloud. With such a resemblance to the firmament he could have been an angel who had floated down to earth to guide me.

I did not fling myself into his arms like a heartsick lover, relieved to have her paramour home from the war, safe and whole, but the sensations of gratitude for his survival were the same nonetheless. "Walk with me," I said excitedly. "I wish to hear about every minute of your absence." And when he gallantly offered his arm, the heat of his body warming mine set aloft a fleet of nervous butterflies in my belly. Had his feelings changed? Had he given his heart to someone in North America? Mr. Franklin had spoken so rhapsodically about the handsome, pragmatic ladies of Boston and Baltimore, Philadelphia and New York. Perhaps one of these *belles* had suited his sober Swedish temperament.

"If I may hazard a guess, Your Majesty will be pleased to learn that there was little opportunity to indulge in pastimes." Axel smiled. "I was quite occupied with more vital matters. Two years ago I saw action, fighting at the Battle of Yorktown—I am sure you read the news of it in the gazette. And when the British general Lord Cornwallis surrendered to Mr. Washington in the presence of General Rochambeau, I had the great privilege of acting as Mr. Washington's translator. I can understand what the American people see in their military commander in chief. Mr. Washington is a very tall man, with the air of a hero about him, although I found him to be somewhat cold, not effusive, as so many Americans are. He speaks but little, but he is polite and a gentleman."

We paused as I showed him the progress Monsieur Mique had made on my rustic little village, or *hameau,* that would support a working farm and dairy. "I have now chosen the dozen indigent farmers and their families who will reside there and cultivate the land. But I have told Monsieur Mique that I wish the buildings to appear charmingly weathered with age, reminiscent of the cottages I used to see on the outskirts of Vienna, so I am engaging scenic painters to 'distress' the façades with their brushes." Axel looked amused. "If you could, why would you not do everything within your power and imagination to make your surroundings as amenable as possible, to create a bulwark against the cruel world? You would be shocked, perhaps, to read some of the *libelles* that are being published about me. I am personally blamed for bad harvests, grain shortages, and every incident of adultery or failed marriages. If any woman dares assert herself against her husband, *I* am faulted for setting her a bad example, because it is believed that I control the king.

"They are all falsehoods, but so cunningly penned that they are roundly credited. Even my own brother believes I have more influence with Louis than I truly do, for the king does not consult me in matters of foreign policy and has made it quite clear that he has no intentions of ever doing so." How fine it felt, how comfortable to be able to unburden my heart to Axel's sympathetic ears!

"You will find France much changed since you left it," I told him. "Monsieur Necker with his confidence in loans—of course he made his career in banking, so it is no wonder—is gone, replaced with Charles Alexandre Calonne as Minister of Finance, and owing to his belief that our economy can only be strengthened if we become a mercantile nation to rival the English, we have embarked on a great campaign to encourage manufacturing by building factories and increasing coal production. Much to the delight of Mademoiselle Bertin and her rival *marchandes de mode,* women may now join trade guilds. *Finalement,* the kingdom is growing more enlightened and the theoretical conversations of the intelligentsia in the Paris salons are being turned into practice. There have been vast improvements in the conditions of prisons and hospitals—can you imagine, the Hôtel-Dieu kept four patients to a single bed when there was room for only two, and half the poor souls had to take turns sleeping on the floor! They did not even change the sheets after someone died." I sighed heavily. "Yet for all the king's good intentions, it is so difficult to effect improvements because someone is always grumbling about forfeiting a perquisite—you should have heard the outcry among the nobility when Louis reduced their pensions by two percent in order to direct the funds to the poor!"

We came upon the *laiterie* and I introduced the count to two of my cows, Bonjour and Bonsoir. The former wore a bell about her neck, tied with a yellow satin ribbon; Bonsoir's ribbon was blue. "How long will you remain in France?" I asked Axel, almost fearing his reply. I could not bear the thought of losing him again.

"I fell ill while I was in America." I felt my heart skip a beat. No wonder he looked drawn. "Not to mention homesick for a woman I deeply esteem." He glanced at me, then refocused his gaze on the pair of cattle. "I should like to call France my home, although this does not sit well with my father. There have been many unpleasant letters between us. The senator feels I am being selfish in not returning to Sweden to further my career and find a wife." At his mention of the word, the muscles in my cheek twitched and I found myself flinching involuntarily.

"However, I believe I have mollified him somewhat by informing him that I intend to seek a bride in France." My stomach clenched. "Monsieur Necker's daughter Germaine, though I find her horribly plain, is an heiress of such vast proportions that he cannot possibly make an objection. Of course," Axel added drily, "Papa does not know that another of our countrymen, Baron Staël-Holstein, is already staking his claim, and by all accounts the young lady favors him highly."

He sighed heavily and stared down at his boots. "My father is also unaware that I have written to my sister Sophie, from whom I spare no confidences. I told her that I do not wish to form any conjugal ties. Since I cannot belong to the one person to whom I want to belong, to the only woman who really loves me, I don't want to belong to anybody."

His words hung in the sultry air, requiring no clarification. My breath caught in my throat. Dare I give voice to the words that dwelled within my breast? Finally I summoned the courage to murmur, "When we said farewell, you promised to claim a kiss upon your return. I would not be so ungenerous as to deny a victorious war hero his due." Perhaps the fact that he had suffered enabled me to speak so boldly, for I have always been drawn to souls in pain—among them Marie Thérèse de Lamballe and Gabrielle de Polignac.

There were no witnesses about. No entourage had shadowed us. And Axel needed no more than a moment's thought before he accepted his reward. Under the indifferent gaze of a pair of livestock, one black and white, the other chestnut red, Count von Fersen enfolded me in his arms and inclined his head, bringing his lips to meet mine, softly at first with a tentative, featherlight touch; and then more confidently and insistently, as I wound my arms about him and clung like a woman who has spent months in the desert and finally stumbles upon a watery oasis.

When she was schooling me in how to respond to my future husband's caresses, Maman had assured me that my body would know what to do and everything would flow naturally. Yet it had never been that way with Louis. Joseph had been right; the king and I were two naïve and clumsy duffers in the bedchamber, and six years' time and the birth of two children had not improved the quality of our conjugal relations. Of late, he came to my bed so infrequently that every time we made love, it seemed as though our loins had to learn the skills anew.

But this—this first kiss I had ever enjoyed that was born out of passion and longing—was a revelation. My body did know what to do, or at least my mouth did, following Axel's lead as easily if we were dancing. My jaw relaxed, widening to receive his tongue—an entirely new sensation—as he explored my own. Shivers of pleasure sent electric tingles along the length of my spine. He pressed me closer, then caressed my neck and ran his fingers through my unpowdered hair. His mouth moved to one of my earlobes and I thought I would burst out of my skin with desire. I had never been kissed by someone who knew how to do it, moreover, someone who cherished me with the ardor of a lover.

Moments later, Axel could feel my body tensing in his arms, and I drew back from his embrace, my face warm and flushed. His eyes, today as blue as his coat, were shining.

I tried to speak. "I . . ." But no more words would come.

We glanced about furtively; mercifully, we remained entirely alone. "*Pardonnez-moi,* Toinette. I will never again compromise you thus," said Axel hoarsely. In the manner of knights of old he sank to one knee and took my hands in his, kissing them respectfully. "But I cannot part from you today without telling you that I breathe only for you and will dedicate the remainder of my life to your happiness and security. And when I am near you, a soft word, your kind regard, a single stolen glance, will define my pleasure."

In the music room at le Petit Trianon I gave him the flacon of toilet water I had commissioned from Monsieur Fargeon. "It will be a sign between us when you wear it," I said. "Every time, I will think of our love."

I accompanied Axel back to the Château de Versailles. There were others he wished to greet upon his return. As we mounted the marble staircase, a commotion behind us heralded the return of the king from whatever private pursuit he had been enjoying. Louis passed us on the stairs, his gaze intently focused on a lock clasped in his hands. It was not until he was several treads above us that he turned and halted as though he had forgotten something.

"Ah, ma chère!" He paused, then regarded Axel, who immediately bowed in acknowledgment of his presence. "*Ah.* So the count did find you, Toinette. I trust you have passed a pleasant afternoon. Mine," Louis said, turning the lock over to admire it again, "has been remarkable."

I could have said the same, but I dared not meet the gaze of either man.

September

In the dining room of the Château de Rohan in Saverne dozens of guests dined on gold plate, while countless beeswax tapers illuminated silver epergnes laden with foodstuffs and hundreds of cut-crystal goblets brimming with France's finest vintages. Among the notables was the marquise de Boulainvilliers who had sought out the renowned Count Cagliostro in the expectation that he would cure her of an ailment her physician had been powerless to assuage. Accompanying the marquise was her charming foster daughter, the twenty-seven-year-old comtesse Jeanne de Lamotte-Valois, the last (but for her brother and younger sister) survivor of that line of illustrious kings, the descendant of an illicit union between Henri II and his mistress, Nicole de Savigny.

The soi-disant comtesse (as Jeanne had bestowed the title upon herself) tried not to goggle at the cardinal's displays of wealth: the Gobelin tapestries that illustrated the great classical myths in silken threads, heavy draperies of velvet and brocade, and gilded mirrors that reflected the painted countenances of some of the highest nobles in the land. She had never seen such opulence, except at Versailles, where she had begun to ingratiate herself in the hopes that the queen would take an interest in her plight. Jeanne had twice attempted her first ploy, deliberately fainting in the presence of Her Majesty, but failed to elicit the queen's notice, the halls being too thronged with people for Marie Antoinette to spy the slender brunette sinking to the parquet, particularly when a crush of people gathered around the poor soul, or so they thought, as though she were some sort of curiosity. At least someone loosened her stays and offered her a sip of brandy to revive her spirits.

Remaining undaunted, the clever comtesse had heard that the king's sister Madame Élisabeth had a kind and sympathetic soul, and so she pretended to swoon in the princesse's antechamber. Informed that a lady of quality had fainted from starvation in her rooms, Madame Élisabeth ordered her servants to bear the young woman on a litter back to her lodgings in the town and requested her own doctors to attend her. After playing upon Élisabeth's compassion for a fellow blueblood fallen on hard times, a gift of two hundred francs soon followed, and the princesse's chaplain undertook to raise an additional three hundred on the comtesse's behalf. With such a powerful patron, Jeanne retained the highest hopes that the royal pension of eight hundred francs a year—won only after refusing to quit the Finance Minister's office, and hardly befitting her birthright—would be substantially increased. Her brother Jacques, a soldier, had been permitted by the king to use the title baron de Valois, but that acknowledgment of their ancestry was merely the beginning of the restitution of her family's estates and the recognition of her lineage that she desired.

Before the splendid meal began, the marquise de Boulainvilliers had presented Jeanne to their host, explaining that she had taken the young woman and her sister under her roof when they were children—"Orphaned waifs, begging by the side of the King's Highway; I insisted that my husband the marquis halt our carriage. Tell the cardinal, *ma chère,* what your mother had taught you to say to people."

Jeanne needed little prompting. Aware, from the appraising glint in his dark eyes, that the prince de Rohan, suave and handsome, though graying at the temples and reeking of costly perfume, had already assumed a certain interest in her welfare, she repeated the litany that had put coins in their pockets and crusts of bread on their table. Widening her eyes and proffering her upturned palm as she had done countless times during her impoverished youth, she said "Kind lady, kind gentleman, take pity on a little orphan child who descends in a direct line from Henri the Second, one of your country's greatest kings."

The presence of an actual descendant of the Valois went to Rohan's head like strong drink. The cardinal took the comtesse's hands in his and, pressing them with an insistence that scarcely concealed his attraction, urged her to tell him more about her origins.

"My father was wrongfully imprisoned for debts and died soon after his release," Jeanne said softly. "Maman, who had once been a lowly serving wench in my grandfather's household, took up with a lover who thought to usurp Papa's place. And then she abandoned us entirely."

Visibly moved by her sorrowful tale, the forty-nine-year-old cardinal claimed her attention for the better part of the evening, stirred by the notion that he might somehow do some service to the charming Valois.

Flattery opened men's doors. Comtesse de Lamotte-Valois admired the unusual signet ring he wore on his pinky, a massive solitaire engraved with the Rohan crest.

"*Merveilleux,* isn't it," the cardinal agreed enthusiastically. "But its provenance is even more remarkable." Gesturing toward his perpetual guest of honor, who was deep in conversation with Jeanne's benefactress Madame de Boulainvilliers, he added, "Count Cagliostro made it for me—created it out of thin air! I saw him do it, madame la comtesse—never removed my eyes from his crucible! It defies every known science. You may have heard the rumors—that he is hoodwinking me and exploiting my patronage for his own ends. But I can assure you that it's nothing but *médisance* from a cadre of malcontents who wish me nothing but ill. The most reputable jewelers in France have estimated the worth of this diamond at twenty-five thousand francs. So, I put it to you, madame de Lamotte-Valois"—the last word tasted like honey on his tongue—"how could Cagliostro be a swindler or a charlatan?" And before she could reply, the cardinal offered to escort her to the count's secret atelier under the eaves.

"He makes gold as well as diamonds," the prince de Rohan said breathlessly, his eyes shimmering with covetousness. He lowered his voice and clasped the comtesse's hands in his. "Five or six thousand francs' worth he manufactured right before my eyes—and he will make much more, rendering me the richest man in Europe. It is not a trick, I assure you; Cagliostro has mastered the skill of transmuting base metals into purest gold."

Jeanne de Lamotte-Valois bit her tongue, quietly marveling at how one of the most powerful men in the kingdom, the most celebrated descendant of an ancient and venerated family, could be so gullible. She had no doubt that Cagliostro's alchemy was little better than a circus trick, but the sheer force of his magnetic personality, combined with the cardinal's utter willingness to believe whatever he wished to see and hear, and de Rohan's evident avarice despite his substantial wealth, had managed to render the cardinal-prince a puppet in the mountebank's clever hands.

The prince de Rohan invited comtesse de Lamotte-Valois to call upon him the following day, but rather than hear her entire tale of woe in one of his numerous public rooms, he escorted her to his boudoir, *le salon des singes,* a chamber more opulent than that of any Eastern potentate. Jeanne had never seen anything quite so exotic. The white paneling was accented with ornately carved and gilded boiserie; on the upper panels the Chinoiserie paintings depicted recognizable members of the French court, including the queen, garbed in Oriental robes. The lower panels were decorated with cavorting monkeys—*les singes*—limned in every conceivable position, most of them lascivious. The beasts' tails were suggestive of the male organ, and in fact one of the monkeys was depicted in a scarlet robe, daintily lifting his tail out of the way so that he might snuff out a candle with his furry derrière.

Jeanne had lived by her wits for most of her life. That the Grand Almoner of France should sleep here, in a room all but designed for debauchery, provided yet another key to the man's character. And when this prince of the church conducted her to the vast bed and, sitting beside her, urged her to tell him everything about herself, she handily summoned a tear or two to her eye and a rosy blush to her cheeks.

"The pension granted by His Majesty is extremely modest; my husband and I cannot support ourselves on eight hundred francs a year. Nicolas tendered his resignation when the commander of his regiment tried to force himself upon me. Life has since been very difficult, monsieur," Jeanne confessed, her lips aquiver. "I should very much wish for an increase to the royal pension, but it is my life's mission to recover our ancestral lands—the Fontette estates in Bar-sur-Aube in Champagne," she told him. "For until the king grants me the permission to reclaim them, the comte and I are compelled to decamp from one apartment to another, each more squalid than the last."

It wasn't entirely the truth, but the comtesse knew when to spin a fanciful web around her prey. Within moments, the cardinal had clasped her hands in his, bringing her closer to his breast. "I wish you had said something sooner, last night, even, for it pains me to see you in such distress when I could have relieved you of many moments' agony." He rose from the bed and unlocked a chest embellished with handpainted Sèvres plaques. Removing a purse stuffed to bursting with gold coins, he bestowed it on the comtesse, urging her to call upon him as often as she wished, whether in Strasbourg, Paris, or Versailles. "I assure you, madame, I shall forward your affairs at court at the first opportunity. With your illustrious name, not to mention your considerable personal charms," he added, with a longing glance at her small but perfectly proportioned bosom, "it should be a simple matter to effect restitution of your property at Fontette. And in return," becoming agitated and breathless the longer he gazed at her, he added, "you must promise to give me your complete . . . confidence."

Both parties knew it would not be long before the comtesse

would give him considerably more than that. Jeanne feigned a demure smile and favored her new benefactor with a doe-eyed look of gratitude. An understanding had been reached.

Throughout the summer Count von Fersen had been corresponding with his father in Sweden in an effort to forestall his return. It had not been my suggestion to find a way for him to remain in France, but once Axel had confided his plan to purchase the Royal Suédois, the regiment of Swedish mercenaries in the service of the king, I would have done anything within my power to help him obtain his dream. Whereas other courtiers most often spoke to me of banalities or endeavored to amuse me, Axel did neither of these things. Not being a Frenchman he lacked both reason and need to ingratiate himself with me, because he could hold no office at court. True, I enjoyed frivolity, but I enjoyed a respite from it in equal measure, and the Count von Fersen supplied it. He and I alone discussed weightier and more personal matters. We each had a domineering parent, forever chastising us, and a sister we adored. I never confided as I did to Axel with the likes of Coigny, Besenval, or even Lauzun, for secrets were currency at Versailles and I was too easily compromised by a friend who might one day become an enemy.

The count and I had gone boating in the Grand Canal on a listless afternoon. Insistent midges hovered above the blue-green water; when they came too close to the boat, attracted perhaps by the scent of my orange flower water or by the fresh blooms I wore in my hair according to the current fashion, I endeavored to fan them away.

"Papa tells me I am being selfish in asking him for a loan. He accuses me of pursuing a foolish and arrogant luxury." Axel exhaled a ponderous sigh, and rested the oars in their brackets. The rowboat bobbed a bit and began to float along of its own volition, borne by the gentle breeze that riffled the placid surface of the water. Reaching into his pocket, he handed me the most recent letter from his father.

> I would gladly consent to this plan of yours if I didn't see one small impediment: neither you nor I have the necessary funds. You say it will cost you 100,000 livres to buy the regiment and that you can secure a loan; but the income it will bring you amounts to only 12,000 a year and you have to factor in 5000 livres in interest on the initial sum of the loan. How do you expect to live on 7000 livres a year? Such a paltry figure would be an impossibility in Paris, where one can barely scrape by on 25,000. Where would you get the money?
>
> Since returning from North America you have cost me between 300 and 500 livres, a sum that is significantly beyond my means, yet amounts to the entire fortune of some families. I ask you, is it fair to your two sisters and to your younger brother, who is about to go forth into the world, and who has an equally valid claim on his paternal rights? Were you to squander such a sum on a whim you will become their ruin, rather than their support.

The elder count's letter reminded me of so many scoldings from Maman that my heart ached for Axel. "I wish to help you," I said softly. "Perhaps it is selfish of me, but I would be tremendously gratified to think that I might see you more often were you to command the Royal Suédois. Have you written to Gustavus?" I asked him, aware that his sovereign might be persuaded to intercede with Senator Fersen.

Axel nodded. "As soon as I received that letter from Papa, I put pen to paper. And I understand that Gustavus has corresponded with the King of France regarding the matter."

Louis had enough to occupy him; as it was he spent sleepless nights in his library poring over documents and decrees. We had not slept together as husband and wife in several months and neither of us seemed to miss the other's presence.

"I will answer Gustavus's letter myself," I promised Axel. At this, illuminated with gratitude, his countenance brightened considerably. He leaned forward to kiss me, but under the open sky with so many courtiers milling about the banks of the Grand Canal, I was certain we were being watched. "I must read your thanks in your eyes rather than receive it from your lips," I murmured.

"Éléphant!" cried Madame Royale, pointing to the baby pachyderm giving himself a mud bath in his enclosure at the royal menagerie. Frowning at the animal, she pouted. "I wish you and *madame la gouvernante* would let me play like that."

"I am certain that Madame de Polignac will scold me for allowing you to become quite dirty enough as it is." Her chubby hands were sticky with a marzipan candy she had been savoring for the better part of our excursion. "Would you like to push your brother for a while?"

Not yet five years old, but with all the arrogance of an older sister, Mousseline shook her head. "He's heavy. It makes me too tired." I knelt down and tucked an errant curl under her linen cap.

"*Ça va,* then. Your job will be to point out all the animals." We continued to stroll about the circular walks that surrounded the charming Baroque pavilion of the menagerie. Beyond the path lay the separate enclosures, cages, and stables for each of the exotic beasts.

"Tigre!" Madame Royale raced to the edge of the path and peered over the low wall. Safely beyond it lay the enclosure for

the large cats. I wheeled the wicker carriage bearing her younger brother, the dauphin. Although Louis Joseph was nearly two years old, he lacked the strength to walk about the menagerie on his own. My son was happily humming to himself, sucking on his fingers and enjoying the warm late summer air as he absorbed the sights.

Mousseline gazed at the large striped cat, as beautiful as she was feral. We watched her for several moments: the graceful stride of her lithe limbs; the uniqueness of her markings; her proud head and emerald eyes daring us to admire her.

"Why is she your favorite, Maman?" my daughter asked, tugging at my skirt with almond candy fingers.

"Because, *ma petite,* as fond as I am of beautiful things, no amount of artifice could duplicate the magnificence—and power—of a tigress." I think, too, because the stunning beast possessed qualities I envied, even coveted for myself; but I could not admit as much to my impressionable child. At that moment, I realized the creature reminded me of my mother. For so many years I had chafed against her myriad admonitions, only to begrudgingly acknowledge, years after I became a maman, that she had been the wisest woman I'd ever known.

"Where is the lion?" inquired Madame Royale, trotting toward the adjacent enclosure. He was sunning himself on the large rock at the center of his habitat, his glorious mane resting upon his great front paws. Mousseline giggled. "The king of the beasts is fast asleep, just like Papa. He is my favorite because he is big and slow and throws his head back and yawns and stretches just like him."

I laughed in spite of myself. "You mustn't say such things. It's not very nice to the lion, or to your papa, who loves you more than any little girl in the world."

We resumed our perambulations about the walking path. I

leaned toward the carriage. "Which is your favorite animal, monsieur le dauphin?" He continued to hum happily to himself, but paused to point to the large bird strutting about a sandy enclosure, oblivious to our presence. *"Tru!"* he exclaimed.

"Ah, so you like the ostrich—*l'autruche.*" I was glad that his only associations with the flightless bird were innocent and pleasant; I could not regard it without recalling the cruel taunts that combined the creature's name with puns on my Austrian heritage. The jibes had also invoked the word for a female dog.

"How can he like *l'autruche*? It's the ugliest thing in the whole menagerie," Mousseline remarked, wrinkling her nose in disgust. But the good-natured dauphin was utterly unperturbed by his sister's insult and resumed his humming.

"Homme!" he said, pointing along the curve of the path. At first I didn't understand him, thinking he was merrily amusing himself with his own private melody. *"Homme,"* the dauphin repeated, so I shaded my eyes and followed my son's gaze. As he had so astutely observed, a *man* was indeed striding briskly toward us.

"Axel," I breathed. As he neared, I could see that he was beaming.

"I have news," he said, greeting me and acknowledging the children.

Madame Royale immediately stuck her thumb in her mouth. *"Homme!"* repeated the dauphin, pointing at the count with a broad smile.

I had only to regard him and my heart did a little fillip. "I am eager to hear it." I smiled down at my children. "We were just finishing our afternoon excursion. If you do not mind escorting us all the way back to Trianon, I shall return *les enfants* to the care of their governess, and then we may converse."

We spent the next hour speaking of inconsequentialities while I continued to entertain my son and daughter, playing guessing games and riddles to pass the time during the long walk back to my little château. Eventually, Madame Royale grew so fatigued that she begrudgingly permitted Count von Fersen to carry her on his shoulders. After a while, she began to enjoy the lofty vantage, although I had to ask her more than once not to dig into the poor man's shoulders as if he were her pony or rap upon the top of his head like a toy drum.

I had been thrumming with anticipation for the entire duration of the walk. At last we reached le Petit Trianon and were able to obtain some privacy by slipping into the Billiard Room. "Well, then, your news," I declared. "You must not keep me in suspense a moment longer."

With triumphant delight, he withdrew a document from the pocket of his coat and brandished the writ awarding him possession as Colonel Proprietor of the Royal Suédois, then sank down to one knee and kissed my hand. "This is your doing, *Majesté,*" he said, humbly bowing his head.

I insisted that he rise at once. "Your presence is all the thanks I require."

"Ahhh." A dark cloud passed over his noble brow.

My belly was seized with a fillip of anxiety. "What is it?"

"Nothing, I regret, comes without conditions." Axel wandered disconsolately over to the clavichord and struck a few random keys in an effort to fill the uncomfortable silence. "Gustavus made the purchase of the regiment possible—he had to offer the prior commander another post—and in so doing he rendered me personally beholden to him. Being youthful and inquisitive, he has decided to make the Grand Tour of the Continent."

As a rite of passage, young men often embarked on a Grand Tour before they settled down; but it was rare for a reigning sovereign to leave his throne for such an extended length of time to gallivant about Europe.

Axel raked his fingers through his lightly powdered hair and shook his head. "His Majesty has asked me to travel with him as his aide-de-camp. We depart next week."

I felt suddenly light-headed. "How long will you be gone?"

He regarded me thoughtfully. "I cannot say." Then, chuckling ruefully, he added, "I suppose Your Majesty would know something about the whims of a king." His eyes grew sorrowful. "And so what we had expected to be a *bonjour* has become an *au revoir.*"

"I will be immeasurably lonely without you," I confessed. "Remarkable, isn't it, how one can be surrounded at nearly all times by countless names and faces, and yet, if none of them belongs to the person one loves . . . and desires . . . one—*I*—could never feel more alone." Blinking back tears, I embraced him, drawing him so close that the buttons of his tunic pressed into my bosom. "If I had a single wish right at this moment, it would be to never leave your arms," I murmured, resting my cheek on his chest.

"*Prenez soin, Majesté;* someone might see us," Axel whispered.

Gabrielle de Polignac was supervising the children of France in the Music Room. They would not intrude upon us. But others might present a danger. My pulse was racing; I feared uttering the words I longed to say yet was equally afraid that I would lose the courage to act. A queen must take the lead with all but the king. "I wish to give you something to remember me by," I said softly, not daring to meet his gaze. "But it is not in this salon. Come." I extended my hand and beckoned Axel to follow me. Room by room I activated the mirrored shades, and then we ascended the cool marble stairs.

In my bedchamber was a single bed covered with a dainty floral coverlet. The pillowcases were embroidered with my cipher in blue silk. I knelt on the little rug, clasping my hands in prayer. "May God forgive me," I murmured. My hands were shaking.

I took off my jewelry, placing it in a cloisonné box on my dressing table, and untied the sash about my waist. The gauzy white *gaulles* were far simpler than court gowns and so much easier to remove. Axel stepped behind me and slid the gown over my shoulder blades, touching his lips to my bare flesh. The *gaulle* puddled to the floor and I stepped out of it gracefully and turned into his embrace, unfastening the silver buttons of his tunic with anxious fingers. We kicked off our shoes and Axel undid the buttons of his breeches and tugged his chemise over his head. His body was that of a soldier, taut and firm. I lightly traced my fingers over the downy Y of dark hair on his chest, then snaked my hands along his shoulders and neck and touched his lips with my fingertips. Axel lowered his mouth to meet mine, claiming it with a lingering kiss.

"My love," he said hoarsely. "My only love. Now and always." With dexterous hands he unlaced my stays and removed my chemise. Cupping my breasts in his hands, he circled my nipples with his thumbs until I thought my skin would burst. Louis had never touched me there. Not until this moment had I realized that my body was so sensitive. I was a naïf of twenty-seven, and despite being a mother of two, still unschooled in the ways of love.

Another kiss, deep and thrilling. Axel scooped me into his arms as if I weighed no more than a willow basket and gently lowered me onto the narrow bed. "You are the loveliest woman in the world," he murmured, tasting my lips. He tantalized me with butterfly kisses along my shoulders and neck, and warmed my earlobes with his tongue until I feared I would scream with pleasure as my body writhed beneath his, craving the union of our flesh as I had never desired anything else.

I ran my hands through his soft brown hair as he explored every curve and hollow of my torso, bathing my nipples with sweet kisses, bestowing caresses, both soft and urgent, on my breasts and the gentle curve of my belly. His hands slid over my hips as he ran his tongue along the length of my thighs, finally lowering his lips to my deepest, most sensitive place. My experience of lovemaking had been so narrow that I was swimming in novel sensations, arching my back against Axel's mouth—my dormant passion fully awakened and hungry for more.

I shuddered, stifling a joyful sob with my fist and invoking the Almighty as I cried out my lover's name. There was no turning back; my body had taken hold of my senses, rapture had replaced reason, and when Axel entered me, clasping me to him and covering my mouth with kisses as our limbs entwined, my fear of God's wrath evanesced into the ether. I wrapped my legs about his back. Desire, need, want; I had become their slave.

"I will always belong to you," he whispered, as we lay in each other's arms. He pressed his mouth to my eyelids, kissing one, then the other, calming my spirit with his soft, cool lips. "Wherever I may be in the world, I am yours."

I wished I could have said the same. But the magic of a late summer afternoon would of necessity fade with the waning sunlight. "I would I had the power to keep you here." He caught my falling tear with his tongue.

"Right here?" he teased, urging his body, excited once more, against me.

I sighed heavily. "I wish it could be so. But we will have to content ourselves with dreaming as much." Cupping his face in my hands, I kissed him, gently at first, but the taste of myself on his lips was so exotic, and so intimate, that it deepened my ardor. "You have my heart," I assured Axel, "even if my body must remain in France while you travel the world." Then I added, "People may talk. I have been traduced by half the kingdom, it seems, for taking lovers. But this is the first time their words will be true." Resting against him, I murmured, "I rely upon your strength and discretion—or we are both ruined." Already, my conscience was troubled, for there was no returning from the fire we had just chosen to walk through.

Looking into my eyes, he said fervently, "May I be struck dead if I were ever to compromise your honor or your name in any way, *ma petite* Toinette."

By the end of the week Axel had set out for Germany, where he was to rendezvous with Gustavus III of Sweden. My heart did go with him, but not my peace of mind. I had become the woman my detractors had limned, the woman I had been raised to scorn and despise with every bit of my anatomy, a Pompadour or du Barry—or my father's mistress, Princess Auersperg. What had it cost me to succumb, not merely to passion and temptation, but to love?

But perhaps the most painful aspect of my betrayal of both God and Louis was that I could never confess my sin.

TWENTY-ONE

Schemers and Dreamers

Spring 1784

The comtesse's town house on the rue Neuve Saint-Gilles in Paris was bustling with activity. She was expecting the prince de Rohan for supper, and such an illustrious guest had to be fêted in a manner befitting a Valois. Every pawnshop in the capital had been scoured for silver plate, candelabras, and crystal. The furniture was on loan from friends she had made at the court of Versailles with the tidy little falsehood that everything she owned had been placed in storage owing to an unfortunate leak in her ceiling, and she had not been able to recover the items in time for the arrival of the cardinal. The Lamottes' fortunes rose and fell according to the comte's luck at the gaming tables. When he won, they spent every sou on luxuries; when he lost, they démenaged in the dead of night and sold or pawned every item of value.

Her royal lineage was Jeanne de Lamotte-Valois's only legitimate possession. Despite her ancestry, she had very little that she could call her own, but she was in the process of remedying her predicament. The prince de Rohan had been exceedingly generous with his purse; she was hardly too proud to refuse his largesse, nor was Nicolas, her husband of four years. If the couple stood to profit by Jeanne's amorous liaisons, the self-styled comte de Lamotte-Valois would be the ultimate *mari complaisant*.

As she had begun seducing the cardinal, Jeanne had discovered that he had a weak spot beyond his lechery: desperation for the favor of the one person who continued to snub him. And so the comtesse returned to Versailles as often as possible in order to be able to describe the rooms with enough detail to convince the prince that she was on the most intimate terms with the object of his obsession, informing him that Her Majesty had expressed the utmost sympathy for her plight, and had even offered to plead her case for restitution of the Fontette estates. The cardinal need not know that despite her best efforts, she had yet to actually meet the queen.

The spirited Jeanne had, however, caught the eye of the comte d'Artois, who dispatched his equerry, the prince de Hénin, to make the necessary arrangements for an assignation. Yet she could hardly boast of her royal conquest to the cardinal, who foolishly believed himself the comtesse's only lover. With her winning smile and lithe limbs, not to mention her talents on the harp and clavichord and her ability to discuss literature and philosophy like the cleverest of Parisienne hostesses, she had cunningly ensnared the Grand Almoner, feigning a fondness for the aging goat, and declaring herself his confidante. He, in turn, was only too happy to become the champion of a Valois.

"Do you realize, *ma chère,*" the prince de Rohan had said to her one afternoon, after a particularly athletic tryst, "Do you realize that my fate as well as your own is entirely in your hands?"

Giggling, for something else entirely was in her hands at the time, she cooed, "How can you seriously believe that, when you are one of the most powerful men in France?" It had been a tall order for her to pretend a passion for a man nearly fifty, his pale flesh flaccid with overindulgence.

"Your friendship with the queen," the prince de Rohan said breathlessly, responding to her caresses. "You and I have no secrets from each other . . . and it is my greatest goal to become the king's Chief Minister. But for the queen, it might have happened years ago; she is convinced for some reason that I have wronged her. If I could only ingratiate myself with her, the appointment would nearly be a surety."

He was angling for Jeanne's offer to intercede, and she did not disappoint him. But like all confidence schemes, her game would take time, months if not longer; and so she continued to bait her hook, informing him at every tryst, banquet, and dinner party that Her Majesty had been so displeased with him that it would take her some time to come around. It was a delicate situation that would require finesse, the comtesse insisted. She counseled patience. In the meantime, Jeanne encouraged the prince to write directly to the queen, explaining his past conduct and pleading his cause before her, offering to deliver the letter herself into Her Majesty's hands.

Several days later, Jeanne handed him the queen's reply, which stated:

> I have read your letter and am pleased that I need no longer regard you as guilty. However, I cannot yet grant the audience you seek; when circumstances permit a *rencontre,* I will advise you. In the meantime, I must caution you to be discreet.

The prince de Rohan had been so overjoyed that he nearly wept in Jeanne's arms. "You are indeed my savior—my guardian angel," he told her, moistening her hands and lips with kisses. That afternoon, he would have given her the moon on a golden cord if the comtesse desired it.

It was difficult for her not to ask for too much too soon. But she did not wish to remain beholden to him for her income. Jeanne was canny enough to acknowledge that men soon tired of their mistresses and abandoned them for the charms of fairer faces. Not only must she keep her noble paramour in her thrall; it was imperative to develop other ways of picking his pocket.

At tonight's supper she would feed the cardinal another crumb.

"You are far too handsome to be a footman, Rétaux," she teased, playfully pinching the only lover who truly satisfied her, her husband's childhood friend, the tall, blond Rétaux de Villette. "But with one glance at those blue eyes of yours, even a ninny will see that you are far too intelligent for your station. You will have to do something about it."

"I shall endeavor to look ignorant, madame," said Rétaux, stooping his shoulders and affecting a vacant expression as he tried to slip a hand beneath her stays.

"Can you keep it up all night?" Jeanne asked him. Acknowledging the double entendre, the conspirators shared a laugh. "Have you finished the letters?"

"The ink is drying on the last of them," he said, toying with her breast. "But we will need to have more sheets made up—which means *I* will need money; the gold embossing is dear."

Jeanne kissed Rétaux full on the mouth. "I shall tap the keg again tonight," she assured him. "Just make sure the correspondence looks authentic."

The comte and comtesse and their illustrious guest supped on filet of sole and, having plied the cardinal with a postprandial goblet of fine brandy, Jeanne confided to the Grand Almoner that the queen had been willing to entertain the prospect of forgiving him, but that he would have to prove himself trustworthy. To that end, she showed him a sheaf of letters, all in Her Majesty's hand, on the queen's own notepaper rimmed in gold and embossed with the fleur-de-lis of France. "You will see, here, her latest note to me in which she asks me to request on her behalf that you aid a friend of hers who is in deep financial distress." She handed the letter to the cardinal, and true enough, Marie Antoinette wished him to deliver sixty thousand livres to the comtesse de Lamotte-Valois, who would discreetly distribute it to Her Majesty's unfortunate friend.

> I cannot be seen to be involved in this endeavor, as I have already exhausted my allowance from the king. He can never know of this gift. And therefore, *ma très chère comtesse,* for the love we bear one another, I entrust you to ask the Grand Almoner, the prince de Rohan, to act as my banker and my emissary. If he can do this for me and keep his counsel when he next crosses paths with my husband, know that he shall have my gratitude.

It was signed by the queen herself. Or appeared to be. Neither the cardinal nor Rétaux de Villette had ever seen her signature.

Noticing the prince's widened eyes, Jeanne took the ruse a step further. A woman who lives by her wits and her wiles learns that people will see what they wish to. "Her Majesty has assured me that once she is informed of your assistance in this most delicate matter, she will acknowledge it. Station yourself in the Oeil de Boeuf at the hour when she passes through the Hall of Mirrors with her entourage on her way to High Mass. The queen has instructed me to tell you that she will be looking for you. If you are there, she will nod to you as a sign of her approbation and approval."

Her scheme worked like the movements of a Swiss clock, so well, in truth, that several weeks later the comtesse de Lamotte-Valois touched the cardinal for an additional fifty thousand livres on the same pretext. By then she had fully convinced the cleric of her intimacy with the queen, staging more than one opportunity for him to witness her departure from Her Majesty's apartments, often escorted by a mysterious man—none other than the clever Rétaux de Villette in disguise. The prince de Rohan had no idea that Marie Antoinette was at le Petit Trianon at the time. And if he began to wonder how the comtesse had acquired her new wardrobe, a complement of jewels, a handsome equipage, and a panoply of sumptuous furnishings, she would reply with the sincerest countenance that she owed her recent acquisitions to the generosity of *Sa Très Puissante Majesté.*

To our sorrow, the dauphin was not developing into a strong child. By now he should have been a plump and sturdy-legged toddler, but Louis Joseph was small and frail, and as the years progressed it was clear that his spine was curved. The king and I nurtured constant fears for the boy's health, but I took a measure of comfort in the knowledge that my sister Marianne, the abbess, suffered from a similar deformity; several years older than I, she still enjoyed good health. And because I was born with one shoulder higher than the other, every time I looked at my beautiful curly-haired dauphin I despaired of having passed him my bad blood.

So on June 7, when I sent Louis an urgent summons to curtail his hunting party and return to Versailles immediately, he feared the worst had befallen our heir. Relief was palpably etched in his broad face when he arrived at the palace, breathless and perspiring, to greet his sovereign brother, King Gustavus III of Sweden, who had arrived with his entourage during his Grand Tour, traveling incognito as the Count de Haga. Louis had so little time to change into his formal clothes that his flustered valet dressed him in one shoe with a red heel and a gold buckle and the other with a black heel and silver buckle.

I was overjoyed to see Axel again, although our reunion took place in the presence of dozens of courtiers. He had brought me a gift—a magnificent Swedish elkhound with blue eyes and a thick gray and white coat. The dog, whom I named Odin, after the king of the Norse gods, was not a surprise; the count and I had corresponded about it during his travels. But Gustavus had been so demanding and so jealous of Axel's time that he had to feign illness just so he would have the time to write me a letter.

"I encountered some difficulty with the breeder," Axel confided when we were able to steal a private moment. "I informed him that the dog was for a woman named Joséphine, but when it took such a long time to acquire him, I was compelled to state that in truth, he was a gift for the Queen of France." I knew, however, that Joséphine was Axel's secret name for me, and that every time he wrote, he would chronicle a letter to "Joséphine" in his journal.

Odin, a large hunting hound—quite the contrast to my bevy of lap dogs—would now assume pride of place in my affections, as my precious pug Mops, the companion of my girlhood, having grown blind and incontinent, had gone to his final reward a few years earlier.

On the twenty-first of June we fêted our foreign guests with a supper party at le Petit Trianon. First I treated them to a command performance of Piccini's opera *Le Dormeur Éveillé* in my intimate little theater, after which the meal was served, course by course, in the park's romantic pavilions, affording our guests the opportunity to fully admire the grounds. Everyone had been asked to wear only white, creating a spectral fantasy as we roamed the estate, each of us resembling a fallen star. My gardens had been transformed into a wonderland; fairy lights were suspended from the trees; torches and pots of colored fire illuminated the grottoes and the lake. Garlanded wherries ferried our invitees across the shimmering water to the colonnaded Temple d'Amour, where they could indulge themselves in strawberries and champagne.

"We are in France only until the twentieth of July," Axel told me. He was wearing the scent I had commissioned for him. "But I promise to see you as often as I may." His eyes glittered in the torchlight. "Even to look at you; to hear your melodic voice as you accompany yourself on the clavichord or harp; to know that you are singing Dido for me"—he touched his hand to his breast—"brings me unalloyed joy." He nodded his head in the direction of his sovereign. "But Gustavus is overfond of diversions, and, like a doting nursemaid, it is my duty to see that he stays out of trouble."

I touched my fan to my lips. "Devoted and always so correct; no one could wish for a more stalwart or trustworthy companion than you, Count von Fersen. I can't say I do not envy the King of Sweden."

He took my hand and bowed, touching his mouth to my fingers. Raising his eyes to meet mine, he murmured, "I will come to you as often as I can."

Throughout the month of July, except for my evening walks on the parterres in the sultry summer air, where I was always accompanied by my ladies, I contrived to be found alone as much as possible. In Axel's presence I was dancing on the edge of a precipice, with the music growing faster the closer my body was to his. And yet I could not step back, although every day I asked myself why it was so impossible. Was it pure desire that drew me to Count von Fersen? Was Louis's clumsiness in the boudoir and his indifference to physical passion to blame? Did *Axel's* noble mien and loyal character transform *me* into a disloyal wife?

JULY

Rétaux de Villette spent the first days of July scouring the shadowed promenades of the Palais Royal for a certain trollop who, according to Jeanne, bore a striking resemblance to the queen. Mademoiselle Nicole Leguay, in her early twenties, could not believe her good fortune when she was told she would be dining in the home of a real comtesse.

Gawking at the velvet drapery and thick carpets, the bronze and onyx sculptures resting on tabletops of exquisitely veined marble in the town home on the rue Neuve Saint-Gilles, the prostitute had never seen such opulence. She was greeted by the comtesse de Lamotte-Valois herself, dripping with rubies that complemented her gown of rose moiré.

After plying her visitor with brandy, Jeanne brusquely informed her, "I am an intimate of the queen and I have chosen you to render a great service to the kingdom."

"Moi?" Mademoiselle Leguay's hand flew to her breast.

"Toi." The comtesse smiled benevolently. "But first I think you should have an aristocratic title." She paused for a moment, thinking. "From now on, you will be a baronne. Baronne Nicole d'Oliva." The newly minted Mademoiselle d'Oliva's services would be required the following night. "What will be expected of me?" she anxiously asked her new benefactress. "Will this grand seigneur expect me to embrace him? And if so, am I to permit him to do so?"

"Undoubtedly," Jeanne replied.

"But . . . what if he should desire still more?"

The comtesse laughed. "I hardly think that probable," she assured the young woman. "You are merely to come with us to Versailles tomorrow evening, where, at a certain spot, you will encounter a great man; when he approaches you, near enough to be heard when you whisper, you will hand him this note and speak the words I tell you to utter." She showed Mademoiselle d'Oliva a folded missive, sealed in red wax with a crest bearing two initials, and told her to return the next afternoon, when she would be attired for her grand role.

While the demimondaine was ensconced in a lavish hotel room for the night, courtesy of the comte and comtesse de Lamotte-Valois, the couple entertained the cardinal, summoning him from the Hôtel de Rohan on the right bank of the Seine.

"I have tremendously exciting news for you," Jeanne told him, removing the crystal stopper from the decanter of brandy and pouring a generous goblet for her illustrious guest. "Your patience and generosity these past several months have finally paid off. The queen herself will meet you tomorrow night below the terraces of Versailles in the bosquet they call the Grove of Venus. A white handkerchief lying at the base of a hedge will mark the place."

The prince de Rohan was well aware that Marie Antoinette's nocturnal strolls along the parterres had for years been the stuff of considerable gossip. And when Jeanne informed the cardinal that the queen remained anxious to ensure his discretion, he, too heady with excitement and ambition, did not question why they were to meet outdoors at midnight on a moonless night.

He saw himself as the hero of a grand adventure, he said to the comtesse, and at that moment would have clasped her to his bosom and smothered her with kisses, had not her husband, puffing away at his clay pipe, been present.

Jeanne smiled and sighed prettily, pursing her lips in a petulant moue at the sight of the cardinal's moist gaze and trembling hands, and pretended to be quite put out that her husband (not to mention Monsieur de Villette), would not quit the room so that she could properly fling herself into the cardinal's arms in a triumphant embrace. A "grand adventure" was indeed about to be staged, not unlike one that had made quite a sensation that season in Paris, when Pierre Augustin Caron de Beaumarchais had penned a romantic comedy that skewered the nobility of France. The king had banned all further performances of *Le Mariage de Figaro,* but after a public outcry, led by the very aristocrats whose class was being mocked, the production was reinstated.

Being the sort of woman who liked to be seen at first nights, the comtesse de Lamotte-Valois was extremely familiar with the scene in which the Countess Almaviva disguises herself as her maid Suzanne in order to catch her own husband in the act of arranging a moonlit assignation in the palace gardens with the maidservant. But the cardinal, for all his worldliness, was too blinded by his own ambitions and his desperate need to be reconciled to the queen to notice the similarities between the stock comedy of Beaumarchais and the plot that Jeanne had contrived.

The following afternoon, the faux baronne d'Oliva was attired by her trio of benefactors in a filmy white dress with a wide blue sash that mimicked the queen's infamous *gaulles.* A flowing cape of white silk completed the ensemble. Nicole's blond hair, lightly powdered to disguise the fact that it was more ash than strawberry, was dressed in fat sausage curls that cascaded from a teased and frizzled coiffure. The comtesse tied a large straw bonnet under her chin; her face was obscured by a *thérèse,* a heavy veil of white lace that was attached to the brim.

Just before dusk, Mademoiselle d'Oliva, with the secret letter in the pocket of her cloak and a pink rose clasped in her hands, was bundled into a coach beside the comte de Lamotte-Valois and the mysterious man whom she had first encountered while sipping chocolate and eyeing prospective patrons outside a café adjacent to the Palais Royal. The carriage clattered out of the rue Neuve Saint-Gilles and into the night.

The coach was left outside the gates and the trio entered the palace grounds, skirting the shadows like so many mice along a baseboard. Just below the Great Terrace and the Hundred Steps was a maze constructed of overlapping *charmilles,* trellises of greenery fanning out every three feet. Less familiar with the gardens than he pretended, Nicolas, guiding Mademoiselle d'Oliva toward the destination appointed for the rendezvous, nearly became lost within the maze of trellises.

"There you are!" he whispered when he spotted another man, who was wearing a voluminous dark cape and a tricorn pulled down over his brow. He was in the company of the comtesse de Lamotte-Valois, who made a discreet fluttering motion with her hand and nodded her head. The prey was in the trap. She approached Mademoiselle d'Oliva and, leading her into a leafy arbor, cautioned her, "Remember, the queen and her maidservant will be watching and listening from behind that hedge. To please her, you will perform this service. You will hand the letter and the rose to the lord who will come to meet you, and as you do so, you will speak only these five words: *You know what this means.*"

She lifted the veil and kissed the girl's cheek. "Wait here. He will arrive presently. *Bonne chance, ma chère.*"

As Nicolas and Rétaux retreated into the darkness, the comtesse de Lamotte-Valois briefly abandoned Mademoiselle d'Oliva and set out through the maze to locate the cloaked and masked cardinal. He was to have waited within the hedges of the Bosquet de la Reine at the spot where she had discreetly dropped the white handkerchief prior to his arrival. She was late for their rendezvous and the anxiety was palpable on his face as he at last recognized her from the voluminous black moiré domino she had promised to wear.

The prince de Rohan clasped her gloved hands in his bare ones. Even through the kidskin she could feel the dampness of his palms. His face was perspiring profusely and she handed him the handkerchief that had lain by the hedge, suggesting that he might wish to make himself more presentable for the queen.

"I apologize for my tardiness," the comtesse said breathlessly, taking the cardinal's arm to guide him through the maze. "I have just come from the queen. She is quite incommoded that Madame and the comtesse d'Artois insist on taking the air with her tonight. They never accompany her, and this has made her quite suspicious. Nevertheless, she insists upon keeping her appointment with you, but it will have to be much briefer, for now she must devise a means of escaping her *belles-soeurs* and they will grow wary if she is absent for too long."

Building the suspense, Jeanne waited a few more minutes, then disappeared into the maze as she told the cardinal, "I think I hear her footsteps! I dare not intrude upon such a private moment, and I am certain that Her Majesty would prefer her words to be for your ears only." A nightingale sang. Or did it? Was it a cue? After the final note a woman appeared, veiled and cloaked, but her overgarment was draped so that it allowed the cardinal a view of a gauzy *chemise à la Reine,* the very style of gown the queen most favored. The woman approached and wordlessly extended the rose to the cardinal.

"*Majesté,* from this moment on, I shall call this the 'rose of happiness.'" He pressed the long-stemmed blossom to his heart and reverently sank to one knee.

"You know what this means," said the woman, finding her tongue at last.

"Oh, yes, Your Majesty," the Grand Almoner breathed. "It means that my hope has been restored. Tonight you have made possible the pinnacle of my joy. To know that all is forgiven. And *you* must know that from this moment on, I am your willing slave." Prostrating himself at her feet, he dared to press his lips to the toe of her silken slipper.

Jeanne decided it was best to end the charade before it exploded. The nightingale sang again. There was a crunching of gravel and from a distant hedge, the sound of voices. From the opposite direction, she emerged with a "*Hsst*—we must leave quickly! The comte d'Artois is approaching with one of his equerries. Hurry, we must make haste! Take cover in the darkness." She shooed the cardinal out of the grove; once she was convinced he had fled, she clasped Mademoiselle d'Oliva by the arm and ushered her toward the *charmilles,* where they rejoined her confederates and left the grove undetected. Only when they clambered into the coach did the courtesan, still a bit flustered by the night's activities, realize that the letter she was supposed to have given to the great gentleman remained in her pocket.

The scheme had worked beyond Jeanne's wildest plans. The cardinal had fairly eaten out of her hand. And from now on, she was convinced, he would never doubt a single word she said.

TWENTY-TWO

The Slave's Collar

September 1, 1784

My dearest brother,

I cannot help but take umbrage at your words. To accuse me of being the "dupe of the French Council of State" is not only inaccurate, it is unwarranted. I had not expected you to credit what half the gossips of France seem to suppose; namely, that I have my husband coiled about my little finger and that I have a tremendous amount of influence, not only on Louis, but on the governance of the realm.

The king is by nature very taciturn and does not share his business with me. Consequently my participation in affairs of state is peripheral at best. In order to learn anything I must slyly wheedle and cajole information from Louis's ministers, to make them believe that the king has already discussed a given situation with me.

Your loving sister,
Antoinette

"Summon the surgeon—*vite! Vite!* The queen has injured her head!"

My horse had thrown me after losing a shoe in the Bois de Boulogne. I lay in the dirt, my skirts belled out about me; the canopy of trees overhead a blur of greenish blue. *"Mes enfants,"* I said deliriously. "I want to see my children."

And then I was lying on my daybed in la Méridienne with my head swathed in a bandage, as I suppose the Queen's Bedchamber was deemed far too public a location for the prostrate body of the sovereign of France. My green and blue décor was, however, just as blurred as that first view of trees and sky. Louis and the abbé Vermond were seated beside me, grave as judges of the Parlement de Paris. My head throbbed, as if someone had clouted me with a plank of wood. I was nauseous and asked for a basin. The king himself held the white Sèvres bowl as I endeavored to relieve myself of the queasiness that had completely overtaken me. I attempted a weak jest. "Maman always warned me about the dangers of riding."

"You are not—?" the abbé left the question hanging in the air.

I smiled and touched my finger to my lips as I regarded my husband, who knew my secret; we enjoyed marital relations so infrequently now, but I knew I was quickening, perhaps a bit less than three months' gone. I blushed for shame. What had I been thinking—going riding in my condition? I had already suffered two miscarriages; the loss of a third baby due to my own foolishness would truly devastate me.

"Où sont nos enfants?" I asked Louis. "I want to see them."

He exchanged glances with the abbé Vermond. "Do you think it a proper idea for them to see their maman like this?" He touched his own head, as if to illustrate his point.

The duchesse de Polignac was summoned with her charges in tow: the tiny dauphin, not yet three years old, and five-year-old Madame Royale. My daughter was sulking and defiantly sucking on her thumb, despite numerous admonitions to cease because it was unbecoming for a girl her age, and moreover, would give her crooked teeth.

"Maman!" The dauphin ran toward me and tried to climb up beside me on the bed.

Rushing to restrain him and glancing at the bloodsoaked bandage about my head, the duchesse leaned down and whispered in my ear, "Perhaps this is too upsetting for them."

I snuggled my son beside me, twining his soft, fine hair about my fingers and gazing blissfully into his open, smiling countenance. It would be my secret that he appeared to have four eyes.

Louis took Marie Thérèse onto his lap, where she immediately nestled into his heavy body as though he were a giant armchair. She regarded me through narrowed eyes, as I lay prostrated on the divan and holding the dauphin to my chest as though he were the most precious object in the world. Her brow furrowed and her rosebud mouth twisted into a frown as though someone had stolen something from her. "Do you regret having a girl, Papa?" she said, stealing a jealous glance at her younger brother.

"*Mon Dieu,* what a question!" Louis replied, genuinely shocked by her words. A tear formed in the corner of his eye. "How can you think such a thing, *ma petite*? I hope that no one stuffed such a notion underneath those brown curls." He looked to me for confirmation and saw the hurt in my eyes. "I most assuredly do not regret for a moment that God and your maman gave you to us, for nothing in the world is prettier to a papa than the sight of his daughter."

"*Mes enfants,* your maman has taken a bad fall," abbé Vermond told the children gently, "but she will soon be all right." He surreptitiously stole a heavenward glance. "Just as good as new. We are all very fortunate that she will be with us for a good while longer."

Madame Royale squirmed in her father's embrace, the better to address the abbé. "She makes me play with baseborn children and take my lessons and share my toys with them. I *hate* little

Ernestine and I *hate* Maman and I wouldn't miss her if she was dead."

The room grew suddenly silent as a tomb, but for the ticking of the seconds as the golden pendulum on the mantel clock swung to and fro. As the adults exchanged shocked looks, Gabrielle de Polignac poured me a glass of orange flower water sweetened with sugar—her usual remedy when she knew I needed soothing. But my head pounded harder than ever and I wished to vomit.

In that moment, I too, wished I were dead.

December

Every few months, the comtesse de Lamotte-Valois had been appealing to the Grand Almoner for another large sum on behalf of the queen, money that would remove the financial distress of some impoverished or indebted friend. And the prince de Rohan never suspected that the friends in question were actually the sharpers who kept touching him for another contribution. By this time the couple had purchased a capacious country home in Bar-sur-Aube, which they had crammed with costly furnishings, and were gleefully flaunting their new wealth and the comtesses's ostensible intimacy with Her Majesty, thumbing their noses at anyone who had been convinced that the ne'er-do-well pair would not amount to much. Owing to the Valois name and to Jeanne's much-vaunted friendship with the sovereign, they lived on credit, never settling a bill, entertaining lavishly, both in Champagne and on the rue Neuve Saint-Gilles in the capital. To owe one's tailor or saddler or shoemaker hundreds of thousands of livres was expected of a person of discerning taste, and in this the comte and comtesse de Lamotte-Valois did not disappoint.

Having thus established themselves as *haut ton,* their guests often included a complement of comtesses, marquises, duchesses, and their red-heeled spouses, all eager to befriend "the little Valois."

After dinner, as her lover Rétaux sang, accompanied on the harp by her husband, a lawyer named Moniseur Laporte admired Jeanne's parure of rubies and amethysts—another purchase made from the cardinal's largesse. "Tell me, do you know a lot about gemstones and jewelry?" Laporte asked his hostess. When she laughed prettily and replied, "Enough to know that I like them," Laporte confided that among his distinguished clientele were the court jewelers, Herren Böhmer and Bassenge. "Swiss-German Hebrews," he whispered behind his hand, "but like so many of their coreligionists, they are connoisseurs of fine diamonds."

He began to rhapsodize about the jewelers' finest work to date, the creation of Herr Bassenge, who was the artiste between the two partners. "They call it the 'slave's collar'—647 diamonds—2800 carats. Absolutely exquisite, if a bit rococo for my own taste. They fashioned it some years ago, after combing the most exclusive markets for the finest stones, in the hope that the *'Bien-Aimé'* would purchase it for Madame du Barry. But," Laporte sighed as though the weight of the world rested upon his pink silk shoulders, "His Majesty went to his heavenly reward and so the necklace remained unsold. It has been their greatest hope to interest the queen in the necklace, but thus far, she has not indicated a willingness to purchase it."

"How much?" The comtesse arched an eyebrow.

"Ah, well." Laporte cleared his throat. "It is rather indelicate to speak of money in such a milieu—but since I believe we may speak the same *lingua franca*"—he chuckled, amused by his own *bon mot*—"I will tell you that they are asking the rather grand sum of one million, eight hundred thousand livres."

Laporte availed himself of a pinch of snuff and took a fortifying gulp of brandy. "As I listened at dinner to your anecdotes about Her Majesty, I admit my mind began to race." He clasped Jeanne's hands and gazed at her with tremendous intensity. "If—if you could, owing to your intimate relationship with the queen—if you could see your way to inducing her to buy the 'slave's collar,' you will have made three men very happy."

The comtesse favored him with a radiant smile. "You know, monsieur, even the closest of her friends cannot make Marie Antoinette do something she does not wish to do. The duchesse de Polignac and I have often remarked upon it. I can promise you that I will speak with her on the subject, but it may take some time to convince her to come around." She bit her lower lip, a subtle suggestion of seduction. "Perhaps if you were to send the court jewelers to call upon me within the next few days—with the necklace—so that I may judge its uniqueness for myself, I will be better able to persuade the queen that no one else must have it."

On the twenty-ninth of the month Jeanne de Lamotte-Valois received two gentlemen in the rue Neuve Saint-Gilles. It took the pair of them, Charles Auguste Böhmer and Paul Bassenge, to carry the gold-tooled case of red Cardan leather, for it was the size of a silver serving platter. Herr Bassenge, the slight, bespectacled designer, and his unprepossessing blond business partner were obsequious in their flattery of the comtesse and her intention to speak to the queen about their prized necklace. Carefully placing the red chest on a marble tabletop, the jewelers opened it to reveal their "slave's collar," resting on a tufted velvet cushion. Jeanne was nearly blinded by its brilliance—and its enormity. "Every stone is flawless," Herr Böhmer explained. "That is why we must sell it. We have sunk our entire credit into creating this *chef d'oeuvre* and cannot imagine breaking up the stones and turning them into other pieces, or selling them off individually."

"May I?" Jeanne breathed, reaching for the necklace. The gentlemen nodded and she lifted the massive collar from its nest. It was almost impossibly heavy and when she held it up to her throat and bosom, it nearly covered the entire expanse, shoulder to shoulder, and fell well below her breasts. In truth the comtesse found the jewelers' masterpiece, a necklace within a necklace, rather gaudy. The choker that sat just below the throat featured three looping festoons anchored by a row of seventeen diamonds as large as filberts, with pear-shaped pendants suspended from the center of each loop. The center section was larger and more ostentatious than the symmetrical side loops, and the stones that dangled from the center swag alone weighed twelve and a half carats apiece. Additional teardrops, even larger than their brethren, hung from the spaces between the festoons. From each shoulder a triple strand of brilliants formed a large M with five-stranded tassels on each end, and two more tassels sprouted from the center V of the design. Above each tassel was an enamel bow in the queen's favorite shade of blue.

Weighed down with the precious gems, the comtesse regarded her reflection. The jewelers' creation was indeed fit for a queen—but not a Bourbon. A secret smile stole across her lips—this "slave's collar" was eminently suitable for a Valois.

Jeanne assured the pair of Jews that Her Majesty, who as everyone knew was fond of diamonds, might indeed be encouraged to make such an extravagant purchase. "It will have to be handled very delicately, however. The king is very modest in his expenditures and she will not want to appeal to him for a loan. But trust me," she added, extending her hand to be kissed, and casting a longing glance at the closed Cardan leather box, "I will see to it that your necklace is taken off your hands."

TWENTY-THREE

Duplicity

JANUARY 1785

"Her Majesty believes you are the only man she can trust in this endeavor." The comtesse de Lamotte-Valois allowed her fingers to play along the contours of the cardinal's naked thigh. Silken sheets, woven to his custom by purveyors in the Orient, puddled about their bodies, immune to the winter's chill thanks to the crackling fire in the enormous hearth. Jeanne outstretched her leg and traced a line along the damask bed hangings with the tip of her toe. "*Naturellement,* your discretion is imperative." She reached for the half-devoured plate of oysters resting beside the bed and tossed back her head to receive one of the succulent delicacies.

"But-but of course," the cardinal stammered. To be singled out by the queen to facilitate this acquisition in her name. Yes—she trusted him implicity. He had read it in her eyes when she inclined her head to him in the Oeil de Boeuf, a glance that spoke volumes.

Time was of the essence, his lover reminded him. "You know the queen's temperament can be mercurial, especially when she's *enceinte.*"

What wouldn't he have done for his sovereign and for his savior, the comtesse!

On January 24, the prince de Rohan stunned the jewelers in their shop in the rue Vendôme by calling upon them in person. Pale blue walls set off with white boiserie reminded him of the interior of a lady's jewel casket. Naturally such a rare specimen as the renowned "slave's collar" would not have been on display in any of the glass vitrines. When the Grand Almoner demanded to see the 2800-carat diamond necklace, the shop assistant, a young gentleman who could scarcely believe he was waiting on a cardinal who was also a prince, rang the bell to summon the owners.

One would have been hard-pressed to determine which of the men was more obsequious—Herr Böhmer, scarcely unable to contain his excitement over the prospect of finally selling his greatest treasure and most costly investment; Herr Bassenge, who could barely suppress his delight, imagining Marie Antoinette wearing his most elaborate creation to date; or the prince, who was already dreaming about how Her Majesty might thank him. To restore the illustrious name of Rohan and be named Chief Minister—oh, his ambition was boundless! And the necklace was truly a work of art; even without a jeweler's loupe the cardinal's discerning eye recognized that the gemstones had no equal.

"Is something troubling you, Your Eminence?" Herr Böhmer noticed the cardinal's furrowed brow and blotted the anxious perspiration from his own with a monogrammed handkerchief.

"I have promised the comtesse de Lamotte-Valois to be the queen's interlocutor in this affair, but"—the cardinal hesitated, unsure of how much to confide—"the sum you request is, even after inspecting the necklace, *ahh,* I believe, somewhat inflated."

"Then what do you propose?" inquired Bassenge, anxiously envisioning the purchaser slipping from his grasp.

The cardinal steeled himself; he was not a man prone to negotiation. "Two hundred thousand livres less: one million, six hundred thousand." He swallowed hard. "Payable in four installments of four hundred thousand apiece every six months over a period of two years, to commence on the first of August."

He accepted a glass of brandy from the proprietors, stalling for time, wondering, when he was indebted to numerous creditors himself, how he could secure the necessary loans and when he might expect reimbursement. Like the queen herself, he was continually exhausting his funds, making improvements to his residences and acquiring exquisite works of art. In one chamber alone, amid pastoral canvases by Fragonard and Boucher, one of the first Gutenburg Bibles reposed in a glass case, on view so that his visitors could admire his discriminating taste.

The jewelers conferred, addressing their concerns in hushed tones. When French failed, they switched to German. Finally they turned to the cardinal and announced, endeavoring to temper their elation, "Congratulations, Your Eminence. We would be happy to accept your proposal!"

Five days later, they delivered the necklace to the Palais Cardinal's gilded salon, shimmering with mirrors and hung with priceless Gobelin tapestries. "I am not in the habit of transacting with my jeweler in this manner," the prince de Rohan informed them. Unlocking an exquisite fruitwood *secrétaire* embellished with vermeil and urging the jewelers to safeguard what he was about to provide, he handed them a letter endorsing the contractual details, signed Marie Antoinette de France. Financially anxious, the cardinal had drawn up this document to indemnify himself, asking the comtesse de Lamotte-Valois to bring it to the queen for her approval. Within a day, she had acquired Marie Antoinette's sanction, and the cardinal became all the more impressed by his lover's intimacy with the queen.

He paid Jeanne a visit on February 1, with the large red leather box containing the priceless "slave's collar" tucked inside an unassuming satchel. Assuring the prince that he had done a great service to France for which both she and Her Majesty would be eternally grateful, the comtesse plied him with compliments and an excellent Bordeaux, then relinquished her charms to him, the better to send him away buoyed with ebullience.

Soon, he believed, he would see the queen wearing the spectacular necklace about her throat and bask in the glow of her reflected gratitude.

March

During my third thus far successful pregnancy, in order to allay my ennui, I commenced rehearsals of Pierre Beaumarchais's comedy *Le Barbier de Séville* in my theater at le Petit Trianon. My detractors, who of course had never seen it, derided the charming pavilion for its preponderance of gilt and marble, but in truth the jewel box décor was nothing more than a trompe l'oeil contrived with white and gold paint and papier-mâché.

My company, *la troupe des seigneurs,* comprised entirely of members of the nobility, was coached by Joseph Dazincourt, a leading actor with the Comédie-Française, and I engaged Louis Michu from the Comédie-Italienne to be our singing master. I had chosen to play the soubrette, Rosine, but as I entered my thirtieth year, I wondered whether I didn't look too old for the role.

The king had been none too pleased about my selection, insisting that Monsieur Beaumarchais was dangerous and subversive, insulting and mocking to persons of rank and title, citing the playwright's *Mariage de Figaro* as an example. But I found *Le Barbier de Séville* a delight and a welcome diversion from the exigencies of my condition, and whenever I was increasing, Louis was exceptionally doting and indulgent.

At 7:30 in the morning on Easter Sunday, the twenty-seventh of March, I was delivered of another son, Louis Charles. France called him the duc de Normandie, but to me, my chubby infant, as fat and rosy as his older brother the dauphin was pale and fragile, would forever be *mon "chou d'amour,"* an affectionate nickname that, as I wrote to my English *amie,* the Duchess of Devonshire, defied a proper translation: "'Love cabbage' is the best I can furnish you, *ma chère duchesse,* but it hardly conveys a sense of charm in your native tongue. He is vigorous and healthy, and as sturdy as a typical peasant youngster. So I suppose I must admit that in this he favors his papa. I do hope that on your next excursion to Paris you will honor us with another visit so that you may meet him." Though he certainly looked nothing like Axel, there were anonymous rumblings from someone who knew of our *affaire de coeur,* questioning the little duc's paternity—the first time in all these years that the count's name and mine had ever been linked. I was entirely certain the duc de Normandie was the king's son, and Louis never for a moment doubted it. Nor did he address the rumors about Axel, which surely reached his ears. I would not dignify the gossip by discussing it with the king, nor did he speak of it to me. It did not lie within his nature to confront a thing directly. Moreover, like his *grand-père,* he avoided any unpleasantness like the pox.

My beloved sister Maria Carolina, the queen of Naples, was our little duc's godmother, although in her absence Gabrielle de Polignac, as royal governess, took her place at the baptismal font. My dear friend became so overcome with emotion as she held the infant prince that her husband had to stand by her elbow in case she swooned. It was all *I* could do not to grow queasy when the odious Grand Almoner kept gazing at me across the font with an ingratiating smirk pasted to his face.

Something changed inside me with the advent of my second son's birth. I had lost my desire to while away the evening hours at the Opéra and masquerades. Dancing no longer held the allure that it had in my youth, and I had even less of a taste for gaming.

"The *gaulles* are for young women," I told Rose Bertin in late May during one of her twice-weekly visits to Versailles. "The last time the royal dressmaker Madame Éloffe measured me, she could only cinch my waist to twenty-three inches in my stays," and my bosom, so much longed for during my girlhood had increased to forty-four inches. "I feel foolish now, looking like *ma petite* Mousseline. It is," I sighed with some resignation, "time for more structure than that afforded by the *chemises à la Reine.*" My untrammeled gaiety was a thing of the distant past, or so it seemed. Motherhood had changed me immeasurably, and my chief desire was to spend as much time as possible playing with my precious sons and daughter.

Mademoiselle Bertin, as ever, was excited about the prospect of creating a different image for me, returning to Versailles bearing armloads of velvets in sumptuous jewel tones—garnet, ruby, amethyst, emerald, and sapphire. The *marchande de modes* was herself gowned in indigo taffeta with minimal embellishments, the taste for overdone furbelows being now on the wane. She was surprised, however, to find me in tears.

"We must present a picture of maturity and restraint," I told Rose, although my voice was breaking. "The scandalmongers are again having their day at my expense, and my husband's censors seem powerless to halt the flood of their defamatory propaganda. If it is at all possible, I wish to limit the amount of fodder for these vultures. Perhaps it is naïve of me to think so, but if I can show them who I really am—a dignified and devoted mother—their pens will cease to scratch so vehemently."

"Regardez-la," I said, handing the *marchande* a pamphlet. "His Majesty found this tucked into his napkin at supper on Tuesday. It could only have come from within the palace."

Mademoiselle Bertin shook her head in disgust. "My heart goes out to you as well as to the duchesse," she muttered, referring to madame de Polignac.

The repulsive engraving depicted me in a lascivious embrace with Gabrielle; one of her hands dandled my breast and the other foraged beneath my raised skirts. "She has been traduced nearly as much as I have for her extravagance," I said bitterly. "And yet, were one to tot up the sums, even taking into account my generosity toward her, my dear friend has spent less in the decade or so since she came to court than Madame de Pompadour did in a single year. Do people truly believe she is my lover? Do they think she is *my* Pompadour? Is that what they mean by this filth?" I sighed heavily. "*Maîtresses en titre* have been tarred by the caricaturists for decades. But what has happened to the respect for the Crown? I warrant I am the first queen of France to be the target of such vulgarity."

As she wordlessly clucked in disgust at the *libelles,* Rose draped the deep blue velvet yardage across my chest. "This brings out your eyes even more, *Majesté.* You absolutely must have a gown made up. It is because you are not a native Frenchwoman that they disparage you so," she said, changing the subject. "*C'est vrai,* la Pompadour also came in for much criticism at the time, but she was one of our own. The French have never taken outsiders to their bosom."

"But my union with the king was not of my choosing," I replied. "Or of Louis's. Everyone knows that."

"Hatred and Reason are natural enemies," said Rose, fussing

with the sapphire velvet. "I would wear diamonds with this. You will resemble the goddess of the moon in the night sky, twinkling with stars."

As she removed the fabric and began to play with the bolt of ruby red, "No more diamonds," I replied. "I have enough already and despite what people have said, although some years ago I purchased a set of bracelets, and I am fond of my *girandole* ear bobs, the brilliants have never been my favorite gem." I glanced at the little duc de Normandie, blissfully asleep in his cradle. "You would think that by breastfeeding him, I would shrink a bit, but *hélas,* that hasn't happened," I chuckled, recalling both the scandal it created when I insisted on feeding Madame Royale myself and Count von Fersen's present appreciation of my pulchritude. He had recently returned from his Grand Tour with the king of Sweden, gratified to be back in France once more. I had not seen him since the previous summer when we fêted Gustavus at Trianon. Axel and I had resumed our liaison, but even now, I was too often burdened with other cares to give myself over to delights of the flesh, and bedeviled with the pangs of a guilty conscience every time my thoughts of him turned amorous. Ours remained a Grand Passion, but what we shared most often now were confidences and dreams, hopes and fears.

Axel listened to me without judgments; he carried all my secrets. How, I marveled, did he always manage to remain above the fray, immune to the petty intrigues and squabbles of the other courtiers? I might have said it was because he was a foreigner at our court, but my Trianon *cercle* alone was filled with them. I preferred to see Count von Fersen as the constant oasis of calm at the eye of a perpetual maelstrom; and in a world of girls and boys, so often the only adult, wise beyond his years.

Where once my coterie, and then Axel, had brought me the most fulfillment, my children had become everything to me, and there were no lengths to which I would not go to see them happy and healthy. When something was wrong with one of them, I suffered just as greatly. That spring Louis had purchased the château of Saint-Cloud in my name after we agreed that the dauphin required the fresh air of a more healthful climate. The king's charming hunting lodge La Muette was too small for our burgeoning family and the entourage necessary to accompany us. Returning to the subject of diamonds, I told Mademoiselle Bertin, "Besides, if I *had* the funds for any new extravagances, I would renovate Saint-Cloud."

JULY

The prince de Rohan had been on edge since April; Comtesse de Lamotte-Valois had delivered the "slave's collar" to the queen several weeks earlier and he had yet to see her wearing it. "Did you not assure me I would see it about her neck at Pentecost?" he murmured to Jeanne during one of their trysts.

Jeanne had cupped his face in her hands; giving him a lingering kiss, she convinced him that Her Majesty had changed her mind and now intended to surprise the king by donning the diamonds when he least expected to see them. The comtesse couldn't admit, of course, that the cardinal would never see the necklace adorning the throat of Marie Antoinette. For as soon as Jeanne had taken possession of the brilliants, her husband and lover prized them from their settings with the intention of selling them to various jewelers. Rétaux had a close call when a suspicious merchant alerted the gendarmes and he was imprisoned while the authorities made some inquiries. Jeanne was terrified that their grand scheme might be smashed like a crystal decanter. But after the police determined that no shops had recently been robbed, the trio exhaled a collective sigh and decided to alter their plans.

Within days the prince de Rohan received a letter in the queen's hand, requesting him to take a holiday at his residence in Alsace, while Nicolas de Lamotte-Valois boarded a ship at Calais, bound for England, where he would retail the diamonds, a few at a time, to the London jewelers, claiming they had come from family heirlooms. Doubtless he would not be paid what they were worth; but, as they were not his to dispose of in the first place, and too much negotiation might raise eyebrows, the conspirators agreed that whatever the comte received would be quite an acceptable sum.

On the tenth of July, back in Paris with only three weeks to spare before he was due to deliver the first installment of 400,000 livres, the prince de Rohan summoned Herren Böhmer and Bassenge to the Palais Cardinal. His Alençon cuffs were limp with perspiration as he confessed, with a good deal of embarrassment, to an unavoidable delay, blotting his panicked brow with a fine cambric handkerchief throughout the interview.

Herr Böhmer's narrow face was pale. "We have a written agreement, Your Eminence."

"*Oui, oui, je sais.* I know that," stammered the cardinal. What could he tell them? That it had been impossible to raise the funds? His eyes darted about the room at the silk tapestries, the oils and bronzes, the objets d'art of porcelain, crystal, and marble; treasures that had been in his family for decades, if not centuries. To part with a single one of them would sully the illustrious name of Rohan.

"Her Majesty has requested an additional discount," said the prince, improvising wildly. "Consequently, until the adjusted sum has been agreed upon, she cannot honor the August first payment date." The doubt and concern in the jewelers' eyes as they exchanged anxious glances prompted him to raise the stakes. "However, the queen has instructed me to inform you that to compensate for the lateness of the payment, she will remit the sum of seven hundred thousand livres shortly after the settlement of the revised price of the necklace." De Rohan knew he was rambling. His throat felt tight. Was his excuse convincing? Beneath his red moiré soutane his legs were trembling.

"Monsieur le Cardinal, I cannot say that we are pleased to hear this." Herr Böhmer held his ground. "We have ourselves borrowed a considerable sum of money agaist the sale of the necklace."

"We have a lengthy association with the Crown and enjoy an excellent reputation as jewelers to the court," added Herr Bassenge. "If we default on our own loan, our credit, as well as our credibility, will be irretrievably embarrassed."

"We stand to be entirely ruined by it," added his business partner bluntly. "In a word—bankrupted."

"It is, *certainement,* an extremely delicate situation," Bassenge interjected, "and we appreciate the difficult position in which you have been placed, Your Eminence. Perhaps, then, being businessmen of long standing with the queen, Herr Böhmer and I might have better luck were we to approach Her Majesty directly."

The cardinal felt his gut plummet. Marie Antoinette had singled him out, relying upon his tact, discretion, and secrecy to complete this commission. What would this bode for his grand ambition to be named France's Chief Minister? Moreover, what would she think of him now, believing he had failed her?

TWENTY-FOUR

Who Is the Spider and Who Is the Fly?

On July 12, a strange letter was delivered while I was in my salon rehearsing my lines for *Le Barbier de Séville* with my lady-in-waiting, Madame Campan. In her youth, this handsome woman, three years my senior, with her broad face and intelligent, dark eyes, had been Mesdames *tantes'* reader and I found her to be an exemplary prompter, for she read aloud with tremendous sensibility.

The note read:

Madame,

We are at the pinnacle of happiness in daring to believe that the latest arrangements proposed to us, which we accepted with both zeal and respect, afford new proof of our submission and devotion to Your Majesty's orders, and we take genuine satisfaction in the thought that the most exquisite set of diamonds in the world will adorn the greatest and best of queens.

Your servants always,

Paul Bassenge and Charles Auguste Böhmer

"*Regardez,* Henriette." I showed the letter to Madame Campan. "Since you are so adept at solving the riddles in *Le Mercure de France,* perhaps you might assay this conundrum, for I haven't the slightest idea what the gentlemen refer to."

She could make neither head nor tail of the note either. Determining that the jewelers must have written it in error, I took it back to my escritoire, rolled it into a spill, and set it alight with the candle I kept illuminated on the desk to melt the sealing wax for my correspondence.

But the strange business reared its head again nearly a month later when Herr Böhmer, in a state of extreme agitation, rode out to Versailles and most vociferously insisted on an interview with me. After being shown to le Petit Trianon, with exquisite politeness he reminded me of the letter he had sent the previous month and, endeavoring to swallow his evident embarrassment, demanded the payment of the first installment on the diamond necklace that he claimed I had agreed to purchase from him for 1.6 million livres. "The 'slave's collar,'" he added, describing it in detail. "In short, Your Majesty, as you have possession of the necklace, and the Grand Almoner insists he does not have the necessary funds, I regret the unpleasantness of appealing to you directly."

Then, taking my confusion for prevarication, the jeweler resorted to threats. "The time for pretense has passed, Madame. Deign to admit that you have my diamond necklace and render me assistance. If not, my bankruptcy will bring the whole affair to light!"

In great distress, reiterating that I had no idea what he was talking about and assuring him that I had neither the necklace nor the money, nor would I be blackmailed, I dismissed Herr Böhmer from my rooms. That same day the puzzle grew even more complex when the abbé Vermond confided that a few hours earlier he had received a visit from Monsieur Saint-James, a prominent Parisian banker. Evidently, the prince de Rohan had approached him to request a loan of 700,000 livres in the queen's name. As the sum was prodigious, Saint-James informed the cardinal that he would have to secure specific orders from Her Majesty before lending him so much money. Sensing that something was amiss, the banker contacted Vermond, aware that the abbé was my trusted confidant.

Events quickly spiraled out of control. Two days later Herr Böhmer returned to the palace in a state of increased agitation.

After affecting a low bow, he spilled the purpose of his errand in a torrent of words. "My dear Majesty," he began, "it seems that we have all been the dupes of a forged contract." He mentioned that a comtesse whose name I did not recognize had visited the jewelers' shop in the rue Vendôme and informed Herr Bassenge that they had been the victims of a hoax involving the Grand Almoner's acquisition of a diamond necklace, ostensibly on my behalf.

"Whyever would I authorize the prince de Rohan to do *anything* for me, let alone purchase a necklace that you say is worth nearly two million livres? I recall perfectly well that back in 1781 when you showed that very piece to the king in the hopes of selling it to him, he was quite taken with it, but I refused such an extravagance. 'Our navy needs the money more than I require the diamonds. I have more than enough,' I told His Majesty, and I am certain my reply was conveyed to you and to Herr Bassenge. In the past I have purchased several bracelets and a pair of earrings from you, and those are all the brilliants I desire. With the crown jewels at my disposal, and the pearls that belonged to Anne of Austria, which are larger than sugared almonds—" I broke off and began to tremble.

"And there are no remittances outstanding, messieurs. Her

Majesty's account was settled in full with you long ago," Madame Campan interjected, her color rising.

I demanded a written report within twenty-four hours detailing the entire sordid business. "I expect you to appear before me tomorrow with the document in your hands, Herr Böhmer. And bring this alleged contract as well."

"I am too distracted to rehearse any more," I told Madame Campan after the jeweler had left. What I dared not admit to my lady-in-waiting was how alarmed I was made by his visit. I had to confide in someone and I was too frightened to speak to Louis, so I wrote to my brother in Vienna, telling Joseph, "I feel sure that the cardinal has used my name like a vile and clumsy counterfeiter. In all probability, temporarily pressed for money, he assumed he would be able to pay the jewelers the first installment before anyone discovered the fraud he had perpetrated."

But nothing prepared me for the contract Herr Böhmer showed me the following day, visiting me in the privacy of la Méridienne. My hands shook as I read it, for I had never seen such a calumny. "Madame Campan, *s'il vous plaît,* summon the baron de Breteuil," I said weakly. The jeweler and I sat in silence while the minutes ticked by inexorably, as we waited for the king's Minister of the Household to arrive.

The burly Louis-Auguste le Tonnelier, baron de Breteuil, impulsive and passionate, had seen much in his fifty-five years. Having served as France's ambassador to Imperial Russia, he had sparred with Catherine the Great and had no qualms about making his opinions known in a stentorian baritone that echoed off the plastered walls. He also had no love for the pompous cardinal, as each was angling for the same plum ministerial appointment.

As he perused Herr Böhmer's recitation of events the baron's face grew more florid by the moment. "And you say you have never met this comtesse de Lamotte-Valois?" he asked me pointedly.

"Not only have I never met her, I have never heard of her." I sniffed. "There are thousands of people milling about Versailles every day—any woman can gain entry. And, it seems, anyone can go about calling themselves a comtesse, or any other member of the nobility as long as there are people gullible enough to believe them." According to Herr Böhmer, it was this soi-disant comtesse who had informed the jewelers that they had handed the cardinal their priceless necklace on the basis of a false contract with a forged signature. How she ascertained this, I knew not.

"And you do not have the necklace?" the baron asked me.

"I do not have it, nor have I ever wanted it, nor did I enter into any arrangement to purchase it," I replied tensely.

Brandishing the purported contract, the baron declared, "I'll wager that this paper is the single greatest crime perpetrated against the Crown in memory! Regrettably, this is far too grave a matter to conceal between us."

My stomach grew weak when he insisted that everything be shared with the king.

Louis's habit of dithering angered me even more. Before he would take the matter in hand he insisted on speaking with one of the cardinal's kinsmen, sending for the prince de Soubise on August 14, to determine what role the Grand Almoner had played in this increasingly confusing charade. But as things transpired, Soubise was nowhere near Versailles. The jewelers wanted their money, and I demanded prompt answers. Consequently, Louis would have to confront the cardinal directly.

The following day, August 15, was a sacred one—the Feast of the Assumption as well as my name day. And the cardinal had a leading role to play in the proceedings. I could scarcely bring myself to look at His Arrogance, adorned for High Mass with an alb worth 10,000 livres, created with millions of infinitesimal petit point stitches depicting the Rohan arms and device.

Before Mass, Louis invited the cardinal into his private study.

Also present were a trio of high-ranking ministers—baron de Breteuil; the comte de Vergennes, France's Foreign Affairs minister; and the Keeper of the Seals, Monsieur de Miromesnil, all clad in their finest silk suits and long waistcoats heavily embroidered with gold and silver bullion.

"Please be seated, Your Eminence." The king's manner was as mild and even-tempered as ever; mine, on the other hand, was swarming with metaphorical hornets. Louis unlocked his desk and removed Herr Böhmer's statement, sworn to and notarized by a Parisian official.

After showing the document to the Grand Almoner, Louis inquired, "Monsieur le prince, did you purchase the necklace the jeweler alludes to?"

As he glanced about the room at the cluster of ministers, I could see that it was an effort for the cardinal to maintain his composure. "I did, Sire—on behalf of the queen."

"But what could possibly have induced you to indulge in this fantasy?" I interrupted. "Are we on such intimate terms that I have made you my errand boy? *Non!* I have not addressed a single word to you since your return from Vienna a decade ago, not even across the font when you baptized my children. No man at court has incurred my displeasure as much as you have done!"

The prince de Rohan leered at me. "Strong words from a woman who met me on a moonless night in the Grove of Venus and handed me a rose. I keep it in a special box, you know. A remembrance of that glorious rendezvous where I dared to kiss your slipper."

A monstrous tale began to emerge: a veiled woman in white, a clandestine tryst. "It-it was all arranged by the-the comtesse de Lamotte-Valois," the cardinal insisted, stammering as he realized he might as well have been standing on a sandy beach during a receding tide. "She gave me to understand that you wished to honor me with the commission."

I threw my hands in the air in utter disgust. "This is the second time I have heard this name mentioned, and I assure you, monsieur, that I do not know such a woman. Not only is she not an intimate of mine, and you may interview any of my ladies—Campan, Polignac, Lamballe, all of whom are longtime companions—for verification, but I have never even met the comtesse you refer to. Frankly, I doubt this personage exists. The baron de Breteuil has quite convinced me that you have devised this entire scheme in order to bring about my downfall."

Breteuil nodded vehemently. "The notion that Her Majesty—who has always detested the cardinal for his weak morals and his antipathy to her Hapsburg relations—would entrust him with such a prodigious and delicate responsibility is preposterous."

Louis raised his arms in a placating gesture. "Please—*everyone.* I wish to get to the bottom of this morass in a rational manner and without further accusations. Your Eminence, who instructed you to purchase the 'slave's collar'?"

Perspiring heavily now, the Grand Almoner said weakly, "The comtesse de Lamotte-Valois, claiming that she was acting as Her Majesty's interlocutor. But as the queen insists that this person is unknown to her, I see that I may have been the dupe of a woman who invented and feigned a friendship that never existed. My honest intention and desire to please Her Majesty blinded me."

Louis removed the contract from his desk and handed it to the cardinal. "So you say, monsieur. But I fail to see how you could be taken in by *this.*"

"That is not even my handwriting!" I cried.

The cardinal's expression was both haughty and disbelieving. "With all due respect, *Majesté,* I do not recall whether I have ever had the occasion to see a document penned by you, in order to form a comparison," he replied testily.

I blushed so furiously that tears came to my eyes.

"Oh, come, come, monsieur!" shouted the baron de Breteuil.

"I have seen much in the past several years—vile cartoons and caricatures, and cruel poems and pamphlets; but I have never been so insulted as *this*. By this man." My shoulders heaved with sobbing.

Moved by my tears, Louis took one of my hands in his, caressing it reassuringly. He raised his other hand in a request for silence. "Perhaps it is true that you have never seen the queen's handwriting—but, sir, how could you possibly—a man of your experience and renown—a *prince*—not be aware that this could never be Her Majesty's signature?! Read that aloud, monsieur."

"Marie Antoinette de France," the cardinal mumbled.

"Louder," commanded the king. The prince de Rohan complied. "Now then: an ignorant forger might not know it, but any genuine member of the nobility, in fact anyone with a rudimentary education, knows that monarchs sign only their Christian names. It is quite understood what country they rule. Not only is this not the queen's hand, but it is clearly not her signature, for if she were to put her name to anything, she would write merely *Marie Antoinette*."

The Grand Almoner grew pale, then turned a sickly shade of green. Louis handed him a paper and quill, and indicating the inkstand, instructed him to compose his statement of events on the spot. Fifteen minutes later, the king collected the document and dismissed the prince from his sight. As all this transpired, I had been unable to contain my weeping, thoroughly convinced that the prince de Rohan was no better than a charlatan bent on destroying my good name.

Louis conferred with the baron de Breteuil, who was emphatically in favor of immediately arresting the cardinal, though I could tell that, true to his wont, the king was unwilling to take a decisive tack. Convulsed with sobs, I became certain that even my husband was betraying me, choosing to favor his duplicitous Grand Almoner over his devoted wife.

The men rose and quit the study, heading for the Hall of Mirrors. A few moments later, I gathered my skirts and followed. Suddenly, above the hubbub of people gathered in the Galerie des Glaces, the baron's booming voice declared, "By the king's order, arrest Cardinal de Rohan!"

A thousand people turned as one shocked body to stare at the Grand Almoner. When they found their respective tongues, a cacophony of excited questions buzzed about the hall. The entire royal family was present, preparing to head to the chapel, our procession witnessed by hundreds of spectactors who considered it a privilege and an honor to be in attendance.

They continued to gawk as the officers of the guard openly humiliated the prince de Rohan by apprehending him in public. At first he endeavored to shrug them off, doubling over as though afflicted with a bellyache. *"Attendez, messieurs,"* he said, with a dismissive wave. "Wait."

"Allow me to adjust the buckle of my garter," said the cardinal smoothly. "My hose are slipping." *Must keep my wits,* he thought as he bent over. Thank heaven for the prescient Cagliostro who had convinced him it was good luck to conceal a stub of pencil and a scrap of paper upon his person at all times.

After being conveyed under guard to his residence at Versailles, his rank allowing him the courtesy of preparing for his inevitable incarceration, the cardinal summoned his valet, Herr Schreiber; and, handing him the hastily scribbled note, murmured, "Take this to the Palais Cardinal and immediately burn all my papers pertaining to this incident." The valet galloped off at full tilt, and by the time the prince and his escorts reached Paris where they were met at his residence by the Lieutenant General of Police, the incriminating documents, as well as the *billets-doux* exchanged between the cardinal and several prominent ladies of the court, had already been consigned to the flames.

At eleven-thirty that evening, another visitor arrived. "I bear a *lettre de cachet,* remanding the Grand Almoner to the Bastille," announced the comte d'Agout. The king's seal was unmistakably imprinted upon it. Incapable of concealing his distress, the cardinal informed the comte of the role that Jeanne de Lamotte-Valois had played in the entire scenario, furnishing the addresses of all her residences.

Upon the arrival of the comte de Launay, the genial elderly governor of the Bastille, come to escort his illustrious detainee to the prison fortress, the prince de Rohan took one last, lingering look at his room full of treasures and priceless furnishings, making a silent vow to return before too much dust had gathered.

At four o'clock the following morning, a heavy knock on the front door of the comtesse de Lamotte-Valois's country estate produced the châtelaine. Though wild-eyed, Jeanne was fully awake. Having heard the news from the royal court, she had spent the night destroying her intimate correspondence with the cardinal, including a considerable number of *billets-doux.*

"Is the warrant written for the arrest of the comte de Lamotte-Valois as well?" she inquired defiantly. After rereading the document, the police lieutenant replied in the negative. Favoring the man with her warmest smile, despite the panic in her belly, she apologized. "*Excusez-moi.* This is all rather frightening, and I find I must relieve myself." With his permission, she darted through the hall on the pretext of locating a chamber pot.

"Hsst!" She prodded her slumbering husband, who groggily tugged the eiderdown coverlet about him. "Wake up! You must

go!" A moment later, Nicolas bolted upright. "Save yourself," she told him hysterically. "Collect as much of our money and plate as you can carry—including the candlesticks—climb out the back window, and mount the fastest horse in the stables. Ride to the coast and board the first ship for England. I don't know where they plan to take me, but I will try to send you word at Nerot's hotel in King Street, Mayfair." They enjoyed one final, desperate embrace before the sturdy former military man accepted his marching orders and fled into the approaching dawn.

The sky was tinged with pearlescent yellow by the time the comtesse was greeted by the Bastille's governor, still wearing his olive silk banyan with a cloth about his head. In this garb, with his morning ablutions still to be made, the comte de Launay interrogated his new prisoner, informing her that she was being charged with stealing a diamond necklace worth 1.8 million livres from the court jewelers.

"Preposterous!" Jeanne exclaimed. "If I were in possession of such a priceless item, would I still be living modestly at Bar-sur-Aube?" She nearly cackled with panic. "I demand that you send someone there—or go and see for yourself! Search the house, every cupboard and closet, from cellar to attic, and see whether the necklace is there. For you won't find a thing, I assure you. If you want to know who controls the cardinal and encourages him to every vice imaginable, question that arch-conjurer who resides under his roof. Cagliostro is the one who alleges that he can make gold and diamonds appear. I'll wager he knows how to make them disappear as well, for how else can he work his alchemy?"

Evidently, there had been other swindlers involved in the mad scheme to depict me as the covetous and covert purchaser of the "slave's collar." On the same afternoon that the comtesse de Lamotte-Valois was apprehended, the vastly popular Count Cagliostro and his illiterate blond wife Serafina were placed under arrest as well. When the police lieutenant demanded of the self-proclaimed mystic whether he knew the reason for his apprehension, Cagliostro declared that he hadn't the faintest suspicion, unless he was finally being taken into custody for the murder of the great Roman general Pompey—protesting that he was blameless, as he had undertaken the assassination on the orders of the pharaoh. I had never even met the renowned mystic and could not imagine what he had to do with the plot, until Madame Campan told me that the cardinal had opened his home to him and believed the mysterious count could create gold and diamonds out of thin air.

"Then why did Cagliostro not conjure a necklace for his deluded host?" I exclaimed bitterly. "It would have saved everyone so much trouble!"

The authorities had trapped nearly all the flies. One culprit, however, had yet to be accounted for. Still on the wing was Rétaux de Villette, the comtesse's erstwhile secretary, who had escaped their notice and flown eastward for the Swiss border.

Imprisonment was only the beginning. I desired the whole of France, nay the world, to know what sort of character the Grand Almoner had. An inquest is not enough, I told Louis. "He must be tried by the Parlement de Paris."

Oddly enough, it was the first time any wish of mine had coincided with the cardinal's.

TWENTY-FIVE

We All Have Much to Prove

November 1785

My Dearest Sophie:

Two more alleged conspirators in *l'affaire* were apprehended in September: a man named Rétaux de Villette, and a fair-haired demimondaine, one Mademoiselle Leguay d'Oliva, well known about the upper reaches of the theater and the cafés near the Palais Royal. The mademoiselle had fled to Brussels after the cardinal's apprehension. No sooner were they arrested than both parties are said to have become quite voluble regarding their involvement in the matter.

That is the good news. The bad, alas, is that the stories being repeated in the provinces, by those who know nothing and are only regurgitating hearsay, are appalling. People refuse to believe that the purchase of the necklace and the forged documents are the real reason for the cardinal's imprisonment. They have heard that he is a long-standing nemesis of Her Majesty's and they are convinced that she forced the king's hand to sign a *lettre de cachet* consigning him to the Bastille. In Paris, where the cardinal's manner of high living is well known, they are saying nonetheless that the queen used her wiles to induce him to buy the diamond necklace and then passed the money on to her brother in Austria.

Yet even His Imperial Majesty, who has had nothing whatsoever to do with the entire business and certainly received no funds from his sister, is unwilling to believe that the cardinal is "light-minded and hopelessly extravagant and capable of such rascality, of so black a crime as that of which he has been accused."

No sooner was the prince arrested but a hue and cry went up from the ranks of the nobility as well as the clergy, who are openly defiant of authority and have become bitter enemies of the queen. One has only to frequent the salons and cafés of Paris, particularly in the vicinity of the Palais Royal, to hear the throne openly censured.

The trial briefs have sold by the thousands, snapped up the moment they are published; some of the defendants' respective attorneys are making their names and all are amassing a small fortune from the sale of this propaganda. These efforts to elicit sympathy and exonerate their clients in the public arena are a pure invention of the testimony given during the depositions; the lawyers are not even permitted to accompany their clients to the preliminary hearings. The testimony is being conducted by the magistrates appointed by the president of the Parlement de Paris, Monsieur d'Aligre, rumored to be among the comtesse de Lamotte-Valois's cadre of lovers—which infuriates the poor queen all the more, for she fears she will never receive justice from such a corrupt body.

Believe me when I say that it is now considered *bon ton* to pay one's respects to the cardinal in the Bastille. Thanks to the influence of the Rohan *famille,* which includes the powerful Guéménés, the Soubises, and the Lorraines—the last being relations of the queen's late father—and to his trial briefs, so cleverly penned by his lawyer, Maître Target, few can believe that such an eminent sophisticate as Prince Louis de Rohan, Grand Almoner of France, a cardinal as well as a bishop, could have been taken in by a provincial woman of little importance.

As the interviews have progressed, Her Majesty withdraws more and more, like a wounded lioness, to le Petit Trianon. She is expecting a fourth child now, and instead of rejoicing in such a blessed event, she despairs. She is most unhappy, and her courage, which is admirable beyond compare, makes her yet more attractive. But her spirit is no longer blithe. She is afraid. And the more unfortunate her state, the more she is forsaken by those who once clamored for her companionship.

We are alone together at Trianon three to four times a week when I am at Versailles. My only trouble is that I cannot compensate for her sufferings, and I can never make her as happy as she deserves. I am completely devoted to her, my dear Sophie, and wish I could dry her lovely tears.

Your affectionate brother,
Axel

Throughout the autumn months of 1785, I endeavored to go about my days as I always had. I was grateful for Axel's strength and solace during these dark days, but I feared I was poor company, for I could do little more than weep. In the late summer, when the court traveled to Saint-Cloud, I became eager to show

France that I was hardly the rapacious ogre depicted in the licentious and libelous pamphlets, opening the gardens to the public so they could witness my promenades with my children. I enjoyed carriage rides through the Bois de Boulogne, and cradled the dauphin in my arms—he was far too tiny for his age—as I strolled through the palace grounds.

I have always been proud, and even in my extremity I would not dignify my detractors by permitting them to see me suffer. And so I endeavored to pass my days as though my reputation was not in jeopardy, trusting (in vain, perhaps) that I had made the right decision by insisting that the cardinal be tried before the Parlement, rather than punished strictly by the king for his lèse-majesté, his crime of treason against me, as his sovereign.

On October 10, we journeyed to Fontainebleau, but even there I could not conceal my anxiety, for all I overheard was gossip about the trial, and the onerous imprisonment of the prince de Rohan. I was shocked to the core to discover that courtiers of the highest rank genuinely believed that I had secretly commissioned him to purchase the diamond necklace on my behalf. Yet I had known absolutely nothing of the entire transaction until Herr Böhmer's visit the previous July and would not be dissuaded from my assumption that the cardinal, aware that he had long run afoul of my esteem, intended to besmirch my good name by using it to swindle the jewelers out of a priceless necklace, which he then planned to sell in order to discharge his embarrassingly massive encumbrances.

But Louis and I had more to fret about than the details emerging from the increasingly sordid trial. France's economic woes had grown steadily worse, compounded by a bad harvest. In August I had summoned our former Minister of Finance, Monsieur Necker—he of the daughter whom Axel had briefly considered marrying—and begged him to return to the government as Treasury Secretary. "*C'est vrai* that in the past I have not been enamored of many of your progressive reforms," I told Necker, "but you have been the only man to have captured the confidence of the people. I appeal to you on behalf of the king and the nation to set aside our differences."

The winter months of 1785–86 were particularly severe. Peasants flocked from the countryside in droves to the capital expecting there to be enough bread, but the bakers of Paris had not the grain to sustain everyone. Prices soared and people starved.

By February, I was nearly as miserable, enduring my most difficult pregnancy thus far, quickly putting on weight as if I was strapping all the burdens of the world to my belly. And I could not admit, even to the abbé Vermond, that I was displeased about the prospect of bearing another child, as he had been conceived not out of love (for my heart now belonged to Axel), but out of duty. Having turned thirty the previous November 2, I was now as old as the prudish *collets-montés* I had mocked in my youth when I dared anyone over the age of one-score-and-ten to show their ancient face at a court devoted to gaiety and youth.

February brought frustrating news as well, regarding the affair of the diamond necklace.

Angered that the cardinal should be tried in a civil forum and believing that he should be the one to sanction him for his frivolity, Pope Pius VI was convinced that such an eminent man as the prince de Rohan could not have committed an actual crime. On February 13, 1786, the Vatican meted out its own punishment when twenty-six cardinals voted to suspend the Grand Almoner of France from the exercise of his cardinalic rights and privileges.

"This amounts to little better than a reprimand," I fumed to Madame Campan. She assured me that, being a civil body, the Parlement would treat the cardinal more harshly. But she could not meet my gaze when she spoke those words. "You have read the trial briefs?" I asked her.

She nodded. "But it was difficult to find them; they are selling like mad. And they are disgusting. Nothing but lies from one lawyer after another. Professionally penned propaganda with but three purposes: to exonerate their client, enrich themselves, and delude an unsuspecting public into believing that the pamphlets contain the truth. Regrettably, these fictions influence the magistrates as well. It seems that everyone would prefer to glean their information from the trial briefs, which are written in some chilly garret across the courtyard, than from the testimony itself. I would not wish Your Majesty to see them, for they might affect your condition," she said, with a glance at my swelling belly. "The best news I can give you is that there was such an outcry over the privileges accorded to the cardinal by the comte de Launay, that once the depositions were completed and the trial itself began, he was remanded from the governor's apartments to a subterranean cell." I was pleased to hear that my nemesis no longer slept on a feather bed and dined on wine and oysters. Nor was he permitted visitors any longer, deprived from spreading his falsehoods and calumnies to the sympathetic souls, many of them his friends and relations from the upper reaches of the nobility, who had made pilgrimages to the prison fortress bearing gifts intended to ease the exigencies of his incarceration. I had heard, however, that he consistently reminded his inquisitors of his rank and title by wearing his full ecclesiastical attire—the scarlet robes of office, calotte, hose, and biretta—whenever he was taken for questioning.

The trial itself had finally commenced in January 1786, after more than three months of depositions. The witnesses testified in the Palais de Justice, while the the prisoners were interrogated in the Bastille's council chamber; the prince de Rohan was personally conducted to each appearance by the prison governor—not a mark of distrust, but of respect.

The magistrates had discussed the unpleasant notion of dispatching a delegation of notaries to Versailles to depose me as well, but the king refused, sparing me the indecency and indignity. Instead, I graciously consented to forward the information in my possession to the Parlement. The document was titled "Information Considered of Sufficient Importance to be Communicated to the Keeper of the Seals for the Purpose of the Enlightenment of the King and of his Parlement de Paris in the Cause of Justice in the Diamond Necklace Affair." There was now nothing for me to do but wait—and pray daily that the magistrates would mete out the proper, weighty sentences commensurate with a crime against the Crown.

TWENTY-SIX

Justice

SPRING 1786

At the beginning of the third week in May, I journeyed to the capital to speak with the marquis d'Aligre, the president of the Parlement de Paris; and Maîtres de Villotran and de Marcé, the two justices chosen to conduct the initial investigation and hearing of the witnesses and defendants. We met at the Tuileries Palace. I scarcely noticed the shabby condition of the château—the peeling paint and crumbling walls—for they were not the subject of my errand.

"I hear they are all accusing one another," I said. "And everything has become like a circus instead of a trial. I have read in the *nouvelles* about all manner of insults flying, even candlesticks being hurled. That must be good for the Crown, *non?*"

Maître de Marcé chuckled. "It is the law, *Majesté.* The defendants have the right to cross-examine one another."

"So if one of them can challenge the lies another has been telling during the investigation, tell me, why has no one stood up and shouted, 'The comtesse de Lamotte-Valois is not the queen's *lover*!'" The magistrates looked at me, their jaws agape. "You are supposed to be reasonable men. Do you believe this woman? It seems to be clear from the testimony of her secretary, Monsieur de Villette—who was also one of her paramours—that he forged all of the letters written in my name, as well as the contract of sale for the diamond necklace, and falsified my signature every time it was required. And yet Madame de Lamotte-Valois has the gall to say in court, in the sight of God, that she and I—*mon Dieu!* I have never yet laid eyes upon this so-called comtesse, who I have heard also testified that I gave her wagonloads of jewelry, plate, and furnishings. And yet not a single voice has been raised in the Grand Chambre to challenge these monstrous lies!" I offered to send my first lady of the bedchamber Madame Campan, the duchesse de Polignac, the princesse de Lamballe, or all three, to testify on my behalf if necessary, but the marquis d'Aligre insisted that there was no need, that it would merely lessen the dignity of the Crown.

"It is best, Your Majesty, if you remain as discreet as possible and allow the wheels of justice to turn without endeavoring to manipulate them," said the president of the Parlement. I regarded his countenance; I have never trusted men with small eyes. Nor would the queen of France be chided by a bureaucrat, especially one who might *truly* be the paramour of the comtesse de Lamotte-Valois.

"And what of the cardinal?" I continued. "He is certainly guilty of lèse-majesté. He has dishonored my name and deserves the harshest possible penalty for compromising the reputation of the monarch." Daily I bore the insult anew when ladies of the court dared to appear wearing the bonnets that were all the mode in Paris—straw birettas *"au Cardinal,"* trimmed with red and yellow ribbons—*couleur du cardinal sur la paille*—the color of the cardinal in straw, a reference to the pallet he was said to sleep on in his damp and chilly prison cell.

As he finally began to appreciate the full measure of my distress, with cautious deference President d'Aligre assured me of his support and that of the pair of examining magistrates. "Maître de Villotran, in particular, is especially persuasive, and he will no doubt exert both his knowledge of the matter and his influence upon the balance of the tribunal during the final interrogation of the accused."

A few days later, Messieurs de Marcé and de Villotran submitted the entire dossier of the case to Maître de Fleury, the Prosecutor General, in an envelope bound with a red wax seal. His report and recommendations would then be presented to the judges of the Grand Chambre and the Tournelle, who would preside over the final phase of the trial.

My anxiety about their verdict weighed heavily upon me, exacerbating my physical discomfort. By now I was more than five months' gone and larger than I had been during any of my previous pregnancies. The duchesse de Polignac had borne the brunt of my irritability, for I had grown exasperated with her perpetual requests for more and greater favors. "When a sovereign raises up favorites in her court, she raises up despots against herself," I lamented to Madame Campan, who had been by my side throughout the affair of the diamond necklace. Heartily sick of the duchesse's domestic tyranny I cheerfully granted Gabrielle's request to visit England, but the gossips spun a different, and fantastical tale, asserting that the Polignac had journeyed to London to convince the comte de Lamotte-Valois to surrender himself.

Public interest in the trial of *l'affaire du collier* was unprecedented, as were the proceedings themselves. Never had one of the highest men in France been accused of a crime against the person of the Crown. The lawyers' trial briefs continued to sell faster than bread and nearly every day the young boys hawking the news sheets could be heard in the streets of the capital crying *"Du nouveau! Du nouveau!"* announcing the publication of yet another preposterous effort to exonerate one of the defendants.

Vile verses and cruel *on-dits* were circulated about the salons and cafés; some had such lengthy tentacles that they found their way to the court of Imperial Russia. And who was most vilified by these poems and songs? *I*—the one innocent figure in the entire sordid ordeal!

Madame Campan insisted I was making myself ill by entertaining them at all. "You should be resting, *Majesté.*"

"Maman can't rest, madame; she's teaching me the satin stitch." Seven-year-old Madame Royale was seated on my lap with an embroidery hoop in her small hands.

"You must lay the stitches right next to each other with equal tension—like this," I said taking the needle and silken thread to demonstrate. "The flower should look just like the one on the princesse's sleeve." I nudged my daughter off my knees. "Why don't you practice in the green chair?"

I rose and removed two of the ugly broadsheets from the hands of the princesse de Lamballe. "If you will not read these calumnies, I will. *Écoutez bien.*" Propped up by the bolster on my daybed at le Petit Trianon, I began to read two of the ditties aloud.

"Oliva says, 'He's such a goose!'
Lamotte insists, 'He's morally loose.'
His Eminence claims he's just obtuse
Hallelujah!
Red are his robes from the Holy See.
'Black is his heart,' said Queen Marie.
'We'll whitewash his name,' the judges agree.
Hallelujah!"

"Regrettably, this completely sums up public opinion," I bemoaned, thinking perhaps I should have held my impressionable daughter's ears. "*Eh bien,* this one pretends to be a dialogue between myself and the demimondaine who impersonated me in the gardens.

" 'Vile harlot, it becomes you ill
To play my role of queen!'
'I think not, my sovereign,
You so often play mine!' "

My hands flew to my breast. "I am going to be sick." Madame Campan fetched a Sèvres basin and held my head while I vomited into the bowl.

Beneath the gilded medieval vaulting a crush of perspiring and over-perfumed spectators sat brocaded elbow to satin elbow on the benches in the two galleries of the Palais de Justice's Grand Chambre. Even the worst seats were being sold for astronomical sums, and on any day a lucky man might make his fortune by retailing his privilege to sit on an unforgiving bench for nine hours to a soul even more desperate for sensationalism. The preliminary investigation had been conducted in secret, with the lawyers' fictionalized trial briefs the only way for the public to learn what was transpiring behind the walls of the Palais de Justice.

Lengthy as those hearings had been, they were, however, merely a tantalizing appetizer. The succulent main course of this bizarre feast was the public trial that was about to commence before the magistrates of the Parlement, all of whom were members of the nobility or the clergy.

The trial was being presided over by a rare joint session of the Grand Chambre and Tournelle magistrates, Paris's two courts of

Parlement. Because of the unusual nature of the case and the illustrious personages involved, the courts would convene as a single body within the larger venue, the Grand Chambre.

The proceedings opened on May 22 with Maître Titon de Villotran's reading of the report detailing the months of preliminary proceedings, a recitation that continued for a full week. The culmination of his recital on May 29 signaled the transfer of the accused from the Bastille to the Conciergerie, the prison fortress adjacent to the Palais de Justice. From there, they would be escorted to the Grand Chambre for the concluding hearing of the trial.

The following morning, the flamboyant Count Cagliostro declared before the sixty periwigged magistrates, "I am a noble voyager, Nature's unfortunate child." His exotic accent and mélange of languages amused the Parlement, but the carnival atmosphere quickly turned grim.

Clad head to toe in black satin, a weeping Rétaux de Villette faced the justices, hoping to avoid the punishment for larceny and forgery by maintaining that he had been acting merely as Madame de Lamotte's secretary.

The lady herself was attired in her lucky gown, blue-gray satin banded in black velvet. About her slender shoulders she had draped an embroidered muslin cape trimmed with fine net. Perched upon the small stool called the *sellette,* reserved for the defendant in a court of law, for the next three hours the comtesse faced the judges and remained regally defiant.

Heightening the curiosity of the spectators on the unforgiving benches in the hall and in the galleries above, she had vowed as she first drew her skirts about her on the *sellette,* "I will expose a great rascal"; yet she proceeded to name no one, instead deflecting the magistrates' questions about the letters purportedly exchanged between the cardinal and the queen. Pretending to protect her sovereign's name, the comtesse laid the guilt upon her ecclesiastical lover, sending the tribunal into an uproar when she confessed that the Grand Almoner had shown her more than two hundred letters sent to him by Marie Antoinette, addressing him as "thou" and "thee," and appointing the times for their clandestine trysts.

Defending his name and honor and that of the House of Rohan, the cardinal refused to sit, preferring to stand before the Parlement. "If I am guilty of anything," he said with a rare display of humility, "it is the crime of having a blinding, overwhelming desire to acquire the good graces of Her Sovereign Majesty."

Dawn had not yet risen when the cardinal's relations, a panoply of sumptuously attired Rohans, Guéménés, and Soubises, filed into the Grand Chambre and like silent sentinels ringed the stone walls frescoed with fleurs-de-lis. An hour later, at five o'clock, in anticipation of His Eminence's testimony that morning the streets surrounding the Cour de Mai, the courtyard of the Palais de Justice, teemed with humanity, sorely testing the resources of the Paris foot guard and the mounted police. The courtyard itself was packed so tightly with people that one couldn't exit through the iron gates without risking bodily injury.

The septuagenarian Prosecutor General Joly de Fleury, stooped and wizened, opened the proceedings at six, unsealing the recommendations for sentencing. The crown was not permitted to make any direct suggestions, although it had been clearly understood that Her Majesty, who was awaiting the news at Versailles, expected the harshest penalties to be levied, especially against the comtesse and the cardinal. The spectators in the galleries grew breathless; gloved hands clutched the embellished sleeves of adjacent strangers.

Having concluded unanimously that the approvals and signature of the queen on the contract of sale for the infamous diamond necklace were false, the forger Rétaux de Villette was to be henceforth banished from France, with all his worldly possessions forefeited to the king.

He had evaded the gallows. As the handsome Villette wept with relief, the galleries hummed with murmurs; was the sentence too lenient? But the spectators were quickly hushed by the guards so the next recommendation could be heard. Nicole Leguay, also known as Mademoiselle de Signy, also known as the baronne d'Oliva, absent sufficient evidence to convict her, was being acquitted with a reprimand from the court for her criminal impersonation of the monarch. The lovely demimondaine, whose face was as pale as her gown, fainted on the spot, resuscitated after a genuine baronne seated in the gallery lobbed her vinaigrette at the *sellette.*

Upon the recommendation of the court, the Count Cagliostro was completely exonerated of all charges against him, at which the galleries, populated by many of the mystic's "patients," erupted into cheers. But they were soon sobered by the reading of the sentence against Marc-Antoine Nicolas de Lamotte. Although he had not been extradited to France from his London mole hole, he was condemned to be flogged naked, scourged with rods, and branded with a hot iron on his right shoulder with the letters GAL, the identification required for His Majesty's galley slaves. Not only was he to be chained to an oar for all eternity, but the entirety of his possessions were also forfeit to the Crown; the public was to be so notified by the affixing of a plaque proclaiming his punishment in the Place de Grève, the plaza where Paris's public executions took place.

"*Sacre Dieu,* how terrible!" a young lady in the gallery commented to her father.

He chuckled. "A mere formality, *ma petite.* Let them try to find him! But hush—here come the bigger fish!"

The spectators grew silent as the judgment was pronounced upon Jeanne de Lamotte-Valois. In another unanimous recommendation, her sentence was much like the one handed down to her husband, except that, judged to be a thief, she was to be branded on both shoulders with the letter V, for *voleuse,* thence to be imprisoned for life in the women's house of correction, the infamous Salpêtrière. Amid a considerable amount of murmurs and whispers, there was a general agreement in the gallery that, although it was shocking for a woman to be accorded so violent a punishment, the penalty was hardly a surprise.

Opinions, barely audible above Jeanne's ear-shattering shrieks, were tossed about in the galleries like so many horseshoes.

"*L'Autrichenne* desecrates the memory of the Valois!"

"Clearly the queen doesn't wish her to reveal everything she knows; remember yesterday when the comtesse said she would name someone powerful?"

"What a terrible price to pay for keeping Her Majesty's secrets!"

It was several minutes before the crowd could be quieted, and the outcry only ceased with the reminder that the cardinal's fate had yet to be pronounced.

The Grand Almoner was attired as if he was preparing to conduct High Mass. Courtly and distinguished, his hair threaded with silver at the temples, he wished to remind the temporal judges of his princely birthright and the clerical magistrates on the tribunal of his lofty ecclesiastical stature. The effect was both humble and intimidating as he stood before the bar, once again refusing to lower his body by accepting the *sellette.*

At last, Monsieur de Fleury intoned the final recommendation of the court. "The cardinal-prince de Rohan is to appear in this hall eight days hence to make a public statement of repentance for the crime of lèse-majesté—the wanton disrespect of his sovereigns—in arranging a midnight rendezvous in the Grove of Venus under the pretext of meeting the queen, and in continuing the deception that Her Majesty was a party to the purchase of the diamond necklace. He is to be stripped of all offices, exiled for life from all royal residences, and compelled to make a contribution of alms to the indigent people of France. And it is the verdict of this court that he remain imprisoned until the completion of this sentence."

The prince de Rohan maintained his composure, permitting himself only the hint of a smile. His punishment had amounted to little more than a formal scolding, a slap on the ruby-ringed hand. He could manage without his offices, and perhaps in time, his family might persuade the king to overturn the sentence and return his sinecures and perquisites. But—he exhaled, the musty air of the Grand Chambre seeming now as fresh as a new-mown meadow—he was alive and would remain unscarred. No flogging, branding, or permanent incarceration! He scarcely heard the clamor of the crowd in the galleries, the hearty congratulations of his smug relations, who had correctly predicted that the clerical justices of the Paris Parlement, which traditionally tussled with the kings of France, would never destroy one of their own by voting to condemn him to indentured servitude, exile, or death. Many of the secular magistrates, too, chafed at the omnipotence of the Crown and might have declared that the moon was red, purely because the king had declared it to be blue.

But they knew that the sovereign was powerless to override a trial verdict. It was not the same as exercising his right to hold a *lit de justice* if the Parlement refused to ratify one of his reforms or edicts. This time, the magistrates had the last word.

The galleries erupted into a clamor, a cacophony of voices, both exultant and disbelieving. Had Justice been served this day? *Peut-être? Non? Oui, absoluement!*

"Vive le cardinal!" they cried, from one man to a chorus of hundreds, who would have leapt from the balconies if they could and hoisted the victorious, if now visibly exhausted and relieved, prince de Rohan on their shoulders.

The dreadful news was broken to me by Madame Campan. I could not curtail my weeping, so I beckoned her to sit beside me, although such proximity to the sovereign was far above her place. I tore at my hair like a madwoman; I clutched at my skirts until the gray-blue satin bore the impressions of my angry fingernails. "If the queen cannot get justice, what does that bode for a woman such as yourself, for your reputation and your fortune?"

Henriette rose and crossed the room as Louis entered, his eyes both sympathetic and sorrowful. "I don't know what to say, *ma chère.*" He sighed heavily, taking my hand in his. He looked as defeated as I. "The Parlement refused to see the cardinal as anything but a man of the church."

"And not the corrupted, over-perfumed swindler that he is!" I interrupted.

The king nodded. "I should like to give him the benefit of the doubt and hope that he will find a way to pay the jewelers. They are honest men and their business should not be made to suffer because the prince was a credulous fool."

I felt sick, from my head to my stomach to my heart. "I feel as though I shall never dance, nor ever smile again," I murmured through my salty tears.

But I did rouse myself; perhaps it was my Hapsburg blood that taught me never to admit defeat. A few days after the verdicts were rendered, I journeyed to Paris to attend the Opéra with my ladies—except for the princesse de Lamballe, for the sympathetic soul had angered me by visiting the comtesse de Lamotte-Valois in her prison cell. Perhaps she sought to learn why the comtesse had so vociferously endeavored to destroy me, and still persisted in maintaining that we shared an intimate bond. Or perhaps Marie Thérèse believed she must have been touched in the head and was in need of prayers.

As my carriage halted outside the Palais Royal, I was peppered with insults as if I were being pelted with stale bread. My fellow Frenchwomen dared to openly insult my virtue, my honor, and the paternity of my children. Boos and hisses from both sexes greeted my entrance inside the Opéra. More frightening still was that in addition to the familiar epithets they had ascribed to me—*"Autrichienne,"* "manipulative harlot"—came a new appellation, even more wounding for its untruth.

"*Et voilà* Madame Deficit," a woman exclaimed as I entered my opera box, escorted by the capital's chief of police, who had come to ensure my safety—a terrifying thought in itself. The woman garnered a laugh and so she repeated the insult. And soon, like a wave crashing upon the shore, a tide of voices, snickers, and murmurs chorused "Madame Deficit."

I turned to the chief of police and tried to mask my fear. "I don't understand, Monsieur de Crosne. What do they want of me? What harm have I done them?"

He shook his head. "You should not have come to Paris tonight," he whispered to me. "And," he added tactfully, "if I were you, I should stay away from the capital for some time."

TWENTY-SEVEN

Punished

SUMMER 1786

How had I become the guilty party?

The court painter, Madame Vigée-Lebrun, paid a respectful call to state, with the greatest delicacy, that she felt compelled to withdraw a portrait of me on display at the Academie, for fear it would be destroyed.

The verdict in *l'affaire du collier* had removed the crystal stoppers from the genies' bottles, loosing a noxious cloud of perfidy perpetuated by caricaturists and pamphleteers not only in France, but from as far away as England and the Low Countries. The king and I were convinced they had been financed by his cousin the new duc d'Orléans, the duc de Chartres having assumed the title upon his father's death the previous year; however, Louis's brother Monsieur was also never above my suspicions. It seemed as though every day there was a new entry in the publishers' stalls along the Seine, although the usual assertions were made: such titles as *A List of All the Persons With Whom the Queen Has Had Debauched Relations* (the lengthy roster included Mesdames de Polignac and Lamballe, as well as the comte d'Artois, *"et toutes les tribades de Paris"*); and *The Royal Bordello: Followed by a Secret Interview between the Queen and Cardinal de Rohan*—a disgusting farce, the setting being "The Queen's Apartments in Versailles."

I could not comprehend such unmitigated hatred; nonetheless, I vowed to change people's minds. "I shall conquer the malicious by trebling the good I have always tried to do," I told Louis.

The king feared for my health, not merely for the sake of the child I carried. Axel was equally solicitous, feeding me like a nursemaid when he came to visit me at Trianon, and insisting I take the medicine Monsieur Lassone had prescribed for my sleeplessness and loss of appetite. Mademoiselle Bertin had told me about a Parisian chemist, Sulpice Debauve, who would distill the remedies into chocolate coins flavored with orange flower water, almond milk, strong coffee, or vanilla in order to render the vile-tasting concoctions more palatable. Rose became responsible for acquiring these "Pistoles de Marie Antoinette," as I was still advised to keep my distance from the capital.

I had thought that once the trial was over, the kingdom would regain its sanity so that Louis and Monsieur Calonne, the Contrôleur-Général, could return their focus to the financial health of the country.

Instead, the trial itself, followed by the spurious verdict that all but exonerated the cardinal-prince, and transformed the scheming comtesse de Lamotte-Valois into the innocent pawn of a debauched court, seemed to have given our subjects carte blanche to attack the monarchy. Had we brought this upon ourselves, I asked Louis, by aiding the American colonies a decade earlier? We had sent Frenchmen across the ocean to fight for another's democratic precepts, and they had come home with the seeds of liberty in their pockets. But cannons and swords alone did not win the day. The initial weapons of revolution and rebirth were words and ideas, powerful enough to bring a nation as great as Britain to its knees. Ever since, the winds of rebellion remained in the air, and conditions in France had put nearly everyone on edge. After the verdict was rendered in the affair of the necklace, I imagined that I heard a slow, steady drumbeat wherever I went.

The world had been turned upside down

By sunrise on the morning of June 21, a massive sea of humanity had gathered in the Cour de Mai to witness the punishment of Jeanne de Lamotte-Valois. I heard she was cheered as though she were a martyr, while curses were rained upon my head, not only by the accused, but by the throngs who viewed her sentence. Soon after her scourging and branding, she was carried off to the Salpêtrière, where the Mother Superior of the prison was so shocked by the violence done to her body that she nearly wept for sympathy.

TWENTY-EIGHT

Reversals

I was brought to bed before my time, giving birth on July 9 to a tiny daughter several weeks early. We named her Sophie Hélène Béatrix, to honor the king's late aunt, who had gone to heaven in 1782, yet another child named for the Bourbons. Young Marie Thérèse, Madame Royale, was the only Hapsburg namesake. But from the start, Sophie was frail; her lungs were weak and it broke my heart to watch my precious infant struggle for breath.

It took several months before I recovered fully from her delivery. My hair had once again fallen out in clumps and Monsieur Léonard determined that the popular fashion for halos of teased and frizzled tresses surmounting a waterfall of curls—styles bearing ludicrous names such as Porcupine, Pomegranate, and Philadelphia (the last being yet another tribute to Mr. Franklin)—would be difficult to create with my scant amount of locks. Powder was falling out of favor as well, and worry over the fragile health of *ma petite* Sophie and the dauphin, as well as heartsickness over the insulting denouement of *l'affaire du collier,* had resulted in the mingling of natural threads of silver with my strands of reddish blond.

Mademoiselle Bertin tried to raise my spirits during one of our twice-weekly tête-à-têtes with an armload of fabric swatches and sketches. Always an advertisement for the latest fashions, she was dressed most *à la mode,* disgusted to be wearing flat leather shoes (though with her height, she did not need a court heel to make her appear more imposing), and skirts that, while full, lacked the underpinnings of panniers.

Much to the king's annoyance, the dandyish comte d'Artois had begun to favor the masculine version of these simple, and (to my taste, somewhat dowdy) clothes—unadorned frock coats, and round hats that made him resemble a country cleric.

"This shade is all the vogue," said Rose, unfurling a bolt of greenish-brown satin. "We call it 'goose droppings.' And this," she added, displaying a length of black-and-white-striped silk, "is an homage to the zebra in His Majesty's royal menagerie. Stripes are *au courant* nowadays, no matter the colors. You will find them in men's breeches, vests, and coats, ladies' skirts and underskirts, full gowns—I have a lovely petal-pink stripe that would suit you exquisitely—and if you prefer a darker, more matronly look, I will show you a green and gold silk taffeta that would emphasize your coloring."

I shook my head sorrowfully. "They call me Madame Deficit now. My accounts have recently been shown to me. And my greatest expenses, apart from renovating and redecorating the royal châteaux, have been the purchases I have made for my wardrobe. In one year alone, I spent almost eight thousand livres for your creations, and who knows how much I paid to the court dressmaker, Madame Éloffe. My riding habits alone have cost me thirty-one thousand francs." Rose began to protest, but I raised my hand to quiet her. I knew she would insist that her own talent was worth the price, but I was, regrettably, forced to make economies.

"I am no more responsible for France's financial ills than for the sun and the moon, but every breath I take is assiduously chronicled and there are numberless people just waiting for yet another exhalation that they can add to their catalogue of my misdeeds. Why, even the comte de Mercy has chided me for playing games with my children in my *petits appartements* when he comes to discuss important business. He says such behavior feeds the false impression that I am a frivolous and superficial woman. I have already laid aside my original plan for the renovation of Saint-Cloud—I had thought to enlarge the Egyptian scheme at Fontainebleau—for the Crown cannot afford it."

My eyes misted over with tears. "For the past dozen years I have relied upon you—and we have made quite a good pair. And I am certain you profited immensely every time I wore one of your lavish creations," I added with a chuckle, "for every woman in France desired the same ensemble. But, through no fault of mine, I was judged a monster for 'forcing' my countrywomen to follow these modes."

I laid my gloved hand across Rose's arm. "But now, *et je le regrette beaucoup, ma très chère amie,* I must, with the heaviest of hearts, give you your congé."

Mademoiselle Bertin's eyes and mouth widened. "I do not believe it!" she declared. "*C'est impossible*—that you should dismiss me. After everything I have done for you!"

"You have always been handsomely paid, Mademoiselle. And, I would hazard, you are one of our rare creditors to have your invoices discharged in a timely manner. Even so, you are forever refusing my *dame d'atours*'s requests to itemize your bills, so how do we know that you have not grossly inflated them, assuming the Crown can pay?" I caught my breath, not wishing to sound cross. "Please, Rose. Please do not make this parting any more difficult than it already is."

She folded her arms, and drew herself up, seeming to grow another half foot in height. *"Je le regrette, Majesté,"* she said evenly, betraying no hint of emotion. I, on the other hand, was in tears.

"J'en suis désolée," I murmured. "Rose, I am so sorry."

Mademoiselle Bertin dropped into a court curtsy, far grander than the circumstances of our meeting required. Then she rose with effortless grace and backed out of the room, eyes not lowered, but fixed on something above my head, determined not to swallow her pride.

Despondency seemed to lurk all about us. It permeated the draperies and tapestries and seeped into our souls. The new year of 1787 opened inauspiciously, with the death in January of the king's ablest minister, the Foreign Secretary, comte de Vergennes.

"I am come unmoored by it," Louis confided in me as we sat alone in his library. Openly sobbing, he gave a frustrated push to his great globe, sending it spinning. "A vessel without a rudder." My brother Joseph had entered an alliance with Catherine the Great and was preparing to go on the defensive against the Turks. Across the Atlantic, in Massachusetts, an armed uprising led by a disgruntled veteran of the American Revolution named Daniel Shays led to the widespread fear that the infant nation's democratic impulse had spiraled out of control. Privately, Louis and I wondered what the impact of their fledgling democratic ideals would have on Continental Europe, now that they had been revealed to be less than Utopian. Perhaps the nation could not survive after all without a king.

The only bright spot was the death the previous August of "the Devil"—Frederick the Great, who had been succeeded by his spectacularly corpulent, but considerably more affable son, Frederick William II. If only Maman had lived to see it.

My husband had gained a significant amount of weight in the last year or so; his already full face was showing the beginnings of a treble chin. His myopic eyes had grown tired and yellow from so much reading, but it was not comme il faut for the king of France to be seen wearing spectacles. Because he reeled a bit on occasion as his heavy body endeavored to compensate for his poor vision, rumors that had begun in the palace, and then pervaded the pamplets, intimated that Louis had taken to drink. They were of course untrue, as he had no taste for wine or spirits, but facts never frustrated the aims of the propagandists.

My husband visited me nearly every day of late; always to commiserate, and often to weep. I endeavored to bolster his confidence. "*You* are the rudder, *mon cher*. You are the captain, not any of your ministers. It is up to you to steer the ship and set its course."

"Yes, but *what* course?" he groaned. "You must help me, Toinette. Help me know what to do."

Finally, after so many years, the moment I had waited for had come, the moment Maman and Mercy and the abbé Vermond had long wished for. The king had solicited my advice and counsel as a full partner in the monarchy. But my husband had deliberately left me unschooled in the governance of France. I knew even less about politics than he. Yet to admit as much to him would only have made Louis more miserable. So I caressed his cheek, and tried to coax him to smile. "You know I will help you in every way I can," I assured him.

In February, the Finance Minister, Charles Alexandre Calonne, addressed the Assembly of Notables, a convocation of 144 literally notable men, from princes to bishops to mayors, to discuss the unsavory issue of taxes. As Louis's adjustments called for both the nobility and the clergy to be taxed for the first time in history, in order to mitigate the burden on the bourgeois and the poor—the untitled persons collectively known as the Third Estate—the news met with resounding ire from the Notables.

That spring we found ourselves saddled with the nation's ills as well as our own domestic woes. Princesse Sophie was not growing properly, like her older sister and our second son, Louis Charles. Her health and that of our older son, the poor little dauphin, weighed heavily upon us. But while Louis saw to the affairs of state, my mind remained predominantly occupied with the children of France.

To honor them, and to remind our subjects that I was a mother above all else, I commissioned Madame Vigée-Lebrun to paint a portrait of the five of us and she set to work, depicting me in my gown of garnet-colored velvet and matching plumed hat. "A Madonna and children?" she replied when I first suggested the composition.

"Well . . . *oui,*" said I.

Regardless of the comte de Mercy's admonishment about playing with my children in the salons, rather than in the privacy of a nursery, after waiting so long to produce my cherished offspring nothing gave me greater pleasure now than to revel in their companionship and watch them grow. Gone were my gaming tables, replaced with wooden hoops, cups and balls, and dolls with painted faces and mohair tresses. Nonetheless, I must have been the only woman in France vilified for loving her children.

The other bright light in my life was Axel von Fersen. "I have a gift for you," I informed him one day that spring, as I led him through my warren of private apartments. After the death of my daughter's namesake, her great-aunt Sophie—Mesdames *tantes* had long since removed themselves to the Château de Bellevue—I had appropriated the late Sophie's rooms for my private apartments, as they were larger and brighter than the warren of chambers that lay behind the State Rooms.

Having recently had a small suite sectioned off from the rest of the apartment, I led Axel to a closed door decorated with gilded boiserie moldings, still pungent from the fresh coat of white paint. *"S'il vous plaît."* With a secret smile I motioned for him to turn the heavy brass handle.

"I thought . . . Why should the Colonel Proprietor of the Royal Suédois be compelled to sleep in a cramped and drafty room under the eaves?" In truth, it would bring me both joy and comfort to know that he was near me during these trying times. Louis and I had not discussed this unusual démenage, although it was not a secret. But the king had greater concerns than the renovation of the queen's private apartments.

Axel regarded the walls, newly papered with a subtle pattern of blue and silver, taking in the furnishings of the room, corner to corner. "Is that a Swedish stove?" he exclaimed incredulously.

I nodded, slipping my hand into his with a lover's ease. "And its installation came at quite a cost." I touched my finger to my lips. "Please don't tell the new Finance Minister." For many reasons, Loménie de Brienne, the sixty-year-old Archbishop of Toulouse who had recently succeeded Calonne, would most certainly have not approved. The previous year, Monsieur Calonne had informed me that during the dozen years of my husband's reign, 1,250 million livres had been borrowed and that the blame for such extravagance fell squarely upon my shoulders. "How can that be?" I had asked him. "How was I expected to know this? When I requested fifty thousand livres, I was given one hundred thousand!"

"I cannot tell *anyone,*" Axel whispered, "Not even Sophie," he added, referring to his sister, "about the reasons my heart is so full." He strode to the stove, the better to inspect and admire it. "And so empty." He drew me to him and stroked my cheek, looking into my eyes as if they held the answer to some inscrutable question. "I was not destined to be happy like other men," he murmured, gently kissing my brow.

His lips were cool and soft against my skin. I closed my eyes and inhaled. He was wearing the scent I had asked Fargeon to create for him six years earlier. "Don't speak like that," I whispered.

"Mais, c'est vrai," Axel insisted, enfolding me in his arms. I rested my cheek against the facings on his coat. "I'm afraid that life will always deny me both luck and happiness." With the tip of his finger he tilted my chin to meet his gaze. "I am indebted to you more than you can ever know," he said softly. "And this gift, this room, what you risked to arrange everything—" He broke off, clasping my hands and kissing them. "You know that people will talk," he cautioned gently.

I nodded. "But I have heard so many insults, I don't think it's possible to wound me any more deeply. *Mon cher coeur . . .*" I reached for him, twining my fingers through his soft brown hair and drew him toward me, claiming his mouth.

"She might have grown up to be a friend," I murmured.

"I am so sorry." Louis held me tightly as our tears commingled. "I fear she never had a chance in this harsh world," he breathed into my hair. I had no words. My mouth could not find them, could not form them. The death of a child is the most searing pain imaginable and all the suffering one endures in giving them life cannot begin to compare to the torment of losing them. The Almighty had given our innocent angel, princesse Sophie Hélène Béatrix, only 345 days on His earth. Barely beginning to cut her tiny teeth she went into convulsions after her lungs began to fail her on the fifteenth of June, and was taken four days later, little more than a week after we had suffered another blow. The woman who had plotted the diamond necklace scheme by claiming me as her intimate, Jeanne de Lamotte-Valois, had escaped from the Salpêtrière, a feat that could never have been achieved without the connivance of highly placed or influential persons.

It was nothing less than a direct insult aimed at the Crown. In the crucible of France a scoundrel had been transformed into a scapegoat; and with the same alchemy had transmogrified her target from an unwitting victim into a villainess.

Count Cagliostro could not have been more successful.

TWENTY-NINE

We Attempt Mitigation

The late summer of 1787 had brought another bad harvest. Thousands could starve by the time the ground turned hard and cold that autumn. Determined to present an example to all three Estates—the clergy, nobility, and the common people—the king endeavored to reduce the treasury's deficit by eliminating several positions in the royal household. In my retinue alone 173 disgruntled souls were given their congé. Renovations to Saint-Cloud were halted as well; and the comte de Vaudreuil was asked to relinquish his sinecure as royal falconer. Baron de Besenval was permitted to maintain his regiment of Swiss Guards, but was visibly provoked by all the reductions. "It is a terrible thing to dwell in a country where one is not assured of possessing one day what one had the day before," he lamented.

The king and I were hard-pressed to conceal the strain. My body, already much thickened by numerous pregnancies, had never fully recovered from Sophie's birth even as I mourned her death. Louis hunted and rode with a near-desperate intensity, and daily gorged himself as if each meal were his last. Madame Vigeé-Lebrun's portrait created a permanent record of our grief when, at my request, she altered the composition, painting out the image of baby Sophie in her cradle, and re-posing the dauphin, who now pointed to the empty *berceau.*

One October afternoon Louis came to my rooms wearing the expression of a drowning man. Wordlessly, he sank into an armchair, completely filling it with his bulk. And without even meeting my gaze, he began to sob. The weight of his grave responsibilities, of his anguish over the loss of our daughter, of the insurmountable deficit, of his enemies' *médisance,* had become far too much for him to bear.

I let him weep, unburdening his heart. And there was no one else in France to whom the king might turn but his queen. Finally, I came around behind him and clasped my arms about his shoulders, resting my cheek against the powdered crown of his head.

"You are the only constant in my life, Toinette," he said, choking back more tears and clasping my hands to his breast. "Have you any idea how much I rely upon you? My ministers . . . the regional Parlements . . . everyone wants what it does not always seem in the interests of France to give." Tightly clutching my hands, he added, "They think I am a weak sovereign who can accomplish nothing but devouring a cold roast chicken in fifteen minutes. And yet they are bent on blocking every remedy I propose. With the Parlements' ability to deny ratification to my edicts, which they do at every turn, how can the country move forward? How will she survive?"

He lowered his head into his hands. Now thirty-three years old, Louis was as lost as he had been at twenty.

Kneeling at his feet, my velvet skirts enveloping me in an indigo pool on the carpet, I vowed to be strong for us both. "Speak to the ministers, *ma chère,*" he implored. "Perhaps they will see reason when it comes from the mouth of a mother, as well as their monarch."

I dared not remind him then, in his distracted state, that I had already proposed a number of pragmatic reforms, but his officials never took me seriously. They persisted in viewing me either as an empty-headed spendthrift or, tainted by their own prejudices, as the perennial outsider—*l'Autrichienne*—not a true Frenchwoman, but one who remained a secret ambassador for Austria despite renouncing my native land to become their future queen some eighteen years earlier.

In November, Louis summoned the Parlement de Paris—the same corrupted magistrates who in my view had all but exonerated Cardinal de Rohan—to a "royal sitting" where the Minister of Finance, Loménie de Brienne, requested their consent to an edict allowing the treasury to borrow 440 million livres over the next five years, a sum that would permit the government to continue functioning. The debate lasted a tense seven hours while the king presided from an armchair, rather than the chaise longue from which he would hold the more autocratic *lits de justice.* Back in July, the Assembly of Notables had refused to ratify Louis's proposed land tax of 2½ to 5 percent of income, payable in kind, depending on the richness of the soil; pressured by ties of family, only his brothers, each presiding over one of the seven sections of the Assembly, had been persuaded to vote for the stamp tax, a tariff levied on contracts and patents. By their very nature, these revenue streams would primarily have affected the upper echelons of society—the clergy and nobility. These two Estates, as they were known, had traditionally been exempt from taxation, and despite their vociferous criticism of the government's vast expenditures, were loath to contribute so much as a sou to the Treasury.

As November's royal *séance* was drawing to a close and the Keeper of the Seals rose to his feet and prepared to announce the formal registration of the new edict increasing the treasury loan, a lone man dared to stand. An imposing figure though his face was pitted with pox scars and his nose ruddy from the enjoyment of too much brandy and fine wine, Philippe d'Orléans, a Prince of the Blood, dared to challenge his cousin. We had always known he bore the temperament of a dissenter. The duc was one of the wealthiest in France, his embroidered pockets as deep as the Seine, the better to finance untold numbers of presses churning antimonarchical propaganda. A leader of the secret Society of Freemasons, the duc d'Orléans was viewed even by the Church as a man to be reckoned with.

Offering the king a nod of his head, the minimal deference required of his rank, he declared loudly, "I consider this registration illegal, Sire."

The room grew uncomfortably silent.

"It *is* legal, because I wish it," Louis replied evenly.

With a flourish, Philippe d'Orléans withdrew a paper from his pocket. Written in his own bold hand this formal protest, clearly premeditated, was designed to sway the opinion of his fellow justices by persuading them that the registration of the king's edict was unlawful because it had not been presented to the Parlement through a formal *lit de justice.* To Louis's dismay, the duc's demagoguery was in large measure successful, for they did vote to declare the registration illegal.

Louis's only semblance of anger was the manner in which he clutched the padded arms of his chair. "My cousin believes he is king," said Louis. "Or perhaps he thinks this is America, where democracy is the order of the day. But we are in France, monsieur le duc, where in case you have forgotten, I rule by divine right and my word is law." He cleared his throat. "From this moment I banish you to your estate at Villers-Cotterets, to be deprived of all society, save that of your nearest relations and servants."

The duc's face grew redder than usual. But he maintained his equanimity even as the king exiled two more councillors of the Parlement, one of them an abbé, for openly supporting the duc's protest.

In banishing these dissenters Louis had exercised an ancient privilege permitted to all kings of France. But the tenor of the times had grown so disrespectful that no one, from the loftiest men in the kingdom to the lowliest *poissardes* in the fish market, thought twice about insulting the person of the sovereign and the very monarchy itself. No longer were the diatribes directed solely against me; nor could they be attributed to the lingering hatred of my Austrian heritage.

And just as I had been vilified by the diamond necklace verdict rather than vindicated by it, Louis was derided for exiling his cousin, whom the people transformed through the alchemy of seditious propaganda from a drunken debaucher into the victim of an arbitrary tyrant.

My husband became sick from the strain, falling ill with erysipelas, an ailment that turned his skin crimson and left him with a raging fever. The Finance Minister Loménie de Brienne suffered from the stress as well, losing his voice.

The spring of 1788 brought more devastating news. In April, the Parlement de Paris rescinded its promise to collect income tax from the clergy and nobility, hardly a surprise as the justices themselves came from those two Estates. But how could reform ever be affected and how could the burdens of the common people ever be eased unless the Parlement was willing to ratify the king's edicts? Livid with their recalcitrance, on May 8, Louis summoned the magistrates to a *lit de justice,* at which he suspended not only the Paris Parlement for their insubordination, but the Parlements of the twelve other regions of France. To take their place in judicial matters, he set up plenary courts.

The Parlements declared their suspension illegal and harnessed the power of the pen to proclaim that the king was endeavoring to circumvent the will of the people of France. It was the worst demagoguery imaginable, for it had been the *Parlements* that were vehemently opposed to levying taxes against those who could well afford to pay them, thus *relieving* the people of their already onerous burden!

Secretly encouraged by the members of the regional Parlements, violence erupted in the provinces. Anger flared in the marketplace at Grenoble, sparking a day of wanton destruction. An innocent hatter was bayoneted in the back. But Louis had given his maréchal orders not to use force against the rioters, believing it would only incite more unrest.

In my salon Mousseline and Louis Charles played with Odin, taking turns rolling a ball across the floor for the elkhound to fetch. "If I began my life again, I should spend even more time with my children," I lamented to Léonard, as he dressed my hair one morning, liberally dusting it with powder to mask the encroaching strands of gray.

My *friseur* reminded me that I had used that nostalgic phrase many times recently.

"Because I have many regrets." A Meissen figurine toppled noisily to the parquet. I turned in the direction of the sound and laughed at the mishap. So many other things were infinitely more fragile. "Every moment with one's children is a precious one, and yet I have been accused of mourning our *petite ange* Sophie overlong. How," I asked incredulously, brushing away a sudden tear, "is such a thing even possible? *Et le pauvre* dauphin—the *médecins* tell us that the curvature in his spine stems from a tubercular complaint. How many more sunrises will he see, and how dare I miss a single one of them in his company? Like my sister the Queen of Naples, I am a mother first.

"The Parlements have demanded that Louis summon a meeting of the Estates General," I sighed. "Such an event has never happened in our lifetimes. Nor did the late king ever call them together. His Majesty reluctantly promised to set a meeting for next May, and so, for the first time since 1614, the three Estates will convene. At least it will give us plenty of time to research the etiquette," I added gloomily. I scrubbed my hands through my hair.

"*Majesté, s'il vous plaît,* I must ask you to stop doing that," Léonard chided gently. "You do it all the time now, and it is very bad for you. It is difficult for me to repair so much damage."

I pressed his hand to my cheek. His long, tapered fingers felt cool against my face. "Ah, *mon cher ami,* what would I do without you?"

As the summer sun scorched the fields the treasury dried up as well. On August 15, the still-ailing Loménie de Brienne announced that the government would no longer honor its debts in cash, instead issuing promissory notes at 5 percent interest. Naturally, a hue and cry was heard across the land, as notes from a bankrupt treasury are worthless. Clearly, the archbishop of Toulouse was failing his duties as Comptroller General.

Louis and I now met daily in his library. If France was a ship in a tempest-tossed sea, he saw the pair of us as her sextant and compass, of necessity navigating together through the gathering storm.

It was the twenty-fourth of August. The heat was oppressive, even with the window sashes raised. My taffeta bodice clung damply to my back and my coiffure could scarcely retain its curl. The king, stouter than he had ever been, perspired heavily in his gray silk suit.

"Why must everything be so difficult?" Louis groaned. "You managed to persuade Necker to return—"

"Despite the fact that we dislike one another and that Artois once called him a fornicating bastard," I interrupted. "He doesn't much care for you, either."

"But the people love him. However, he will not work with the archbishop, nor will Brienne work with *him.*" The king mopped his brow with an exasperated swipe of his handkerchief.

"But they need each other," I insisted. "Necker's visions for France are too radical and may anger the people if they are implemented too quickly, or at all, for that matter. Loménie de Brienne's less progressive outlook will rein him in."

Louis unfurled my fan and began to cool himself. "The archbishop views our recall of Necker as a personal affront to his ability." He began to pace about the carpet. "I fear, *ma chère,* that we must choose between the lesser of the two evils: the progressive Swiss or the ineffective cleric."

The following day, Loménie de Brienne was dismissed and the mercurial Jacques Necker reinstated as France's Côntroleur-Général of Finance. "Long live Necker," the people cried when they heard the news. For a few shining moments, the nation rejoiced. The government's stocks rose and there were celebrations in the streets. But then the mood grew dark. An effigy of the archbishop was burned in the Place Dauphine. Tens of thousands participated in the violence, wielding clubs and lobbing stones. Their swords drawn, the guardsmen attempted to repel them. France, it seemed, could not exult without going mad.

It had been my idea to recall Necker; I had convinced Louis that it was best for the nation if he rejoined the government. I prayed I had done the right thing.

Only to Axel could I confide my true feelings about the entire state of affairs. "It seems to be my fate to bring misfortune, and if Necker should fail, like his predecessors, or damage the king's authority, I shall be hated even more than I am now. I am blamed for every misfortune, but never ceded a scintilla of credit when anything good occurs. My happy days are over, since they made me into an *intrigante.*" I reclined on a yellow-striped sofa at le Petit Trianon, resting my head in his lap. The color lifted my spirits and the touch of his hand as he gently stroked my hair soothed my brow.

"There is nothing to be gained from blaming yourself," he chided. "No matter what people may say, you and I know that you do nothing out of malice. If it would change anything, I would ride from house to house and tell every citizen in France the truth." Odin padded over to us, demanding a caress.

"I am frightened," I whispered.

I looked into Axel's eyes; his expression had grown suddenly grave. "Now and always, I offer you my devotion." He stroked the dog's muzzle affectionately. "And while I cannot speak for my friend here, I would hazard that he is as loyal as I, and if necessary we would most willingly risk our lives to aid the Queen of France."

THIRTY

Our Thoughts Divided

January 1789

My dearest Sophie,

Things grow steadily worse here. The queen is in a state of perpetual despair over the health of the dauphin. He has rickets as well as a malformed, protruding spine, and weighs significantly less than any boy of seven should.

The landscape of France is bleaker than ever. It has been an unseasonably cold winter; three weeks of thirteen-degree weather, without respite. It rarely snows here the way it does at home, but this season so much has fallen that the carters have been unable to remove the refuse, so it has been left to accumulate and stink. Garbage freezes in the gutters because it is too frigid for the water to wash it away, and the Seine has frozen as well. With the river a ribbon of ice no boats can traverse it, which of course means no grain can get through. No grain, no bread; and so the price of a single loaf has risen to an astronomical fourteen sous, and countless poor are starving. Cheaper English goods are flooding the French markets, which makes things even worse. Workshops are shutting down, and so unemployment is rising. The stock market, which had briefly risen after Monsieur Necker resumed the financial reins, has returned to the sewers.

There was a frightening hailstorm a few weeks ago but the people have conveniently forgotten about the king's twelve-million-franc lottery to benefit the families ruined by the national disaster. They talk only of his avarice and his insensitivity, which, if you knew His Majesty, are qualities one could scarce attribute to him.

What they conveniently remembered was the grand gesture made by the king's cousin, the duc d'Orléans, who sold his finest paintings and donated the eight million francs he received for them to charity.

Taking advantage of the increasing discontent with the monarchs and the ministers and courtiers who are loyal to them are two distinct factions: the increasingly literate populace who have read and appreciated the writings of such *philosophes* as Voltaire and Rousseau, as well as those who ascribe to American ideals, and have swallowed the belief that all men have rights and are equal under God; and those who have been antagonized by the court in the past—a cabal led by none other than the duc d'Orléans. I fear for the sovereigns. Philippe d'Orléans is not merely powerful, but dangerous. For all his democratic posturing, I believe that his deepest desire is to wear the crown himself.

As with my previous letters, I trust you will also burn this one.

Your affectionate brother,

Axel

The king had begun to seek the advice of men who had their fingers on the pulse of the people, among them a lawyer who was also a talented botanist—such accomplishments were de rigueur in our enlightened society—named Lamoignon de Malesherbes. Both of them were avid students of world history, and the evident malaise among the representatives of the three Estates in advance of May's assembly was a subject of some concern.

"Pause, Sire, for a moment or two, to consider the predicament of Charles the First of England," urged Monsieur Malesherbes. "Your position, like his, lies in the conflict between the earlier customs of authority, and the present demands of the citizens." With a faint smile, he added, "Fortunately, in this case, religious disagreement is not involved."

"*Ah, oui,* we are indeed fortunate. One can thank heaven for that," Louis readily agreed, taking the commoner's arm in an unprecedented gesture of equality. "So the ferocity will not be the same."

"Besides, the gentler ways of our time guarantee you against the excesses of those days. I can assure you that things will not reach the stage they did with Charles the First; but *Majesté,* although France is a nation of high-principled idealists, I cannot answer for the absence of any other forms of excess, and you must turn your mind to preventing them."

Their conversation sent shivers along my spine. My husband had always been an assiduous student of the life of this particular British monarch, although he had never countenanced the possibility of civil war until now. He took Malesherbes's words to heart and grew determined to make the gathering of the Estates General a resounding success. To ensure that it would be truly representative of the entire nation, Louis decided that the Third Estate should, for the first time, be comprised of as many deputies as the first two Estates combined, ignoring the suggestion of the Princes of the Blood who insisted that the Estates should be constituted just as they had been in 1614, with each order possessing the same numerical strength, which of course would mean that the clergy and nobility would always outnumber the populace two to one.

"What matter if my authority suffer, provided my people are happy," my husband declared. His words, published in every newspaper in France, elevated his popularity and banished our fears.

On May second, before the assemblage formally convened, etiquette demanded that they be received by the king in the Royal Chamber at the Château de Versailles. In accordance with protocol, both doors were open to admit the nobility; only one door was open for the clergy to file through; and the portals remained shut in the face of the Third Estate, which had to request permission to enter.

The folderol commenced on the morning of May 4, when the royal family rode in state from the palace to the church of Notre Dame in the town of Versailles. Our cavalcade left the palace precisely at ten. Cherub-cheeked pages in bright liveries re-created from the reign of the venerated Henri IV, complete with white goffered neck ruffs and billowing breeches, led the way, followed by the falconers with their majestic hooded birds sporting tinkling bells on their leather jesses. Thousands had turned out to witness the pageantry and to see their king and queen ride by in their respective coaches, even as they anticipated the dawn of a new era and the possibility of a Constitution or a similar document granting all men equality in the sight of God.

Although I was displeased with the political climate, the weather could not have been more salubrious. Rays of sunshine caught the ornate gilding of Louis's carriage at just the proper angles, lending the conveyance—drawn by six white horses caparisoned and festively plumed in the same red, white, and blue of the royal livery—an otherworldly glow as it rolled along the cobbled *rues.* Although the Bourbon brothers often disagreed, that morning they presented a portrait of unity, with Monsieur seated to the king's right, and the still-dashing Artois perched on the box. On the back seat, Artois's sons, the ducs d'Angoulême, de Berri, and de Bourbon squirmed and fidgeted with their unfamiliar costumes, for everyone but Louis had sartorially stepped back in time to the late sixteenth century.

"Vive le roi!" A cheer rose up from the crowd, echoed by the voices of the onlookers above the tapestry-bedecked windowsills, souls who had paid dearly for such an exceptional vantage. Men had clambered up to the rooftops; young boys precariously straddled chimneys. My carriage followed the king's. I was clad in rose-colored silk taffeta, and Monsieur Léonard had dressed my hair with false plaits threaded with matching silk flowers. To my left sat ten-year-old Madame Royale, in buttercup yellow, with a fetching straw bonnet to protect her from the sun; at my right hand, Louis's sister, the gentle princesse Élisabeth, in hyacinth blue. When it became clear that we were passing in stony silence as if we were riding in a hearse, my *belle-soeur* withdrew a handkerchief of finely woven cambric and blotted away her tears.

"It is not right," Élisabeth whispered to me. "We have done them no harm."

"It is not 'we' to whom they show such disrespect," I murmured. "Neither you nor my daughter have done a thing to incur their displeasure."

The silent journey to Notre Dame seemed interminable. Upon reaching the broad square in front of the church the royal family was met by the entire complement of the Estates General, clad according to centuries-old protocol: the nobles draped in silken cloaks trimmed with gold lace, their hats adorned with enormous white plumes; the clergy—scarlet-robed cardinals and bishops in their purple cassocks; and, most unnerving, the soberly garbed representatives of the common people. They were dressed in black coats, vests, and breeches. Even their hose and tricorns were black. The severity of their wardrobe was relieved only by the white jabots at their throats. To a man, every deputy carried a candle.

Now the second leg of the procession began, more martial than regal, threading its way through the narrow streets of Versailles from Notre Dame to the gleaming white cathedral of Saint-Louis. The page boys and falconers were replaced with fife and drum, beating a brisk tattoo as the entire delegation started out on foot, this time led by the lowliest participants, the deputies from the Third Estate, proudly marching in two parallel lines.

As the last of their group went by, a great gasp, followed by a cheer, rose up from those nearest the delegations, for the rabble-rousing Philippe d'Orléans had chosen to walk with the representatives of the Third Estate, rather than take his place among the nobility. After such an extraordinary event, the sight of their resplendently garbed monarch—the massive Regent diamond gleaming in his hat—held little excitement for the clamorous crowd. Louis strode with tremendous pomp and dignity behind the baldachin; beneath that arch walked the venerated archbishop of Paris, whose surplice, sparkling with countless diamonds, glittered even more spectacularly; but it was the duplicitous duc, dressed in sober black silk, who received the loudest acclamation of the morning.

As I passed a group of market women, a brawny butcher darted out of the crowd, startling me. *"Vive le duc d'Orléans!"* she cried, as if to lob the words into my face. She had come so close that I could smell the perspiration on her chemise. For a moment I lost my equilibrium and felt my knees give way beneath me.

A man's voice pierced the silence. A stage whisper. *"Voilà la victime."* I turned toward the sound and located the source—a shaggy bear of a man, the comte de Mirabeau, one of my loudest detractors, walking with the black-clad delegation of the Third Estate.

My head swam, and I began to swoon. A moment or two later I felt someone at my elbow. It was Madame Élisabeth, supporting my weight. At my other side was the princesse de Lamballe, whom I had long ago forgiven for visiting the comtesse de Lamotte-Valois during her incarceration. The duchesse de Polignac and I had repaired our differences as well, but she was so roundly despised by the people that I thought it safest if she remained at the palace and did not take part in the procession.

"*Voici.* Inhale." The princesse held a vinaigrette of my beloved orange flower water under my nose.

I took a quick sniff and blinked hard. "I cannot let them see me this way," I whispered. I could never permit anyone with cruelty or malice on their mind the satisfaction of seeing that they had affected me. I would be lost forever if I did.

"*Regardez!* There is the dauphin!" cried Élisabeth. He had wished to watch the procession and so we set up a mattress on the little balcony of the royal stables. The future king was swathed in a velvet cloak, nestled amid a pile of silken cushions, for he had long been too weak to stand. Swallowing my tears, "We must smile for him," I told his doting aunt. Madame Élisabeth and I raised our gloved hands and waved. "Would they accuse me of being undignified if I blew my dying son a kiss?" I wondered aloud.

At the church of Saint-Louis, the archbishop of Nancy blessed the gathering; then, with his notorious oratorical gifts—and to the delight of the deputies of the Third Estate—he began to inveigh against the excesses of the monarchy and the insensitive extravagance of the courtiers—but most particularly the queen. When he promulgated the lie that the walls of my little theater at Trianon were covered with precious stones, my lower lip trembled with anger. Had the acquittal of the cardinal in the affair of the necklace given the clergy carte blanche to be insolent to us? I glanced at the king, but he had fallen asleep and was snoring softly beside me, blissfully oblivious to the insults raining down upon us from the pulpit. Now I would be compelled to invite a delegation of deputies from the Third Estate to my private idyll simply to prove that not only the décor, but the archbishop's words, were false.

I passed a sleepless night. Louis, however, always enjoyed the deep slumber of the unencumbered—how well I recall our wedding night—no matter the circumstances. We had spent the better part of the evening drafting the speech he was to present the following day at the inaugural session of the Estates General. Much of the time had been spent arguing over the tone: The king had wished to be conciliatory, while Artois and I most adamantly felt that the sovereign must stand firmly against these adversarial, even antimonarchical, voices. "The duc d'Orléans must be silenced," I insisted. "You are the father of France and they are as unruly children testing the limits of their leading strings. What they truly require is the guidance of a wise and authoritarian parent."

"And if they refuse to accept it, they must be told they shall be punished," added Artois.

I nodded emphatically. And if it had been up to me, the meeting of the Estates General would have been held far from Versailles, where it would have been more difficult for spectators, especially the clamorous Parisians, to attend. But Louis had heeded Necker instead. "These rebellious firebrands must be reminded that it is their duty to obey their king." I began to pace about Louis's study, nervously tying and untying my linen fichu.

"Write this," I said, dictating to my husband, who had been reluctant to commit to any particular tack. But if someone did not grasp the reins we were headed for the abyss. "'To the burden of the taxes and the debts of the state there has been added a spirit of restlessness that will bring about the greatest disasters if it is not promptly checked.'" I came around behind him and made certain he had transcribed my words.

What would Maman tell the deputies under these circumstances? I wondered. I imagined myself in the stiff black gown of the late Empress Maria Theresa, unafraid, impervious, rather than the thin-skinned Marie Antoinette who could only feign her mother's formidability. Resuming my dictation I added, "'I hope that this assembly'—no, 'this *distinguished* assembly'; we can allow them that—'will show the obedience which is as necessary to the people's happiness as it is to the conservation of the monarchy.'"

I clung to my opinion the following morning, as I instructed Léonard to dress my hair for the procession. "I must go like an actress, exhibit myself to a public that may hiss me," I said, sighing. As I appraised my reflection in the mirror I caught him doing the same. Had he noticed that my shoulders had become a bit stooped and my bosom, which not too recently had measured forty-four inches, looked shrunken, as though I were considerably older than thirty-three?

Madame Campan helped me dress in the last of the gala gowns I had ordered from Mademoiselle Bertin, a robe of purple satin and cloth of silver with a white underskirt that sparkled with countless diamonds and paillettes. My tresses were swept into a violet bandeau studded with brilliants and crested with a single white heron feather.

Louis, too, was every inch the monarch in his glittering robes and plumed hat. His ample person coruscated with diamonds—on his cloth-of-gold suit, on the jewel-encrusted hilt of the court sword at his hip, on his shoe buckles, his garters, and on the orders of the Golden Fleece and the Saint-Esprit that he wore pinned to his bosom. Once again, he wore the enormous, and flawless, Regent diamond pinned to his hat.

Outside the palace gates, in the town of Versailles, stood an enormous hall known as the Salle des Menus Plaisirs. This repository of theatrical scenery and properties had always been the purview of the now gout-afflicted Papillon de la Ferté, the royal Steward of Small Pleasures; and for the purposes of the meeting of the Estates General he had transformed it into an ancient Greek temple, a triumph of gilded and faux marble and papier-mâché. The allusions to the birthplace of democracy were not lost on the Third Estate. The fact that the trappings were sham was not wasted on the first two delegations.

A broad center aisle was delineated by two lines of Doric columns leading to a raised dais upon which the king would repose beneath a carved baldachin of purple and gold and a canopy bearing the fleur-de-lis of France. Designated for me, a padded armchair was placed slightly to Louis's left. The 1,214 deputies of the three Estates were seated according to strict etiquette, with the First Estate, the clergy, to the king's right; the Second Estate, the nobility, to his left; and the representatives from the Third Estate arranged along the back of the *salle,* facing the throne. The balconies opposite us were thronged with spectators, eager to witness history in the making.

We had been compelled to wait for several hours before entering the hall while the roll was called and each of the delegates' names was formally inscribed. It was after noon when the king and I entered the *salle.* Neither of us knew what to expect. Louis looked anxious. I expect I looked a bit haggard. Between the frustrations of composing his speech, my anger over the convening of the three Estates in the first place, and my fears for the dauphin's failing health, how could I ever convey the portrait of regal serenity?

Cries of *"Vive le roi!"* greeted our arrival, yet as I crossed the threshold a frosty silence descended. The room grew horribly still. Beneath my stays, my belly fluttered with tiny convulsions.

Their hatred of me was palpable. Was that why the king jettisoned the words I had so assiduously helped him pen the previous day? A frisson of shock reverberated through my core and I fanned myself with undignified agitation.

My husband rose from the throne, his stature appearing the more imposing, for he had gained so much weight of late that seated he resembled a fur-trimmed fleshpot. Never comfortable before a large audience, Louis nonetheless relied on one of his strengths; he spoke plainly and with compassion for his people.

"The day my heart has been awaiting has finally come," he began sonorously, "as I stand amid the delegates of the nation I take so much pride in ruling. You have come before me to address the financial condition of France and to reestablish order where chaos has begun to rear its head. As your king, my power is great, bestowed by divine right, but my concern for my subjects is of equal magnitude. *Messieurs, mes amis,* everything you may expect of the most loving interest in the public happiness, all that can be asked of a sovereign who is also his subjects' best friend, you may, you *must,* expect from my feelings."

I was so relieved when his speech was interrupted by applause several times, not just from the clergy and nobility, but from members of the Third Estate as well. I frequently found myself gazing across this sea, hundreds deep, of pale, dour faces set off above by ink-hued tricorns they had refused to remove, and below by their mandated garments of the same shade. Who were they, these angry men, who so despised the monarchy, and so detested their queen? What had I done to them, or to their wives and children, their cousins and sisters, their mothers, brothers, and fathers? Was it any one of them, I wondered, who had written, or published, the vile tract called "*Le Godemiche,* or

The Royal Dildo" or the "operatic proverb" titled "The Austrian Woman on the Rampage, or The Royal Orgy"? *Veni Vidi* was the farce's bawdy Latin epigraph—I came, I saw. I blinked back tears imagining what Maman might have made of this denigration of her youngest daughter.

I felt sick. I had one son whose span of days was clearly numbered, as had been those of the daughter taken from me in her infancy. And over the past few years these antiroyalist monsters had stolen precious hours I could have spent with my children, even robbed me of thoughts I might have devoted to them by wasting my time instead on these vicious tracts. If the representatives of the three Estates and the spectators in the galleries, eager to find something unpleasant to say about the queen of France, returned home to write in their journals or told their friends that I looked sour or peevish, I was certain they dared not look within to divine the cause.

When the king finished speaking, he lowered himself into the throne and gave Monsieur Necker a nod. The Minister of Finance took the floor to resounding cheers, but after a few minutes it became painfully clear that at the pinnacle of his career the great Swiss banker was losing the courage of his progressive convictions. What followed for the next three hours—he became so hoarse that his assistant had to read the remainder of his speech—was a monotonous recitation of financial statistics. Where was the call for a Constitution that the Third Estate had expected him to proclaim? A tide of murmurs spread throughout the hall. Had the king forbidden him to mention it?

By the end of the session no one came away satisfied. I was becoming convinced that the entire assembly was not only a waste of time but a dangerous referendum against the monarchy in general, and most specifically, against the royal family.

THIRTY-ONE

Struggling for Life

Over the next several days, the deputies—308 from the First Estate, 285 from the Second, and 621 from the Third, presented their *cahiers,* or lists of grievances, to the king. These consisted of complaints that the price of salt was too high, that farmlands had been greatly reduced because of hailstorms, or abused due to foot traffic caused by a detour from the roadway. High taxes, or the fact that taxes and duties were levied at all, was a perpetual objection. No progress had been made in weeks other than the decision by some of the lower orders of the clergy to join the ranks of the Third Estate. By the end of May, although most of the Second Estate firmly insisted on retaining their aristocratic perquisites, there were a few members of the nobility, most notably the duc d'Orléans, and one of our heroes of the American Revolution, the russet-haired marquis de Lafayette, who declared that they would not mind forfeiting a few of their privileges in exchange for a Constitution.

I had no stomach for their political haranguing. The dauphin had been conveyed a few miles away to Meudon where his doctors had insisted on assuming control of his care. Tiny Louis Joseph, covered with sores and as wizened and misshapen as an old man, lay atop the green baize of the brand-new billiard table—an odd wish, for he looked as though he were laid upon a bier; but it had been his own, and I was determined to indulge him, knowing it would be one of his final requests.

Every day I rode out to visit my son, and all too often I was met with "You may not see him, *Majesté,*" from one of his *médecins.*

"But I must—I am his mother!" I would implore, clasping the physician by the arms, and when they remained impassive, I would beseech the dauphin's preceptor, the duc d'Harcourt, to intercede for me and allow me to attend him.

"You know the etiquette, *Majesté.* I can only accept instructions from one of His Royal Highness's doctors," the duc would reply stiffly.

There is something remarkable about children who know they are about to enter the kingdom of Heaven; they are stronger than we can ever imagine ourselves, were we to be faced with the same fate. When Louis and I were granted permission to visit the dauphin, my son would insist that his cooks prepare *my* favorite dishes; he would gallantly play the host, propped up on the green velvet cushions of his mechanical wheelchair, although his diminutive body was nearly swallowed up by the metal and wicker contraption. And he could not bear to dismiss the footman who served us merely because the man was clumsy. "He is only shortsighted like Papa, and if a servant can suffer the same malady as a king, why should he be punished for it when the sovereign is not?"

I endeavored to assume a bright countenance in his presence, foolishly tried to convince the dauphin that I was at least as brave as he. He told me he had wished for the room to be painted the color of the summer sky so he could pretend to be outdoors. But finally, he admitted his true reason for choosing that particular shade of blue. "I want to grow accustomed to looking at Paradise, Maman."

There was not one specific day when I was summoned, told that the end was near, for his doctors truly did not know. Each hour was much like the last and would be like the next. And so I made certain to travel from Versailles to Meudon every day, unable to concentrate on the contentious meetings of the Estates General as my son was slipping further and further from our earthly grasp. Special prayers for the dauphin were ordered to be said in all the churches on June 2. And on the morning of June 4, shortly after the hour of one, as I held my firstborn son in my arms, he looked at me as if to tell me something, and then his eyelids gently fluttered closed for the last time.

I had been sent to France for one purpose: to bear this little boy. And now he was gone. Wracked with agonized convulsions, I rocked his ruined body in my arms, raining tears upon his lifeless form.

A few minutes later, Monsieur Lamartine, the dauphine's *premier médecin,* entered the room. "*Pardon, Majesté,* but I must ask you to leave. Etiquette demands that the monarchs remain absent during the examination of the corpse and the ensuing autopsy."

"But he is my son," I cried, choking on my sobs. "*Je m'en fous!* I *never* gave a damn for etiquette and I certainly do not care a whit for it now." I saw Lamartine look to another physician for assistance. "Try to restrain the Queen of France—try to stop me from staying with *mon pauvre petit*—"

Madame Campan rushed into the chamber and helped me to my feet. Her round face was wet with tears. "Come, Madame," she soothed. "His Majesty will have need of you most."

When we reached Versailles, Louis, whose temperament was maddeningly placid even on the direst of occasions, was in a foul mood. His valet, the faithful Hanet Cléry, was collecting discarded handkerchiefs from the floor of his study. My husband's light eyes, like mine, were rimmed with red, the lids puffy and swollen. He threw his hands in the air. "The Paris deputy from the Third Estate, the astronomer fellow—Bailly," he began. "He insisted on seeing me today. Today! 'I must have an audience with the king,' he said. I sent a man to tell him 'Monsieur, His Majesty is grieving. The dauphin died this morning.' But the heathen only said, 'I am mightily sorry for His Majesty's loss. Nevertheless, I and a delegation of others need to speak with him as soon as possible.' So I went to the threshold myself and opened the door and let him see my face. And before he could say a word, I asked him, 'Are there no fathers among you?'"

All they cared about was politics. At the death of my poor little dauphin, the nation hardly seemed to notice.

I slipped into Louis's embrace and we clung to each other. I wept anew, my tears staining his embroidered waistcoat, while he rested his cheek against my hair, claiming one new handkerchief after another from Cléry.

"We must tell the children," I said tearfully, and summoned the duchesse de Polignac. When Gabrielle entered the room, it was clear that she, too, had been crying. "Please bring Mousseline *et mon chou d'amour* here," I said, using my pet names for Madame Royale and Louis Charles.

As ever, our daughter's countenance was grave. "What will happen now, Papa?" she asked, addressing her father directly.

Louis pulled her onto his knee. Balanced in the crook of his arm was our surviving son, as pink and sturdy of limb as his late brother had been sickly and pale. "You are the dauphin now, *mon brave,*" said the king, chucking the tot under the chin. Still only four, Louis Charles giggled uncomprehendingly, bringing the first smile in weeks to his father's broad face.

"What then shall *I* be?"

"You shall marry your charming cousin the duc d'Angoulême, and become a great lady, *ma petite,* just like we always talk about," I said without hesitation. But I knew what Marie Thérèse was really asking. Royal daughters were simply not as important as their brothers. I did not make the rules. She thought I loved her the less for it. And that knowledge daily cracked my heart.

The dauphin lay in state for several days; his tiny form reposed inside a coffin lined with royal blue velvet and draped with a silver cloth that was embroidered with a crown, a sword, and the Order of the Dauphin of France.

The political insults heaped upon us by the three Estates continued to inflict deeply personal wounds as well. According to royal custom, Louis Joseph's heart was not to be buried with his body. The honors of escorting the urn that contained the vital organ to the Benedictine convent of Val-de-Grâce fell to the highest-ranking Prince of the Blood.

"He will not go," Louis informed me angrily.

"Quoi?!"

"Philippe d'Orléans will not escort the heart of his cousin to the convent."

I was brushing my hair at the time and noticed with each stroke how many strands remained in the boar-bristle brush. "Does he give a reason?" I demanded, my hatred for the duc increasing with each passing moment.

Louis hesitated. "I don't wish to vex you. You are distraught enough," he said gently.

"Then another moment of pique will hardly make things much worse."

He came behind me and affectionately stroked my cheek.

"Philippe says that his role as deputy and the affairs of the Estates keep him too busy to depart on other business. He has offered to send his oldest son in his stead."

I rested my chin in my hands and gazed at my husband in the mirror. "I should not be surprised, I suppose." I sighed with regret to think that our son had not been conceived in as much intimacy as the pair of us now shared while we prepared to discuss his funeral arrangements.

The dauphin was buried on June 12. In keeping with tradition, the king and I were not permitted to attend the rites at the Cathedral of Saint-Denis, but that night I dreamt of him. And I did so for several nights thereafter. I was no longer able to fall asleep with ease. One evening, I was telling Madame Campan about my dreams, how the dauphin looked, what he said to me. Four guttering candles illuminated my mirrored dressing table. As one went out, I assumed that a slight draft had extinguished the flame. Campan relit it, but a minute or so later two of the others died out. As Madame Campan went to relight them, I clasped her wrist. "My mother taught her children not to be superstitious, but we talk of shades tonight. If that fourth candle goes out, with all that has happened of late, I will regard it as a very bad omen."

As if on cue, the flame sputtered, hissed, and expired.

THIRTY-TWO

Confusion Reigns

"They shout 'Down with the rich!' and cry for 'Democracy' and 'Liberty' outside the Palais Royal where it seems every hour a new pamphlet is being hawked by the newsboys. Three or four madmen lead the whole thing. They have frightened a waxworker named Curtius into lending them his busts of Necker and the duc d'Orléans and the rabble parade them through the streets as through they are holy relics."

"You must be our eyes and ears," I urged Axel. "For we could not travel to the capital even if we dared." Louis was equally appreciative that we had a trusted advocate to keep us apprised of the ever-changing mood in the Parisian *rues.* In the two short weeks since the death of the dauphin, an insolent new order was emerging with little interest, it seemed, in the way of the world for the past thousand years. The king's blue and gold library with its leather-bound monogrammed volumes and thick soft carpets had become an oasis from the storm.

"I do not know from whence they derive such power, such

authority." Louis groaned, speaking of the Third Estate. "Other than sheer numbers. Perhaps, in hindsight, it was a mistake for me to extend them the privilege of voting by head rather than *en bloc*."

He had experimented with being a progressive leader in an attempt to mollify the bourgeoisie, a course I had not supported in the least; in fact I had strongly advised him against it. I could almost hear Maman's warning in my head: *Give the rabble an inch and they will take a country.*

"The duc d'Orléans has become the most popular man in Paris, even if he has to subsidize his acclaim," Artois declared rhetorically, thumbing through a volume of *Candide*. "I am certain it is he who convinced the clergy and nobility to join the Third Estate."

"I would agree. It is all part of a plot to discredit you and to turn himself into a man of the people. Something must be done to stop him. To stop all of them," I insisted. "How much longer are you going to wait?" My husband's indecisiveness was costing us precious time.

"I would advise you, Sire, to issue an edict immediately disbanding them," said the comte de Mercy. "Two days ago, the Third Estate managed to convince most of the deputies from the first two Estates to make common cause with them. Some of the men have been highly persuasive—Mirabeau, Malesherbes, a provincial lawyer named Maximilien Robespierre, and of course your turncoat cousin Philippe. And this morning the entirety declared themselves a wholly new body—a *legislative* body that has decreed all taxes illegal and immoral. They are calling themselves the National Assembly."

My skin pebbled with fear; I wanted to vomit. The Bourbon brothers released a torrent of exclamations.

"Idiot bourgeoisie! If *no one* pays taxes, how is anything supposed to run?" Monsieur snorted, his perennial distaste for the lower orders evident in every sneered syllable. Of course, my brother-in-law paid no taxes himself, but was adamant that the populace should know its place and continue to finance the well-being of those who belonged to the two superior Estates.

Artois dropped the novel and thumped his fist on the gilded table. "I vote we separate the ringleaders from the rabble and execute them. A lesson like that becomes an immediate deterrent."

Mercy concurred. "Violence may be the only viable way to save the monarchy, *Vôtre Majesté*."

I clutched the padded arm of my chair, digging my nails into the silk, scarcely able to believe what I was hearing. The monarchy of France, venerated, ancient, courtly, sophisticated—was it all to be blown away in a fetid puff of angry rhetoric, fanned by the powerful bellows of men like the conniving duc d'Orléans and the unkempt comte de Mirabeau?

Louis raised his hand for silence. "*Mes frères! I* am the king," he said weakly. "And, monsieur le comte," he said to Mercy, with a sidelong glance at me, "France does not receive her instructions from Austria."

More haranguing followed. But the king remained disinclined to make any abrupt decisions. The following day he decided to conduct a special royal session of the Estates General five days hence, on the twenty-third of the month. But every hour of delay seemed like two that were lost to our cause. The self-proclaimed National Assembly continued to convene, and on the twentieth of June, when they arrived at the Salle des Menus Plaisirs to find troops guarding the great iron padlocks that had been placed across the front doors, did they stop to wonder that perhaps it was because of the extensive preparations taking place inside, arrangements that were necessary for their unprecedented convocation only three days later?

Of course not! The hotheads who called themselves statesmen were immediately convinced that a royal conspiracy was underfoot, and they handily managed to sway their colleagues into believing the same.

Despite the downpour, nearly twelve hundred strong sought shelter elsewhere, a frightening sea of humanity flooding the narrow *rues* in search of a venue large enough to house them all, ultimately finding it in a *jeu de paume,* an enclosed tennis court.

"What do they want?" Louis lamented, his question nearly rhetorical.

Once again we were in the king's library. The collective mood was as gloomy as the weather; outside the raindrops spattered upon the Cour Royale, staining the white pebbles ochre.

"The National Assembly is determined to remain in the tennis court, meeting day and night if need be, until France has a Constitution," Necker told us.

"What?" I glanced at the marble clock atop the mantel and watched the golden pendulum sway for a few beats between a pair of Doric columns. It was barely eleven in the morning. "This is not America!" My cheeks and *poitrine* flushed with choler. "I regret now that we sent those rebellious colonists a single sou, for our ill-conceived alliance fed revolutionary ideas into the bellies of loyal and honest Frenchmen. *Here* the monarch does not share his power with anyone. Louis—will you permit a pack of madmen to dictate to a king?"

"They need the whip, *Majesté,*" shouted Artois. The king's brothers wished to send the royal guards into the *jeu de paume,* trapping the hogs in their pen and spitting each of the new legislators upon the point of a bayonet.

But Necker advised conciliation. "Sire, they only want to be heard. If you give them a voice—"

I looked at Axel, who had been journeying back and forth to

Paris to keep us apprised of the mood in the capital. "If you give the people a voice they will shout *'À bas la monarchie!'* Count von Fersen has heard them! They are jubilant. There is one man in particular, a man with a stammer, even! Camille . . . ?" I turned to Axel, for I had forgotten the name.

"Desmoulins."

"*Oui*—Desmoulins. A failed lawyer from nowhere with pretensions to journalism. And he cannot even speak well. Yet he climbs a tree or a bench and shouts obscene things about us and people rally around him. Give the people a voice? Monsieur Necker, you have lost your mind!"

More interested in devising a solution to the dilemma than in decimating his enemies, Louis split the difference—which frustrated all concerned. He sent four thousand soldiers to clear the tennis court but the *jeu de paume* was like a tinderbox waiting for the aggressive strike of a flint; and so the troops never even entered the hall.

On June 23, at the *séance royale,* the king declared the National Assembly not only null but illegal, continuing to recognize the three Estates only as distinct entities. But the deputies of the Third Estate refused to depart to their separate chambers. "I warn you, if you endeavor to interfere with my efforts to improve the lot of my people, there will be consequences," Louis cautioned, "and I will continue my labors *alone.*" But his threats were perceived as empty and the deputies defiantly stood pat. The king raged and stormed and fumed, but finally, afraid he was being made to appear the fool, caved in to the Third Estate, shouting, "Damn it! Then let them stay!"

Louis's only conciliations to Necker at the *séance royale* were a begrudging acquiescence to the principles of individual freedom, a free press, and equal taxation for all. No one ended the day satisfied.

Axel's assessment of the situation in Paris worried the king enough to order reinforcements to join the troops already garrisoned there. The men were commanded to prepare themselves, should they be required to keep the peace. As the days went by we seemed to be holding our breath, terrified to exhale. I would awaken each morning hoping I had merely dreamt the events of the previous day. But Louis was invariably of two minds on any given thing, which meant that ultimately, he refused to act at all. "Don't you realize that the duc d'Orléans is bribing the laborers of the Parisan faubourgs to rise up against the crown?" I would cry. "Where is your pride?" I demanded. "What legacy will Louis Seize leave? And what will be left of France for your little son to govern?" I would actually tear my hair in exasperation, for my husband had become so petrified that he would sit for hours in his study staring at a volume of world history as if it held the answer to our woes.

He would not be consoled, nor was there time for coddling. "If you will not strike a blow, Monsieur will do it for you. Or Artois, Or *Necker*!" I exclaimed. "Any one of them will act in your name so that Philippe d'Orléans and the National Assembly do not declare your obsolescence."

Jacques Necker had handed the king his resignation and Louis was panic-stricken. "You mustn't let him leave, Toinette. It will be a disaster if he departs, for everyone will believe that I dismissed him. He is the only minister who is popular with the people."

"His Majesty does not heed a word of my advice," Necker said, when I went to plead the king's case. He had already begun to pack his quills and inkstands in a large wooden box. His thin lips were pressed together in an expression of resolution.

I laid my hand on his arm to halt the progress of this proud, intelligent man. "You and I have not always agreed, Monsieur

Necker. But I respect your gifts. And I am fond of your family. Do not forget that His Majesty and I had the honor of attending your daughter's wedding." I drew a deep breath. "We are witnessing an unprecedented series of events. The king rules by divine right, but he is not immortal. He is entitled to doubt. And he is entitled to be afraid. Permit yourself, monsieur, the secret satisfaction of knowing that in many circles you are more beloved than he. And continue to endear yourself to his royal person by remaining in his government."

So Necker stayed. But the citizens of France remained restless. On the first of July Louis ordered another ten regiments—twelve thousand troops—most of them German and Swiss mercenaries, to march to Paris under the command of baron de Besenval.

Upon hearing that the National Assembly had become alarmed over the mustering, Louis maintained, "Only the ill disposed could mislead my people about the precautionary measures I am taking." While the royal family and the court fretted about the future, the king himself remained resolutely optimistic. "The people of France are good," he continued to insist. "They have always had an unbreakable, sacred bond with their sovereign." And when I would weep he reminded me that the people had rioted in the days of his grandfather and even in the time of the Sun King, protesting high taxes and shortages of bread, harsh winters, and bad harvests. And *their* queens had been foreign-born as well. "Kings have been called names before. I did not permit their adulation to swell my head when they called me *'Louis le Desiré'* on the day of my ascension, nor do I countenance their cruel sobriquets now." He placed his hands on my shoulders and leaned over to kiss my cheek. "You shall see; we will weather this storm, *ma petite*."

I wanted to believe him.

"*Rien.* Departure of Monsieur Necker," read the entry in Louis's hunting journal on the twelfth of July—*rien* because he had not ridden to hounds that day. What the king did not write was that he had dismissed every one of his ministers, not just the progressive Contrôleur-Général. Charged now with overseeing a brand-new administration was the competent and loyal baron de Breteuil, who as the king's Minister of the Household had stood by the Crown during the diamond necklace debacle.

At Versailles we went about our day, tamping down our apprehension as we awaited news from Paris. The weather was stifling hot, so I took Mousseline and the dauphin for a boat ride on the Grand Canal, and then we strolled about the *hameau* at le Petit Trianon, visiting the *laiterie* because the walls of whitewashed stucco made a cool and inviting spot for two cranky children on such a sultry day. The dauphin wished to milk one of the cows and as I was explaining that such things took some skill, one of the farmers happened by and offered to teach the children of France how to do it. Madame Royale disdained to touch either Bonjour or Bonsoir—"They smell!" she declared, wrinkling her nose—but the dauphin cheerfully sat upon the farmer's broad lap as the pair of them perched on the milking stool.

"*Pour toi,* Maman," said my son, offering me a monogrammed Sèvres jug of warm milk some minutes later.

Upon our return to the palace we were met with a sea of anxious faces. I summoned the duchesse de Polignac and asked her to see to the children. Her nails were bitten to the quick with worry. "They are rioting in the capital," she whispered to me, drawing me aside. "When word reached Paris of Necker's dismissal, rumors spread like fire over dry straw, and no one has paused to wonder whether or not they are true."

With one eye still on my son and daughter, I asked the duchesse, "What has happened?"

Though her voice was low, her tone was angry, becoming increasingly cynical as she described the situation. "After the hussars and dragoons from the baron de Besenval's regiments took up their positions in the Place Louis Quinze near the Swiss Guards, the tale was given out that the king had ordered them to plant explosive devices under the meeting hall of the National Assembly, intending to detonate the building and incinerate everyone inside. That awful stammering Desmoulins—he jumped upon a chair and shouted that the mustering was a 's-s-signal' for another 'S-S-Saint' Bartholomew's Day Massacre."

"That's the most preposterous thing I've ever heard! What possible parallel could he draw to an attack perpetrated hundreds of years ago by a Catholic government against Paris's Protestants to the king's efforts to safeguard all of his subjects against a potential threat from a crowd of political rabble-rousers? And in any event, not a word of what this man said was true!"

Gabrielle nodded vehemently. "I'm sure that most of the people listening to him were impoverished citizens who had no idea what he meant, but he managed to terrify them by claiming that Besenval's mercenaries had come to cut their throats."

I gasped, my own hand reflexively flying to my neck. "But this is madness."

"It gets worse." The duchesse began to say something, but when the dauphin, who had grown bored as his maman and governess conversed, began to run down the hall, gathering speed with each waddling step, I feared he might do himself some injury, and sent Gabrielle after him. "Does His Majesty know?" I cried.

I entered Louis's library in the midst of another argument. "There will be absolutely no show of force. I will never fire upon my people!" Louis thundered, his broad face scarlet with rage.

"Besenval has retreated," Artois announced as I closed the

door behind me. "He cannot countenance the notion of one Frenchman shedding another's blood."

"Permit me to speak for myself, Your Royal Highness." Older, of course, than he was when he was the *eminence grise* of my Trianon set, the courtly baron rose to his feet. "The comte d'Artois simplifies the picture. We did experiment with the use of force at first, something that would have satisfied both yourself, *Majesté,* and monsieur le comte. Your cousin, the prince de Lambesc, an excellent horseman, rode at the head of the Royal-Allemand, one of the mercenary regiments under my command. To break up a group of rioters he rode straight into their midst, saber aloft. Women, children, and an unarmed guardsman who had deserted his post and joined the citizenry, were trampled under the hooves of his mount. Needless to say, the violent display on behalf of the Crown had the worst repercussions—resulting in a call to arms among the hostile elements of the populace. And that is merely point one."

The baron gave Louis's enormous globe a savage spin. "Point two: I regret to say that having spent these past few days in Paris, we cannot rely upon the loyalty of the guardsmen, Your Majesty. This summer's oppressive heat has made every temper testy, and the troops are exhausted and demoralized. For nearly a year they have had to contend with riots over the lack of bread and keeping order in a city that is flooded with destitute families from the countryside hoping to find employment. Many of these soldiers rather like the notion of a free press, even if they don't understand what one is. And they *very much* like the idea of a comte d'Artois or a Cardinal de Rohan paying as much tax as they do."

"Are you saying that it is unwise of us to arm our own guards?" Louis asked incredulously.

A tense silence hung over the room like a fetid cloud. After pacing about the library for several moments the sixty-seven-year-old baron finally came to roost beside the king's chair. He opened and closed his snuffbox repeatedly, punctuating his phrases with nervous clicks. "Afraid that the Crown intends to crush the National Assembly's infant cries for democratic reforms, the citizens have formed their own militia. Owing to his substantial military expertise, they have asked the marquis de Lafayette to command it—and he has accepted."

Louis, who, uncharacteristically, had not slept blissfully through the previous night, seemed to deflate before my eyes with the news that a creature of his own advancement had betrayed him. "I cannot comprehend it," he muttered, repeating the phrase many times, and *bien sûr,* each time it was employed it could have been applied to yet another stunning turn of events.

And still, perhaps surprisingly, Versailles remained much as it ever was, the most democratic of palaces, where anyone properly attired, from a duchesse to a *poissarde,* could gain admission. The uprisings in Paris and even the violent roistering that attended the final meetings of the Estates General just beyond the château grounds had not changed the age-old etiquette governing entry to the residence of the royal family, no matter how viciously we were derided.

Among the visitors on the morning of July 14 was the seventy-one-year-old Maréchal-Général Broglie, arriving in such a state of agitation that he did not even pause to remove his hat upon reaching the Salon d'Hercule at the top of the grand marble staircase. He nearly sprinted down the length of the Hall of Mirrors, though his legs were bowed not only with the frailties of his age, but from so many years in the saddle. After halting in the Salon de Mars to see if the king was holding court there, he resumed his progress through the Galerie des Glaces, rounding the corner into the Oeil de Boeuf hoping to find his sovereign in the King's Bedchamber, where the former monarch customarily received petitions. A footman finally directed the bewildered maréchal to the king's private apartments, where he found Louis in heated conference with his cousin the prince de Condé, freshly arrived from Chantilly.

"Ah, Broglie!" The king hailed the newly appointed Minister of War, who offered him a reverence. "Condé here has just offered his services to lead an army against the rebellious citizens. He is of course the only professional soldier among us Bourbons. What say you?" But before the elderly maréchal could furnish his reply, the king had offered one of his own. "I have all but graciously refused. I cannot countenance the idea of civil war in France."

Maréchal Broglie's moon-shaped face looked as if it might explode. "But perhaps you should bend your mind to it, *Majesté*. You might be persuaded to reconsider your refusal after you hear this intelligence." Close to apoplexy, he finally paused to catch his breath. "Parts of the countryside have been utterly decimated. Lawlessness reigns. Half the soldiers are disaffected; they are, I fear, in no manner prepared to march on Paris to keep the peace or to protect the royalists there."

Louis seemed to become lost in thought. What was there to deliberate? I wondered. How could he remain so unruffled? He did not know that I had spent the wee hours of the morning packing my jewels and burning compromising papers in case we had to flee. Even so, like the comte d'Artois, I was in favor of resistance. At present, there was no legitimate reason to head for the border, to abandon crown and country.

An airless chamber filled with anxious relations and courtiers staining their garments with perspiration and fear waited for the king to speak. The seconds ticked by. A sweaty rivulet snaked through my hair, and down the back of my neck, trickling uncomfortably beneath my stays. "I am not an ignorant man," the king said. "Nor am I naïve. But history bears me out. And," he added—either stalwartly or stubbornly, depending on one's opinion—"I will not believe that Frenchmen would rebel against the Crown."

The rest of the day was passed with as much normalcy as we could muster. As he had not gone hunting for the third day running, Louis succinctly penned the word *rien* in his journal. That night he retired at his customary bedtime of ten o'clock. He did not visit my boudoir, and according to court etiquette he was not to be disturbed or awakened. But at two in the morning the doors of his bedchamber were thrown open and the Master of the Wardrobe, the duc de la Rochefoucauld-Liancourt, his red damask banyan unbuttoned, burst into the room as if a pack of rabid dogs was at his heels.

"Arise, Sire, the Bastille has been taken!"

Bleary-eyed and disoriented, the king tossed off the silken coverlet and hefted his legs over the edge of the bed. As it seemed clear that his sovereign was having difficulty processing the news, the duc delivered an even more devastating blow. "A mob twenty thousand strong, *Majesté*—they commandeered the muskets and cannon from Les Invalides. Claiming to be in possession of twenty kilos of gunpowder they threatened the prison governor that if he did not surrender the fortress they would blow up the entire *quartier* of Paris. The comte de Launay surrendered without a single show of resistance, and all seven prisoners in the Bastille were released. But then the rabble . . . they"—the old duc's voice became choked with tears—"they murdered the governor, spitting the poor comte's head upon a pike and parading it through the streets of Paris."

The king shuddered, and blinked disbelievingly at the duc de la Rochefoucauld-Liancourt. "Is it a revolt?" he breathed.

"No, Sire," came the horrified reply. "It is a revolution."

THIRTY-THREE

Stay or Go?

In window after window candles were illuminated as the residents of Versailles were awakened by their servants in the small hours of the morning. Rousing herself, the duchesse de Polignac observed ruefully, "There was a time when we could not have been dragged away from the pharaon tables at such an o'clock—when we would not have dreamt of retiring so early; and tonight we would give much for another hour of untrammeled slumber."

The members of the royal family and their respective households assembled in the Hall of Mirrors. Monsieur and Madame waddled into the Galerie in their quilted satin dressing gowns, looking like a pair of pepper pots. In the past they had entertained rival factions at court and had behaved quite cruelly to Louis and me. But the petty intrigues of Versailles were clearly laid aside for the grave matters that now faced us and a common enemy that threatened the very fiber of the monarchy. Madame Élisabeth was hugging her nephews, the sons of the comte and comtesse d'Artois, and murmuring words of reassurance, as much for her own sake as for theirs. My body had not stopped trembling since we had heard the news from Paris. My face was barren of all cosmetics and my hair was disarranged. Who could imagine a coiffure at such a time?

His silk banyan half untied, Louis moved lethargically, as if in a dream, his face drained of all color. "There is nothing for it but to abdicate," he declared numbly, before anyone else had uttered a word.

Frightened, disbelieving glances were exchanged. Had a King of France ever abandoned his throne?

I proposed that we immediately set out for Metz, convinced that the fortified town in Lorraine not far from the German border would provide a safe haven. "The garrison will protect us," I reasoned.

"Yes, of course you can go to Metz—we can *all* go to Metz—but what shall we do when we get there?" Without his wig Maréchal-Général Broglie resembled a plucked chicken. He had lit a clay pipe and was anxiously puffing away. "With officers who dare not shoot, what good are the soldiers?"

"The princesse has fainted!" A cry went up and I saw that Madame de Lamballe had swooned, surely overcome at the thought of the dangers that might befall us in Metz, or perhaps by the ones that might attend us, should we elect to remain at Versailles. Several attendants began to root about in their pockets for vinaigrettes.

"*Mon frère,* you cannot flee!" Monsieur was adamant. Louis looked from his brother to me and back as if he were watching a *jeu de paume.* Although their fraternal rivalry had always been intense, my husband genuinely esteemed Monsieur's judgment and intelligence. Stanislas had always been considered the cleverest of the brothers. Now was the time to bend his fine mind toward preserving the monarchy.

"To fly now is to abandon your crown forever." Monsieur grew more insistent as he watched the king waver on the brink of a decision. "Her Majesty is deluding herself if she thinks we can all take a holiday in Lorraine and expect the fervor of democracy to blow away like an ill wind. If you quit the throne, I guarantee that you will not be able to win it back without a war, and the old maréchal here has just informed us that our soliders are unwilling to raise their muskets and prime their cannon. Look!" He seized Louis by the shoulders and spun him about to face the mirrored walls. "*Regardez, mon Sire!* Look at all of us! Regardless of our hasty toilettes this morning, in these *glaces* is reflected the glory of France, the forms and features belonging to the most ancient and venerated families in the kingdom."

Louis was quite moved by his brother's eloquence and I could tell that he was allowing himself to be persuaded to remain, but the prospect of staying had clearly unnerved Gabrielle de Polignac. Pointing toward the king's Master of the Wardrobe, she whispered to me, "The duc says the mob shouted 'Death to Artois and the Polignacs!'" She threw her arms about my neck and began to weep. "Your Majesty, I am so afraid."

I held her while she sobbed and stroked her back to soothe her nerves. Even the king's eyes were moist; for despite our occasional differences about her he, too, greatly esteemed the duchesse. "In your situation, there is no question of it—you must depart for safety as soon as possible. Go while there is still time; remember that you are a mother. You will not be the only ones to flee. The prince de Condé is headed for the border as well. Perhaps he will escort your family."

"Please know that I do not want to leave you, *ma chère Majesté,*" she insisted, but I continued to assure her that the violence in Paris, albeit terrifying, was a temporary political hiccough and before long she would be able to return. Still, with people chanting for her blood, we thought it best for her to assume a disguise, and so she donned the mobcap and skirts of a chambermaid.

We clung to each other like sisters. I was reminded of the tearful partings I had endured with Charlotte before she left for Naples and with Josepha when Maman had demanded that she descend into the Kaisergruft to pay her respects to our late sister-in-law; Josepha had been overcome by the premonition that we would never see each other again.

"*Adieu, ma très chère amie.* Farewell, dearest of friends," I murmured into her rose-scented hair. "Such a dreadful word—*'adieu'*—as if one of us is really going to God. *Attends!*" She waited while I absented myself for a few minutes, returning with a small but weighty purse. "There are five hundred louis in here. Guard them carefully. It might arouse suspicion if a chambermaid is found with so much wealth about her."

We embraced one last time. *"Je t'aime, ma chère coeur."* I was sobbing, for how could I not love someone who had been a dear and trusted friend for the better part of fifteen years?

It was just as dangerous for the comte d'Artois and his family to remain as it was for the Polignacs. Relieving them of the awkwardness of choosing whether to flee or stay, Louis issued a royal order for them to depart. After the children had said good-bye to their governess, I encouraged Mousseline, "Now bid farewell to your cousin." She bashfully approached Louis-Antoine, the duc d'Angoulême, nearly fourteen now, with just the glimmer of a shadow of hair above his upper lip. My memory journeyed back to a spring day in 1770; his father, the comte d'Artois, had been even younger when first we met.

The two young cousins, promised to each other in marriage since my daughter's birth, shyly, but affectionately, embraced. I stole a glance at Louis, who was saying good-bye to his youngest, devil-may-care brother, the audacious young man who had brought the sport of horse racing to France, flouted the conventions of fashion, and encouraged us to embark on so many delightful adventures. Would we live to attend the nuptials of our innocent children who now so fondly said *adieu*?

By the time the pale light of dawn rose on the morning of July 15, the Polignacs and the Artois *famille* were already hours away.

Ever since I came to France I had watched Monsieur do everything imaginable to undermine his older brother's confidence. Yet today, when the very fate of the throne was at stake, petty differences, grudges, and jealousies melted away. Or . . . for a fleeting moment I thought Monsieur was so extraordinarily clever that by insisting the king appear before the National Assembly, he was sending him to certain death, leaving the field open for a regency, for who else would rule during little Louis Charles's minority?

I tried to push those black thoughts from my mind. Monsieur was a cunning man, but I dared not think his heart was fratricidal.

Finally, Louis reached a decision. Blotting his brow, he conceded, "Even a king can have a moment of weakness. He is, after all, just a man, although I am comforted by the thought that only those who are dearest to me have witnessed my craven behavior this night. But a sovereign is the father of his people. And to abandon them at the hour when they most have need of his guidance and governance would be akin to leaving one's children at the mercy of wild beasts in the wilderness." He turned to me and caught my trembling hand in his. "I must remain, *ma chère,*" he said with a ponderous sigh of finality.

My heart beat wildly; my eyes filled with tears. "Then we stay. And stay together *en famille.* I would never dream of leaving without you. My duty is to remain where Providence has placed me and to present my body to the daggers of the assassins who wish to reach the king." It was inconceivable to depart without our children, to separate from them, or to leave Louis behind to face his enemies alone.

On the seventeenth of July, Louis traveled to Paris to address the National Assembly, unescorted, in an unadorned black carriage. In an atmosphere that was already highly charged with agitation, we feared that any sign of ostentation would have increased the risk of harm to his person. When I kissed him good-bye that morning, pinning the Order of Saint-Louis to his brown silk jacket and making certain his tricorn was adjusted at the proper angle, we pretended that his leave-taking was as ordinary as any other, as if he were merely going hunting in the Bois de Boulogne. But his jowls were quivering as if he were close to tears, and my stomach was rumbling and knotted with fear.

The king returned to the château in the late afternoon, perspiring heavily and looking somewhat relieved. As soon as I heard his carriage clattering into the Cour Royale I ran out to meet him with the dauphin in my arms. Madame Élisabeth and Mousseline were on my heels. Louis descended from the coach and I nearly fell, weeping, into his embrace, so relieved I was to see him home. Soon he was drying all our tears with a handkerchief in each hand.

"What is this?" I demanded, once I got a better look at him and determined that he was in one piece. Affixed to the king's hat was a red, white, and blue cockade—the colors of Paris wedded to the white of the Bourbons, he explained. An insignia to denote the concord achieved between the National Assembly and the monarchy.

"What happened?" I inquired eagerly. Closeted within la Méridienne, I wished to hear the news before Louis shared it with anyone else.

"I approved the appointment of the marquis de Lafayette as commander of the National Guard—I hope he remembers the day when he served the Crown so admirably in North America—as well as that of Jean-Sylvain Bailly, the astronomer who wouldn't let me mourn the passing of the dauphin, as mayor of Paris." My husband removed his hat and regarded the tricolor cockade. "Perhaps if they look to the stars for guidance they will be offered the hand of God and begin to walk in His way instead of seeking to deny and destroy what has made France the envy of other nations. Nonetheless," Louis said, sinking into a *fauteuil* upholstered in celadon-colored silk, "I assured the Assembly that my people could always count on the love of their king."

He handed me the tricorn and I quickly hid the hat behind the doors of a tallboy so that I should not have to look at the offensive cockade.

"They believe the monarch has been restored to their bosom, now that his 'evil counselors' have been exiled," Louis said, bitter at the sacrifice of his youngest brother and my beloved Gabrielle. "But if that is the price of harmony from now on, you must admit, it is not as dear as it might have been. Happily there was no bloodshed." His wan smile broadened into a relaxed grin. Enfolding me in his arms he added, "And I swear to you, Toinette, French blood will never be shed by my order."

"And although hardships and misfortunes surround us at every turn, *I* promise that adversity hasn't lessened my strength or my courage." I clasped my husband's hands in mine and brought my lips to them. His palms were as moist as the day we first met, timid adolescents thoroughly schooled in our royal duties, yet utterly unprepared to navigate the vicissitudes of life. Since the day we exchanged our vows I had been accused of every vice imaginable from frivolity to extravagance to adultery to tribadism. And the king's had always been the first and loudest voice to defend me. Now, more than nineteen years later, stouter, graying, and perhaps a bit wiser, we were facing challenges that as newlyweds, scarcely older than children, our minds and hearts never could have imagined.

Three nights earlier I thought the world we knew was ending. In hindsight, it was merely heralding another dawn. The day could only grow brighter. It was the law of Nature.

Acknowledgments

Un très grand merci to my editor Caitlin Alexander for her enthusiasm, her vision, her passion, and her patience; to my agent extraordinaire Irene Goodman who has always been everything one could wish for and whose devotion to my career in macrocosm and to the Marie Antoinette trilogy in microcosm has never flagged; to the historical fiction blogging community for being so supportive of the genre in general and my Marie Antoinette novels in particular; to the spectacularly talented authors who took time from their own prolific careers to blurb the first novel in the trilogy, which was in print before I could publicly acknowledge my gratitude to them; to Christine Trent for spurring me to stay on schedule (as much as possible) by threatening to create a spreadsheet for me; to Pauline Gardner and my classmates at the Equinox Spa in Manchester, Vermont, for their encouragement throughout the birthing process and for being sympathetic ears, and soft shoulders to cry on when I felt overwhelmed by deadlines. *Et finalement, à mon très cher mari* Scott, for making my life a better place every day, which makes it infinitely easier to be creative.

Bibliography

Although it is not customary to provide a bibliography for a work of fiction, my research for the Marie Antoinette trilogy has been so extensive that I wished to share my sources with my readers. I am indebted to the following fine scholars and historians.

Abbott, John S. C. *History of Maria Antoinette.* New York: Harper & Brothers, 1849.

Administration of Schönbrunn Palace. *Schönbrunn.* Vienna: Verlag der Österreichischen Staatsdruckerei, 1971.

Asquith, Annunziata. *Marie Antoinette.* New York: Taplinger Publishing Company, 1976.

Bernier, Olivier. *Secrets of Marie Antoinette: A Collection of Letters.* New York: Fromm International Publishing Corporation, 1986.

Boyer, Marie-France, and Halard, François. *The Private Realm of Marie Antoinette.* New York: Thames & Hudson, 1996.

Cadbury, Deborah. *The Lost King of France: How DNA Solved the Mystery of the Murdered Son of Louis XVI and Marie Antoinette.* New York: St. Martin's Griffin, 2002.

Castelot, André. (trans. Denise Folliot). *Queen of France: A Biography of Marie Antoinette.* New York: Harper & Brothers, 1957.

Cronin, Vincent. *Louis & Antoinette.* New York: William Morrow & Co., 1974.

De Feydeau, Elisabeth, *A Scented Palace: The Secret History of Marie Antoinette's Perfumer.* London & New York: I. B. Tauris, 2006.

Erickson, Carolly. *To The Scaffold: The Life of Marie Antoinette.* New York: St. Martin's Griffin, 1991.

Fraser, Antonia. *Marie Antoinette: The Journey.* New York: Anchor Books, 2002.

Haslip, Joan. *Marie Antoinette.* New York: Weidenfeld & Nicolson, 1987.

Hearsey, John. *Marie Antoinette.* New York: E. P. Dutton & Co., Inc., 1973.

Hibbert, Christopher and the editors of the Newsweek Book Division. *Versailles.* New York: Newsweek Book Division, 1972.

Lady Younghusband. *Marie Antoinette: Her Youth.* London: Macmillan and Co., Ltd., 1912.

Lever, Evelyne. *Marie Antoinette: The Last Queen of France.* New York: Farrar, Straus & Giroux, 2000.

Loomis, Stanley. *The Fatal Friendship: Marie Antoinette, Count Fersen, and the Flight to Varennes.* New York: Avon Books, 1972.

Mossiker, Frances. *The Queen's Necklace: Marie Antoinette and the Scandal that Shocked and Mystified France.* London: Orion Books, Ltd., 2004. Originally published in Great Britain by Victor Gollancz, Ltd. in 1961.

Pick, Robert. *Empress Maria Theresa.* New York: Harper & Row, 1966.

Thomas, Chantal. (trans. Julie Rose). *The Wicked Queen: The Origins of the Myth of Marie Antoinette.* New York: Zone Books, 2001.

Weber, Caroline. *What Marie Antoinette Wore to the Revolution.* New York, Picador, 2006.

Webster, Nesta H. *Louis XVI and Marie Antoinette During the Revolution.* New York: Gordon Press, 1976.

Zweig, Stefan. (trans. Cedar and Eden Paul). *Marie Antoinette: The Portrait of an Average Woman.* New York: Grove Press, 2002. Originally published in the United States by Viking Press in 1933.

Glossary

Below are most of the French words and phrases found in the novel that are not obvious cognates, with their English definitions.

À bas la monarchie	Down with the monarchy (expression chanted in the streets during the French Revolution)
allées	paths
allez-vous	Go
attends	Wait (a command)
au fond	basically, really
au revoir	good-bye
bal masqué	masquerade ball
baume samaritain	a specific type of balm or ointment
beau-frère	brother-in-law

belle-soeur	sister-in-law
berceau	cradle
bien sûr	of course
bonjour	Hello, good day, good morning
bonne chance	good luck
bonne nuit	good night
bon soir	good evening
bourreau	executioner
carosse de gala	large, fancy carriage used on special occasions
ça suffit	that's enough (a command)
ça va	it's all right, that's okay
c'est charmant, oui	it's charming, yes (isn't it)
c'est défendu	it's forbidden
c'est divine, n'est-ce pas	it's divine, isn't it
c'est vrai	it's true
chef d'oeuvre	a masterpiece
chère amie	dear friend (feminine)
cheveux	hair
collets-montés	strait-laced prudes
comme il faut	proper, correct
congé	leave, dismissal

coucher	a royal's formal, public ritual of getting undressed and into bed each night.
coup de foudre	literally a thunderclap; colloquially an expression used to denote the sensation of falling in love at first sight
dame d'atours	mistress of the robes
dame d'honneur	superintendent of a royal lady's household; the highest ranking woman in her retinue
dîtes-moi	tell me (a command)
écu	monetary unit; a coin. Its value varied and there were both gold and silver *écus*. A silver *écu* was also known as a *louis d'argent*.
enceinte	pregnant
enfants	children
est-ce tellement vrai?	is it really true?
femme	wife
fenêtre	window
fête champêtre	an outdoor repast, picnic, or event
gazette des atours	the book that catalogued all of the queen's garments, from which she made her daily wardrobe selections
gitane	a gypsy
glaces	mirrors

grand-père	grandfather
hameau	hamlet; rustic village
homme	a man
hôtel	mansion
il etait si noble, si gentil	he was so noble, so kind
Je m'en fous	I'll be damned/I don't give a damn (slang)
Je t'aime, ma chère coeur	I love you, my dear heart
Je vous prie	I beg you
jolie	pretty
la reine	the queen
la tête	the head
laiterie	dairy
le Bien-Aimé	the Well-Loved (Louis XV)
lettre de cachet	official document issued by the king consigning someone to banishment, or remanding someone to prison without having to specify the reason
lever	the reverse ritual of the *coucher,* performed every morning, where the royal is publicly dressed and makes his/her toilette; getting dressed, made up, coiffed, etc., can take hours. *Levers* were also business and social times where they heard petitions and chatted as they were

	dressed. Meanwhile, invited spectators and guests could enjoy a snack.
lit de justice	a formal session of the Parlement de Paris, the capital city's judicial body, for the compulsory registration of the king's edicts. The king would recline on a divan or "bed" (*lit*)
Louis le Desiré	Louis the Desired (nickname of Louis XVI upon his accession to the throne)
ma belle	my beauty (a term of endearment)
ma chère (feminine)	my dear
mon cher (masculine)	
ma pauvre petite	my poor little one (feminine)
ma très chère amie	my very dear friend
mais	but
maîtresse en titre	a royal's official mistress; a formal role at the French court
marchande de modes	fashion merchant; stylist
mari	husband
mari complaisant	the term for a complacent or compliant husband aware of, if not complicit in, his wife's extramarital affair
médecin	doctor
médisance	backbiting, mean-spirited gossip

moi, aussi	me, too
mon frère	my brother
mouche	artificial beauty mark; literally a fly; a patch to cover a pockmark, but often used purely for cosmetic reasons.
parfums	perfumes
pas pour moi	not for me
passementerie	a type of elaborate, dimensional trimming stitched onto garments, usually in looping patterns
pauvre	poor, unfortunate
Permettez-moi de vous offrir mes condoléances. J'en suis désolée	Permit me to offer you my condolences. I am so sorry [about it].
petit déjeuner	breakfast
petite armée	little army
petits bisous	little kisses
peut-être	perhaps, maybe
poissarde	fishmonger (female)
poitrine	a woman's chest, bosom area
premier chirugien	first surgeon
prenez soin	take care, be careful
quoi	what
rien	nothing

robe de cour	a formal court gown, typically elaborate, enormous, and weighing several pounds
rue	street, avenue
sois courageux	Take courage (literally, be courageous)
suis prête	I'm ready
tant pis	too bad (as in, tough noogies)
tapissiers	upholsterers
tellement fatigué	much fatigued
une étrangère	a foreigner (female)
vendeuse	saleswoman
vite	quickly, fast
Vive le roi Louis Seize	Long live King Louis XVI
voici	here is/here are
voleuse	thief
Votre Majesté, Vos Majestés	Your Majesty, Your Majesties
Vous l'avez détesté	You hated him
vraiment	really, truly

DAYS *of* SPLENDOR, DAYS *of* SORROW

JULIET GREY

A READER'S GUIDE

Juliet Grey on Writing *Days of Splendor, Days of Sorrow*

It provided great pleasure, but also left me with a measure of sadness, to continue the story of Marie Antoinette's life in *Days of Splendor, Days of Sorrow,* because of course we know the tragic denouement. I felt that part of my role in this middle novel in the trilogy was to show how Marie Antoinette's journey continued along its fatal path. It's clear from the book's epigraph, taken from a quote at the time she ascended to the throne as the queen consort of Louis XVI, that she was considered a liability. Add that to all the animosity that had built up against her, particularly within the French court, during the four years she was dauphine—an effervescent teenage girl making enemies right and left as she pushed with all her might against the rigid etiquette of Versailles.

One can go back even further to the 950 years of enmity that existed between France and Marie Antoinette's native Austria, a political albatross hung around her pale and slender neck almost as soon as her betrothal to the future Louis XVI was arranged. When her mother, the Hapsburg Empress Maria Theresa, sent her to France in April 1770, she exhorted her youngest daughter to make the French love her. With a few notable exceptions, that admiration came mostly during the late reign of Louis XV, who by then was roundly despised by his subjects. The charming (and morally upright) strawberry-blond dauphine and her husband were seen as the great young hopes for France's future.

But Marie Antoinette's popularity soon faded as the propaganda spread that she was not comporting herself with the dignity of a French queen and was, moreover, behaving like a royal mistress by decking herself out in increasingly elaborate jewels, gowns, and other accoutrements such as the outrageous (and outrageously expensive) towering "pouf" coiffures. Her subjects, convinced by propaganda disseminated from within Versailles itself, published by nobles she had angered by ostracizing them from her intimate circle, soon saw her as the queen of excess.

Marie Antoinette's behavior predates the study and practice of psychoanalysis, but in *Days of Splendor, Days of Sorrow* I aimed to convey the genesis of her extravagance and what lay behind her increasing mania for pleasure. It was of course primarily a substitute for what she most desired—a child, especially a son and heir—not only for the security of the Bourbon dynasty, but because she adored children. Her life might have taken a different trajectory had she conceived early in her marriage. Instead, her first child, a daughter, was born in the waning days of 1778, a frustrating and embarrassing eight and a half years after her nuptials—ample time for her enemies to recast the religiously devout and faithfully wed young queen as a promiscuous hedonist.

What happened on her wedding night was immortalized by Louis in his hunting journal with a single word: *rien*. Nothing—although the reference was really a notation that the bridegroom had not killed any woodland creatures that day because he'd not gone hunting. Not only was Louis shy and uncomfortable around his new bride, but he may have suffered from a mild deformity of the penis known as phimosis, where the foreskin is too tight to retract. This condition made intercourse, and even an erection, painful.

Historians' opinions are divided as to whether Louis suffered from phimosis and underwent a minor procedure (not as radical as circumcision) in late 1773 to correct the defect (for narrative reasons I placed the event in 1774, after he became king); or whether his inability to make love to Marie Antoinette was purely psychological or psychosomatic. The latter is harder to believe because Louis admitted that he both loved and respected Marie Antoinette and found her very beautiful. While a number of present-day scholars vehemently dispute the phimosis speculation as being the pet theory of Marie Antoinette's twentieth-century biographer, the Freudian Stefan Zweig, they cannot explain away the preponderance of correspondence that came out of the Bourbon court at the time. This included not merely the dispatch from the Spanish ambassador to his sovereign graphically discussing the issue of Louis's penis (which could be dismissed as gossip), but a number of letters written between Marie Antoinette and her mother discussing whether or not Louis was prepared to submit to the operation, and the medical opinions of the various court physicians on the subject. The language of that correspondence most clearly refers to a physical problem. Whether it was compounded by psychological and emotional issues is also a possibility. Unfortunately, Louis's boyhood tutor, the duc de la Vauguyon, had instilled in him a hatred of women and a particular distrust of Austrian females. But by 1773, the dauphin and dauphine had become close friends, and presented a united front against the duc's malevolent influence. This was even truer by the time they ascended the throne in 1774.

The subject of Louis's phimosis and how it was treated is one of a couple of controversial topics I explore in this novel. I do believe that he suffered from a mild physical deformity and that he underwent a corrective procedure. The operation detailed in the novel is taken from a procedure performed in France around 1780 so it is about as accurate a description as one can get of what Louis's medical treatment might have been like.

Another of my aims in writing the Marie Antoinette trilogy was to convey the humanity (and sometimes not) within these historical figures. Too often they have been depicted in film and literature as archetypes, stereotypes, or dusty relics of an era long past. As I breathed life into characters who to some readers may be little more than names from a history book, I saw them as vibrant and vital, complex and flawed. It was also my intention to depict some of the lesser-known (but equally fact-based) events of their lives. For example, the silk merchants of Lyon really did pay a call on Mesdames asking for their support after Marie Antoinette began to dress almost entirely in the muslin *gaulles;* Marie Antoinette really did suffer a terrible fall and hit her head, and Madame Royale's shocking reaction to her mother's injury, as well as the conversation she had with her father about whether he would have preferred a son instead of her, really happened. I was stunned when I first read about the incident in the many biographies because it revealed so much about the characters of the precocious and envious Madame Royale and the king, who was a tremendously sentimental man. Louis indeed adored his little girl from the moment of her birth and never resented her gender, despite the immense pressure upon both him and Marie Antoinette to produce a son and heir. The fact that both of them were such sentimental, vulnerable, and fairly hands-on parents made them quite anomalous, especially for royals, even in the Age of Enlightenment. In another fascinating moment "ripped from real life," the queen did indeed summon Jean-Louis Fargeon to le Petit Trianon to create a perfume that captured the essence of her private idyll (I own a replica of the fresh, floral scent, which made my research all the more redolent!). And she did ask Fargeon to develop a unique fragrance for a man she described as "virile as one can possibly be," that phrase, in translation of course, taken from the perfumer's own diary. In a subsequent event, to be depicted in *The Last October Sky,* the third novel of the Marie Antoinette trilogy, many years later the aroma of that custom-made toilet water will come back to haunt Fargeon's nostrils.

One of the central aspects of this novel is the developing relationship between Count Axel von Fersen and Marie Antoinette. Historically, there has been some controversy as to how far it went, whether it remained strictly platonic, whether (and when) it may have blossomed into a physical love affair, and whether Marie Antoinette ever violated her deeply held marriage vows and consummated her passion for Fersen.

I have a cardinal rule about writing historical fiction: If it *could* have happened, bolstered by solid research, then it's fair game to be included in a novel. Stanley Loomis, in *The Fatal Friendship: Marie Antoinette, Count Fersen, and the Flight to Varennes,* offers enough compelling evidence for a relationship between them that may indeed have eventually been consummated. Biographers Antonia Fraser, Stefan Zweig, Vincent Cronin, and André Castelot share that opinion. We have the culture of the eighteenth century to thank for the plethora of diaries and memoirs left to posterity. Some may be more reliable than others. After Marie Antoinette's death, Fersen's beloved sister Sophie, to whom he was especially close, burned a number of his letters; and at some point (perhaps after his gruesome murder on June 20, 1810, which took place exactly nineteen years to the day from the royal family's fateful flight to Varennes in June of 1791, an event that will be dramatized in *The Last October Sky*), his diaries were heavily redacted. However, enough of Fersen's own words remain to obliquely hint at a relationship with Marie Antoinette that went far deeper than the proper bounds of a common friendship. We have his declaration to Sophie that he would never wed because he could not be united with the one woman he really loved and who loved him in return. As historians cannot document any abiding yet for some reason inappropriate or equally illicit relationship with another woman (his other love affairs, regardless of their duration, were fairly inconsequential by comparison), the conclusion is viable (certainly by a novelist), that he gave his heart and soul (and the case can be made for giving his body) to Marie Antoinette.

There is no denying that Fersen risked his life more than once to save the queen—and the king, of course, whom he also admired, possibly making his transgression all the more guilt-inducing.

The events that I used to build the relationship between Marie Antoinette and Axel von Fersen are rooted in fact. As for the issue of privacy in a royal court, Marie Antoinette, who detested being surrounded by an enormous entourage while she was dauphine, immediately changed the rules when she became queen, reducing the size of her retinue (most of whom had been assigned to her upon her arrival in 1770) to a handful of trusted attendants. Moreover, she was roundly criticized for turning le Petit Trianon into her exclusive haven. Whereas Versailles had traditionally been open to the people, she had signage posted on the gates of her little château and about its acreage stipulating that entrance to the premises was by permission of the queen alone, and that all visitors had to be escorted inside by her servants or attendants.

The existence of the mechanical mirrored window shades that closed off the view inside to all would-be trespassers or intruders, who would find themselves staring at their own reflections if they dared to pry, is a fact. At le Petit Trianon, therefore, it was simple enough to dismiss the servants from a room, to enjoy private tête-à-têtes with her confidants of both sexes, or even with a room full of people. It was precisely this exclusivity, and the maddening notion that all sorts of goings-on were taking place at le Petit Trianon to which they were not invited, which gave rise to the rumors spread by her detractors of Marie Antoinette's rampant debauchery there. Ironic, isn't it, how the very aristocrats who derided the queen for having a personal fairyland were so desperate to secure an invitation. They never received one because Marie Antoinette, who knew what was being said about her, did not feel the need to surround herself with, in twenty-first-century parlance, "toxic" people.

But le Petit Trianon was indeed a private idyll where Marie Antoinette could truly be herself. Insofar as being able to consummate a romance there with Axel von Fersen, a lawyer would no doubt concede that she had both motive and opportunity.

The more I considered what is essentially a love triangle with the queen at its apex (because I do believe that by the time Axel returned to France in 1778 Marie Antoinette and Louis had grown to love each other in a quiet, solid way), the more the three of them began to remind me of another trio of royals: King Arthur, Guinevere, and Lancelot. Although those archetypal characters (who may have been actual historical figures) are English, their story was first set down by Chrétien de Troyes, a French romance writer in the Middle Ages. The elements of Guinevere and Lancelot's star-crossed love affair, and their shared affection for Arthur, as well as Arthur's deep respect for Lancelot, are also present in the Louis/Antoinette/Fersen triangle.

At bottom is a very human dynamic that has played itself out countless times in myriad marriages, along with the woman's struggle to reconcile the parts of herself that are satisfied by each of the men: the physical passion she finds with a handsome soul mate, and the solidity and devotion of a faithful husband to whom she is not sexually attracted. She must also battle the demons of guilt, betrayal, and remorse that cannot fail to rear their gargoyle-like heads once she has made the difficult decision to violate the marriage vows she had previously held so sacred.

Although Marie Antoinette was raised from the cradle to despise adulterers (because her father had a mistress, a relationship that deeply wounded her mother, the Empress Maria Theresa), I believe she ultimately became one. I imagine the emotional cost (not to mention the obvious risks) must have been enormous for her, to have spent her entire life up to a point with an unshakable view that is finally shattered by her own volition.

As to the famous Affair of the Diamond Necklace, the French system of justice at the time worked in a fairly arcane manner. Defendants were arrested and incarcerated without being told what they were accused of or who their accusers were. They could hire lawyers but their attorneys were not permitted to be present during the inquisitions; they could only publish trial briefs which were based on hearsay (and which in this case were truly sensational). These trial briefs were little more than professionally penned scandal sheets that sought to exonerate their clients by influencing not only the magistrates of the Parlement, the region's judicial body, but the public as well—a public that was entirely ignorant of the facts of the case being investigated and tried.

To answer the inevitable question, "How many of the events of this book really happened?" nearly all of them are based on the historical record, both the larger picture as well as many of the more intimate details regarding the events of the characters' interrelationships, with the exception of the sexual relationship between Marie Antoinette and Axel von Fersen, where, as a novelist, I chose to explore the possibility propounded by numerous biographers that their friendship blossomed into an affair. Although this position is controversial, when all is said and done, *Days of Splendor, Days of Sorrow* is a work of historical fiction.

Yet their friendship, as well as the other interrelationships in the novel, has been thoroughly researched. In some instances I even put actual quotes into my characters' mouths; die-hard Marie Antoinette aficionados may spot them. To that end, much of the correspondence in the novel is based on the genuine letters as well. In a couple of cases I moved things around; for example, the letter that opens chapter four was in reality written exactly a year earlier. And with regard to the events leading up to and surrounding the Affair of the Diamond Necklace, the movements of the key and supporting players are so complicated they could merit an entire novel of their own. So I truncated the timeline just a bit and excised a few of the supernumeraries because they weren't germane to Marie Antoinette's knowledge of events.

For narrative flow, I also combined the circumstances of two of Marie Antoinette's miscarriages into a single tragedy. In actuality, the miscarriage brought on by the coach ride was a separate incident from the one that occurred on her birthday. And Marie Antoinette's renovation of rooms within her own apartment at Versailles for Axel von Fersen, complete with a Swedish stove, occurred in October 1787, rather than during the spring.

A third aim in writing *Days of Splendor, Days of Sorrow* was to set forth some of the real reasons France was financially bankrupt by the time the Bastille was stormed on July 14, 1789. Discontent had existed for well over a generation—for several decades, in fact, going all the way back to Louis XV's expenditures on the Seven Years' War (1756–63); although it was his mistresses' extravagances, particularly those of Madame de Pompadour, that angered the French just as much because these were tangible, visible reflections of excess: the clothes, the jewels, the amount of money lavished on furnishings and interior design, and of course the construction of le Petit Trianon, which later became a code phrase for the debauchery that was corrupting the nation, thanks to the outrageous behavior that the anti–Marie Antoinette propagandists ascribed to the queen.

Both Louis XV and Louis XVI emptied the treasury to fight foreign wars, which cost the French exponentially more than any royal mistress (or Marie Antoinette) ever spent, even at the zenith of their acquisitiveness. Americans might want to look long and hard at this period of history because if Louis XVI had not supplied the colonists with so much financial and military aid, including providing soldiers, sailors, and ships, throwing the might of France's navy into their struggle for liberty, the British might have ultimately prevailed.

This decision cost the French crown in more ways than one. Many of their aristocrats fighting in North America returned not only victorious, but infused with the spirit of liberty, watering the seedlings that had already begun to sprout in the fashionable salons and coffeehouses of Paris and behind the gilded paneling of the Palais Royal—spearheaded by the king's cousins, the duc d'Orléans and his son, the even more ambitious duc de Chartres, who inherited his father's title in 1785. Their radical ideas were bolstered by the writings of the French philosophers of the Enlightenment such as Voltaire and Jean-Jacques Rousseau, who suggested that all men had equal rights under God, no matter the circumstances of their birth.

By July 14, 1789, the storm clouds of revolution had already gathered over Paris, but just a few leagues away at Versailles, the monarchs were convinced that the republican fervor was no more than a temporary ill wind. How they met the realization that the world as they had always known it was changing all about them, with a velocity they neither predicted nor were equipped to handle, will be dramatized in the final novel of the Marie Antoinette trilogy, *The Last October Sky*.

Questions and Topics for Discussion

1. France and Austria had been at odds for more than 950 years by the time Marie Antoinette married Louis. This was a huge weight to bear at the age of fourteen. In what other ways was her marriage to Louis troubled before she even moved to France?

2. "I am terrified of being bored" and "I felt so useless." These statements seem to be at the root of Marie Antoinette's struggles. Do you think that if she'd been able to have children earlier in her marriage this general sense of ennui would have been as prevalent? In what ways do you imagine things in the royal world would have been different if she had been able sooner to fulfill her dream of becoming a mother?

3. Marie Antoinette comments that she felt pressure to keep up with the fashion and luxury of Paris. Do you think that she ever felt truly guilty about her overspending and

debt-accruing ways? Have you ever found yourself in a similar situation? What parallels do you see between the financial troubles in France and those of the United States and other countries today? What about the political climate?

4. Do you think that Marie Antoinette's interest in getting involved in the politics of the monarchy was a direct result of the problems that she and Louis had in their marriage? Was Marie Antoinette too strong-willed for Louis? Was Louis threatened by her? How did you interpret the dynamics of their relationship?

5. In what ways was le Petit Trianon a symbol of who Marie Antoinette was? If she had been more open to interacting with the public, do you think she would she have ended up so alienated from her people?

6. Were you cheering for Marie Antoinette's kiss with Count Axel von Fersen or did you feel that she should have been loyal to her husband regardless of their problems? *Days of Splendor, Days of Sorrow* takes a controversial approach in positing, based on circumstance and some of Axel's letters to his sister, that Marie Antoinette and Axel consummated their *affaire de coeur*. What do you think really happened?

7. At the zoo, Marie Antoinette says that the tiger is her favorite animal there because it reminded her of her mother. If her mother is a tiger, what kind of animal would Marie Antoinette be? What kind of animal do you think that she herself would identify with?

8. In what ways were Marie Antoinette and Louis alike? In what ways were they different?

9. Do you think the punishments meted out to Jeanne de Lamotte-Valois, her husband, and Cardinal de Rohan following the Affair of the Diamond Necklace were just? Were you surprised by how easy it was for Marie Antoinette's detractors to convince the public that she was at fault?

10. "I will not believe that Frenchmen would rebel against the Crown," Louis says. How do you think he was able to remain so naïve about what would happen to France?

11. Do you think the French Revolution was inevitable? If there was any one moment at which Louis and his advisors could have turned the tide of public opinion, what was it? After reading *Days of Splendor, Days of Sorrow,* how much responsibility for the revolution do you attribute to Marie Antoinette's actions?

12. What scene in *Days of Splendor, Days of Sorrow* surprised you most? Do you feel more sympathetic toward Marie Antoinette than you did before reading this novel? Why or why not?

ABOUT THE AUTHOR

JULIET GREY is the author of *Becoming Marie Antoinette*. She has extensively researched European royal history and is a particular devotee of Marie Antoinette, as well as a classically trained professional actress with numerous portrayals of virgins, vixens, and villainesses to her credit. She and her husband divide their time between New York City and southern Vermont.

www.becomingmarie.com